Praise for *Abo...*

Jody Ferguson makes great use of t ....que city as a backdrop
to his story of war, love, and loss... colorfully drawing characters
who, like Shanghai itself, are desperately seeking a way out
of one world and into the next.

James Carter, author of *Champions Day: The End of Old Shanghai*

The writing is superb, poetic and historically authentic.
Mr. Ferguson has done his homework. His depiction of
wartime Shanghai with its eclectic classes of people
adapting to the Japanese occupation reads with chilling accuracy.
His description of the battles is captivating and masterful,
exhibiting his extensive knowledge of this time in world history.
And through it all, he has woven this enchanting story
of two lovers who never stop loving each other though
war has ripped them and their worlds apart.

Steve Warren, author of *The Confessions of Davy Crockett*

Above the Water is engaging and educational,
and you'll feel its *thrum* on your emotions as well.

Dana Frank, author of *The Moon Can Tell*

From its vivid portrayal of Russian expatriate life in China to
his stark scenes of men in combat...Jody Ferguson makes us feel
we know these people, and their fates are bound up in our own.
The author's extensive background in Russia and East Asia
lends a rare authenticity to the worlds he surveys.

Russell Working, author of *The Irish Martyr*

ABOVE THE WATER

JODY FERGUSON

PHALINA
PRESS

Above the Water is a publication of Phalina Press,
which is a subdivision of Phalina, LLC.
PO Box 300040
Austin, TX 78703

Cover design and interior design by David Provolo

Cover image: *Glance at the Bund*, Virtual Shanghai Collection, 1933,
Photographer: Zhenchang Tang

Shanghai Map:
Shanghai, International Settlements 1932
Stock Image by Historia for editorial use, 1932

Cataloging-in-Publication data
Library of Congress Control Number: 2020914445
ISBN 978-1-7352334-3-7

Printed in the United States of America on acid-free paper.

19 20 21 22 23 10 9 8 7 6 5 4 3 2 1

First Edition

For MAPP

He had passed through an ordeal of wretchedness which had given him more than it had taken away . . . there was left to him a dignified calm he had never before known, and that indifference to fate which, though it often makes a villain of a man, is the basis of his sublimity when it does not. And thus the abasement had been exaltation, and the loss gain.
—Thomas Hardy

Each could feel
The sly and simple current run,
The juice between them, flicking forth,
The anode-cathode of themselves—
The mighty earnestness so small
They couldn't see it—might not even
Speak of it. And yet it lived, would always live
Between them day or dark.
—MacKinlay Kantor

Author's note

For Chinese place names I utilize the Wades-Giles system that was the standard during the 1940s and before. So, for example, whereas today we use the Pinyin system, and say and write Beijing or Chongqing, Westerners in in the early twentieth century would have said and written Peking or Chungking. Shanghai's Huangpu River was spelled Whangpoo, and Suzhou Creek was spelled Soochow. Larger place names in the novel such as bodies of water, streets, landmark buildings, and neighborhoods are the actual names as they existed; I did not make these up. The 5th Marine Regiment was active in the Pacific War, and fought at Guadalcanal, Cape Gloucester, Peleliu, and Okinawa. The 5th Marine Regiment is one of four regiments (along with the 1st, the 7th, and the 11th) that make up the First Marine Division. In wartime each Marine regiment is normally composed of four battalions of eight hundred men each. Each battalion is composed of three rifle companies of roughly two hundred men each (as well as smaller headquarters and weapons companies). The companies are commanded by a captain. Although many of the characters in this novel are partially based on actual people, only historical figures have kept their real names, such as admirals, generals, politicians, musicians, actors, etc.

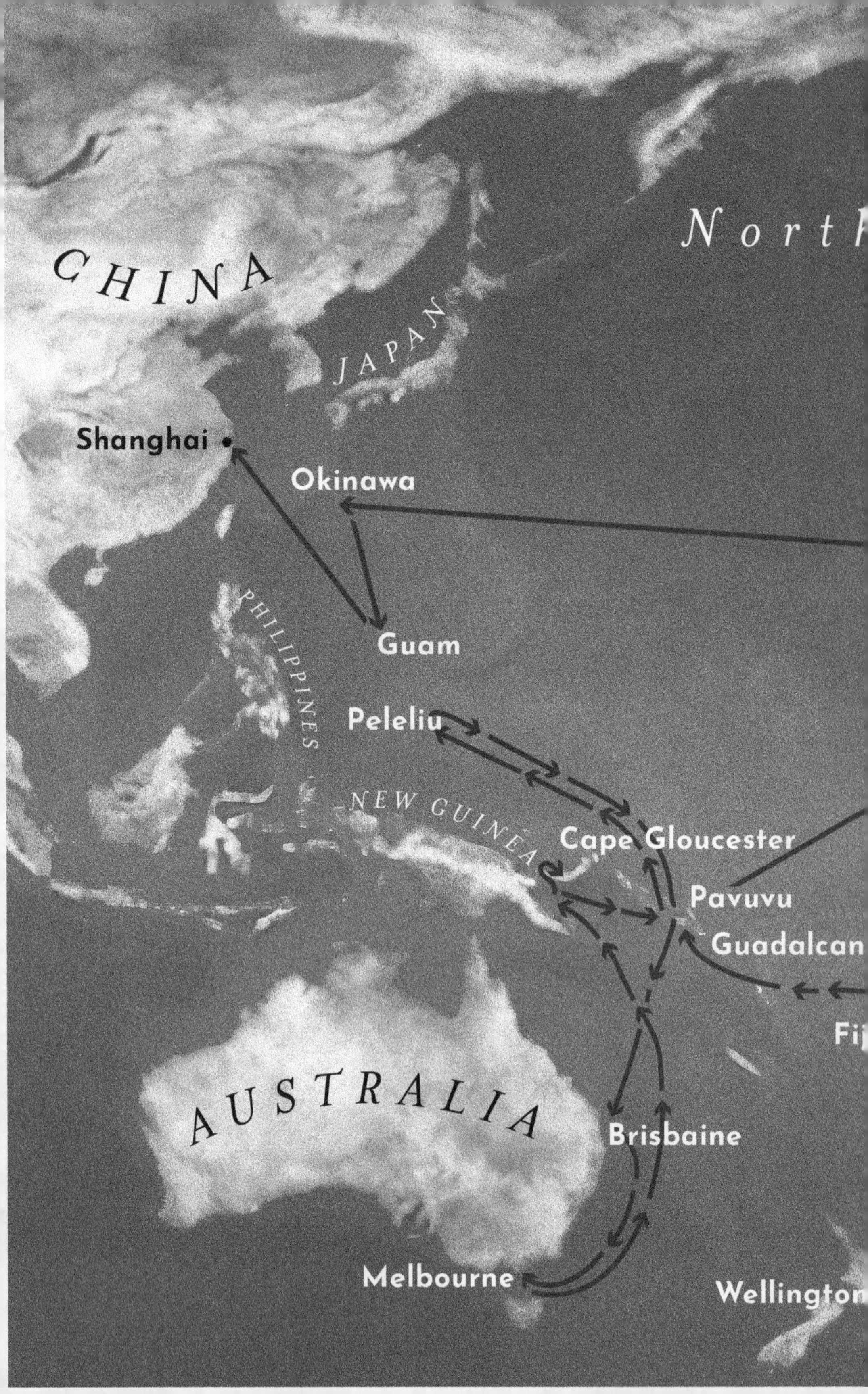

CHINA
JAPAN
North
Shanghai
Okinawa
PHILIPPINES
Guam
Peleliu
NEW GUINEA
Cape Gloucester
Pavuvu
Guadalcan
Fi
AUSTRALIA
Brisbaine
Melbourne
Wellington

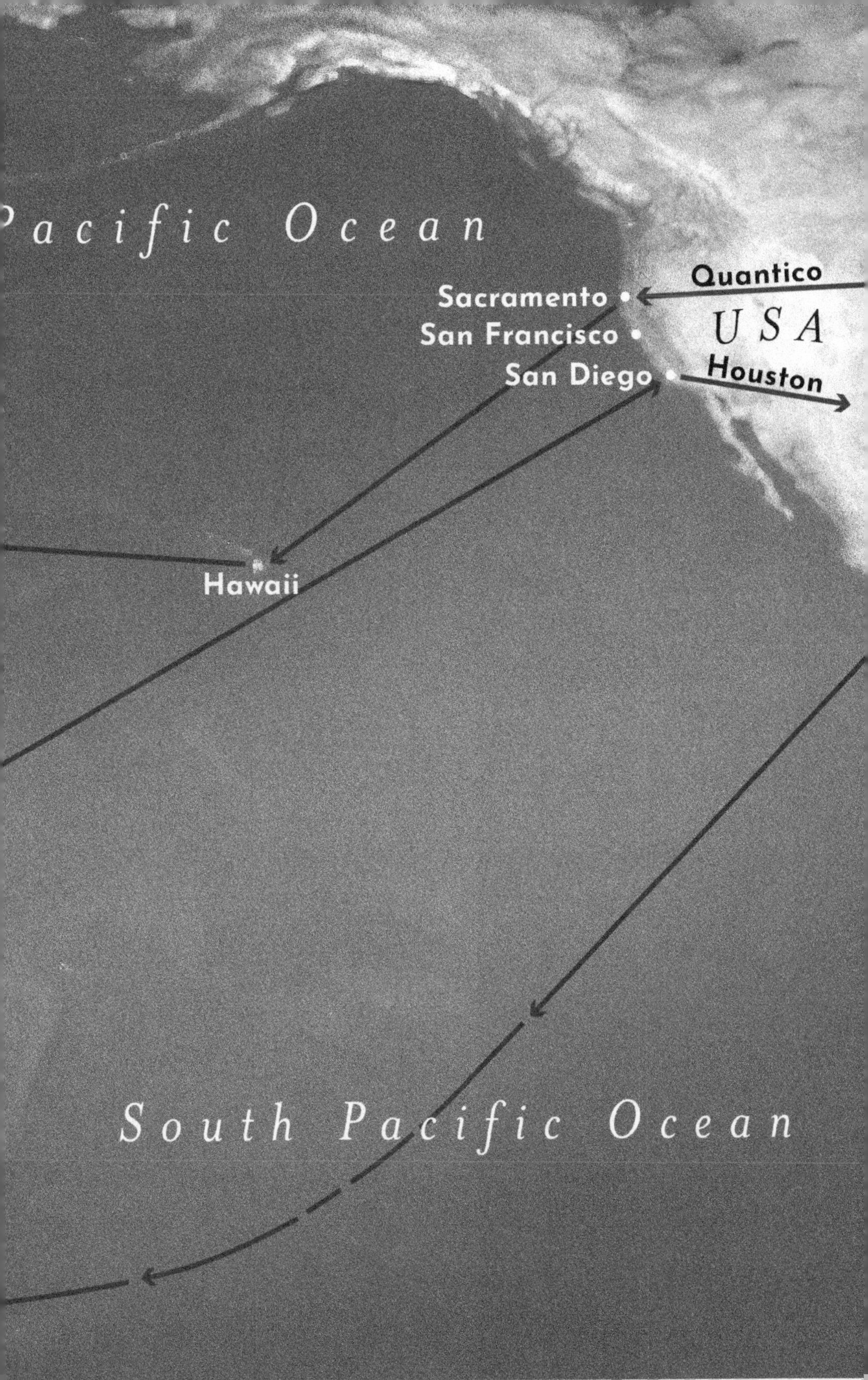

Pacific Ocean
Quantico
Sacramento
USA
San Francisco
San Diego
Houston
Hawaii
South Pacific Ocean

Prologue

September 19, 1945

There it was. He instantly recognized the smell. He hadn't been in Shanghai for years, but this was a malodor so redolent of the city that it couldn't be mistaken for any other place. Long ago he had surmised that the foulness started with the river and eventually pervaded everything it came in contact with—the people, their clothes, the streets, the food. This peculiar odor transported him back to the first moment he had come to the city, six long years ago. It may just as well have been sixty. Years filled with war, friendships, wrenching losses, the struggle to get back to Viktoria.

Harry's return was somewhat unexpected, and though he had prepared himself mentally as best as he could, it had not really hit him until today that he would be in Shanghai. Now, as he sat in the passenger seat of an old Citroën, gazing out the window at the crowded streets of a liberated but desperate city, the realization of his return washed over him along with the cloying stench of the Whangpoo River.

The convoy of vehicles slowly made its way west on Nanking Road. The main commercial street of Shanghai's prewar International Settlement was still lined with shops and department stores. For a short while, a group of revelers blocked the road. Once the crowd had dispersed, the convoy continued on until forced to halt at an intersection packed with pedestrians and rickshaws.

Harry asked his driver, Alston, to stop, and he got out to see what the holdup was. Standing on the sidewalk Harry spotted what he thought was a European face in the crowd. It was a woman. Perhaps she was Eurasian. He quickly lost sight of her. Looking farther west he could make out the building where the Savin teashop was located. It was near the Sincere Department Store, a notable landmark on Nanking Road.

Harry reflexively ducked his head when a small explosion of fireworks erupted nearby. He cursed under his breath as he climbed back into the Citroën. Once more the convoy advanced, moving slowly to avoid crushing anyone.

Soon afterward Harry again asked Alston to stop the car.

"Sir?"

"Let the trucks go on ahead. They know where they're going. I want to see something for a moment."

Harry got out. The Cyrillic lettering over the entrance was still visible. Harry went inside; Alston followed behind him. The stately tearoom had been ransacked, the furniture and most of the fixtures gone. Harry's mind filled with memories of this place, where he had first gotten to know Viktoria—drinking tea together and eating *piroshky*, the Russian stuffed pastries he had so come to love. He remembered the blue dress she'd worn and the scent of her perfume the first time they met there. He could even have identified the booth where they had sat, had it still been there.

Alston conspicuously displayed a Thompson, slung over his right shoulder. He remained near the door to keep an eye on the car. Harry's .45 was in its holster, but he was conscious of it at all times. Three Chinese merchants were selling various wares inside the shop. They stood and mutely watched the two Americans with suspicion. Harry went toward the back to investigate, hoping to gain some clue as to the tea merchant's whereabouts. In the old kitchen the aroma of cakes and tea had been replaced by the pungency of garlic and fish. Harry turned and walked back into the main room. He looked at one of the merchants and tried out his rusty Pidgin English.

"My wanchee savvy, s'pose Russia man have got, no got?"

The man shook his head and said something, but Harry couldn't understand.

Harry answered in Pidgin. "Me no savvy."

A burly middle-aged woman walked over to Harry, took his left arm, and pointed toward the door, saying something loudly in Chinese. Harry gently took hold of her arm and removed it from his. She said something again, shouting now and angrily gesturing toward the exit. Alston took the Thompson from his shoulder and held it ready. Harry motioned to him that it was okay. "They've gotten to where they have an innate distrust of anyone in uniform. Can't blame them."

Harry turned to the woman and said in English, "I'm looking for the people who used to be here. The Russians? Savvy?"

She shook her head and gave Harry a hostile look.

Harry used the only Chinese he could remember. "*Mei-yu fa-tze.*" He looked at Alston and repeated himself in English. "I guess it can't be helped."

They walked back outside, where a crowd had gathered beside the car. Two young boys were crouched in front of it. When they saw Harry and Alston, they jumped up and offered to shine their boots, speaking in rudimentary English.

Alston shooed them away, and he and Harry climbed back into the coupe. Alston started the engine and it backfired. The onlookers scattered rapidly.

Harry smiled and looked over at Alston. "Did you do that on purpose, Corporal?"

"No, sir. Just lucky." He put the car in gear, and they drove farther west on Nanking Road to where it merged with Bubbling Well Road.

After several minutes, Alston's curiosity got the better of him. "None of my business, Major Dietrichson, but what was all that about at the shop back there? The Russians, I mean?"

"The owners were a family I knew when I lived here before the war. They were good to me. I just wanted to find out what happened to them." Harry said nothing more about it. But his mind raced with an array of feelings. The Whangpoo's foul-smelling waters spurred many untold—yet not forgotten—memories of his days in what some had once called the Paris of the East. He had to find Viktoria.

Chapter One

June 28, 1941

The liner slipped down the Whangpoo to the estuary of the Yangtze River, China's artery and lifeline to the world. As Shanghai's skyline faded from view, Harry saw the imposing Japanese naval presence anchored on the roadstead. A dozen warships—the largest a cruiser—sat like a pack of wolves, silently and patiently observing a herd of caribou at a distance. The few smaller British and American warships anchored farther to the south, closer to the Bund, seemed almost quaint in comparison.

Harry stood at the rail and looked down. As the estuary gave way to the ocean, the turgid brown water of the Yangtze met the dull green water of the East China Sea. The river appeared to flow above the adjoining sea, and the ship seemed to be sailing down a hill, as if being poured out onto the plain of the ocean. Here, the two bodies of liquid were hesitant to mingle, and they sat side by side like vinegar and oil. The muddled, confused waters expressed Harry's feelings well, and he found himself immersed in dark thoughts.

He had been left standing on the quay in Shanghai that morning, hoping against hope that Viktoria would arrive to accompany him back to the United States. Instead, she had informed him that she would not be coming with him after all. It seemed to Harry that all the people he had ever loved either died or pushed him away. Viktoria proved the rule, not the exception. And now here he was, sailing back to America alone, with a cable from the War Department in his breast pocket, informing him that he was to report to the United States Naval Station in New Orleans at the end of July.

In the gathering storm, the United States was calling its young men back home. Harry had but one week to pack up and say his good-byes in Shanghai. It was during this time he and Viktoria had secretly agreed to be married. Her family was against the marriage, but he had convinced her to leave Shanghai and come with him. Like Harry, she had been adopted by an aunt and uncle upon the death of her parents. Harry and Viktoria often jokingly called themselves "the lost orphans." Their stories were so similar. But whereas Viktoria maintained a close relationship with her family, Harry's relationship with his uncle had been strained at best, and often contentious.

Harry Dietrichson was twenty-five years old. He was tall, with straw-colored hair and bright blue-gray eyes that seemed to bore right through you. His hair was already thinning, and his nose was slightly crooked, which kept him from being classically handsome. But he possessed a genuine sincerity that attracted people. His knowing eyes and unassuming personality made people both curious and comfortable in his presence. He could make them feel within the first few minutes of conversation as though they had known him for a long time. But Harry rarely spoke about himself, because he understood that most people really wanted to know only just *so* much about another person.

Harry kept to himself mostly because what he had seen and experienced in his scant years of existence had been lamentable. When people asked him personal questions, he usually tried to change the subject. And if dark thoughts—his own way of describing his recurring bouts of depression—came over him, he would suddenly turn inward, leaving others to wonder whether he was the same person they had known previously.

But what truly set Harry apart from other young men his age was his ability to interact with people older and more powerful than he was. He could almost immediately put himself on the same footing with them. He made them feel not just as if he were their equal but also grateful that he was bringing them into *his* confidence. He showed respect but never abject deference. Powerful individuals have an innate sense for obsequiousness, and although some revel in it, the truly great ones despise it. Harry understood this long before most of his peers did.

Travelers on ocean liners usually looked forward to dining with fellow passengers on the long crossing where they could engage in lively discussions on culture, politics, and the world situation. That was especially true now, with America on the cusp of war. Harry, however, stayed to himself on this voyage. He read to distract his thoughts, primarily from *The Pilgrim's Progress*, his grandmother Sarah's favorite book. A precocious child, Harry thought that Bunyan's descriptions of the Celestial City were descriptions of a faraway Shangri-La somewhere in the Orient. He joked to others during his time in the Far East that *The Pilgrim's Progress* was as responsible for his being out there as anything else. Now Harry felt as far away from Bunyan's allegory of paradise as any man could feel.

Harry was relieved when they finally docked in San Francisco. The familiarity of the language, the people, and the surroundings all put him at ease. Before he caught the evening train east, he sent a cable to his family in Texas. He took a cab into Chinatown to have an early supper at a chop suey parlor. The food on the ship had been bland. In Shanghai he had developed a taste for Chinese food, and he felt an urge to have some. Although the chow mein they served was a poor imitation, Harry enjoyed it. For the first time in quite a while he felt hungry. He sat alone at a table below a photo of the restaurant owner standing with Joe DiMaggio, and ate ravenously.

After the meal, as Harry walked down the street, he passed a young Chinese girl standing on the corner in the summer evening's light. Spread in front of her was a blanket on which four Chow Chow puppies sat. He stopped and smiled. He had bought a Chow Chow puppy for Viktoria in Shanghai the previous year. She was delighted and had named the puppy Lev. Harry clearly remembered the vexed expression on her uncle's face when he and Viktoria returned to her house with the puppy. The young girl picked up one of the puppies and offered it to Harry. He shook his head, but then he thought of his cousin Henry back in Houston. On an impulse, he bought one of the puppies. His uncle wouldn't be happy about it, but he didn't care. Henry and his older sister, Jolyn, were the two people Harry felt closest to back home. Later, after a short conversation with the Pullman conductor, Harry was able to find an old birdcage that had been left at the train station. It would suffice as a pet carrier. For the first time since leaving Shanghai, Harry accepted the companionship of another being.

Two days later the train pulled into the station in Houston. Harry's tow-headed cousin Henry stood out in front of the crowd. He was wearing the sailor suit—now much too small for him—that Harry had given him upon receiving his commission as a naval officer after college. Jolyn, now almost thirteen years old, stood behind him. When they made eye contact they both bounded forward to greet Harry and smother him in hugs. Their exuberance doubled when they saw the puppy.

Aunt Jo was wearing a blue cotton dress and a white hat. She came forward and greeted Harry with a tender hug. A vivacious, petite ginger-haired woman from Mobile Bay, she had always been caring and loving toward Harry. Uncle Walter, the younger brother of Harry's deceased father, was wearing a beige poplin suit and a brown fedora. He was clearly not happy about the dog, but he said nothing. He took Harry's hand in a firm shake. "Welcome home, boy," was all he could muster, even though they hadn't seen one another since 1939. Over the years Harry had gotten used to this, but he grudgingly admitted to himself that Walter had shown immense generosity bringing Harry in during the Depression, when most people were having a hard time putting food on the table.

"Did ya git 'im in China, Harry?" Jolyn asked as she pet the puppy, which squirmed in Henry's arms. She had her mother's ginger hair and happy eyes.

"I got him in Frisco, in Chinatown. He's a Chow Chow. He'll get big . . . and look like a lion. They use them as hunting dogs in China."

"What are we gonna name him?" Jolyn asked.

"I'm gonna call him Harry," said Henry.

"That's dumb, Lefty. We can't have two Harrys!" Jolyn said disdainfully.

Harry had begun calling Henry by the nickname "Lefty" for obvious reasons when his cousin was a young boy. But also because Harry's favorite ballplayer growing up was Lefty Grove of the Philadelphia A's. Uncle Walter and Aunt Jo hated the nickname, but it stuck.

Aunt Jo looked at Harry. "We're so glad to have you back."

"It won't be for long," Walter said, biting off the end of a cigar. "He's got to be in New Orleans by the end of the month." Walter, who was growing portly in middle age, had the same piercing blue-gray eyes that they both had in common with Harry's grandmother Sarah.

"Well, let's not push him out the door just yet." Aunt Jo took Harry's arm, and they began walking. "You're skin and bones. We need to fatten you up for the Navy."

As they drove home in Walter's Studebaker Commander, Harry

fished two silver coins from his pocket and gave them to the kids. "Another present. These are from China."

Jolyn turned the coin over in her hand. "It's from Mexico, Harry."

"I know. They use the Mexican silver dollar all over China."

"Really?" piped up Henry. "Why?"

"Well, Mexico traded with the Philippines when they were both part of Spain, so somehow a lot of these coins got into circulation. Everyone got used to Mexican silver dollars, and so the Chinese traders still use them. The Chinese Red Army even pays their soldiers in this coin."

"Are they the ones fighting the Japanese?" Jolyn asked.

"No—I mean, yes. Well, they're fighting the Japanese, but they're also fighting the Chinese Nationalists under Chiang Kai-shek, who's also fighting against the Japanese."

"But why are the Chinese fighting each other?"

Harry shook his head. "It's complicated."

"Hey, this one's from 1929!" Jolyn exclaimed. "The year I was born. Lefty, let me see yours." She grabbed it out of her brother's hand as he struggled with the squirming puppy. "Wow, 1931! That's when *you* were born!"

"Hold on to those. Don't lose them. They bring good luck."

"Gee, thanks, Harry. These are swell." Jolyn leaned over and hugged him. "We're so glad you're back."

Jo turned toward the backseat with a big smile. "How does it feel to be back, Harry?"

"Well, I'm glad to see all of you. But there's so much going on in the Far East right now. Covering turbulent times like this is what all correspondents dream about."

"So, do you think the Japs will attack the East Indies?" Walter asked. "What's the correspondent's take?"

Harry sensed a sarcastic tone in the last part of his uncle's question. He thought a moment and looked out the window before answering. "I don't know. They may go after the Russians first. The army faction in Japan wants to clear the Soviets out and set up a buffer state in the Russian Far East—like Manchuria." He went on, "The Japanese Navy really wants to get at those resources in Malaya and the East Indies, but I just don't see them taking that next step against Great Britain. They'd be biting off more than they could chew."

"Even with the war in Europe going so badly for the British?"

"Yes, well, that *could* change things, but you see, many of their naval officers were educated in England and the U.S. Although they recognize that the British and Dutch colonies may be ripe for the picking, they don't want to antagonize the West. I just don't see them making that big leap from war in China to war with England and potentially America."

"Well, I hope nothing happens, especially now that you're being called back into the service," Jo said as she gazed out the window at the traffic on Westheimer Road.

"You may be sent out to the Atlantic for convoy duty," Walter said. "Anyway, it's bound to heat up somewhere, and that's where our Navy will be, sure as shootin'."

Harry quietly shook his head in the backseat. His uncle had a way of turning any conversation negative. "By the way, Uncle Walter, I appreciate everything you did. You know, introducing me to your friend. Without that, I'd never have landed that job."

Walter shook his head imperceptibly, keeping his eyes on the road. "You got the job because you were qualified. I didn't have anything to do with it."

"I think I got the job because no correspondent worth his salt would agree to be posted to Tokyo."

"Why is that?" Jo asked.

"It's really oppressive for foreigners in Japan. The secret police followed me everywhere. Shanghai was much better in that regard."

"Anyway, you got the job in Shanghai on your own."

Although the remark was made as a compliment, Harry felt more like Walter was simply tossing him a bone. Harry knew that the best correspondents were in Chungking, the provisional capital of the Chinese Nationalist government, which had been fighting against the Japanese since 1937. He understood that Shanghai had been a demotion of sorts after Tokyo, but he didn't care, which was often the case when he became depressed. He felt he had to leave Tokyo, and he might as well go to Shanghai.

"I'm gonna call him Popeye," Henry blurted out. "He'll be a sailor-man just like you, Harry."

"That's a great name, Lefty!" Harry rubbed the puppy's head.

Aunt Jo laughed. "That boy of ours has got *quite* an imagination."

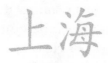

Chapter Two

With Walter busy at work, Harry spent most of his time at the Dietrichson house in the River Oaks neighborhood of Houston. There he regaled Aunt Jo and his two young cousins with his tales about the Far East. Naturally, some of the stories were about Viktoria, but Aunt Jo didn't say anything at the mention of her name. Later, during a quiet moment together, Jo asked Harry to tell her more about Viktoria. He sighed, leaned back in his chair, and told his aunt about Shanghai—and the woman he'd fallen in love with there.

Shanghai is the door to the Yangtze River Valley and hence the hinterland of all Central China. That is why both the British and the Japanese felt they needed to control it. The British for economic reasons, and the Japanese for strategic reasons. Although most of northern and eastern China was in Japanese hands by 1941, the international concession territories in Shanghai and in other cities along the Chinese seaboard were still neutral bastions. Shanghai's importance in the ongoing war between China and Japan had taken Harry there as a correspondent for United Press in 1939. As far as he knew, he was the youngest Western correspondent in China at the time.

Stretching inland for miles from the Whangpoo River was Shanghai's International Settlement—the British concession. Behind high compound walls, grand homes—built in typical English fashion—were occupied by wealthy families and their Chinese servants. Within the International Settlement one found Gothic and Romanesque churches as well as the manicured grounds of exclusive country clubs. Just to the south of the International Settlement was the French Concession, or "Frenchtown" to the other Westerners. The French Concession was a more eclectic mix of Western residences, Chinese-style homes and temples, and Russian churches. To the north of the International Settlement, across Soochow Creek, was the district named Hongkew, situated on a large bend of the Whangpoo. Hongkew dominates the waterborne approach to the city from the Yangtze. Originally it had been the American Concession, Harry explained to Jo, but the Japanese now controlled it.

Soon after his arrival there, in the spring of 1939, Harry agreed to meet an acquaintance for drinks on the top floor of the Cathay Hotel on the Bund. The Bund, the center of Shanghai's International Settlement, is a road hugging the embankment of the river. Its ornate neoclassical skyscrapers would have fit perfectly in New York or Chicago. Some were beautifully—if garishly—decorated in a Moorish or Baroque style that included columns, sculptures, and bas-reliefs. The grand Western-style Hong Kong and Shanghai Bank building looked more like an Italian church than a bank. The pair of bronze lions that flanked the entrance gave comfort to the citizens of the British Empire who passed through its doors every day. The most prominent of these buildings on the Bund was the Cathay Hotel, with its high peaked roof.

While waiting for the elevator in the lobby of the Cathay, Harry heard Russian voices. He turned and saw three women emerging from the elevator on the opposite side. They seemed to be about his age. He realized he'd seen them once before. One of the young ladies had flowing blond hair—rare in the days when most women bobbed their hair—and the high cheekbones of a Slav. She was wearing a green cocktail dress with short sleeves. She gave Harry a sidelong glance, smiling discreetly. A large Cossack bodyguard escorted them out of the hotel into a waiting car. Harry stood and watched as they walked out of the lobby. He noticed a purple scarf that had fallen near the door. He went over, picked it up, and hurried out to the car. Just as they were set to drive off, Harry knocked on the back door. The young blond woman rolled down her window.

"Excuse me, miss, but I think you may have dropped this," he said holding out the scarf. "Is it yours?"

"No, it belongs to my cousin, but thank you. You are a gentleman." She reached and took the scarf. She looked at him with warm blue eyes.

"I was on the boat last week from Yokohama with your father, I believe. You came with your family to meet him at the quay?"

"Yes, I remember. That was my uncle." She smiled, and only at that moment did Harry notice the other passengers, who shifted in their seats, impatient to move on.

Harry liked her eyes, her smile, her voice. He sensed a familiarity, though they had never before exchanged a word in their lives. She held his gaze momentarily, seeming to confirm the feeling. He tried to prolong the conversation. But by the time he finally thought of something to say, she had rolled the window up and the car sped off. Harry stood and watched as it merged into the traffic heading south down the Bund.

"That's so romantic, like the slipper from Cinderella." Aunt Jo interrupted his reverie. "Who was her uncle?"

"Hmm? Her uncle?" Harry exhaled. "That's another long story."

"Well, I mean, it's just so interesting, you know? The Russian émigrés? No country, no passports, no prospects. Poor souls."

Harry went on to explain that most White Russians were in Shanghai out of necessity, not by choice like the British and the French. Mostly middle-class professionals, the White Russians—called "White" because of their opposition to the Bolshevik "Red" forces during the Civil War—had fled into northern China and Manchuria after the Bolshevik triumph. There they built their own towns and communities, just as the British and the French had done across China and the Far East. But with the Japanese takeover of Manchuria in the early 1930s, more and more Russians were streaming into Shanghai. Although the White Russians were stateless and powerless before both Western extraterritorial laws and the Chinese judiciary, they constituted a powerful presence in their own right.

The ubiquitous White Russians made up a large part of the mosaic of daily life in Shanghai. Russian merchants sold everything from jewels and furs to pleasures of the flesh. Russian officers served with the Shanghai Municipal Police and as private bodyguards for wealthy Westerners and Chinese. But mostly the Russians came to dominate the cultural world of the International Settlement and the French Concession: Russian musicians and dancers populated almost every cabaret and nightclub; Russian artists sold cheap portraits on the street and fine sculptures out of studios; and Russian fashion stores and jewelry makers were the rage, especially among wealthy Chinese clients. Young (and not-so-young) Russian women dominated the Shanghai nightlife as pretty accoutrements, dance partners, or lowly prostitutes.

But Viktoria's family was in Shanghai by choice. "Viktoria's uncle, Grigorii Savin, is a legend in Shanghai," Harry explained to Jo. "He's been out in the Far East since before the Revolution. He was originally a high official of the Romanovs. He made a fortune in China, exporting tea. He has a big shop on Nanking Road and several warehouses in the region. Everyone in Shanghai knows him or has heard of the Savins. He has clients in Europe, Japan, and North and South America. They say he even sells tea to the Soviets, and that he is politically connected there."

Harry lit a cigarette before he went on wistfully. "The family lives in a mansion in the French Concession. They throw these wonderful soirées, Aunt Jo. You should see it: acrobats, jugglers, dancers—one time they had even dancing bears. Savin and his wife, Maria, support an extended family that fled Moscow when the Bolsheviks came to power."

"And his niece, Viktoria?"

"We were in love." He paused for a moment and then corrected himself. "Well, we *are* in love, I mean."

"What happened?"

"I don't know, really, and I guess I'll never fully understand the whole story. But she left me waiting at the boat alone. She told me she couldn't leave her family, under the circumstances."

"From your letters we thought you might be coming back with her. You must be so disappointed, poor dear." Jo patted Harry's arm. "I should think her family would be happy to see her get away, to come to America."

"Her uncle has queer notions of returning to Russia one day and restoring the Romanovs to the throne."

"Well, that's crazy."

"I totally agree. The Tsar will never come back."

"No, no, Harry, I mean . . . I don't know much about the politics, but she could never find a better man than *you*."

"I wanted to marry her and spend my life with her, Aunt Jo. And now, I don't know." He shook his head. "I'm angry with her, and I don't know if it's even worth writing to her anymore."

"Well, as I said, she's missing out. You're a good man."

"Thanks, but all the same, I'd prefer not to speak about her anymore."

Jo sighed and then stood to put a record on the Victrola. It was

a record Harry had brought back as a gift to her from Shanghai—
Rimsky-Korsakov's symphonic masterpiece *Scheherazade*. As the music
commenced, Harry closed his eyes for a moment, remembering.

It was a humid Saturday afternoon in Shanghai, with rain show-
ers off and on. Harry was in Arnaud's, a French-owned store that had
Shanghai's best collection of jazz and classical records. Harry asked the
owner to recommend some pieces by Tchaikovsky and Rachmaninoff to
satisfy his newfound interest in Russian composers. Just then a young
woman wearing a light-gray beret and a red raincoat walked into the
store. She and Arnaud greeted one another familiarly. As she proceeded
to browse, Harry realized he recognized her. It was Viktoria Savina. As
soon as she saw Harry, she too flashed a smile of recognition.

Her blue eyes were as mesmerizing as Harry remembered from their
encounter in front of the Cathay. Harry guessed she was about twenty
years old. Arnaud formally introduced the two of them by name and
explained to Viktoria that since Harry was looking for Russian composers, she was better placed to steer him in the right direction. She agreed
and said she would be happy to give Harry some ideas.

Once Arnaud had returned to the front of the store Harry spoke first.
"Do you remember me? From the Cathay a few nights ago? I returned
your scarf."

She blushed slightly. "Yes, of course. It was my cousin's scarf. That
was kind of you. Shanghai is a small city: you run into the same people
all the time." She changed the subject. "I'm surprised to see an American
interested in buying music by Russian composers. Shouldn't you be looking for swing records?" She spoke English with a crisp, clean accent. Harry
guessed it was from long hours studying with tutors and governesses.

"Well, you may not know this, but American jazz and swing music
have deep Russian connections. George Gershwin, Irving Berlin. I guess
you could say that I'm getting back to the roots of it all."

She smiled, her eyes observing him from above her smooth cheeks.
"Well, Mr. Dietrichson, I'm happy to help you look." Harry noticed that
she pronounced his name perfectly.

Together again, they reassumed the easy, unaffected familiarity of the
brief encounter at the Cathay. As they spoke, Harry never thought to try
to impress her; there was no pretense, no attempt at bluster. That wasn't

Harry's way. With Viktoria, more than ever before, he felt an instant connection, and he hoped she felt the same way.

As they browsed the selections, she explained to him, "Your collection should contain a copy of Rimsky-Korsakov's *Scheherazade*. It is one of my favorites. Unlike Tchaikovsky and others, who were heavily influenced by German and Austrian composers, Rimsky-Korsakov looked to capture the essence of Russia in his music." Harry noticed she spoke with great conviction, and with a hint of pride. "You must also buy Mussorgsky; he uses Russian themes too. Their music is so much bolder and richer than Tchaikovsky's or Rachmaninoff's. *Pictures at an Exhibition* is one of my favorite Mussorgsky pieces."

Viktoria could have told Harry to buy a fur hat on that hot day, and he would have gone and done so. She spoke with an easy affability. She was also a good listener, and she met his eyes throughout their conversation. They laughed easily together a few times. Although they spoke for about ten minutes, to Harry it seemed like only ten seconds. Try as he might, he could think of no way to prolong the conversation. He thought about inviting her to tea or coffee, but as he considered it, suddenly she seemed too unreachable. He thought to himself, *What could a woman like her ever see in a fellow like me?* He was an orphan from a pitiable household in Pennsylvania. A correspondent with no money. This young woman was educated in all the arts; she probably plays a musical instrument. She's used to country clubs and social gatherings of the wealthiest people in Shanghai. Her clothes come from the best shops, in the latest fashions. What could he possibly offer her? With a feeling of unworthiness that stuck in his craw, Harry doubted whether he could ever manage to attract and hold the affection of a young woman as sophisticated as Viktoria.

And so, lost in those thoughts, Harry was surprised as they parted to hear her say, "I hope we will see each other again, Mr. Dietrichson."

During his time with the children in Houston, Harry told them humorous anecdotes about life in Tokyo or Shanghai. He liked to retell the story of how strangers in Japan would tell him they spoke no English, even when he approached them speaking Japanese. They did not seem to understand that a foreigner could speak their language and would evince great surprise—which Harry artfully mimicked—when they realized this young American was speaking Japanese.

"What do they speak in China, Harry?" Henry asked him one day as they walked in a park near their home.

"Lefty, you dummy, they speak Chinese," Jolyn said.

"That's a great question, Lefty. In Shanghai they speak a lot of different languages. Most people can get by with English, but people there speak French, Russian, and Portuguese. They also speak different dialects of Chinese."

"What's a dialect?" Henry asked.

"It means that the languages are similar but not exactly the same. It's like when I first moved to Texas, when I was about Jolyn's age, if I used a Pennsylvania Dutch expression like 'Outen the lights,' or asked for scrapple in the diner, people would give me strange looks. But most everybody in Shanghai speaks Pidgin English."

"Pigeons, like the birds?"

"No, Lefty. It's a way people talk that mixes up the languages to make it easier for everyone to understand one another. It comes from the word 'business.' The Chinese had a hard time pronouncing it, so they started saying 'Pidgin' instead. I had to speak it with delivery boys and other people I dealt with, like rickshaw drivers."

Henry looked up quizzically. "Did you have a wife there too, Harry?"

"No, Lefty, just a gal I was friendly with."

"Is it true you were engaged?" Jolyn asked.

"Yes, but she didn't want to be married to me." He quickly changed the subject. "You know, Lefty, when I get my orders, I might just have to take Popeye with me shipboard, him being a sailor and all."

"*No!*" the boy protested. He scooped the puppy into his arms and ran ahead.

Chapter Three

Viktoria Savina sat staring out of a window into the garden, watching raindrops bounce off the leaves of the pear tree. Recently, she often found herself sitting alone, lost in thought. Harry had been gone now for several weeks. Time and time again she asked herself whether she had made the right decision. She tortured herself each day replaying her last conversation with him. Was she better off staying? Was her family better off because she stayed? Was she wrong to think her uncle and aunt expected this sacrifice from her—their niece, not their daughter?

The walls of the house seemed to close in on her. She hardly heard or understood what other people were telling her. She became curt with everyone, especially her younger cousins. And Tanya was no longer there for support when she needed it most. Viktoria had never been so alone in her life. She tried to find comfort in reading the copy of *The Pilgrim's Progress* Harry had given her on her birthday the year before. But Viktoria found that trying to follow the parables of Christian only made her think more about Harry—and she was heartsick.

Entirely bereft of emotional support, Viktoria decided to go each day to St. Nicholas Cathedral, Shanghai's Russian Orthodox church that had served the community for close to sixty years. She found solace in the dark interior, surrounded by the rich colors of the religious paintings and icons. The Sunday service gave her the most comfort. The beautiful choral singing in Church Slavonic and the aromatic incense enveloped her in warmth and gave her a sense of belonging. She felt part of a community when she was at the church. When she confessed to her *Batushka*, Dmitry, for the first time after Harry left, she told him that she had sinned and had lain with a man before marriage. It was her first confession in almost two years. She had avoided the confessional ever since she became intimate with Harry. She didn't want to hide the fact from Father Dmitry, so she chose simply not attend confession. Until now. Viktoria asked Father Dmitry many of the questions that had nagged her since Harry left.

"Would it have been wrong to leave my family, Father, even if was with the man I love?"

"Why did you choose *not* to leave, my child?"

"I felt that I would be abandoning them. You see, Father, my cousin Tanya eloped with her English boyfriend just before Harry and I were due to set sail for San Francisco."

"The decision you made was the only decision you could have made. Was it correct? The correct decision was the only one you could have chosen. Had you chosen to leave with your young man, that would have been the correct decision. I'm not necessarily saying that it was preordained, but God was with you in spirit when you made the decision. And He supports you and loves you as you make your way forward."

"I see, Father."

"As for your cousin Tanya, she left without the permission of her parents, but that does not make hers a bad decision. She has her own reasons for leaving. She felt differently than you did, but God will bless her just the same as He blesses you, my dear."

"Thank you, Father."

Father Dmitry asked Viktoria to return more often, to open up her heart to him and to confess before God.

Now that she was back in the fold of the church, Viktoria felt better spiritually for having confessed, but emotionally she was still adrift. She no longer had her parents, and though she was close to her aunt and uncle, she felt she couldn't talk to them about Harry. She wasn't even sure she could have gone to her own parents. She sighed and looked over at a framed photo of her father. He looked earnestly at the camera from under a fur hat, somewhere in Siberia. She barely remembered the long train ride across the frozen vastness of Russia to escape the Red Army during the Civil War. The crowded, stinking railcars, the frozen sleigh rides. Didn't she remember huddling in her father's arms? She brushed the idea away. He hadn't even been with them for the journey from Moscow. He was somewhere in Russia's Far East. Her mother had been with her, as had her older brother, Boris. Perhaps she had remembered huddling in Boris' arms. Not long after arriving in Vladivostok on Russia's Pacific coast, Viktoria's mother lost a child at birth. It was a boy. Medicines and care were in short supply throughout that time. After the tragedy, Viktoria's father sent them onward to Shanghai, to be with his older brother. He left for the front, leading a regiment of Cossacks fighting near Mongolia. They never saw him again.

After they learned of her father's death, Viktoria's mother withdrew and ceased being a mother. She was unable to forgive herself for the loss of the baby. By this time Viktoria's brother had been sent to the Russian military academy in Harbin, where sons of Tsarist officers prepared to one day retake Mother Russia from the hated Bolsheviks. Viktoria remembered more moments of her childhood in the company of her beloved Aunt Maria, learning to cook or to tend the garden. Even before her mother passed away from pneumonia when Viktoria was fifteen, she seemed more the daughter of Maria than her own mother. The resemblance between her and Maria's oldest daughter, Tatiana—or Tanya—seemed to cement in the mind of the Russian community around Shanghai that Viktoria was in fact the daughter of Grigorii and Maria. Viktoria and Tanya were inseparable. They were closer than sisters or even best friends. It was almost as if they were twins, because they thought and acted so similarly.

Tanya had dark hair and deep brown eyes, but her resemblance to Viktoria was remarkable, especially the high cheekbones and the soft chin. Tanya was intelligent and well spoken, and Viktoria looked up to her. Tanya's beau, Edward Muncy, was a tall, square-shouldered young Englishman whom everyone said looked like a twin of Douglas Fairbanks Jr. He and the stunning Tatiana Savina were considered the most handsome couple in Shanghai. They were seen about town frequently, often in the company of Harry and Viktoria.

Edward Muncy was from a well-connected family that had been prominent in Britain's Far Eastern colonies for generations. After university in England, he returned to China—where he was born—to work in the company where his father was a director. His family and everyone in the British community in Shanghai disapproved of Edward's romance with Tanya. Chafing at the stilted conventions of society, Edward and Tanya eloped to Hong Kong in June 1941, a few days before Harry set sail for San Francisco.

Tanya's decision to elope with Edward the day before Viktoria was supposed to leave with Harry to America had been like a bolt from the sky. Tanya and Viktoria were *so* alike they had even—unknowingly—hatched similar plans to leave Shanghai. Tanya had acted more quickly. When Vickoria saw how devastated her aunt was, she hesitated to bring this misfortune down onto the family twice.

Viktoria had initially pushed back against Harry's pleas for her to leave with him for America. She tried to make him understand the importance she placed in trust and fidelity to family. "Even if I did agree to come with you back to America, I would like to have the permission of my aunt and uncle. Maybe you feel differently about your family, but I can't do anything without their blessing. Besides, I'm still so young. You're so young."

Harry kept up his persistence. "My family would understand if I had to give everything up and abandon them for someone I love."

"Harry, please understand the enormity of the decision I'm making. You have lived away from your family for almost four years. You have your own life, your own profession. I have never been apart from my family. And to leave them entirely behind in a time like this? Not knowing what might happen to them? I'm not saying I'm not prepared to leave with you or that I do not love you, but I need more time to think about it."

"Of course," he answered. "I understand. It was selfish of me to not think of it from your perspective."

Eventually, Viktoria relented. They met at the American Club several days after Harry received word that he had been called back to the States. The heat that day was overbearing, and the summer smells of Shanghai had reawakened, leaving the pleasant spring only a distant memory. Viktoria was dressed in a short beige dress. She left her hair down, and it shone gorgeously in the bright sunlight as she walked in. Harry was wearing a gray seersucker suit and a dark-blue bow tie. He stood to greet her. She smiled and leaned forward to kiss him on each cheek.

After they had settled in their seats, she said, "You know, Harry, it's been a difficult time for me recently, being torn between you and my family. But with you being forced to leave now, I'm able to think more clearly. I've decided I *will* go with you."

Harry could hardly believe his ears. "I'm speechless. I can't believe this isn't a dream. Pinch me."

She leaned across the table and took his hand, squeezing it. "That's right, I'm going to be your wife." She smiled radiantly.

Harry shouted out, "Hot damn!" The people sitting at other tables turned to look at the two young lovers. Harry winced, then said quietly but rapturously, "I'm sorry. I'm just so happy." He tightly gripped both of her hands. "I've booked passage on the boat through Manila leaving six days from now. We can be married here at the consulate. Or we can be married in San Francisco. I can arrange it easily." He paused and leaned over the table to kiss her. "I still can't believe it."

"I can't bear the idea of you leaving and never seeing you again."

"I feel the same way."

She asked Harry to come to her house and say farewell to her family, as he had been planning to do anyway. Viktoria's aunt and uncle had grown fond of Harry over the course of his relationship with their niece—but not to the point of seeing her married to him. Viktoria met him at the door of the Savin residence when he arrived the next evening. He could see that she had been crying.

Harry's heart dropped for a moment. "What's the matter, Love?"

"Oh, nothing. At least nothing for you to worry about." She wiped her eyes. "I'm just sad about my family. Uncle Grisha and Aunty Masha suspect nothing, and I might never see them again. They have been so good to me."

Harry hugged her. "I know it's tough. And you may regret your decision for a while, but I'm sure one day you'll realize that it was the right decision." He pulled back and looked her in the eyes. "I love you. And I understand how you feel. But it's going to be rough here, very soon, and we won't want to be here when that happens."

They went inside. Harry greeted Grigorii, Maria, and other family members. The dinner was a subdued affair. Everyone was genuinely saddened by the news that Harry—whom everybody truly liked—was leaving Shanghai. Both Grigorii and Maria made a special effort to show their affection for Harry, and that whatever may have come between them on the subject of Viktoria, they bore him no ill will. Harry tried to avoid looking at Viktoria, afraid that a knowing look could betray their impending elopement.

On the verandah after the digestifs had been drunk and the cigars smoked, Harry and Viktoria had time alone together. She lamented again how painful it was to be forced to make a decision between love and family. But she assured him she would be ready. No one knew—not even Tanya. She kissed him tenderly and whispered in his ear that she would come to his apartment tomorrow for tea at five o'clock.

The next evening Viktoria came to Harry's apartment. He made a dinner for her of scrambled eggs and toast. They sat around the rest of the evening listening to records on the Victrola and talking quietly about the future. As they made love they felt completely as one. In bed they spoke quietly and tenderly. She stayed with him until midnight. He took her down the elevator and had a driver take them to her house. As she prepared to get out of the car in the driveway, she told Harry that she would call him, and as a last resort meet him at the quay on the day the ship sailed. He kissed her deeply and told her he wished they could leave right at that moment.

And so, when Viktoria made her last-minute decision to stay with her family, she felt as if she were betraying him. She came to see him at his apartment the morning of his departure with a heavy heart. She hugged him and then took hold of his arm. She couldn't hide the look of desperation on her face, and she saw that Harry sensed immediately something was amiss.

He said quietly, "It's off, isn't it?"

"I just can't do it."

Harry nodded and bit his lip. He then closed his eyes for a moment. He started to say something, then stopped.

"I was ready to leave with you, Harry, to leave everything behind. But I can't." She paused for a moment as Harry waited expectantly. "Tanya has eloped with Edward. They were wed in a civil ceremony a week ago."

"What?"

"They left for Hong Kong yesterday." She shook her head. "My uncle and my aunt are in shock."

"But what does that have to do with us?"

"Don't you see? They would be losing two daughters. I just don't know if they could bear this." She shook her head and looked down. "I've made this decision, Harry, only out of devotion to my family, not because I don't love you. It's just that I can't bear the idea of deserting them now."

"Please, don't do this, Vika. I'll do anything you want. Just tell me what I can do to change your mind."

"Oh, Harry, it's not you. It's just that…I just can't leave them now."

Harry clenched his jaw and then said in a tone of slight desperation, "Viktoria, *dusha moya*, how can I go anywhere? How can I do anything without you? I just don't understand. You do love me? Don't you?"

"Of course."

"Then what's the problem?"

"I love my family more, Harry. It's as simple as that. To abandon my family and leave for a land I know nothing about, to completely change my life, to change who I am."

"Viktoria, I can't wait for you; I have to leave now. There is no way of putting this off. Do you understand? After today you may never see me again."

"Harry, I'm trying to be strong on the outside, but inside I'm dying."

Harry closed his eyes and remained silent. They stood quietly for a few moments.

"I'm so sorry." Viktoria hugged him tightly and began to cry again.

"I love you, Viktoria."

She pulled away from him and looked into his eyes. "Harry, I'm heartbroken, but you must understand."

Harry had no answer. He started to leave, and then turned and said to her, "You haven't seen the last of me."

And so, over the course of the hot summer of 1941 in Shanghai, Viktoria found herself frequenting places where she and Harry had spent time together. On occasion she'd drop into Arnaud's record shop and buy a jazz or swing record of an artist Harry liked. At home she'd put on the music and daydream. Sometimes she'd have a coffee at the Cathay Hotel, another one of their haunts, and each time she walked by the Hamilton House, where Harry had rented an apartment, her heart sank. And if a place didn't remind her of Harry, it might remind her of Tanya. When she accompanied her uncle and aunt to the horse races that summer, she thought fondly of the many times she, Harry, Tanya, and Edward attended the races and bet on the horses.

And each evening before she lay in bed, she prayed for Harry. She prayed that he would patch up the relationship with his family, something she knew he needed but had been deprived of. She saw him in dreams, but each morning she awoke to the sad realization that she had jilted him and that he was probably angry. And though she wrote him several letters, his only reply was one terse, short letter telling her that he was leaving soon for officer training and would likely be too busy to write. Sensing Harry's anger, Viktoria wondered again whether she had made the right decision.

Chapter Four

One Saturday evening shortly after Harry arrived back in Houston, the Dietrichsons sat at the table over a supper of fried chicken. Halfway through the meal, Walter announced that he would take Harry to Smith Point on East Galveston Bay for a fishing trip the next day. Young Henry interjected, saying that he wanted to go too, but his father cut him off, saying, "I'd like to spend some time with Harry before he leaves." During high school and college Harry sometimes accompanied his uncle and his uncle's friends on day trips along the coast, where they would fish for speckled trout and redfish atop the saltwater flats. Harry loved to wade out in the bays and find serenity among the shorebirds and the marsh grasses.

They took the Studebaker down early the next morning. Since it was a Sunday, few cars were on the road and they were able to make the drive in just over an hour. They stopped in a bait shop and bought some live shrimp and crawdads. They put on their waders, hooked the bait buckets to their belts, donned their Abercrombie fishing hats, and started out into the warm waters of the bay. They had done this so many times before there was little need for conversation. In the still, hot morning the only noise was the muddy bottom sucking at their boots. They waded for a bit, searching for telltale signs such as bubbles or jumping bait fish. They cast their lines and waited. Harry had the first strike. As he reeled the fish in, he could sense his uncle's expectant eyes. He pulled up a small redfish.

Walter took an unlit cigar from his between clenched teeth and spit. "That's not a keeper."

Harry gently released the fish, rebaited his hook, and cast. Almost immediately a fish struck his line again, and he yanked his rod to set the hook. The fish got off. Walter was quick to offer advice, but his tone was typically negative. "You're setting your hook too early. Don't be so impatient." Harry waded off in a different direction. He heard his uncle yelp and turned to watch him reel in a nice-sized redfish. "Supper, my boy," he shouted to Harry.

Harry removed his hat and wiped his brow. He kept going, wading past a small bend. When he was satisfied that he could no longer see or hear his uncle, he began casting again. Over the next two hours he caught five speckled trout, three of them keepers, which he attached to his waistline through their gills.

Just before twelve o'clock, Walter appeared from around the bend. He had sweated through his vest. "How's the fishing over here?"

Harry looked at him. "Came across some specks. Haven't caught any reds, though." He pulled his waistline up and showed Walter the three trout, which were still alive but sluggish, offering almost no resistance.

"Good work. We're bringing home the bacon tonight. I got three more reds and one huge speck, bigger than any of yours." He smiled broadly, proud of his haul. "Whaddya say we go back and get the picnic basket from the car? I'm gettin' hungry. Besides, the fish are gonna lay up now."

"Sounds good. I could use a beer."

Once they had climbed out of their waders and put their gear away, they took their lunch and found a stunted oak tree near the shore. There they sat in the shade. Walter opened two bottles of Pearl beer that had been sitting in an ice chest. Harry was so thirsty he drank down nearly half the bottle. After Walter had drained his beer, he stood up and belched. He went to the car and took a wooden board from the back, brought it to the edge of the water, and expertly fileted the seven fish in no time. Harry always admired his uncle's dexterity with the thin filet knife. After Walter had finished and put the filets in the ice chest, he sat next to Harry and they silently ate bacon and tomato sandwiches. Harry thought to himself how ironic that the only person he could never feel fully comfortable around was his uncle, his own flesh and blood.

After a bit, Walter started to talk about a trip he had taken the previous fall to Port Aransas, where he and some friends fished for tarpon. "You know FDR likes to go fishing there," he said.

Harry nodded. He finished his beer and took another sandwich from the wax paper.

While he was on the topic of Roosevelt, Walter continued. "I just don't know how the Brits led him this far down the road toward war, with Lend-Lease and all. Like we need this now. We're just climbing out of the Depression, just getting our footing, and now we're getting hauled into a war in Europe again. Didn't we learn anything twenty-five years ago? Your own father died because of the last war."

Harry didn't correct this last statement, which wasn't quite true, but he offered a response anyway. "Seems to me it's a bit different now. Besides, our war may not be in Europe. We might be fighting in China instead. Or the Philippines."

"Hell, China's not our war. Europe's not our war either."

"Well, I'm not an expert and I wasn't around for the big war, but Hitler and Mussolini seem like a different kettle of fish altogether."

"You're right, you're not an expert," his uncle said, seeming to relish the opportunity for rebuttal. "You weren't around then. I'll tell you this: it was a fool's errand. And we got suckered into it. Our mother was heartbroken. I don't think she was ever the same after your pa died."

Harry nodded imperceptibly. He took another bottle of beer, opened it, and drank deeply. He lit a cigarette and sat silently for a while.

Then he brought up the topic that had been a point of contention between them for the past three years. "Uncle Walter? Why didn't you let me know earlier that Grandma Sarah had died? I would have at least liked to try and come back for her burial."

"What, with you halfway around the world in Japan? It would have taken too long."

"I might have splurged for the Pan Am Clipper."

"Sure, and you might have spent a year's salary doing so."

"But at least I would've liked to have had the option."

Walter took a bite out of a cigar and spit the end out. "Listen, I didn't expect to rehash this again. But we really didn't think it was appropriate to wait so long for her service and burial." He softened his tone a bit and said, "Look, Harry, I know it hit you hard. It hit us all. But I think she would have wanted you to keep on doing what you were doing: reporting. She wouldn't have wanted you to traipse all the way back. It wouldn't have changed anything anyway."

Harry nodded and drank his beer. They stayed quiet for some time. After they had finished smoking, they loaded up the car and drove back to Houston.

Walter and his half-brother, Henry—Harry's father—had an antagonistic relationship growing up in Reading, Pennsylvania. The boys were separated by five years and were sons of different fathers. Henry's father—Harry's grandfather—had died of pneumonia. Walter's father was their mother's second husband. He had been alcoholic and died in a work accident at the rail yards. Before he died, the man did not spare his own son or his stepson any of his abuse. But he seemed to especially relish tormenting his stepson, Henry. Out of this poisonous atmosphere, an adversarial relationship had developed between the two half-brothers, who fought mainly for the affection of their mother, Sarah. Harry's father Henry died during the Spanish influenza epidemic in the winter of 1918 on an Army base in Kansas, before he was shipped out to France. Harry was only two years old. Harry's mother, Elizabeth, succumbed several years later to cancer.

Sarah took in her grandson Harry when he was nine. She raised him and instilled in him the same values and humility that she had tried to instill in her own sons. But she quickly realized that her grandson was different. He was thoughtful and intelligent and much less impetuous than her two sons had been. More importantly, Sarah saw compassion in Harry. She saw to it that he was educated properly, and well read. Through her he developed his fascination for the world.

As she grew frail and sickly, Sarah decided in early 1930 to send Harry to live with his uncle in Texas. She felt that it would be better for her grandson—on the cusp of puberty—to live in a home with a male role model. In spite of the magnanimous gesture she was making, a gesture born of love, Harry—too young to understand—felt betrayed. His grandmother, the person he loved more than anybody in his entire life, was giving him up.

He pleaded and protested. "I can do everything for you. I can cook. I can get a job. I'll do whatever it takes. Just let me stay with you."

"Trust me, Harry, when I tell you this is for the best."

He ran out of the house and kept running until he had reached the foothills of Mt. Penn. It was dusk on a cold, raw day. Harry had no coat to guard against the chill, but he continued walking up the ridge. There, shivering in the oncoming darkness, he questioned God and questioned the whole world. He had not directly mourned his father's death; he had been too young. But growing up without a father was difficult for him, and he suffered from that absence. His mother and his grandmother had doted upon him, but the lack of a father to bond with was a void the women could not fill. He tried to understand what Sarah was trying to do for him, but he still resisted the idea.

Now in the gathering darkness of Mt. Penn, Harry found himself confronting this ugly reality at the tender age of thirteen. After a while the cold got to him and he made his way down the serpentine mountain road to their row house on West Douglass Street. He came in before midnight, took off his wet clothes, and sat before the fire, bereft of any more emotion. Sarah understood his need to be alone. She prepared him a cup of strong tea, which he drank intently. When he had finished, he lay back and fell deeply asleep.

Harry joined Walter in Texas, and he spent the next four years trying to fit in at his new home with his new family. All the while he dreamt of one day leaving and finding the Celestial City. When he had completed four years of high school, he knew he wanted to study composition in college with the aim of becoming a correspondent in the Far East. He learned that the University of Texas didn't offer Oriental languages, so he applied to Princeton, where they taught Chinese and Japanese. He was accepted and chose to study Japanese, only because the class for Chinese was already full when he arrived in the fall of 1933. Harry stayed at Princeton only a semester. He suffered a bad bout of depression that forced him to take a leave of absence. Uncle Walter had Harry committed to a psychiatric hospital near Reading. Once he returned to Texas and enrolled at the university in Austin, Harry—unwilling to ask his uncle to pay for his college tuition—joined the Naval Reserve Officer Training Program. He wrote for the *Daily Texan*, the student-run paper. Through his instructor at Princeton, Harry was able to find a Japanese language teacher in San Antonio. He traveled there from Austin when he could for language lessons. Eventually, that launched him to the Far East. Now arriving back in Texas after four years as a correspondent in Japan and China was almost as strange for Harry as his arrival in the Far East had been.

Chapter Five

In early July, a few days after his fishing expedition with Uncle Walter, Harry placed a call to his ROTC instructor at the University of Texas, Lieutenant Commander Elwood Dewar. Dewar had helped Harry arrange a training cruise on board a destroyer out of Pearl Harbor in the summer of 1936, and he had given Harry useful advice about how to avoid call-up after graduation. He was also the first person to start calling Harry "Dutch" once he found out Harry had been born in Pennsylvania Dutch country.

Over the phone Harry told Dewar that he was having second thoughts about serving on board a ship. "I'm thinking about joining up with the Marines instead. Is that possible? It's all under the Navy Department. I'm sure they'd allow me to switch over."

"You don't need to do anything more as far as the Navy is concerned. You're ready for shipboard activity as a commissioned ensign," Dewar told him. "But, if you ask to have your commission transferred to the Marine Corps, you'd have to go through ten more weeks of training, plus a platoon leadership course. I wouldn't recommend it."

"I know, but let's just say I admire the Marines. I saw them do a lot of good things in Shanghai. Can you help me out?"

"Now, why in hell would you want to become a saltwater cowboy, Dutch?"

Harry asked him again patiently, "Can you help me out, El?"

"Okay, I'll see what I can do."

Harry laid down the receiver and pondered for a moment as he listened to the rain falling through the pines outside. He thought about the Marine with the scar across his cheek he had encountered his first summer in Shanghai.

One smililarly rainy afternoon Harry took Viktoria to the cinema on Amoy Road. They had just started seeing one another, and Harry knew only the sweet, delicate side of Viktoria. The picture they saw that afternoon was *The Adventures of Robin Hood,* starring Errol Flynn. It was the sort of Hollywood escapism that Westerners in Shanghai so enjoyed. It was jolting to walk out of a darkened theater to find oneself again on the streets of an Asian metropolis. After he and Viktoria left the cinema hall, they strolled along Soochow Creek, which separates the International Settlement from Hongkew—the Japanese Settlement. Soochow Creek had been widened over the years to about one hundred yards, and it had been deepened to allow river-borne traffic.

There was a loud commotion on the embankment across the way. Shanghai was chaotic and violent incidents occurred on a daily basis, even within the confines of the International Settlement. Not only did two warring armies surround the city, but gang warfare among various competing groups was rife as well. Harry and Viktoria looked across the creek to the Hongkew side and saw several Japanese policemen shouting and pointing down into the water. A figure was struggling to stay afloat. It appeared to be a Chinese man. He thrashed at the water and swam badly, but he had been able to get halfway across. Viktoria gasped and grabbed Harry's arm. She pointed to an oncoming cargo barge headed directly for the man.

"Don't look." He took Viktoria into his arms blocking her view of the creek. He could feel her heart beating rapidly against his chest. He couldn't avert his eyes from the barge boring down on the drowning man.

Just then the Japanese policemen drew their revolvers and began shooting at the bobbing head. The bullets created small geysers of dirty water. The man doggedly swam on. The barge soon passed right over him. After a moment Harry pulled Viktoria away and they started to walk off. The shouting started again. Harry looked back and saw that the man had miraculously escaped being chopped up by the barge and was close to reaching the near embankment, where several elderly Chinese women were washing clothes on the shelf. The Japanese policemen stopped firing to avoid shooting them. The women impassively continued with their chores, seemingly ignorant—or indifferent—to the chaotic scene around them.

Viktoria tugged Harry's jacket. "You have to help him, Harry."

"But what can *I* do?"

"Come on," she grabbed his arm.

They reached a narrow staircase leading to the embankment below and went down to the shelf. Viktoria grabbed one of the bamboo poles used by the women to balance their laundry baskets across their shoulders. One woman said something harshly to Viktoria, but she ignored it and handed Harry the pole. He suspended the pole above the struggling man, who grabbed hold of it with one hand. The Japanese policemen continued shouting. Harry pulled the man toward the embankment. His nose and mouth were bloody, and there was a huge tear in his cotton jacket. Viktoria wrapped her arms around Harry's hips from behind as he leaned over and extracted the man from the river. Harry understood why the man couldn't swim very well. His left hand was missing. Harry dragged him away from the creek. The man sat leaning his back against the wall, staring mutely ahead, breathing heavily. The Japanese across the way numbered five patrolmen. Harry understood what they were saying, but he ignored their calls. Just then he heard some whistles from Amoy Road, above them.

Viktoria nudged Harry's arm. "Let's get him up the stairs. There are policemen up there."

They lifted the man from either side, draping his arms over their shoulders. He was filthy and smelled of the creek. Harry could see Viktoria grimacing with distaste, but she continued to support him. He admired her determination. They reached the top of the stairs and found three U.S. Marines standing at the rail, looking across the creek at the Japanese patrolmen. The Japanese now had a megaphone and were demanding, in English, that the Marines return the "criminal." Harry and Viktoria sat the man down on the curb of Amoy Road while traffic continued to whiz by them. One of the Marines, who had a prominent scar across his cheek, shouted back to the Japanese policemen, "You can come get him yourself, boys, or you can go to hell!"

A young Marine officer approached Harry and said, "That was brave of you to bring him up from the creek."

Panting, Harry simply shrugged his shoulders and shook his head.

The Marine continued. "But it was damned stupid, brother. The Japs mighta shot you and your girl."

"This one here wouldn't back down," Harry nodded toward Viktoria. In fact, he was in awe of her at that moment. She had insisted they help the poor man. He had to admit to himself that he would probably have walked on by, had he been alone. It was the first of many living examples in which Viktoria would demonstrate her strong sense of right and wrong.

"You won't give him back, will you?" Viktoria asked with obvious concern. The officer looked at Viktoria, whose blouse was stained with mud and blood.

"No, ma'am. He's a political prisoner. He's got no left hand. The Japanese sometimes chop off their hands as a warning. That way, when they let them go, they can find 'em easier later."

"Well, we know you'll take care of him," Harry said. He turned to Viktoria. "We'll take a cab back to my apartment and get you cleaned up. We don't want your family to think ill of me, do we?" They waded out into the traffic on Amoy Road to hail a cab. Behind them they heard the officer shout to his men, "Okay, let's take this poor fellow down to the SMP station."

The "China Marines" had been in Shanghai since the early 1920s. After the Germans conquered France, in the spring of 1940, many Westerners in Shanghai speculated that the Japanese military would turn its attention to the International Settlement and the French Concession, as well as the other foreign concessions in China. The siege mentality in the city increased with each passing day. The U.S. 4th Marine Regiment patrolled the south side of the Garden Bridge as well as checkpoints just across from the Badlands and Chapei. They became one of the International Settlement's more colorful and beloved institutions. Harry recalled the emotional words of an English friend when the British pulled out the last of their forces—the Seaforth Highlanders—from Shanghai in August 1940. "Now the 4th Marines are all that are left between us and the Japanese. God bless 'em."

Harry hadn't shared with Dewar his deepest motive for joining the Marines. On the voyage to San Francisco, once his anger at Viktoria had subsided a bit, Harry realized that if he joined the Marines there was a chance he would be sent back to Shanghai.

Three days before he was due to report to New Orleans, Harry received a phone call from Dewar. Harry had been given the green light to report to Quantico, Virginia, for the Marine platoon leaders' course in August. Although that was exactly what he wanted, as the day approached, Harry became melancholic. What lay ahead in the coming months was anybody's guess. He knew that a phase of his life was ending. He no longer felt like a young man. He had suffered so many personal losses to this point that he felt middle-aged. Viktoria had jilted him, and now he would have to say good-bye to the only family he had left.

The night before Harry's departure Walter took the entire family out to Brenner's for steaks. Henry wore the too-small sailor outfit again, much to Jo's chagrin. But the boy wanted to be with his older cousin in spirit even if Harry was no longer going into the Navy. Jolyn peppered Harry with more questions about Shanghai and Tokyo. Walter listened impassively, seeming to enjoy his steak more than the conversation. Harry didn't eat much; he nervously smoked cigarettes and sipped his beer. When they returned home, Jo went upstairs to put the children to bed. Walter took a bottle of whiskey and two glasses and bade Harry to follow him to the screened porch at the back of the house. It was a sticky night, and the crickets chirped loudly. At first, they drank in silence, but once Walter lit a cigar, he cleared his throat and began to talk.

"Listen, Harry, I know you've had it rugged. Jo and I tried to make you comfortable as best we could. And I know it hasn't always been a bed of roses for you, what with my work and the kids and all. But Jo adores you, and, well, I feel as if you're like a son—I don't know—or a younger brother maybe." He shifted his body in the wicker chair. Harry knew this was uncomfortable for his uncle. But he let him—needed him to—go on.

"We've tried to be there for you. I know I'm not the easiest fellow to get along with sometimes." He paused and chuckled. "Your father knew all about that."

Harry nodded and pulled on his whiskey, remaining silent.

"Anyway, sometimes we weren't sure, Jo and I, how to talk to you. You know that whole thing with your leaving Princeton, and the hospital . . ." His voice trailed off.

"You mean the psychiatric ward?"

"Come on, Harry, it wasn't as simple as that. You'd been through a lot. Any normal person could have cracked under much less difficult circumstances. Losing your parents, having to uproot."

"Uncle Walter, I know you took me in at a rough time. But you don't need to explain anything."

"I know, but you seemed to resent us trying to help you. We did the best we could…"

Harry interrupted him. "It just seems that every time I've been close to somebody, they go away—or they push me away. I mean, I guess I understand what Grandma Sarah was trying to do, but I felt like she just abandoned me."

"Like I said, a lesser man wouldn't have survived what you have." Walter shook his head. "You know, you remind in that way of your father. We fought and argued a lot, but I admired him. He stood up to my old man and never backed down."

Harry continued to listen.

"Anyway, I just wanted to let you know that we're proud of what you're doing now, answering the nation's call, even if I don't agree with our policy. And if you get sent off somewhere, well, we'll be with you, you know—in spirit. Know that you have a home here."

Jo came out to the porch and joined them. Harry offered her a cigarette. She took it and sat next to him on the small wicker sofa. Harry struck a match and lit her cigarette. She exhaled a stream of smoke and sat back. After a moment she put her hand on Harry's knee. "Big day for you tomorrow. Why does it seem you're always leaving us?"

"Oh, I'll probably be back soon, Aunt Jo. This gathering storm probably won't amount to much."

"I just hope we don't get hoodwinked again this time," Walter said.

Jo nodded and put her head on Harry's shoulder.

That night Harry had the first of many dreams to come about Viktoria. In the dreams she was drowning, and he struggled to save her.

Chapter Six

Over the course of the summer and autumn, Aunt Jo forwarded several letters from Viktoria to Harry, who was now in Virginia. Viktoria explained her anguish at having been forced to make such a decision. She hoped that he could understand. She promised they would see one another again, and she vowed to make it right. Harry wrote her back only one time. The words he put down on paper were unresponsive. He was tormented. He so wished to be with her, but at the same time he still harbored anger toward her and an inability to fully understand why she had refused to come with him. Had the roles been reversed, he thought, he'd leave his family every time. In his sleep now, he saw her almost every night.

Pearl Harbor changed everything. The Japanese occupied Shanghai's International Settlement and the French Concession. From that time on, Harry heard nothing more from Viktoria. Although he was anxious, the feverish activity of the training kept him occupied. Having no one to talk to about Viktoria—he couldn't even write Aunt Jo about his jumble of feelings—he reluctantly decided then and there to try to put her out of his mind . . . permanently.

On that calm Sunday afternoon of December 7, Harry sat with two other newly minted second lieutenants around a sandy bivouac under pine trees in the New River area of North Carolina, where the Marines were conducting amphibious exercises. Sam Emtman was a husky young man with curly sand-colored hair who hailed from a farm near Pullman in eastern Washington. The other men called him "Country." Joseph "Frenchy" LaSalle was a University of Wisconsin graduate from Sheboygan. Because he was lean and handsome, with a dark complexion, everyone said he looked like Cary Grant.

Harry—known as "Dutch" to the others—Country, and Frenchy were all new platoon leaders in I Company, a rifle company of the 3rd Battalion in the 5th Marine Regiment, Harry's new home in the 1st Marine Division.

The breeze from the ocean that afternoon was cool, but the sunshine was warm. The smell of the pines reminded Harry of Houston. They were finishing a snack of canned cheese and crackers with raisins when the company sergeant came and told them the news.

"The Japs bombed Pearl Harbor this morning."

Country sat up. "Where's that? The Philippines?"

"Hawaii," the sergeant replied. "They came from carriers."

After recovering from his initial shock, Harry said calmly, "*Iacta alea est.*"

"What the hell does that mean, Dutch?" Country asked.

"That's what Caesar said when he crossed the Rubicon River on his way to Rome," Frenchy answered. "It means no going back. Well, literally, it means 'the die is cast.' What, didn't they teach Latin on your farm, Country?"

"What, you mean they threw some kinda dye in the river? Like to color it?"

Frenchy chuckled and winked at Harry. "Country, you never played craps? You *are* aware that die is the singular of dice, right?"

"Seems to me that it means the Japs are fucked now anyway," Country said and spat into the sand.

Harry lit a cigarette. "Well, boys, what it means is that we are in it now. No more play fighting. This is the real deal."

"Boy, I can't *wait* to teach those sorry bastards a lesson."

"You ever met a Japanese person, Country?" Harry asked.

"A Jap? Sure, I seen 'em in Spokane and around some of the other farms. Can't trust 'em a lick."

"Maybe, but just remember, most of them are fighting for the same reasons we are. They got caught up in a fast-flowing current they couldn't avoid."

"What are you saying, Dutch? That I don't understand what we're getting into?"

"No, no. Just that you should respect them as soldiers. They'll be a tough opponent."

"How come you know so much about the Japs?"

Frenchy interjected, "All he's saying, Country, is don't go thinking you're Sergeant York out there. Be careful. That's all."

Harry hadn't mentioned to any other Marines that he had lived in Japan, that he understood the language, and that although he could never abide their actions in China, he knew them as individuals. And some Japanese he respected greatly, especially Jingu-sensei.

After Harry withdrew from Princeton, his former language instructor sent a letter to Jingu, recommending he take Harry on as a student so he could keep up with his Japanese in Texas. A widower, Jingu lived with his two daughters, their husbands, and a number of grandchildren in San Antonio. They ran a teahouse and sold Oriental paintings and scrolls, as well as various garden items. The teahouse sat in a beautifully sculpted landscape that was surrounded by pools and lily ponds and waterfalls right off the San Antonio River. It was a peaceful place.

When Harry drove down from Austin for their first meeting, in the fall of 1935, he was greeted by a grandfatherly yet lively figure attired in a blue cotton robe, or *yukata*. Jingu invited Harry to sit on a reed mat, known as *tatami*, and the two became acquainted. Harry liked Jingu from the start. He had immigrated to Texas in 1910 via California, where he had lived for ten years after coming over from Shikoku, the smallest of the four major Japanese home islands.

Jingu liked Harry too, and he agreed to teach him each Monday after Harry's morning classes at the university. Harry traveled the seventy miles from Austin, usually in a borrowed car, sometimes on a bus. Jingu would spend an hour with simple lessons. Afterward, they would have a big afternoon meal, and then they would walk around the gardens. Jingu conducted the conversations in simple Japanese. Harry kept up this pattern for two years. When he left the United States to take the correspondent's job in Tokyo in 1937, he was well prepared, thanks to Jingu, not just linguistically but also in understanding Japanese mores and culture. Little did Harry know at the time that he would one day be forced to employ the language in ghastly circumstances among the most vulnerable of people.

The 5th Marines' training intensified through the winter and into the spring of 1942. When he was able to get home leave, in late March, Harry traveled back to Houston. Aunt Jo was pregnant again. It was an unexpected but welcome surprise for the entire family. Harry spent much of his time with Henry and Jolyn walking Popeye the puppy, going to the movie theater, or having lunch at the counter in the Avalon drugstore. They were thrilled to be seen in public with Harry when he wore his uniform.

During his leave in Houston, Harry kept forcing himself to push any thought of Viktoria out of his mind. Each memory of her was a cruel reminder of his failed effort to bring her home with him. In that mind-set Harry reestablished a connection with an old college flame, Ellen Lowry. She had recently moved back to Houston after a brief and unhappy marriage to a banker in New York City. She had a young daughter and was living with her parents. Motherhood, Harry thought, had made Ellen even more beautiful. He and Ellen saw one another almost every day. Both rebounding from disappointments, they threw themselves headfirst into an intense whirlwind romance. They had passionate trysts in hotel rooms, under assumed names. Although no verbal promises were made, it was assumed they would be together once Harry returned from the war. Harry convinced himself that he had purged any remaining feelings he had for Viktoria once and for all.

Just before his leave ended, Harry decided to take a bus to San Antonio to pay his respects to Jingu, the man who, more than anyone, was responsible for his positive experiences in the Far East. On the bus ride to San Antonio, Harry marveled at the carpets of azure along the highway, bluebonnets interspersed with the patches of red and yellow of the Indian paintbrush. Texas seemed so peaceful, even as the rest of the world imploded. He grew morose again, thinking of the end of this phase of his life. He would never know inner peace, he felt. He had seen the brutality firsthand in Shanghai, and he understood what he was getting into better than most of the young men leaving for the war.

Jingu received Harry warmly, and the two spent the afternoon together in the garden. As they lunched on fried shrimp and cold soba noodles, Harry thanked Jingu for his introductions to so many people in Japan and in Shanghai, telling him how they had been invaluable in more than one way. Jingu was delighted to hear the stories about Harry's experiences both in Japan and in China, and doubly glad that Harry had returned safely.

"Still," Jingu lamented over a cup of tea after lunch, "it is a shame how it has all come to pass." He smoked a long, thin pipe called a *kiseru*, and every once in a while, he banged the ashes out into a ceramic ashtray. "And now, you are in uniform, off to do battle with my countrymen." Jingu sighed. "It truly makes me sad."

"Yes, it is sad," Harry responded, speaking in Japanese. "I learned a lot about myself and about people during my time in the Far East. I hope I have become more patient and have come to understand more about human beings."

Jingu sat impassively and listened. Finally, after some moments of silence, he said, "I see in your eyes, Harry-san, that you have suffered greatly in your life. Suffering is something one cannot hide." He sighed and put down his pipe. "But you have become a wise young man because you have suffered. And because of this you have empathy for others who are unlucky. You are young, but in your wisdom I detect a ripeness of age. I consider myself fortunate that you are my friend. You may think you have learned much from me, but I have also learned much from you. And for this, I thank you."

Harry looked down and shook his head. "No, sensei, I can never thank you enough for all that you have done. It is *my* fortune to be your student and your friend."

They spoke quietly into the early evening. At seven o'clock, Harry boarded the last bus for Houston. He never saw Jingu again. After the war, Harry learned from one of Jingu's sons-in-law that the old man had passed away in the summer of 1945, shortly after the atomic bombings of Japan. Harry suspected it was from a broken heart.

Chapter Seven

December 10, 1941

My Dearest Harry,

I hope that one day you read this in good health and in happiness. Although I cannot communicate with you directly for the time being, it is still a comfort to continue writing you so that you remain in my thoughts. I will save this diary for you alone to read when this horrid war has ended and peace returns.

Right now there seems to be no happiness in the world.

Late Sunday night loud explosions awakened us. They came from the direction of the river, and they lasted for nearly an hour. We also heard rifle fire and some aeroplanes. We all settled back into bed but slept poorly.

Imagine our shock the next morning upon hearing the dreadful news that the Japanese had attacked Hong Kong, the Philippines, and America! I hope you were not in Hawaii, but even if you weren't, it saddened me to hear of this attack. It must have been quite a shock for you as well. We further learned that what we had heard during the night was the Japanese sinking a British warship on the Whangpoo River. All day Monday we sat in front of the radio and numbly listened. We are also beside ourselves, wondering about Tanya and Edward. We can assume that the Japanese will not be kind to the British in Hong Kong.

The Japanese Army has taken over complete control of Shanghai, including the international concessions. The British and French authorities submitted immediately. We stayed in the house for the entire day. When Uncle Grisha went downtown to the warehouse the next day, he said that Japanese troops were stationed at every corner. He was stopped numerous times but was allowed to continue.

For now the Japanese are telling all foreigners that we must stay in our homes. A curfew has been established. We will be given word soon of our fate. We are told that the Japanese will register all of the names of the foreigners living in Shanghai so that they can have an accounting, and then we will be left alone. We are so worried!

In Shanghai, American and British administrators will be allowed to continue working at essential enterprises like the telephone exchange and the rail company. But the banks, the merchant houses, and the newspapers have all been closed. My aunt worries about her sister, who is in Japan, and about my brother in Tientsin. God only knows what fate has in store for my brother Boris and his family.

The German army, we hear, is now only fifty kilometers from Moscow. Uncle Grisha thinks that Stalin and the Bolsheviks will be chased from Russia. He has become even more obsessed by this thought and he speaks of being ready to leave for Russia at a moment's notice. You remember how he felt about this. Aunt Masha agrees with him, but I am unsure. My only concern is to see you again. What the future holds is too unbearable to even think of. With the world collapsing around us, there will be no way for us to keep in touch, and this pains me, for I have so much to tell you about myself, and about us.

Please know that I love you dearly. And I think about you all the time. We have prayed for you and lit candles at the church. I pray that all this will soon come to an end. And I pray that we will see one another soon.

With all my love,

V

As she closed the entry Viktoria wanted more than ever to speak with Tanya to find comfort and companionship in her hugs and caresses. At times, she would forget that Tanya was gone, and she would look up, expecting to see her across the dining table, or bent over in the garden, or reading in the sunroom. They had always been inseparable. Now everyone looked to Viktoria, as the eldest unmarried member of the extended family, to be strong and loyal. They had no idea that she was ready to leave any day with Harry. Yes, she had chosen to stay with her family, but now she was starting to have regrets at not having gone. Especially given what had been revealed as the autumn months approached.

Viktoria had been feeling weak and sick through most of August.

She also had a hard time holding down food. One day in early September when she was hanging laundry in the courtyard behind the kitchen, she swooned and fell to the ground.

Aunt Maria insisted that a doctor be called to the house. Viktoria had suspected for weeks, since she had missed her last period. The young French doctor examined Viktoria in her room. Dr. Rabbino had curly black hair and splashed himself liberally with eau de cologne. Viktoria thought he looked close to twenty years of age, but many of the more experienced doctors had long since left Shanghai, even the White Russians.

Natasha, a short, plump Buryat maid who hailed from the Russian Far East and had been with the Savins for years, sat with Viktoria during the examination.

Upon completing his examination, Dr. Rabbino looked at Viktoria and said cautiously in French, "It seems, mademoiselle, that you are with child."

Viktoria crossed herself and looked at Natasha, who kept her eyes fixed on the floor. Although the maid spoke no French, it was fairly clear what the doctor's prognosis was.

"Thank you, Doctor. I ask you please for now not to tell my family about this."

"As you wish, mademoiselle," he said with the utmost discretion. "I will contact you again soon to set up appointments for the remainder of your pregnancy." After the doctor left, Viktoria looked at Natasha and said sternly in Russian, "Nata, not one word of this to the family. Do you understand?"

Nastasha nodded and took her leave. Alone with the startling news, Viktoria thought through all the various scenarios. Even if Natasha could keep the secret, Viktoria couldn't hide her condition forever from the family.

By the beginning of October, Viktoria started to show. She went first to Aunt Maria, who was stunned by the news but supported her niece and adroitly steered her husband into an awareness and acceptance of Viktoria's situation. At first, the Savins considered a quick Orthodox marriage to avoid the shame of an illegitimate child, but they understood that no Russian man of a comparable upbringing would be willing to enter into such a marriage of convenience, nor would Viktoria agree to it. Instead, the Savin family embraced the fact that they would be blessed with the arrival of a new member. Maria prepared a nursery in Viktoria's room and, as the days passed, seemed more and more excited about the arrival of the baby.

Viktoria, on the other hand, was distressed. She sometimes sat in her room feeling lonelier than she had ever felt in her life. In one such moment she decided to keep a diary in hopes that one day Harry might read it. Inside the diary she kept a photo of Harry taken at the racetrack in the summer of 1940. He was dressed in a white suit and wore a straw skimmer. She agonized constantly over his whereabouts, but she tried to be positive and assure herself that he had not been in Hawaii on December 7. She knew how hurt and angry he was when he left Shanghai. Maybe it was best for him to get on with his life without her, she reasoned. Meanwhile, she had to manage the day-to-day struggle everyone faced in Shanghai. As lonely as she was, Viktoria was determined to love her baby unfailingly and to make its father proud.

上海

Chapter Eight

Harry's physical journey to war began in June 1942. It was drizzling and overcast dockside at Norfolk Naval Base, and even though it was early summer, it was chilly. The weather matched Harry's black mood. He looked over the faces of the young men in green twill fatigues who shouldered their seabags in one simultaneous movement, like automatons, and filed onto the transport. He knew these would be their last footsteps on American soil for a long time; for some, these would be their final steps on their home ground forever.

They sailed out onto the tidewater, and within the hour they passed out of the Chesapeake Bay, leaving the East Coast behind them. The transport sailed for seven days, zigzagging to avoid German submarines on its way south to the Panama Canal Zone. Transiting the Isthmus of Panama took a full day. Again the weather was wet, but now it was hot and sticky. As the ship pushed through the last lock and bobbed out onto the Pacific Ocean, Harry looked back at the shore installations. On a platform high above the last lock stood an Army sentry in a rain slicker wearing a Kelly helmet. His rifle stuck up above him like an antenna. Some of the Marines called out and waved to the soldier, but the lone figure stood motionless in the drizzle. He seemed to have locked eyes with Harry, who stood quietly, watching the helmeted figure grow smaller and smaller.

For most of the young men, fresh out of small towns, the voyage was the first of many adventures to come. In their minds, they were bound for glory. They spoke about medals and about killing Japs. But no one spoke or thought about his own death. Harry was an exception. Throughout the long journey across the Pacific, his dark thoughts hung above him like an ominous cloud. He brooded to himself about death. Although some fellow officers kept diaries (against regulations) and wrote letters home, Harry for once in his life wrote nothing. He wondered if he was killed, would anyone even care? Sometimes, it just didn't matter to him anymore.

That night, after they had sailed away from the Panama coast, Harry was awoken by the bursts of two signal flares. He sat up in the dark, forgetting momentarily where he was. Then he remembered another time he had awoken with a start on a liner—his first voyage to Shanghai in 1939.

Harry's bunk shuddered at the sound of two successive rattling booms. He sat upright, and remembered that he was aboard a liner off the coast of China. He wondered whether they had been fired upon or had run into a mine. It was, after all, a Japanese-registered ship coming from Yokohama to a war zone. But after a few moments he could tell from the absence of an alarm that the vessel was in no danger. The explosions must have come from inland.

He got out of the bunk in his small cabin below, splashed water onto his face, and then hastily dressed to go topside. He emerged on the port side of the ship. It was just past sunrise. When he saw nobody else along the rails, he walked around to starboard. There he saw a group of passengers gazing west toward two plumes of black smoke cutting across the bank of low clouds that reflected pink and yellow from the opposing sunrise. The source of the plumes was hidden by an enormous earthen berm that spanned the western horizon. The ship had sailed into the estuary of the Yangtze. Harry walked up to the railing and stood next to another Westerner, who looked out toward the looming landmass that was China.

"China in a nutshell," the man spoke with an accent that Harry couldn't place. "No explanation. Nobody knows what happened." The man sighed and shook his head. "It's all very sad." He turned to look at Harry and asked, "New arrival or returning?"

Harry paused for a moment, not expecting the question. He said, "It's my first time in Shanghai."

"Ah, then you are uninitiated to the wonders and tragedies of our fair city on the Whangpoo River," the man said grimly. "This all takes a bit of getting used to, but you'll learn to ignore most of it—until it becomes too close to ignore."

"Yes, I've heard the stories. I've been in Tokyo for the past eighteen months."

The man, who was big and burly, wore a trimmed beard peppered with red and gray. "Well, what do you Americans say? Out of the boiling pot and into the fire?"

"Actually, it's from the frying pan into the fire."

"Ah, yes, that's right. You'll forgive me. I'm bad with American colloquialisms." The man paused for a moment and then extended his hand, "Terribly rude of me. I should have introduced myself. I'm Grigorii Savin."

"I'm Harry Dietrichson. It's a pleasure to meet you."

"Dietrichson, you say?"

"Yes, that's right."

Just then a well-dressed elderly Japanese man came to the railing. He held a bamboo cane, which looked oddly out of place given the rest of his expensive wardrobe. He pointed out to the west with the cane and said in heavily accented French, "*C'est la guerre.*"

"*Oui,*" Savin nodded, affirming what the old man said. "*C'est la guerre.*" He turned back to Harry and said, "It looks like something happened on Chungming. It's the largest island in the estuary. Perhaps the Japanese had an ammunition dump there and the Nationalists got to it. Anyway, *somebody's* not having a good morning."

The group of passengers stood for a while, their gaze riveted on the horizon as if some clue to the explosions would present itself. After about half an hour, other passengers started to turn away and head back inside.

A man with a long mustache and a wool hat walked out on deck and approached Savin. A Cossack. He said something to Savin in Russian. Savin turned and said to Harry, "I must take my leave now. Have an enjoyable stay. Maybe we will run into one another again. The Western community is growing smaller by the day in Shanghai."

"Thank you, Monsieur Savin. A pleasure meeting you."

Harry would see Savin again as they disembarked later that day. The stately gentleman's family greeted him on the quay along the Bund, and it was then that Harry had first laid eyes on Viktoria.

The military transport convoy sailed for twelve more days, zigzagging across the South Pacific, before arriving in New Zealand in late June.

There, Harry's unit joined up with the remainder of the 5th Marine Regiment. The winter weather in Wellington matched that of Virginia when they had embarked: cool and rainy. At times, Harry wondered whether rain had broken out perpetually all over the world and would continue until the fighting stopped.

They spent more than a month in Wellington, on the southern tip of the northern island. The 5th Marines built a tent encampment north of town at McKay's Crossing. At almost every opportunity, the other young Marines would go into town for drinks at the pubs. Harry stayed to himself mostly, although he did once accompany fellow officers to the home of Wellington's mayor for a Sunday brunch of beer and raw oysters.

Harry had become close with three other second lieutenants in the 3rd Battalion of the 5th Regiment. Frenchy LaSalle was one of them. Another was a lean, tall Texan named Billy Swanson, who hailed from a ranching family in northwest Texas, just south of the Panhandle. In K company they called him "Swede." The third was a short, stocky fellow from Santa Monica, California, named Fred Derry. They called him "Ozzie" because he was the product of an Australian father and an American mother. Derry, who was also in K Company, spoke with a slight Australian accent, even though he had moved to California—his mother's home—after spending the first twelve years of his life in Perth. Like Frenchy, he was married to his high school sweetheart. The four of them—Dutch, Frenchy, Swede, and Ozzie—called themselves the League of Nations. They were all close to the same age, had attended college, and had worked for a couple of years before the war. They discussed world politics, sports, swing music, and women, in no particular order.

Swede and Harry had long before figured out they both attended the University of Texas around the same time. They had mutual acquaintances but had never been introduced. Swede was two years younger than Harry, yet they grew especially close given that connection. One afternoon the group sat around the mess hall over coffee discussing the upcoming college football season.

Frenchy, a graduate of the University of Wisconsin in Madison, was a Badger fan. "They're gonna be something special this year. Watch out for Crazylegs Hirsch and Dave Schreiner."

Ozzie chimed in, "You should have seen the team my UCLA Bruins had in '39. Boy, they were something. We had three colored players that were dynamite. There was one, Kenny Washington, who was one of the best players I've ever seen."

"Sure, I remember. Kenny Washington, Woody Strode, and Jackie Robinson, right?" Frenchy asked.

"Yup. The 'Gold Dust gang.' The three fastest football players to ever play the game."

"Did you fellows see much football back in Texas?" Ozzie asked, looking at Swede and Harry.

Swede answered modestly, "I actually played briefly, but I hurt my shoulder. We weren't very good when I was there. Our coach—Jack Chevigny—played under Knute Rockne. And we did have one big victory over Notre Dame. Our new coach, Dana Bible, is gonna turn things around."

"How 'bout you, Dutch?"

"Oh, I played in high school. But I follow baseball more. I'm a fan of the Athletics. You know, I met Lefty Grove once?"

"Yeah?" they chimed. "No kiddin'?" "Yeah. When I was a kid, I stayed after one of their games at Schibe Park in Philly. I milled around outside the stadium, waiting for the players to come out of the locker room. Lefty finally comes out and looks in my direction and waves. He starts walking right toward me. I just freeze. Just as he comes right up next to me, I put out my hand. He brushes right by me without even pausing. I turn and see this gorgeous brunette parked at the curb in a shiny tan Chrysler Imperial Coupe. She was wearing a blue tam and had perfect teeth. Lefty climbed in beside her, and they sped off down Lehigh Avenue."

The entire group of Marines burst out laughing.

"Guess he had other plans, Dutch!" Frenchy said, slapping his knee.

In spite of these new friendships, Harry remained morose throughout the time in New Zealand. He was tired of the drilling and the exercises, and ready to get into the fight. Often he thought to himself that he wasn't going to come out of the war alive anyway, so there was no use worrying about it.

Harry led a platoon of 43 young men. It was a diverse group, hailing primarily from east of the Mississippi. They included a good number of New Englanders. The youngest was seventeen, and the oldest was thirty-one. The men often mistook Harry's disconsolate behavior for aloofness, but they all thought him to be fair, unlike some other young officers who were considered martinets. Harry addressed the men in a respectful tone and meted out punishments sparingly. They looked up to Harry because he was older and more experienced than most of the other second lieutenants.

Harry had the good fortune of being assigned an excellent platoon sergeant. He was told in the platoon leaders' course that a sergeant could make or break a second lieutenant. Staff Sergeant Elmer Burns was a giant man from North Platte, Nebraska, who had once wrestled steers and broken horses. Burns possessed a sardonic sense of humor that Harry appreciated. He was just a year older than Harry, so there was none of the disdain that sometimes prejudiced the relationship between a platoon sergeant and a young, green lieutenant. Burns had been in the Marine Corps for eight years and had seen his fair share of the world. He had been involved in minor skirmishes around the Caribbean. Harry knew this would be a good man to have behind him in a fight. Burns had no family and had never been married. His nickname was "Bull." Harry once asked him whether he got the nickname from his calf-roping days.

"Nope. When I first joined up, they called me Tiny. But one time we got liberty off our ship in Tampico and we went to see a bullfight. I got liquored up and jumped into the ring." He pulled up his shirt and indicated a scar under his ribs. "See? I got gored by a bull."

"Jesus!" Harry grimaced. "What about the one on your arm there?"

"Oh, that? Knife fight in Haiti." He shrugged. "It didn't end well for the other fellow." He looked at Harry. "How 'bout you, Lieutenant? Seen much of the world?"

"A little bit. I was a foreign correspondent in the Far East."

"On the level?"

"Yeah, but no knife fights. I was on the sidelines. Just reporting the news."

"What about that scar on your neck?"

"Collateral damage."

Harry and Viktoria had been walking back from a visit to an old Chinese temple in the walled Nantao section of town on a sunny afternoon in August 1940. The humidity had abated somewhat, and there was a nice breeze coming from the north. They were held up at an intersection by police officers. They stood with other pedestrians and watched a fancy limousine standing in front of a building in lower Frenchtown. A group of people had gathered round the car, and Harry figured it must be somebody important. Just then a man in Chinese clothing ran out of the crowd to their right and threw an object under the car. Harry instinctively pulled Viktoria to the ground and shielded her with his body. A thunderous explosion pierced the peaceful afternoon. As they lay on the ground, pieces of glass and shards of metal dropped around them. "A Shanghai special" was what the Westerners called these attacks, which were political assassinations.

Once the air was clear, Harry and Viktoria hesitantly stood up and looked around. Harry's ears rang. Wounded people all around them lay moaning.

"Are you okay, dear?" he asked.

"Yes, yes. I'm fine. Are you hurt?"

"No. I'm fine."

"But, Harry, your neck! You're bleeding!"

He put his hand to his neck, withdrew it, and stared at the blood. A fragment of glass had lodged itself below his right ear. He pulled it out and put pressure on the wound with his handkerchief.

They went to a nearby bench on the embankment and sat, momentarily listening to the sirens wail. Several constables from the Shanghai Municipal Police soon arrived to help the victims.

Viktoria approached one of them, who stood next to a squad car.

"Can you help us? My friend has been hurt."

The constable walked over to Harry. "You okay, buddy?"

Harry noticed the man's American accent. "I think it's just a cut."

"It's a pretty big gash. Better you go see a doctor just in case. We're gonna have to go back up to the Nanking Road station; we'll give you a ride."

"No. I'm fine. Thank you."

"Listen, pal, we're going up there anyway. You and your friend might as well come with us."

"Thank you," Viktoria said. "We accept your kind offer."

Harry and Viktoria climbed into the backseat of the car. The driver was a tall Sikh policeman wearing a tan turban. Around his neck on a red lanyard was a nickel-plated whistle.

Harry asked the first constable, "Any idea who the victim was?"

"Yes, it was the mayor."

"The mayor of Shanghai?"

"Yes, the mayor of the Chinese city."

Harry knew the mayor was a Japanese puppet who had many enemies. "Did they catch the culprit?"

"No, he was blown to smithereens," the constable said. "Say," he
turned to Harry, "you're an American, aren't you?"

"Yes. You too?"

"Chicago."

"How did a cop from Chicago end up here?"

The man replied with a wry smile. "Exchange program."

"What do you mean?"

"The SMP sends five constables over to Chicago every six months,
and the Chicago PD sends five over here."

Shanghai was given many names, but one of the more accurate com-
parisons was the Chicago of the East. Chicago in the Roaring Twen-
ties was known worldwide as the playground of gangsters, including Al
Capone. Intrigued by that analogy, an enterprising British member of
the Municipal Council came up with the idea of promoting an exchange
between the SMP and Chicago police forces. It was assumed that the
officers could share lessons learned on the embattled streets of their
respective cities. The SMP constables viewed their stay in America as a
sort of holiday, but the Chicago policemen quickly became unnerved by
life in Shanghai.

The constable went on to explain. "Most of the fellows who came
over from Chicago got scared by all the killings. Bombings every day can
catch up with you. We don't even know who's fighting who. The Japs
have the whole city surrounded, but the Chinese keep killing each other.
Nationalists versus Communists. Pro-Japanese versus anti-Japanese. It's
crazy. You know that I fired more rounds on the job here in my first
month than I did during my entire career in Chicago? The other fellows
took off after a few weeks. I'm the last one."

"Why?"

"No more volunteers. The SMP cops are still going over to Chicago.
I know several of them stayed on for good. Mostly Russians."

Viktoria chimed in. "Yes, I know of a Russian man, Strelnikov, who
went to Chicago. He worked for my uncle as a bodyguard."

The constable turned and looked out the front windshield, "Plus, with all the war stuff going on, they'll be calling us all home."

"What have you heard?"

He turned around again. "You didn't know they're bringing back the draft?"

"No. I didn't."

"FDR just announced it." The constable looked again at Viktoria. "Are you Russian?" She nodded. "Ma'am, they are all welcome in Chicago, your boys. They are good, dependable fellows, each and every one of them. They know how to run a beat, and they are fearless."

Rumors swirled around the encampments outside Wellington. One day the 5th Regiment was going to be deployed with the 7th Marine Regiment in Samoa. The next day it was said they would be going to New Guinea, to fight alongside the Army and the Australians. The general consensus was: "I don't care where we go, so long as we get to kill Japs."

By the end of July 1942, it became clear they would be re-embarking soon. Liberties were curtailed, equipment was loaded onto ships, and the tension was palpable.

On July 21, a brilliant sunny day—the first in weeks—the men boarded transports, and a huge convoy sailed north out of Wellington Harbor. Initially, the convoy consisted of twenty-five transports escorted by five cruisers and seven destroyers. On the fifth day, a lookout spotted a large number of ships on the horizon. Curious and bored Marines moved to the port rail to look. In the distance a peak slowly emerged on the horizon. At first it looked like a typical superstructure of a cruiser or a battleship. Then a long, flat deck appeared, lifting like an elevator straight out of the water. An excited voice cried out, "It's a flattop!" Within another two hours, two more carrier groups had appeared. Now the convoy consisted of three carrier battle groups: the *Enterprise*, the *Saratoga*, and the *Wasp*. The men's morale soared.

Soon the officers learned that Guadalcanal was their destination. They were issued crude maps, which they feverishly studied. They spent hours each day going over the plans and then rehashing them with their respective units. Harry was told that D-day was set for August 7. He shook his head and looked to the sky. It was Viktoria's birthday. Somehow, she always came back to him, try as he might to forget her.

Just then Harry remembered the photograph of her he carried in his wallet. It had been taken in the backyard of her house in Shanghai, in the garden. Tanya had given it to him. Viktoria protested at the time, saying she didn't like the photo. It was a candid shot, with her squinting slightly in the bright sun, but she seemed to be just breaking into a smile. Harry treasured it. He took it out and looked at it for a while. He closed his eyes and then put it back into his wallet, next to the only other photo he carried—of Jolyn, Popeye, and Henry in his favorite sailor outfit.

Chapter Nine

The transports lay at anchor in stunningly blue waters off of an impossibly jagged dark-green island. A shimmering silver-green line, which was miles of swaying palm trees, was visible along the shore. Above the tree line stood high peaks shrouded in cottony clouds. The large green shape they were drawing toward was the culmination of all their training. The months of grueling physical exercise and mental stress were about to be played out. It was August 7, D-day. The 5th Marine Regiment would be part of the first wave to land. Harry and the other men and officers of rifle companies I and K of the 3rd Battalion would be on the first boats to come ashore—the tip of the spear. The 1st Marine Regiment was to land in the second wave and move inland to secure the airstrip the Japanese were building. They were told that as many as three thousand crack Japanese naval troops would be there to greet them on the beach.

Before he sat down to breakfast, Harry circulated among his platoon dispensing encouragement and last-minute advice. "Remember, keep your heads down, fellows, and do your job. Don't try to be heroes. You will be asked to do plenty of dangerous things, so don't go looking for extra trouble." Some of the men—boys, really—chuckled nervously at Harry's admonition.

He made sure that each man was given an orange to take with him when he disembarked. In the service, canned fruit was rare; fresh fruit even more so. Someone said out loud, "Thanks, sir, but heck, I'd just as soon have a Clark Bar." The comment elicited a guffaw of laughter from the tables.

Harry turned and answered Marion Hargrove, a thin young man from Billings, Montana. "Tell you what, Happy, if I scrounge up a Clark Bar, I'll be sure and let you know."

"Gee, thanks, Lieutenant. And, um, I'd even settle for a Baby Ruth or a Butterfinger." Happy looked like he was about fifteen, although he was really eighteen. He went about each day on a cloud of boyish insouciance. He never complained, never spoke poorly about anyone else. There wasn't a guy in the company who had a bad thing to say about him.

"Okay, Happy, duly noted. But now I guess I'll have to scrounge up several dozen candy bars for the whole platoon—or at least all you fellows within earshot."

Happy—his shrill voice cracking like a teenager's—shouted, "Pogey bait for the platoon!" When Harry left, the platoon was jabbering about their favorite candy bars. He was glad they had a temporary distraction.

In the officers' mess things were much quieter. They were served cream chipped beef, canned pineapple, and white bread with jam and margarine. Hardly anyone spoke. Harry noticed that some of the others ate with gusto, especially Country, but his own stomach churned as he tried to choke down his food. He gave up and instead sipped coffee and smoked a couple of Lucky Strikes.

After they had finished eating, the tremendous boom of the naval bombardment commenced. Harry looked at his Hamilton watch, the type issued to every officer. It was a quarter past six. The officers were given cotton balls with which to plug their ears and permitted to go up on deck to witness the awe-inspiring spectacle of battleships, cruisers, and destroyers loosing their enormous projectiles in great arcs of flame onto the beaches and positions further inland.

Harry decided to stay belowdecks. After smoking a cigarette, he started to write a farewell letter to Uncle Walter. But after several minutes, he put down his pen. He figured that if he was going to die, he had already told his relatives everything he needed to say in the last letter he had sent them from New Zealand.

Instead, he decided to write a short note to Ellen Lowry.

He and Ellen had written often during the summer, but their intimacy was never openly expressed in their correspondence. Instead, the factual and mundane news they shared was akin to letters exchanged between a couple that had been married for years. Although Viktoria was a constant presence in his thoughts and dreams, Harry had given up ever seeing her again. When he reflected on his experiences with her, he was no longer angry. He was worried about how she would survive the war in Shanghai now that the Japanese had occupied the city.

After composing his note to Ellen, Harry went to rejoin his platoon. He descended several sets of ladder wells and circulated among the men. In the hold, where the bunks were piled five levels high, the smell was a mixture of body odor, hair oil, soap, and urine. When the blower went out, the stench from the head was overwhelming. Some of the fellows were casually shooting the breeze, but most spoke in muted tones. A chorus of young men accompanied by a harmonica was singing "Blues in the Night."

Harry sensed that the men felt more comfortable around him than before. It was probably due to the gathering fear among them of the impending battle. They needed a figure of authority for comfort and reassurance that everything was going to be okay. Harry exhorted his men to check their weapons for excess oil. "Wipe 'em clean, Marines. You don't want sand getting mixed into that oil and jamming things up."

Most of the enlisted men carried a Springfield .30-06 Model 1903, a bolt-action rifle that could carry five cartridges. They affectionately called it the "thirty ought six." Harry loved the Springfield. It was similar to the rifle with which he and Uncle Walter had hunted deer and javelinas in Texas. But he was concerned that the bolt action would be too cumbersome to operate in a close jungle encounter. So, instead, he was going ashore with a Reising forty-five-caliber submachine gun, like most other platoon commanders.

Most of the company commanders carried the Thompson thirty-caliber submachine gun. Tommy Guns were famous from gangster movies, although the version the Marines carried had a straight ammunition clip rather than a round drum clip. Harry didn't like the weight of the Thompson. He knew it would be tough lugging around an extra eleven pounds of metal in the heat and the thick underbrush of the Solomons. He felt better with the Reising, which weighed only seven pounds. He would also be a carrying a Colt .45 sidearm. The heavy pistol would stop anything at fifty yards. Some men—mainly the noncommissioned officers, like Bull Burns—carried a Browning Automatic Rifle. Known as the BAR, this weapon was even heavier than a Tommy Gun, but it put out a murderous hail of 30.06 and could be fired from the hip during close engagements. The enlisted men were not so lucky. In a close engagement they had only their bayonets and knives.

Harry found Bull leaning against a bulkhead, whittling a stick with his Ka-Bar knife.

"Shouldn't you be sharpening that thing instead, Sergeant?"

"Oh, Lieutenant, as long as I keep this baby greased," he motioned with his knife toward his BAR, "I don't plan on using this. 'Sides, I don't much care to get my hands all messy with Jap guts."

"How are the men?"

"Morale seems fine. They've prepared well."

"How about *you*?"

"This ain't my first rodeo."

"Good," Harry answered. "I'm counting on you. I can't say for sure how I'll react out there."

"Lieutenant, you'll do just fine."

I Company's commander was Captain Timothy Tuttle. A Yale man, he had been a banker in New York but had enlisted in the Marine Reserves in 1938. He was of medium height and had curly brown hair. He had a pair of smiling eyes under his wire-rim glasses. He stayed fit, and never drank or smoked. Harry liked Tuttle and respected his intellect. Burns was less sure about him and wondered out loud on more than one occasion to Harry whether Tuttle would hold up under fire. But Harry knew there was no telling who would succumb to the stresses and inner fears they were sure to confront on the island.

A bell sounded, indicating the hour to go atop decks. By this time the bantering among the men had ceased. Now the shouting of the coxswains and transport officers had become the only audible noise above the din of the winches and the bubbling grumble of the Higgins Boats, bobbing alongside the transport. Company by company, the 3rd Battalion, 5th Marines filed out topside, climbed over the sides, and clambered down the cargo nets. No matter how much one practiced on the nets, the climb down was not easy. Each man was weighted down by more than fifty pounds of equipment on his back. The nets were rough hewn, and sometimes the man above you stepped on your hands. But you held on no matter what.

Harry was the last to board his Higgins Boat. The small boats circled until the entire group of vessels was ready to approach the beach in unison. The smell of diesel and the bobbing of the sea made the nervous men feel nauseous, though very few actually vomited, having been on ships for so long.

They had orders to remain crouched or seated, but Harry couldn't. He stood next to the coxswain. He watched the island grow larger and was relieved to see that no fire was coming from inland. As they drew closer, the coxswain reversed the engine and then put the boat in neutral, letting the waves bring them in the final few yards. The men jumped over the sides into the warm surf. They scrambled up onto the soft beach, which was littered with coconut husks, logs, and palm fronds that had all been shattered during the American naval bombardment. The men plopped down onto their bellies below a small embankment. The tension suddenly broke as they realized that nobody was shooting at them. The entire platoon audibly exhaled with relief. It was not long before the joking started. "Lieutenant, you promised us Japs. Is this any way to run a war?"

Bull growled, "Shut up, Marines. You'll get plenty of Japs."

They stayed and waited on the beach. Some of the men gathered green coconuts, opened them with bayonets, and drank the salty-sweet liquid inside. Word was then passed that the entire 3rd Battalion was safely ashore. The command was given to march inland. Captain Tuttle moved among the company. "Men, no talking. I want five paces, single file. Sergeant," he motioned to Bull, "you take Corporal Vargas and get your BARs up on point. Wait until you hear my orders." Virgil Vargas was a burly Mexican fellow who had played on the football team at New Mexico A&M in Las Cruces. They called him "Jefe."

As the men assembled, Tuttle gathered the company staff. The four platoon leaders were Harry, Frenchy, Country, and "Woody" Woodring, from Sausalito, California. Woody was in charge of the heavy weapons platoon. The company executive officer was First Lieutenant Jeremiah "Jerry" Lindauer, an enlisted veteran who had been promoted from the ranks. Like Harry, Lindauer was an orphan, and he'd been raised in a hardscrabble neighborhood in Louisville, Kentucky. Nathan Moore, the company first sergeant, was an old salt from the 4th Marines in China. They called him "Pith" because he wore a tropical pith helmet when he wasn't in combat.

Tuttle quietly told the group, "First platoon will lead, followed by third platoon, then weapons platoon, then second platoon." He looked straight at Harry. "Dutch, when you get first platoon to the river, cross it, then advance one hundred yards, set up a perimeter, and hold until third platoon gets across. They will join you on the perimeter. Then hold till the weapons platoon is across. Got it?"

"Aye, skipper." Harry understood that the river would be the most likely spot for a Japanese ambush. If he was going to die today, he thought to himself, it would most likely be at the river.

They marched quietly through a grove of coconut trees on what was once a British copra plantation. The platoon passed through the grove and entered a large patch of kunai grass, a tall tropical plant that grows as high as ripe corn and is sharp along the edges. In the kunai patch, visibility was minimal. The relief of having landed unopposed gave way again to the terror of not knowing what stood four feet ahead in the thick growth.

The maps turned out to be inaccurate and utterly useless. The Marines' mouths, already dry from the oppressive heat, became cottony with fear. At one point, Harry came upon Bull and Jefe, who were both kneeling on the ground. In front of them lay the corpse of a Japanese man dressed in pale tan coveralls. On his feet were two-toed *tabi* boots made of canvas, like sneakers. The corpse lay face down on blood-soaked ground. Bull silently pointed with the barrel of his BAR to a trail of blood going back through the grass toward the beach. The man must have been wounded in the early morning bombardment and then crawled into the grass to die. He had no weapon. Harry quietly instructed Bull to lead the men away from the corpse so they would not stop to gawk.

After an hour of slowly making their way through the kunai grass, first platoon came to the banks of the river, just east of the airfield. Bull and a private slowly waded across the small sluggish stream. Harry and a group of men crouched tensely in a line on the bank, weapons at the ready. After ten minutes, the entire platoon had crossed the river. As they waded into the muddy water, some of the men filled their canteens and drank. They had been warned about parasites and leeches, but they didn't care. They were thirsty. Harry filled his canteen. From his shirt pocket he produced a halazone iodine tablet, put it in the canteen, and shook it. He drank the tepid metallic-tasting water after waiting fifteen minutes.

About an hour later, when the entire company had made its way across the river, the men started talking again in low voices. The order was passed up to continue the march. Still no sign of the enemy. The unbearable tension of not knowing was almost worse than encountering opposition.

After several hours of alternately marching and pausing they came to another coconut grove, which was situated on a slight rise, affording a view of the sound where convoy was visible far off at anchor. It was reassuring to see the mass of gray steel in the sound, knowing that the might of the U.S. Navy was within gun range. Somewhere south of the island, out of sight, stood the three carrier groups launching a constant rotation of flight patrols.

The order was made to bivouac. The hungry Marines broke out C-rations, pulling spoons out of their pockets to eat canned corned beef hash and potatoes. Over the course of the afternoon the men dug fox-holes and gathered palm fronds in an attempt to fashion crude beds and camouflage. Darkness came at six o'clock and was immediate. Although everyone was bone-tired from the heat, the exertion, and the constant tension, nobody slept.

The nighttime sounds of the jungle were foreign to the men: birds, bats, insects, the swaying of fronds overhead, and the occasional crashing noise of a falling palm tree, having been weakened during the bombardment. Everyone was on edge. The men craved cigarettes, but there was a strict policy against smoking. Swarms of mosquitoes were another unpleasant aspect of the night. Men put their heads under their rain ponchos to ward off the nuisances, but that only made it stifling and hard to breathe. Then, in the middle of the night, the rain came.

Huge droplets pelted them at the beginning, which soon gave way to a steady downpour. Although the rain took care of the heat and the mosquitoes, now the men were wet and cold. They huddled and shivered under their ponchos. Each man again felt the distance from home as he sat alone in the dark, sunk in his own thoughts, hearing and seeing the enemy behind every bush and in every shadow. When the rain lifted, the sounds of the jungle came alive again, seemingly even more shrill and intense than before. And then the mosquitoes returned.

At one point, Frenchy came to Harry's foxhole and dropped down beside him.

"Well, Dutch, so far so good."

"Yeah, I don't know what to make of it."

"Where are they?"

"It's a mystery to me. You hear Bull found a body?"

"Yeah, Pith told me. Said the Jap was about four feet tall," Frenchy chuckled with grim amusement.

"Yeah, he was a little fellow, but that doesn't mean anything. I've seen 'em up close. They can be as mean as hell."

Frenchy slapped at a mosquito on his neck. "God, I hate these drill bugs. What I wouldn't give for a cold beer right now."

Just then automatic fire broke out to their left.

"That must be it: they've made contact," Harry said.

"I'm gonna get back to my platoon." Frenchy quietly slipped out of the foxhole.

Harry waited for a while, but there was no more fire. Two men from his platoon approached stealthily and asked him what the scuttlebutt was. Harry remained evasive. "We'll get our orders. Just get back to your foxholes and stay vigilant." He then left his own foxhole and went around the platoon, telling everyone to sit tight and be ready. But there was nothing more than the continual jungle rhythm of screeches and chirping noises.

They stayed that way the rest of the night: tense and alert.

Captain Tuttle gathered the platoon leaders just after dawn. He explained the ruckus during the night. "A corpsman went out of the perimeter to take a piss, and several men in L Company got itchy trigger fingers. Now he's dead."

"*Merde!*" Frenchy said. "Come all this way and get killed by your own people."

"And it won't be the last time that happens," chimed in Pith. "Plenty of fellas got knocked off that way in France in '18."

"Who was it?" Country asked.

"Hubert. He was an E-3," Tuttle answered.

"I know him," Harry said. "Knew him." He felt silly for correcting himself.

"Listen," Tuttle took control of the huddle again, "that's why we maintain weapons and perimeter discipline. Better to relieve yourself in your foxhole than wander out into the jungle. Lieutenant Lindauer will give you the day's orders. I've got to go back to battalion for a briefing. Go ahead, Jerry."

Lindauer chomped on an unlit cigar and waited until Tuttle had left. He then drew a crude map in the sandy soil with a stick. He explained that the original plan for the 1st Marine Regiment to take the airfield was off. The 5th Marines would take the airfield instead. This time I Company was to advance on the airfield abreast in a long skirmishing line rather than in column. "Intelligence doesn't think we'll meet any resistance. Our patrols didn't find anything last night. The Japs seem to have slipped away somewhere." He took the cigar out of his mouth and spit before continuing. "I know we are all short on water, so the quicker we take the airfield, the quicker we can replenish. There's another river just on the other side of the airfield. We're supposed to move across it and set up a perimeter there. They say the water there runs clear and cold. May even get some hot chow tonight."

The 5th Marines took the northern approaches to the airfield—closest to the sound—without a shot being fired. The only Japanese they found were mutilated corpses that had bloated in the fetid air. Intelligence noted the lack of battle dress and weapons. The "enemy" seemed to be workers from a construction battalion, which meant that the real soldiers were somewhere out there, maybe even watching their every movement from the hills. "It's the damnedest thing, Lieutenant," Bull remarked to Harry as they stood on the edge of the airfield. "Can't figure them Japs out."

Within the wrecked airfield installations, the Marines found a bounty of supplies and equipment: howitzers, trucks, road-graders, generators, radio transmitters, refrigerators, and gasoline. Among these were large quantities of canned food, sacks of rice, and large bottles of sake. The 1st Marines followed the 5th Marines onto the airfield and subsequently pushed onto the slopes of the high ridge overlooking the field from the south. The men felt a little more at ease during the second night. During the day they had bathed in the clear Lunga River and filled their canteens. The cooks had been able to prepare some hot chow. The officers decided to let the men release some of the built-up tension and rationed out the sake.

After midnight, most of the men were nodding off to sleep. It was raining again but not as heavily as the night before. They had been without real sleep for more than forty-eight hours. Harry and Frenchy were sitting under palm trees in a coconut grove to the north of the airfield, where they had a view of the sound. At one point, they noticed an eerie green light hovering off a small island in the channel to the northwest. "Must be flares," Harry said. Just then a series of bright flashes lit up the sky in the channel to the north. A few seconds later a wave of thunderous explosions sounded, bringing everyone in the grove to their feet.

"*Mon Dieu!*" Frenchy exclaimed.

"It's a naval battle," Harry said.

At one point a heavier explosion sounded and they could see an orange pillar of fire billowing up from a ship, as if the vessel were being sucked up into the heavens. The firing continued intensely for another hour and then started to die off. No one was sure what had happened or whose ships still stood on the sound. The men all suddenly felt small and inconsequential. By then it was almost dawn again.

"That was quite a show," an enlisted man said.

Happy Hargrove sang glibly, "I haven't seen a show like that since Broadway . . ."

Harry admired the boys who could introduce moments of levity in terrifying situations. He lay down to try to get a few minutes' sleep. He dozed off quickly. His dreams were vivid. In one of them, he relived an evening with Viktoria, when they had gone to watch a show at a Russian restaurant in Shanghai.

The restaurant was called *Samovar* and was located off Route Père Robert in the French Concession. The inside of the restaurant was laid out in a circle, with a sunken interior where the tables and patrons sat. A circular walkway ringed the dining area, with a set of steps to the tables in four places. This gave the waiters and—more importantly—the performers a stage surrounding the guests where they could perform and easily circulate. Throughout the meal there was never a break in the entertainment.

Samovar was one of dozens of such restaurants that doubled as night-clubs in Shanghai. It was considered one of the best. The show, which lasted almost three hours, was a well-choreographed, endless parade of talented performers: Contortionists shared the stage with jugglers. Clowns—proficient in half a dozen languages—toyed with both the players and the audience. There were always beautiful singers, switching between Russian ballads and English songs and French chansons. The main singer in Samovar was a forty-year-old Russian woman with lustrous tresses of copper hair and the figure of a twenty-year-old. She was draped in a slit Chinese *cheongsam* dress that showed off her shapely legs. As alluring as she was, however, the lines around her eyes conveyed a litany of sad stories and experiences. Even though she sang in Russian, Harry needed no translation. Her songs were plainly about love and loss. Viktoria laid her head on his shoulder as they listened to the dolorous voice.

Viktoria ordered the meal for them, starting with *kholodets*, a jellied beef aspic dish, followed by *golubtsy*, a dish of stuffed cabbage, and grilled sturgeon. They washed their supper down with chilled vodka flavored with buffalo grass. Harry was surprised to find that the vodka seemed to have little effect on him.

"No Russian drinks without a table full of food," Viktoria explained during one of the few breaks in the evening's program. "At least, not when friends and family gather. That's why, when we open a bottle of vodka, we throw the cork away. It shows that we will all finish the bottle together." Then she added demurely, "But we don't have to finish the bottle if we can't." Harry leaned over and kissed her on the lips. Their mouths grew warm together.

Harry felt a hand shaking his shoulder, and he awoke to see a man wearing a tan tropical helmet crouching over him. Startled momentarily, Harry recognized Pith. "Lieutenant, get yourself some chow. The captain wants to see the platoon leaders at 0700." Harry looked at his watch. It was six o'clock. Day was breaking over the sound. He had slept only an hour. He got up and made the rounds to check on the men. He found that most of them were still asleep. He decided to let them continue their slumber. He told the ones that were awake to go eat. He took his own mess kit, walked to the edge of the airfield, where a hot kitchen had been set up, and waited in line with the others. Harry walked back to the grove, ate his breakfast, and then wandered down to the Lunga River. There he filled his canteen, brushed his teeth, and shaved.

Walking to Captain Tuttle's foxhole near the spit of the river, Harry looked out over the water and stopped. His mouth dropped open. Beyond the piles of crated supplies that had been stacked on the beach during the previous two days he stared at an empty horizon. There were no more ships in the sound. No cruisers, no destroyers, no transports. The Navy was gone. He walked further out toward the beach and saw several transports steaming to the west and one sole cruiser moving slowly to the northwest. He could see a large hole in the cruiser's bow even from a long distance.

When Harry arrived for the briefing, Tuttle, Lindauer, Pith, and the platoon leaders had already assembled and were discussing the naval engagement. No one knew exactly what had happened, but the aftereffects were clear: The Marines were alone for now. Someone asked about the carriers. Tuttle pointed out that no planes were patrolling. "I think it's safe to assume that they're gone too, which is why the transports are skedaddling. I just hope the Japs didn't get 'em."

"Well, shit, I hope this doesn't end up like Wake Island," Country said, "and we get left out to dry."

"Yeah," someone added, "like Bataan."

Tuttle tried to reassure them. "Listen, we have almost fifteen thousand men ashore here, an entire division. And, as you can see," he swept his arm out toward the beach, "we have a mountain of supplies. Not to mention all the loot we got from the Japs." Then he shrugged. "But, fellows, we have no longshoremen to unpack for us, so the 5th Marines are going to be pulling that duty today. Division says we can't afford to leave all our supplies out in the open. So each of you will gather your platoons and report to the northern edge of the airfield at 0800 to learn about being wharf rats." Tuttle then dismissed them sternly. "Gentlemen, we have a fine fighting force here, and we *will* hold this airfield. And you need to reassure your men. No talk of Wake or Bataan. Is that clear?"

"Aye, sir," they said in unison.

The next day the Japanese air raids began. Like clockwork, every day at noon a squadron of light bombers flew down from the Japanese base at Rabaul, three hundred miles to the northwest. Men scattered in all directions to foxholes and slit trenches that had been dug along the perimeter of the airfield. It was terrifying at first, but they grew used to it. Nightly air raids began soon thereafter. Since most of their planes were not outfitted to fly at night, the Japanese usually sent one floatplane just to harass the Marines. Sometimes the bombs hit way off in the jungle. Sometimes they splashed harmlessly in the sound. The plane's engine made a peculiar looping noise that everyone likened to the sound of a washing machine. Soon the men started calling the flying bucket Washing Machine Charlie. The Japanese just wanted to keep the Marines from sleeping regularly, and Charlie was effective at that. They learned to hate him . . . and to keep their boots on when they slept.

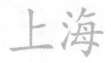

Chapter Ten

After a week on the island, Harry was ordered to begin leading night patrols to scout west of the Lunga River for Japanese troop concentrations. Usually a company's executive officer would fill this role, and Jerry Lindauer had led the first few patrols. But on the fifth night a sniper put a bullet into Lindauer's elbow as he raised his arm to motion the men forward. The bullet traveled through his right forearm, exiting through his palm.

Now it was Harry's turn.

Although the other young officers spoke jealously of Harry's getting to lead the patrols, much of it was bluster. The truth was, most men were terrified at the thought of leaving the relative security of the perimeter at night. When the Marines walked out through the veil of dark vines into the jungle, it was almost as if they were passing through a portal into another world. Moonless nights in the tropics have a black thickness to them that seems to envelop you, almost as if the darkness itself is one and the same with the humidity. The rain and the jungle give the darkness an extra cloaking quality. It was hard to see the man in front of you, much less anything or anyone that might be hidden by a tree ten yards ahead of or behind you.

Before Harry set out on his first patrol, Swede joked with him good-naturedly. "Aim low, Dutch. Those Nips ain't too tall. Just act like you're shooting jackrabbits in Texas."

He reiterated this exhortation each time Harry went out, and it became a ritual. Harry would answer, "Sure thing, Swede. Make sure you have my breakfast ready when I get back."

The patrol squad always consisted of ten men, plus a corpsman. During the first few patrols they walked cautiously, stepping forward without lifting their back foot until the first foot was firmly planted on the ground. They halted at every sound. The rain, the mud, and the terrain impeded them, and as such, at first they rarely patrolled very far. The officers at battalion berated Harry for this. Harry would simply report that his squad had covered more ground than they actually had. He was ashamed of his misprision, but he was more ashamed to admit that the black jungle terrified them. Soon they became used to the rhythm of the jungle sounds and learned to quicken their pace. Whenever they found themselves atop a ridge, on an open patch of ground where the enveloping jungle gave way to the dark sky, the men would audibly exhale, as if coming out of water for a breath. But Harry knew that in those clearings they were easier targets for snipers, so he urged the men to move on. They would reluctantly resume their march and pass once again through the curtain into the black jungle with constricted throats and dry mouths.

It was on such a murky night in late August that the patrol encountered a Japanese sniper, who had tricked them into showing themselves by crying out in American-accented English that he was a wounded Marine.

"Corpsman!" a voice cried through the rainy gloom.

Harry whispered to Bull, "You think there's another patrol out here?"

Again, the voice cried out. "Corpsman! It's me, Smith. Please come and help me!"

Bull craned his neck, looking out toward the call. "Not unless maybe a patrol from the 1st is also out here, sir. Would they be?"

"I'm not sure. I thought their patrols were staying close to the beach." Harry shook his head and whispered, "But with these useless maps, who knows where we are."

"Corpsman!" the voice cried again. "They shot me! Please come, I'm hurt!"

They waited a minute. Bull whispered to Harry, "It's a Jap trying to get us to come forward and expose ourselves."

"How can you be sure?"

"No Marine would say, 'They shot me!' He'd say, 'I'm hit!' or 'They got me!'"

"Yeah, his grammar is a little too precise. But I want to make sure. I don't want to leave a wounded Marine behind."

"I'm telling you, Dutch, it's a Jap. If you send anyone out that way, he's gonna get shot."

"I'm not sending anyone out, Bull. I'm going myself."

"Okay. Then I'm going with you."

Harry started to protest, then thought better of it. "Okay. But we'll need another man. Tell Happy to come up with his Springfield."

Besides being a fan of Clark Bars, Happy was the best shot in the platoon.

Harry signaled for the men to stay put while they slowly crawled toward the area from which they thought the cries arose.

After they advanced about twenty yards, Harry felt through the darkness and the mud and found a sturdy stick. He slowly rose and hurled the stick as far as he could through the undergrowth to the right of their position. He quickly fell back down to the ground. As soon as the stick crashed into the foliage another shot rang out. This time they saw the flash and heard where the shot hit, close to where the stick had landed. Harry was sure the sniper had lost sight of them. He nudged Happy. They slowly rose to a crouching position and quietly moved forward.

Another shot rang out. Happy let out a groan and fell down by Harry. Harry dropped into a prone position. A third shot rang out, and Harry heard the bullet pop just overhead. Harry heard a groan behind him. He turned and looked. Bull was leaning against a stump with his hands near his face.

"Bull?!" Harry whispered. He crawled back to him.

"I'm okay, I think he just grazed me," Bull said holding his neck. Harry could see that his fingers were streaked with a dark liquid. He quickly looked to Happy.

"Happy? Is it bad?" Harry whispered. No response.

Harry called out in a low voice for their corpsman, Pharmacist's Mate First Class Herbert Sullivan. "Sully! Get over here quick!" Harry admired the Iowan's almost unnerving calm, even during the most chaotic situations.

Together Harry and Sully dragged Happy back down the jungle trail to where the rest of the squad was lying in wait. Harry clasped Happy's hand as Sully probed the teenager's wound, while rain dropped onto their faces.

"There's an entry wound through his ribs and an exit wound just a few inches above it here on the side." Sully indicated the exit point with bloody hands. "It's a good thing the bullet went through him. Assuming it didn't hit anything vital, he should heal okay. He's probably got busted ribs, though."

Harry said, "It didn't go through his lungs, I hope."

"Do you taste blood in your mouth?" the corpsman asked him. Happy shook his head. Sully deftly applied a compress and bandage. "Think you can walk? A young buck like you should be tough enough to walk out."

Harry couldn't see the other men, but he felt the fear and tension among them. He looked at his own trembling hands then took a sip from his canteen. He noticed that he felt hot in spite of the cool rain. No more shots were fired, suggesting the sniper had left.

Sully was looking at Bull's neck. "It's just a flesh wound," he confirmed. As he put a compress to the wound he whispered, "You're lucky. Two more inches and you'd have been KIA."

Sully looked up at Harry. "We need to get them both back, Lieutenant."

Harry ordered the squad to fall out. His voice shook. He was ashamed to look the men in the eyes because he felt that he had failed them. And now two of them—two of his favorites—had been shot because of his mistake.

It had stopped raining. Harry stayed by Happy's side as they trudged eastward toward the Lunga, supporting him as they ascended the ridges. They decided to skirt the bare ridge tops to avoid any other contact with the enemy. The men seemed to move quicker the closer they got to the perimeter. They got back to base camp in just over two hours, neither Bull nor Happy slowing the squad's pace.

An hour after they arrived Harry sat alone at the mouth of the Lunga River in the morning light, smoking a cigarette. He had a piece of paper stretched out in front of him on the back of a ration box. He was attempting to sketch a crude map of the area they had scouted, making note of its ridges and ravines. Battalion Intelligence (B-2) would want a rundown of the patrol.

After he finished drawing the crude map, Harry wolfed down half the can of chicken à la king that Swede had given him upon their return. The transports had managed to unload plenty of ammunition and medical equipment before they weighed anchor, but they had been forced to leave before all the food had been brought ashore. Once the 1st Marine

Division exhausted their C-rations, they would have to subsist on dry K-rations and captured Japanese rice. They were already restricted to two meals a day.

Harry went to the battalion command post north of the airfield for a debriefing with the B-2 exec, Lieutenant Ferdinand Goff. Goff was of medium height, with black hair and a prominent cleft chin. Goff was a first lieutenant and thus outranked Harry, but he made Harry feel at ease in his presence. They sat on a fallen palm log outside a group of tents and went over Harry's map. Comparing the two drawings Harry noticed the great detail on Goff's map and wished out loud that he had had it on his patrol.

"We can't take the risk of the Japs getting their hands on our maps." Goff smiled. "We don't want them to know how ignorant we really are."

Goff produced a small hip flask, opened it, and passed it to Harry, who took a long sip. The bourbon burned his throat, but it gave him a burst of energy. Harry handed it back to Goff, saying, "You boys living it up at battalion, huh?"

Goff took a sip from the flask, smiled, screwed the top back on, and said, "Old Granddad. Nothing but the finest for Mrs. Goff's baby boy."

They continued to talk for a while. Goff had a sardonic sense of humor that all Marines seemed to develop eventually. When Harry asked how he got into intelligence, Goff explained that he had a degree in classics from the University of Chicago.

"Oh? Your Latin coming in handy these days?"

"No, but my background in Byzantine history sure helped prepare me for the court intrigues here at battalion," he said, gesturing with his thumb to the tents behind them.

Harry smiled. "I wonder what Belisarius would make of all this."

"Oh, he'd feel right at home. The enmity, the mendacity, the petty grudges, the everlasting injustices—and that's just among us Marines."

Harry nodded. "The chickenshit."

"You said it, brother. They say it's worse in the Army."

Goff took out his flask and offered it again to Harry. "I think all this history calls for one last drink."

Harry took another sip and gave it back to Goff. He paused and then asked, "What do you hear about the Navy? Are the carriers really gone?"

Goff looked at Harry directly for a moment without responding.

Then he said, "As you probably guessed, the Navy took a real licking last week. We lost a couple of cruisers, and rather than risk the carriers, Admiral Fletcher withdrew them south to Espiritu Santo."

Harry just nodded and said, "I figured."

Goff continued. "We can expect the carriers to make occasional forays up this way, but until we get fighters permanently onto the airfield, we're going to have to make do without air support. The Seabees are making good time on the airstrip, and we think that within four or five days—certainly within a week—we can have the strip serviceable for our planes. Anyway, the 7th Marines will be here soon, and they'll bring more supplies. We're also getting reports from Jap stragglers that they're low on food, a lot of them have malaria, and they're getting desperate."

"Is that the opinion of a battalion intel officer, or are you on the level?"

"It's the word of a gentleman—and hopefully a friend."

Harry extended his hand. "Yes, a friend. And my friends call me Dutch."

Goff took his hand. "And my friends call me Ferdie."

"Ferdie," Harry said as he stood up, "count on me to come by from time to time for a friendly visit and the latest scuttlebutt—and to avail myself occasionally of some Old Grandad."

Ferdie tipped his flask in Harry's direction. "What's mine is yours—until it runs out."

Harry waved as he left. "So long."

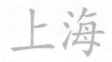

Chapter Eleven

August 1, 1942

My Dearest Harry,
I've barely had the energy to take up pen and paper since the end of last year. Writing to you may be a useless exercise, but I'm doing so in hopes that you can one day know what we have had to endure since your departure a year ago.

The news of the fall of Malaya, Singapore, and the Philippines in the spring was such a blow to us. All summer I have found myself wondering whether you were serving in the Philippines. I have no way of knowing whether you are okay or even alive.

Life in Shanghai without you and Tanya is bad enough. And life in Shanghai under Japanese rule is simply awful. All foreign nationals have been forced to register at the Hamilton House—your old apartment build-ing! You can imagine how I felt going there for the first time since you left. Foreigners in Shanghai are forced to wear silly armbands in public, iden-tifying their nationality with the letter A, B, or F printed boldly above a registration number. Not the Germans, of course, and, ironically, not the Russians. But we are still second-class citizens in Shanghai.

The Shanghai Club is now an officers' club for the Imperial Navy, and the American Club has become a club for Japanese civilians. They removed the two bronze lions from in front of the Hong Kong Shanghai Bank on the Bund. I remember walking arm in arm many times with you under the gaze of those very lions. I miss them too, like long-lost friends. Most of the restaurants are closed except in Hongkew. There is no vibrancy in Shanghai as there once was. The city is now dreary and gray where it was once brilliant in neon.

My uncle continues to manage his financial and business affairs, but the conditions are not good, especially now that the Japanese have gone to war with the British. Losing French and American markets has also made it difficult, though he does still sell tea to the Japanese. But he pays an exorbitant tax, and he has to trade in the occupied Chinese currency. Many Russian émigrés lost their jobs once the American and British trading firms were shut down. Friends and colleagues come to Uncle Grisha for handouts, and to the extent he can be, he is quite generous with them. Interestingly, he rarely speaks of going back to Russia now that the Germans have been stopped—at least for the present.

Aunt Maria sees to it that nobody in the family goes hungry. The garden flourishes under her tireless care, and the children and I help with feeding the chickens and rabbits. For now, we are all in good health because our diet includes eggs and meat and fresh vegetables. How I long for piroshky, *like the ones you and I used to eat at the teahouse!*

We've had no word from Tanya and Edward. Perhaps they got out of Hong Kong before the Japanese attacked. We can only hope so. At least she was able to get out of Shanghai.

Our cars have been confiscated, so when we go out—which is not often— we go by bicycle or on the tram. The French buses run on coal, so they are absolutely filthy and we avoid taking them unless absolutely necessary. The city has become much more lawless and dangerous, so for the most part we stay at home, except when we go as a family to functions such as at church.

I miss you so much, Harry, My Love. And I dearly miss my Tanya. I feel at such a loss to be unable to do anything, to be unable to know anything, to be unable to hear anything from those I love the most. Perhaps you feel the same way. Not having either of you to confide in makes it even more difficult for me. I pray for you that you are safe and that your family is well.

With all my love,
Your Viktoria

Viktoria had been unable to write much in her diary during the long winter months and into the spring. She couldn't find the strength, nor could she ward off her despondency. Then came the birth of a boy on March 21, 1942. Maria, several female cousins, and an older Russian friend who had once been a nurse attended at the birth in the room that Viktoria had shared with Tanya. Doctor Rabbino was also present.

The delivery was mercifully short, and Viktoria got through it, although the pain was almost unbearable. The baby was born with a shock of white hair, bright blue eyes, and a very loud voice. From the moment she found out she was carrying Harry's child, Viktoria knew that if she had a son she would name him Henry, in honor of Harry's father and his favorite cousin. So when the boy was christened in August at St. Nicholas Cathedral, with Grigorii Savin standing in as the father, he was given the name Henry Garrievich Dietrichson. At times Viktoria wanted to shout out at the top of her lungs that Harry now had a son, but she knew it was pointless. Harry had no way of knowing. She wasn't even sure he was alive or whether he even cared to remember her anymore.

At the christening of Henry, Viktoria was able to have a short conversation with Father Dmitry. She knew he was making a tremendous exception by christening a child born out of wedlock, something the church was deeply opposed to. But Father Dmitry understood the situation and the absurdity of life for Russians in Shanghai, especially under Japanese occupation. In his eyes, welcoming another soul into the church was his duty, wedlock or no.

"Thank you so much, Father, for agreeing to baptize my son."

"Vika, dear, he is a child of God. There was never any question in my mind." Father Dmitry then chuckled. "Of course, your aunt is not an easy woman to say no to."

Viktoria nodded and smiled. "Neither is my uncle."

"Tell me about Henry's father. He is an American, but what of his profession, his views, his philosophy on life?"

"He is a correspondent, Father. Or rather *was* a correspondent. Now he is in uniform, like so many other young men these days."

"He is a Catholic?"

"No, Father, he is a Protestant, of Norwegian and Scottish origin."

"I see, a Viking *and* a Highlander. Does he practice?"

"He is well read and knows the Bible intimately. But he has mixed emotions about religion, Father. You see, like me, he was orphaned at a young age." Viktoria's thoughts drifted back to the first time she and Harry sat together and discussed each other's lives. It was at the Savin teahouse, several days after they had encountered one another at Arnaud's, in the spring of 1939.

"Nice to see you," Harry said as they settled into a booth at the teahouse.

"I'm glad to see you too." Viktoria shifted in her seat to catch a glimpse of her reflection in the mirror on the opposite wall.

"I hope you didn't think I was being too forward."

"No, not at all."

"It's just that when I saw you the second time at Arnaud's, I thought to myself, 'Harry, you go ask that charming young lady to coffee before she gets away again.' Besides, you didn't drop a scarf or anything that I could use as an excuse to chase you down."

Viktoria smiled and blushed. "Well, I'm glad you chased me down, Mr. Dietrichson. And I'm glad you are here now."

"Please call me Harry." He asked if he could call her Viktoria. He then asked her the name of her father.

"Sergey," she answered, somewhat taken aback.

"Then I shall call you Viktoria Sergeyevna." Russians often call friends and colleagues by their first name and what they call a patronymic—a derivative of that person's father's name—out of respect. He had learned that in Tokyo when he met with Soviet officials.

Viktoria was surprised. "You seem to know a lot about Russia."

"I try to keep up. The country fascinates me." He asked her where she learned to speak English so well.

"I have lived in China practically my entire life, and my cousins and I were all educated together at my uncle's house by French and English governesses."

"So you were born in Russia?"

"Yes, I was born in Moscow. My father was an officer in the Imperial Army. He was wounded at the front in the Great War and had been sent out to the Far East for convalescence. My mother chose to keep us in Moscow with her family. And then, of course, the civil war broke out, so we made our way east to join our father in Vladivostok."

"Do you have brothers or sisters?"

"Yes, I have an older brother, Boris, and he lives in Tientsin."

"And your parents are here in Shanghai with you?"

She looked down uncomfortably for a moment. "My mother lived here for a while. She died of pneumonia when I was fifteen. My father disappeared during the civil war. I don't remember him well. I was just three."

"I'm sorry to hear that."

"No, that's okay. It was a long time ago."

As Viktoria spoke, a middle-aged woman brought a bronze samovar to the table. Viktoria explained to Harry the process of pouring strong black tea from the teapot and then filling the glass with boiling water from the samovar to the desired strength of tea. The glass tumblers were placed in carved tin receptacles with handles.

"In Russia, tea drinking is a big part of our culture. You must read Pushkin to better understand the role of tea in my motherland."

Just then a young woman brought them a plate of sweet and savory pastries, or *piroshky*, stuffed with different fillings. Viktoria explained how they were comfort food for Russians, bringing back childhood memories of snowy days and warm kitchens. Harry took one filled with cabbage and egg and bit into it. "It's delicious."

Viktoria then asked Harry questions about his own background. Without pain or hesitation, he began to tell her his life story. "My father also died when I was young, but I don't remember him. My mother died of cancer when I was nine. After that I was raised by my grandmother and then my uncle."

"What part of America do you come from?"

"Texas," he said, then paused. "Well, Pennsylvania, actually. I moved to Texas to live with my uncle and his family when my grandmother grew old. So, though I hail from Texas, my most formative years were in Pennsylvania with my grandmother. She was the biggest influence in my life."

"How did she influence you most?"

Harry thought for a moment and took a sip of tea before answering. "She introduced me to books. She opened the world up for me. We were living in a small town in the hills of southern Pennsylvania. But she helped me to understand that there is so much out in the world, and that I could see it for myself one day. I guess you could say that I'm here having tea with you because of her. She never traveled more than the fifty miles from her home, yet she was a worldly woman. I miss her more than I miss my own mother."

They sat in comfortable silence while Viktoria absorbed the information. She sensed a warmth and intelligence in Harry beyond any person her own age she'd met. She was surprised how easily he had opened up with her from the beginning. Clearly it was because she spoke of losing her own parents.

She smiled. "We have a lot in common, Harry."

"Yes. Partners in misery, I guess."

After another sip of tea Harry continued his story. "My uncle has worked hard and made a successful life for himself as an engineer in Texas. I was educated even more broadly under his roof. His wife, Jo, is a wonderful lady. They have two young children—Jolyn and Henry—so I wasn't always the center of their attention. Anyway, my uncle and my aunt helped put me through college and helped me get a job as a correspondent. But . . ." Harry paused for a moment.

"But what?" she asked.

"It's hard to explain. I'm very fond of my uncle and my aunt, but something holds me back from showing them as much affection as I should. I don't know why exactly. But I often felt like a stranger in their home. Like I was an uninvited guest."

"I understand. My uncle has been a great influence in my life as well. He has taken care of us all. He has done well in China, and he has never forgotten his family. But sometimes I also feel like—what's the proper word—a decoration? An unwanted part?"

"An appendage."

"I've never heard that word used like that before."

"You just described what it means perfectly."

She turned the conversation back to Harry. "How did you end up in Shanghai? Why did you choose to be a correspondent?"

He couldn't even begin to list the serendipitous chain of events that led to his being in Shanghai. How he had ended up in Japan, his friendship with Jingu. He tried to narrow it all down. "I suppose I've been fascinated with Asia ever since I read Bunyan as a child. Do you know *The Pilgrim's Progress*?"

She shook her head.

"*The Pilgrim's Progress* was written by an Englishman during the 17th century. It's a fantastic account of Heaven, written as an allegory. In the story there's a place called the Celestial City. It's meant to represent paradise—or Heaven." He paused to sip his tea. "It describes a man's journey through life, with all its difficulties. My grandmother read it to me every Sunday after church. For some reason, as I listened to the descriptive chapters, I associated the Celestial City with Asia."

"Are you very religious?" she asked.

"It's hard to say. It interests me for the history. But I have a hard time coming to grips with the question of suffering. Sometimes I find myself asking the question: If Jesus suffered for us, then why do we continue to suffer so much here on earth?"

"I think it's a natural question for someone who has suffered in life, someone who has lost loved ones, to ask. I sometimes ask myself the same thing as I wander around Shanghai. It is horrible what people here are going through."

"That's why I continue to grapple with religion, Viktoria. I'm just not sure about everything." He paused. "It's complicated."

"Of course, but I *do* believe, and I'm certain that the more people believe, the less suffering there will be, ultimately."

Henry was a fussy baby in the beginning and sleep was hard to come by. Fortunately, family members surrounded Viktoria, and she could count on any number of them to help spell her when she was overtaken by exhaustion. Maria absolutely doted on the boy, and she loved to sing him to sleep when he suffered from colic.

Henry kept Viktoria occupied and distracted, but he could never fill the void left by the departure of Harry. She often thought about their days together. They were the best days of her young life. She understood that war was a deprivation for all, and she carried on, maintaining a stoic demeanor, but inside she cried to herself each day. As comforting as the presence of the extended family was to her, she felt overwhelmed at times and was always lonely. Viktoria's loneliness was compounded by the arrival of postpartum depression.

Viktoria looked on the writing in her diary as a form of escape from the difficulties and drudgery of motherhood. But she chose not to write about Henry; she could not find the words to put down on paper something as important as a birth of a child. As much as she longed for Harry to know, she was unable to convey the idea in words, not that he would know anyway.

August 1942 was one of the hottest months on record for Shanghai, and the entire Savin family suffered through the heat wave. The stench of the city—the combination of the river, the night soil, and the number of people dying from sickness, starvation, and heat stroke—made some areas unbearable to traverse. The great fear was that an epidemic, such as typhus or cholera, would break out and kill even more inhabitants of the city.

Viktoria took extra care of Henry, and she did her best to maintain her own health. It had now been more than a year since she had seen Harry. She could only wonder how many more months or years would pass before she would see him again.

One day as she sat in her room, rocking Henry to sleep, her aunt came into the room. She looked down at the baby and smiled sweetly. "He is our angel."

Viktoria smiled and continued rocking. Maria stood beside her and hummed softly a child's song. When he had fallen asleep, Viktoria stood and placed him in the cradle.

She turned and looked at Maria. "I was thinking of Harry. Where he might be. What he might be doing. Whether he's even . . ." Her voice trailed off. She sighed and sat down next to her aunt on the bed.

Maria put her arm around Viktoria. "Oh, Vika, dear, I hope and pray that he is fine. And I feel, deep down in my heart, that he senses he is a father."

"How could he possibly know?"

"God works in mysterious ways. I'm sure one day Harry will return to you." She looked over at the cradle and said, "And to him."

"You don't know how much your kindness and understanding mean to me, Aunty Masha." She looked down. "I know I have brought shame down on our family."

Maria grasped Viktoria's arm gently and said, "No, dear. You have brought us joy. Henry is a beautiful addition to our family. We are lucky."

Viktoria shook her head. "But I know Uncle Grigorii is ashamed. Sometimes the way he looks at me."

Maria shook her head. "Dearest Vika, I know for a fact that he loves you and supports you—and Henry. But some people have a harder time adjusting to new realities and they have a hard time expressing their feelings. Your uncle is like this. He has always been this way. Is it the optimal outcome? No, of course we would prefer your husband, Henry's father, be here with us. But he cannot. The war has imposed all sorts of hardships on the world. This is just another hurdle we must overcome. But never, ever doubt that you have our unending support and our undying love." She stroked Viktoria's cheek.

"You are too kind." Viktoria hugged her aunt.

As they embraced, Maria spoke over Viktoria's shoulder. "These are difficult times. But we must face them with courage and resolve. And, most importantly, we must face them together as a family."

"I just wish Tanya were also here."

"I know, dear. So do I. God be merciful, that we will be reunited one day. Just as you will one day be reunited with Harry. But we must hold on and survive this tempest. Better days will come."

"I just wish I had *any* news about him. He never wrote me after the letter last summer. I never told you, but we had agreed to be married. And when I refused to go with him, he was so mad. I can't say I blame him."

Maria was surprised by the news, but she responded with composure. "He may have been angry, but that is because he loves you. This will make him even more determined to come back for you." She looked again toward the crib. "And what a joyous surprise he will have!"

"Aunt Maria, you are such a wise soul. I am so lucky to have you with me. I couldn't handle any of this were you not beside me."

Maria smiled. "I promised your mother."

Chapter Twelve

One hot, dry afternoon in late August—several days after the bloody night patrol—the men lolled in their bivouacs around the airfield. The naval engineers, known as the Seabees, had made good progress, and the matted strip was now ready to accommodate American planes. General Alexander Vandergrift, the commanding general of the 1st Marine Division, had christened the strip Henderson Field for a Marine pilot killed at Midway. As they dozed or gossiped, the men heard the faint hum of aircraft engines. Although it was later in the afternoon than the regular Japanese raids, they all instinctively looked for cover. Harry noticed that the engines didn't make the regular tinny sound of the Mitsubishi motors. Instead, the aircraft made a guttural, roaring sound like motorcycles. A rifleman shouted and pointed, "Look, fellows—they're ours!" At first the Marines warily squinted up at the sky, their hands shielding their eyes from the sun. After a few moments, white stars on the wings and fuselages became visible. Faces lit up with smiles and shouts as each man confirmed the truth of the spotter's words. Jeeps and trucks raced to the end of the runway, horns blaring, to greet the first planes coming in.

"God bless the Seabees!" another leatherneck shouted.

Harry stood with Frenchy, Swede, and Ozzie just west of the airfield. They counted one plane after the other as they touched down.

"Another Wildcat," Ozzie said. "That makes fifteen."

"Here comes a Douglas," Swede said. "What's that? Eight?"

"Nine," Frenchy said. "Nine beautiful torpedo bombers."

The last of the planes, a Wildcat, swooped down and made a hard landing. For a moment it looked as though its tail might flip forward, sending the plane over onto its back.

"Coney Island pilot," Ozzie chuckled.

"I don't care," Swede said wistfully, "he's beautiful to me." He wiped a dirty sleeve across his face. He looked over at Harry and the others. His eyes glistened with tears.

The morale of the men, which had been rock bottom, soared. Now, at least, the planes would keep the Japanese from dominating the air. But they all knew that they were not out of the woods. As long as the Japanese fleet controlled the waters, they couldn't get the supplies they needed.

That night, the Japanese made their first attempt to recapture the airfield. Automatic weapons and mortar fire erupted within a few hours after the arrival of the American planes, shattering the temporary peace that had lulled many of the men into a false sense of security. Harry awoke to the vibrations of an explosion. He initially thought it was an air raid and ran to a foxhole. It was soon apparent that a large-scale attack was under way. Pith escorted the platoon leaders to the battalion command post to consult with Major Armbruster, the battalion commander. Armbruster was a small, irascible man, who had a booming voice.

"A big Japanese push is in progress at the river to the east. We aren't sure how many of the enemy we're talking about, but it seems there's at least a battalion, maybe even a whole regiment."

"How did they get an entire regiment onto the island, sir?" someone asked.

Ferdie Goff, who spoke up. "We explained to Major Armbruster that we think they were landed last night by destroyer. The Japs want that airstrip before we get a full complement of planes."

Major Armbruster spoke again. "The 1st Marines have met a concentrated push from the east at the Tenaru River. We will consolidate two battalions—ours and the 2nd—at the eastern edge of Henderson. Either we go in as replacements at the river or worst case—if the Japs break through—we fight them here in the grove."

The Marines of I Company stood by tensely all night, gripping their weapons. Harry went around and spoke with his platoon. He joked, trying to lighten up the atmosphere. "I think the Japanese came to bring us a delivery of more rice."

The firefight's intensity peaked after about two hours, and it gradually subsided and died off around four in the morning. Now and again there was sporadic rifle fire, but automatic weapons and mortar fire had ceased. Harry heard .45 pistols being shot randomly, one at a time. Before sunrise it was reported that hundreds of Japanese were dead and that Marine casualties were light.

The next morning Harry, Ozzie, Frenchy, Ferdie, Swede, and a few other officers from the 5th Regiment walked along the beach surveying the carnage. Japanese corpses littered the spit and others floated in the green river. Hundreds of others were said to be piled waist-high in the grove beyond the river. The sightseeing group came across a strand of tumescent guts trailing across the sand. To Harry, the entrails resembled Portuguese man o' wars that often washed up on the beaches along Galveston Island. A leg, severed at the hip, stood at an oblique angle in the sand, its white femur peeking out the top. It looked like a misplaced leg from a storefront mannequin. Harry remembered Bunyan's description of the River of Death. *How appropriate*, he thought.

An older gunnery sergeant from the 1st Marines walked around with them, explaining what had happened. "I've never seen mortars being walked backward like they were last night. The Japs were chased to the river, right into our fire, *toward* our lines. We just mowed 'em down. I ain't ever seen nothin' like it."

Harry picked up a discarded Arisaka rifle on the beach. He opened the magazine and an unfired round popped out. He sniffed at the barrel. It didn't appear to have been discharged.

Ferdie asked if there were any prisoners.

The grizzled sergeant shook his head. "No. A corpsman tried to help a wounded Jap. The fucker rolled over and blew himself up with a grenade. Took the poor corpsman with him. We shot all the wounded ones we found after that." He took a puff and then threw a cigarette down onto the sand. He added, "Goddam savages."

Just then a loud splash came from the river. They all turned to look. A Japanese corpse seemed to be swimming across the surface of the water. The sergeant said blithely, "We leave 'em for the crocs to eat." He then laughed out loud. "This mornin' one fella shouts out, 'Hey! Look at them 'gators!' and a college boy next to him says, 'They're crocodiles; there are no alligators in this part of the world.' Everyone laughed and started callin' college boy Smithsonian. That's his name now. Smithsonian."

Harry and the others chuckled, but they quickly regained their grim demeanors as they walked among the dead. Harry stared at the piles of

Japanese corpses that would be left to rot in the jungle. What if it had been the reverse? He felt bad for the families of these men, the parents who had given their sons over to the cause of the emperor. Mothers like Mrs. Tsurugawa.

During Harry's stint as a United Press correspondent in Shanghai, one of his most invaluable contacts was a Japanese naval officer named Commander Tsurugawa. Their paths crossed after Harry first arrived, in 1939. Harry had a letter of introduction from Jingu to Tsurugawa. As a child Tsurugawa had been a calligraphy student of Jingu's before the master immigrated to America. Tsurugawa had also lived in America; he studied for two years at the University of Michigan back in the mid-twenties. When he and Harry met, Tsurugawa had already been in Shanghai for three years at the naval command in Hongkew.

He and Harry met at cafés or restaurants. But most often they met at the American Club, where Tsurugawa liked to listen to early Sunday morning football games, especially when the broadcast featured Michigan. During their discussions, Tsurugawa explained to Harry the back-and-forth game of bombing and assassination being played between the pro-Japanese and the pro-Nationalist forces in Shanghai. Harry had been surprised how readily Tsurugawa volunteered his thoughts on the political situation. But Harry wasn't naïve. He knew the Japanese were likely looking to establish channels for information about the United States in the Far East. And Tsurugawa knew Harry was a reserve naval officer. Perhaps Tsurugawa, unsure about Harry's true métier, was looking to pass false information about Japanese intentions in China. Disinformation in the early stages of the worldwide conflict could be as valuable as the most accurate intelligence.

It was remarkable, Harry thought, just how balanced Tsurugawa was in his assessments of China. He was not fanatical like so many other Japanese officers Harry had met while living in Tokyo. Tsurugawa fully recognized the desires and rights of the Chinese, although he clearly felt that China would be better off with Japan as overseer. He doggedly believed in Japan's vision of the Far East without an ounce of hypocrisy. When Harry brought up incidents such as the massacres at Nanking, the violation of Tientsin, and the bombings of Canton and Chungking, Tsurugawa never argued that the end justified the means. He was clearly pained by the suffering of the Chinese, and he loathed the Western colonization of Asians. Harry truly respected him.

One day in the spring of 1940 Tsurugawa paid Harry the ultimate compliment by inviting him to his home, a comfortable apartment in Hongkew he shared with his wife and teenaged daughter. Their son, Shigeki, who was hoping to secure a spot in the Imperial Japanese Naval Academy in Etajima, was eighteen and had just begun military training in Japan. The evening Harry arrived the family had learned that Shigeki had been accepted into the cadet program at Etajima. Tsurugawa was in a jubilant mood, and he appeared to have been drinking already. His wife, however, seemed somewhat subdued.

Mrs. Tsurugawa prepared a delicious meal of ginger mackerel and fresh grilled vegetables. She did not eat with Harry and her husband; instead, she sat near the table, served the dishes, and poured cold sake when the cups were empty. Tsurugawa offered toast after toast to his son. Harry imbibed freely and relished the opportunity to be in a Japanese home, where he could practice speaking the language. Near the end of the meal, Tsurugawa tipsily began to offer a toast to the Imperial Navy, but he stopped himself. He raised his cup toward Harry. "To the great *American* Navy. And to my many friends who serve in her."

They drank, and then watched as Mrs. Tsurugawa refilled their cups once more. Harry then offered his own toast. "To the Imperial Japanese Navy, and to my friends who serve in her."

Tsurugawa smiled broadly and emptied his cup. Soon thereafter Tsurugawa's chin dropped to his chest. His head nodded up and down several times as sleep overcame him.

Mrs. Tsurugawa came back into the room from the small kitchen and saw her husband. "*Ara!*" she exclaimed. She squatted on the tatami and then bowed deeply toward Harry. "Please forgive my husband. Now that Shigeki has been accepted at Etajima, he is letting off steam. This is the culmination of many years of preparation."

Harry shook his hand in front of his face in the Japanese manner. "It's perfectly fine. I understand how proud both of you must be."

She bowed a second time and thanked him. Her face assumed a sad demeanor. Harry could tell she worried about her son. Japanese losses in China had been mounting in recent months. After a moment of silence, Mrs. Tsurugawa sighed and said to no one in particular, "Boys

. . . we look after them only for our emperor. Until we give them back, it's nerve-racking." She used the words *hara-hara shimasu*, an expression that Harry had learned in Shanghai, used often by the Japanese residents when describing the terror bombings. She then quoted from the "Imperial Rescript to Soldiers and Sailors"—an oath that each man made upon enlisting. "Duty is heavier than a mountain; death is lighter than a feather." Harry was moved by her sentiment. She was prepared to sacrifice her son. For the Japanese, family started with the nation and the emperor. They were willing to give all. He thought to himself at the time, *How can the Chinese ever expect to beat them?* As he rose to leave, Harry offered to help Mrs. Tsurugawa clean up some of the dishes, but she wouldn't have it. He knew that to insist would be an insult to her. So instead he offered to carry Tsurugawa to his futon in the back room. She gratefully accepted his offer. "Otherwise, he will sleep here," she said. Harry gently pulled Tsurugawa up. He opened his red eyes in surprise, saw Harry, and began mumbling something about fishing.

"I'll take you to your room, *Chuusa*," Harry said, using the Japanese word for commander. "Shigeki-san would want you to sleep now that you have celebrated his success."

When he heard Shigeki's name, Tsurugawa pulled his head up, smiled broadly, and said, "Wonderful."

Harry walked his venerable friend to the prepared futon, where he eased him down and pulled a blanket over him. Harry went back into the main room and thanked Mrs. Tsurugawa. She thanked him profusely in return. "Please, Harry-san, come again."

Harry took in the sight of the slaughtered Japanese men on the beach. What if one of the corpses was Shigeki?

Harry then thought of Shakespeare's words in *Henry V*: "I am afeard there are few die well that die in a battle; for how can they charitably dispose of any thing when blood is their argument?"

As summer ended, the rains grew heavier on Guadalcanal. Staying dry became impossible. There had been as of yet no resupply of rations. By now, with their monotonous rice diet, almost all the men had shed more than ten pounds. Rats and land crabs were endemic. Mosquitoes tormented them at night. Many men developed dysentery. Some suffered from malaria. The men often resisted taking Atabrine antimalarial tablets because it made them nauseous and they complained it was turning their skin yellow. "I don't want to be mistaken for a Jap, sir," one Marine told Harry. "Tropical ulcers" were perhaps the biggest scourge to the men. These skin lesions grew and festered on the body, most often in the groin or on the feet. When the rough twill of their dungarees or their boots rubbed against the sores, it was agony. Their uniforms were in tatters. Men quit bathing. The latrines overflowed with the rains, adding to the stench.

One day in early September a group of Navy supply ships returned to the sound, and for the first time in several weeks, the Marines ate hot chow. It was also the first mail call since they had landed a month before. The men waited expectantly as the letters were distributed. After their names were called, they filed off individually to read their letters. Some of the men read their letters aloud, either to tell a funny story or to mock a trivial complaint made by the person who sent it. The happiest leathernecks were those lucky enough to receive a care package. Some contained Ritz Crackers, candy bars, or canned food, like sardines or peaches. Some included sweaters or socks, which were both luxuries on the island.

Harry encouraged the men to answer the letters before the ships left again. "Remember, no doom and gloom. Tell them you're quartered safe out here. And keep in mind, Marines, Uncle Sam will be reading your letters to scrub any intel from them."

Harry received a letter from Aunt Jo and one from Ellen. He read Ellen's letter first. It was scented with perfume. He sniffed it longingly. He ached to see her and to hold her. He grew aroused as he remembered their lovemaking sessions. Their time together had been short but passionate. Their bodies seemed to fit into one another perfectly, and they usually brought one another to climax several times when they lay together. He hungered for any sort of intimate companionship at this stage, and he even began to think he was in love with Ellen. She enclosed a photo in the letter. It was a studio photo of her. She looked alluringly at the camera.

Ozzie saw the photo and let out a wolf whistle. "Woo, Dutch. You got yourself a looker!"

He self-consciously put the photo away in his wallet, momentarily forgetting the one of Viktoria that lay in there as well.

Aunt Jo's letter was dated early July. Two months ago. In it she mentioned that Henry had been sick frequently and had developed some sort of ailment or allergies. They were concerned for him. Otherwise, the news from Houston was the same.

Harry decided to write a letter to Henry and Jolyn. He told Henry he would take him to Austin to watch a baseball game at the university, as he had done in years past. He also penned a short note to Ellen. What else could he say to her or anyone other than he was fine and that he missed her? How could he tell her that he saw crocodiles eating corpses? Or that the jungle conditions were squeezing the life out of him and his men?

That very night Harry had a vivid dream about Ellen. She was swimming on the Whangpoo River and struggling to stay above the water. Then her face became Viktoria's face. Viktoria called out to him. Crocodiles swam in the river. He awoke with a start and found that he was short of breath, as if he had been in the water with her. He lay back down and tried to sleep, but he could only doze for a few minutes at a time.

Most nights he led a squad that patrolled the area west of the airfield. No one ever got used to the tension of being in the jungle after dark. Snipers continued their deadly arcade game from the trees; casualties steadily increased. Cases of sickness and fatigue were even higher. And every night the Japanese sent fast destroyers down the Slot—as they called the sound to the northwest—to disgorge several companies of Japanese troops along with supplies and ammunition. Before the Japanese destroyers turned north to return to Rabaul, they'd turn their guns on the airfield. They would then race home before sunrise to avoid the Marine flyers, who were augmented by Navy pilots from the carrier *Wasp*. The Marines started calling this resupply run the Tokyo Express. In a testament to the seesaw nature of this particular campaign, the men learned in mid-September that the *Wasp* had been sunk by a torpedo in the waters south of Guadalcanal, but most of the accompanying aircraft were able to escape to the *Hornet* or onto the field at Guadalcanal.

The 5th Marines were ordered to make a push west to keep the Japanese away from the airfield. The 2nd and 3rd battalions (around 1,500 men) were to set out from the village of Kukum, just west of the Lunga River, cross the Matanikau River at the spit, and seek out enemy contact. Additionally, a battalion of eight hundred Marine Raiders was to ford the Matanikau at a point further upstream, just north of the ridgelines. The two groups of Marines would meet in a pincer movement on the morning of September 27. Harry was happy to have Bull Burns, who had rejoined the company after his short convalescence.

On the morning of the engagement, the three companies of 3rd Battalion—including Harry's I Company—easily crossed the Matanikau at the spit and continued several hundred yards into a coconut grove. They could hear firing upriver, which meant the Raiders had engaged the Japanese inland to the south. I Company was ordered to move south along the river's bank to meet up with the Raiders, while K and L companies would push further west before turning south. Captain Tuttle instructed I Company's new exec, Lieutenant Bill Auldin, who had come from regiment headquarters, to lead the advance. They had moved one hundred yards downriver when the first shots rang out. Auldin took a sniper's shot straight through the neck. Then the *whump* of Japanese mortars started. As the Marines hunkered down, Harry went to Sully who was crouching over Auldin. His eyes were wide open, but they had the lifeless look of a shot deer.

Sully looked up at Harry and said, "He lasted a second; then he just gurgled and died."

A shot kicked up sand next to them. It came from behind. Harry shouted back to his platoon to cease fire. He saw two men behind him go down. "Sully!" Harry shook his shoulder and pointed to the downed men. "Go!"

Japanese snipers in the grove behind them had waited for the Marines to pass by before springing an ambush from the treetops. The platoon crouched behind fallen logs and whatever cover they could find. Shots seemed to come from every direction. Japanese machine guns began pouring a withering fire onto I Company from the south. Though most of the men had been on patrols, this was their first experience in a set battle. The terrified men looked to Harry, who quickly assessed the situation and instructed weapons platoons to form a horseshoe defense, with their backs to the north, toward the beach.

The cry for "Corpsman!" sounded every few minutes. The men all blindly discharged their weapons toward the Japanese lines. Harry quickly went through a clip of ammo on his Reising gun. He was as frightened and overwhelmed as the men were.

After roughly twenty minutes, Harry was given word that Captain Tuttle wanted the platoon officers to gather at the command post in a dry creek bed. When he arrived, Harry noticed that Tuttle was bleeding from his upper arm. He was pale and seemed in a partial state of shock. Harry asked, pointing to his arm, "Shouldn't a corpsman take a look at that, Skipper?" Tuttle looked down at this arm with wild eyes. He seemed unaware that he had been shot. Harry then noticed that Frenchy and Country weren't there.

"Anyone seen Frenchy?" There was no answer. "What about Country?"

"Dead," answered someone.

Tuttle told the men to maintain their positions for now. He sent two teams of sharpshooters to hunt the snipers that were creating a killing zone from the trees. Once they had been cleared out, he would make a reassessment. "Get back to your men and keep up the fire!" He gasped after he made the exhortation.

Harry rejoined his platoon facing south in the bottom of the horseshoe. He had positioned himself behind a barrier of two fallen palm trees. There they continued firing at the Nambu machine-gun nests. Harry fired occasional bursts with his Reising gun. The Japanese mortars were having a deadly effect. A man nearby cried out, "Corpsman!" Harry turned to call for Sully, and at that instant a mortar round splintered a log, sending fragments of wood into his eyes and his forehead. A piercing pain came through his temples and across the bridge of his nose. He tried to open his eyes, but they stung sharply. He poured the contents of his canteen onto his blurry eyes. He sat helplessly as explosions rocked the ground. Harry knew that if the Japanese overran him, he wouldn't be able to see them.

Just then Frenchy jumped down beside Harry. He was panting, sweat pouring over his face. "Dutch, have you heard anything from Captain Tuttle?"

"Frenchy? Where the hell have you been?"

"Been trying to not get shot or blown up. What's the situation?"

"We're ordered to hold, until the snipers are neutralized. The skipper's been hit, and he's losing blood."

"What happened to your nose?"

"Splinters. Look, I can't see a damned thing, so you'll need to go to the command post and tell Tuttle to call in the artillery. If he doesn't, you call it in. Can you find the coordinates? They're coming from the south-west. I estimate two hundred yards." He pointed his arm in the general direction. He felt blood running down the bridge of his nose.

"You sure you're okay, Dutch?"

"Yeah, just got some debris in my eyes. Go!"

"Okay. I'll go find him." Frenchy sprinted away.

Unable to see anything, Harry suddenly grew calm. He realized that he was no longer frightened. As if he could say to himself, *You can't do anything about it, so why worry?* He could think things through clearly without caring about what was going on around him. The battle raged on, but as bad as it was, Harry could tell that the situation upriver with the Raiders was worse. The din from that direction was louder. Harry hunkered down alone, waiting for Frenchy to return. Suddenly Corporal Vargas stumbled over the fallen palm trunks and nearly fell on top of Harry.

He sat up and shouted toward the unseen enemy, "*Hijos de su puta madre!*" He panted for a moment and then looked at Harry. "Sir, I just came from the command post. Captain Tuttle wants to withdraw across the spit. Sergeant Moore and Bull want to move up the river and take out those machine-gun nests. They're arguing about it."

"What about Lieutenant LaSalle? Did you see him there?"

"No, sir."

"Damn," Harry said. "*Jefe,* stay here. You have the platoon until I get back. Make sure they stick to positions perpendicular to the riverbank. It's the safest place. Is that clear?" He called for a runner. A short, stocky youth named Sergetti came to their position. "Corporal, give me your canteen." Harry took it and poured the contents into his eyes. "Now take me to Captain Tuttle."

They waited until there was a slight diminution of fire. Sergetti gripped Harry's upper arm and together they sprinted from one cover to the next. After five minutes of sprinting and diving for cover, they found the command post.

The group was huddled in the same dry creek bed. Tuttle, whose face was now ghastly white, addressed Harry. "Dutch, we're going to pull out across the spit." Tuttle then motioned to Bull and Pith, who sat sullenly on the ground. "I know they want to go upriver, but the mortars will kill us if we do that. And we can't call in the artillery. It's too close and I don't know where the other companies are exactly."

Harry interjected, "Skipper, I'm not sure it'll be safe on that spit. The Japanese probably got it pre-sited." He didn't envy Tuttle. The decision he made could get them all killed.

Tuttle exhaled and said. "Then we'll have to make our withdrawal orderly and continue pouring fire to the south. I've called in extra stretcher details. They'll meet us at the spit."

"Aye, sir," they all said.

Harry then asked, "Anyone know where Frenchy is?" No one answered.

Bull came to Harry with a look of concern, "Dutch, are you alright?"

"Yes, it's superficial."

They returned together to the platoon. They began a gradual and orderly withdrawal down the river in the direction of the beach. By now Harry could see a little better. He instructed Bull to lead the withdrawal, and then he sought out and asked Sergetti to help him look for Frenchy. They retraced the path between Harry's foxhole and the command post. They found Frenchy lying behind a palm tree fifty yards from the foxhole. His helmet was gone, and the left side of his body from the waist up was a bloody mess.

"Oh, good God, no! Frenchy?" Harry cried aloud. He immediately called for a corpsman before crouching down beside his friend. "Frenchy, can you hear me?"

He was breathing but unconscious. His face was contorted. Harry stayed with him until two men came with a stretcher. He helped them carefully lay Frenchy down. They managed to get to the spit, and to Harry's immense relief, he noticed that they were no longer being fired upon. Tuttle had made the correct decision. They carried Frenchy to a grove just east of the river, where all the wounded were put into jeeps and driven back to the perimeter.

Once safely back across the river, I Company joined the Marines from the other two companies of the 3rd Battalion, who filtered in over the course of the next hour. The men filed back in a green column down the beach road. The firing to the south and west was dying down. Many of the men were dazed while others limped pitifully. Bull offered Harry a cigarette. "We sure as hell took a licking back there, Dutch."

Harry took the cigarette gratefully. "We sure did. Felt like there was an entire regiment of Japanese back there in that grove, but I never saw a single one of 'em."

"That's a helluva cut on your nose."

Harry put his hand on his forehead. "I know, but I got some splinters in my eyes, and that smarts a lot more."

"I reckon half the company are wounded." Bull pulled on his cigarette, then added, "I think you're the only ranking officer still walking on two feet. Or maybe Woody, if he's alive."

Harry didn't answer. He didn't care to think about having that awesome responsibility at this moment. He walked on, silently smoking his cigarette, trying to steady his shaking body. He agonized about Frenchy.

上海

Chapter Thirteen

The 5th Regiment and the Raider battalion lost sixty-seven dead and more than two hundred wounded at the battle on the Matanikau River. I Company lost nine men plus twenty-eight wounded. Captain Tuttle received wounds in his chest and upper left arm. He was evacuated on the first transport. The new company executive officer, Auldin, was shot and killed by a sniper in the first minute of the battle. Sam "Country" Emtman was also killed. Four of the company's six officers were now out of action, two of them dead. Worst of all for Harry, his close friend Frenchy was in critical condition and had been flown off the island the day after the battle. By the time Harry arrived at the hospital the next morning to check up on Frenchy, he was already gone. He had no idea whether or not his friend would live.

Harry was treated for the splinters he'd taken in his eyes. The sclera—the whites of both eyes—were bloodstained. He had to return to the field hospital each day to have his eyes flushed with saline solution and boric acid. During those few days he wrote letters to all the families of the men killed in action, a job that normally would have fallen to Captain Tuttle. Harry barely knew four of the nine men, and he found it especially hard to write their loved ones. What could he say?

Even though his own experience with family was luckless, on Guadalcanal Harry began to appreciate the importance of family for the men and for morale. No matter how dire the situation and how beleaguered they were, a respite for mail call lifted the spirits of everybody. Harry understood that the "home front" was more than just a name. It embodied everything that was good, everything that they were fighting for. And at the core of this was family. For the first time in a long while he thought of his parents and his grandmother. He desperately wished they were alive to write to him.

Harry did receive news several days later, but not the kind he'd wished for. It was a letter from Uncle Walter, who wrote that Henry had been diagnosed with leukemia. Harry was unsure what the long-term prognosis was, but from the tone in the letter he sensed that things were not good. He was devastated. Later that night Harry confided in Swede about Henry's illness and the special relationship they had.

"You know, he's the first person in my life that I really feel is *mine*. Everyone I've ever known already existed before I came to know them. Do you know what I mean? They've lived and had their own experiences. Henry, though, was born not long after I moved in with my aunt and uncle. He's never known life without me. He probably misses me more than anybody else on this earth does."

"Damn, Dutch. I'm sorry."

"You know I used to take him to the baseball games at Clark Field when he came up to Austin with his parents to visit me." Harry chuckled. "He could never get over the idea of Billy Goat Hill in the outfield, that the centerfielder may have to run up onto it to field a ball. He'd always say, 'It doesn't seem fair to make the fielder run all the way up there.' He'd go on about it all game long."

"He's right. Nothing seems fair," Swede agreed. "Take this war. Us having to come out all this way, so far from the folks back home."

"I just feel so helpless."

"My kid brother back on the ranch talks all day every day about going off to fight in the war. He's fourteen years old. My parents are worried sick. I write him letters telling him that he needs to stay home and be a man on the ranch. I try and tell him he doesn't need to come out here. Charley, my other brother, is a fighter pilot. He's out here somewhere in the South Pacific."

Harry nodded and looked at the ground. He tried to hold back his emotions. He was glad that it was night, and that nobody besides Swede could see his anguish. He felt that only Swede could understand him.

A week had passed since the battle on the Matanikau, and the men of I Company sat on the beach near the Lunga on a sunny afternoon watching dogfights taking place over the sound. They spoke about home, about food, about women, but they mostly wondered when the Army would come to relieve them. At one point a Wildcat caught up to a Zero and began firing. Soon a plume of smoke followed the Zero. The men stood cheering and watched as the Japanese pilot parachuted from his spiraling plane. With the wind blowing onshore it became apparent that the pilot would come down somewhere near the airfield. As he passed over the beach, the men could see his face. He looked back at them. They all stood and some ran to follow the chute.

Swede said, "That bastard's gonna feel real sorry when he hits the ground."

Then, suddenly, the Japanese pilot deliberately unbuckled his harness and fell to the ground, crashing through the foliage of the grove.

"Jesus!" they all gasped. Some men ran to inspect the remains. Most of the men nonchalantly returned to the beach. They had seen enough Japanese corpses.

After a while, the other Japanese planes quit the engagement and flew north over the sound to return to Rabaul. The men gathered on the beach, turned their backs on the planes, pulled their pants down to their ankles, and showed the Japanese pilots what they thought of their performance.

In mid-October good news arrived in the form of the 164th Infantry Regiment. The Army had finally come. The Marines thought that they would now be withdrawn. It had been two long months, and they were exhausted, hungry, and sick. But it was not to be. Rather than an entire Army division, it was only a regiment—not enough men yet to relieve them. Still, the three thousand big Swedes from North Dakota were itching for a fight, and they joined the 5th Marines on the west side of the perimeter facing the Matanikau River. The same convoy brought in more supplies, including more rations.

Nobody's fools, however, every man who had been on Guadalcanal since the beginning understood that there was a clear pattern to events. Things happened in pairs: Every bit of good news would be followed by bad. So, as soon as the Marines got over their happiness in seeing more men and more supplies, they instinctively braced themselves for the inevitable backlash to come.

It didn't take long. That very night, the men rested in their bivouacs, their bellies full of hot chow. It was raining hard. Harry lay on his cot in a tent with Woody, Swede, and Ozzie. Just past midnight Harry shifted to adjust his blanket and saw through the trees the entire airfield lit up momentarily. He assumed it was a lightning flash. Seconds later the earth shook so violently that the men, accustomed to making nightly foxhole dashes, couldn't keep their feet. Harry was thrown down twice before he began crawling on all fours toward the closest hole he could find.

For ninety minutes, Japanese battleships in the sound released a wall of fire on the Marines and soldiers. Fourteen-inch shells shrieked into the compound, obliterating planes, huts, supply dumps, trees, and men. Harry squeezed his eyes shut and balled up and put his hands over his ears; in this quasi-protective cocoon, he lay wishing it all away. He tried to think of something else—home, Henry, friends—but nothing helped. He could hear some of the men in the sodden foxhole praying and weeping like children. Men gasped for breath as the tremendous concussion shells sucked the oxygen out of the air. An enlisted man in their hole lost his nerve and tried to run out, but some others held him back. He lay there sobbing. Soon a stench came over their foxhole. The man had lost control of his bowels. Thousands of miles away from home, at the mercy of a pitiless enemy bombarding them with a hellish fire, they all suddenly felt orphaned.

Harry's right eye began to throb again, and the pain almost made him forget the shelling. He thought about being blown up beyond identity. *Maybe,* he said to himself, *it's just better to go this way. No pain, no lingering. Just blown to atoms.* He was too exhausted to care anymore. He was tired of being hopeful, only to see all hope crumble the next moment. He looked at his watch. It was almost one-thirty. Just then, Zeus and the Titans set their thunderbolts down as suddenly as they had taken them up. Within two minutes of the slackening of the shell bursts, all firing ceased. The Japanese ships turned back to the north.

At first, everyone was too afraid—or shocked—to leave the security of their dugout shelters. Then, slowly, the men crawled out and staggered toward the airfield. Nobody spoke. Men walked with blood streaming from their ears. Others walked holding their sides and whimpering in pain, their chest cavities pushed in, their lungs collapsed. As Bull put it, "Clean on the outside, jelly on the inside."

Later that morning the butcher's reckoning was made: More than forty men had died in the shelling, many of them blown to pieces beyond recognition. But what was of more immediate importance was the loss of forty-nine planes, and almost all the aviation fuel. Fires burned amid the shattered wreckage and shredded tents. The runway had been badly cratered. The Japanese had succeeded in badly demoralizing the men. Then it began raining harder than ever before.

Two days later the sun finally reappeared after an incessant week of rain. Harry sat on the bank of the Lunga enjoying the warmth for a change. He shaved his scruffy beard and washed his tattered dungarees—in the process tearing them even more. A young Army lieutenant came and sat nearby, about twenty yards down the bank. The man also shaved and then brushed his teeth. After a while, conscious of Harry's gaze, he waved. Harry waved back.

"Sorry to stare, but I haven't seen a clean toothbrush in a long time."

The Marines tried to keep two toothbrushes at all times: one to clean their teeth and one to clean their weapons. If you did without one, it was the former.

The young soldier stood up and walked over. He offered Harry his toothbrush. "Wouldn't want the Marines getting cavities."

Harry laughed, and then let out a long sigh. He took the toothbrush, mainly to show his appreciation at the gesture. He didn't care anymore whether he brushed his teeth. "Much obliged, Lieutenant . . ."

"Linscott. Sidney Linscott." The man offered his hand. Linscott wore glasses and was slightly pudgy, which made him seem out of place on this island of raggedy scarecrows.

Harry shook it. "North Dakota?"

"No, Holton, Kansas. I'm one of the odd men out."

"Didn't think that name sounded Scandinavian. I'm Harry Dietrichson, from Houston, Texas."

"Now, *that* sounds Scandinavian to me," Linscott said, sitting down next to Harry.

"Yeah, it's Norwegian, like Babe Didrikson, the Olympian." Harry hastily and perfunctorily added, "But, no, we're not related. I spell my name differently, though a long time ago the names were probably spelled the same."

"You have that line well-rehearsed."

"I memorized it. Everyone asks how to pronounce my name, and the conversation usually goes something like that."

"Well, Dietrichson, go ahead and use that toothbrush. Sorry I don't have any powder."

"That's okay. As you know, our general-purpose soap does it all."

Harry held up a small green soap bar. He then rubbed it on the toothbrush and brushed for a full minute before rinsing with water from his canteen. Harry returned the toothbrush to Linscott, rubbing his tongue along his clean teeth. They felt new.

The two of them fell into an easy conversation about the finer points of life on Guadalcanal: the jungle, the mosquitoes, the red ants, the rats, the air raids, the cuisine.

Linscott asked Harry, "Are you with the 7th?"

"No, the 5th."

"So, you've been here since the beginning?"

"Yup, August the seventh. Can't you tell from my fine attire and my coiffure?" Harry raised his left arm and pointed to a festering jungle sore in his armpit. "And how about this beauty mark?"

"Holy Toledo, that must hurt." After a pause Linscott asked, "What was your job?"

"Oh, you know, lots of things, but mostly walking around in the jungle at night and getting shot at."

"I mean back home. What did you do? You know, before the war?"

"Oh, yeah. Back home? I've almost forgotten about that. I went to the University of Texas. Drank a lot of beer and wrote for the school newspaper. After college I was a correspondent for United Press. I was posted overseas, in Japan and China."

"Yeah, no kidding? *Japan*?!"

"Hmmm." Harry slowly nodded and threw a stick into the river.

"You must have a lot of stories to tell," Linscott said, and then quickly put his hands up. "Don't worry. I'm not gonna pester you about that now. Maybe some other time."

"Yeah, I do have some crazy stories. China was even crazier. I'd love to share them with you sometime." Harry took out a cigarette and offered it to Linscott, who declined. Harry lit up, took a puff, exhaled, and then picked a piece of tobacco off his tongue. "You know, when I joined the Marines, I never told anyone about Japan or that I spoke the language. I didn't want to be behind some desk, filing intelligence reports. So I kept mum. I wanted to see action and serve like a regular fellow." He looked around at the jungle surrounding them. "And now I have to question my own sanity."

Linscott nodded his head. "Yeah, I was offered a commission with the Army's finance department in Washington because I studied business at the University of Kansas. I turned it down for the same reason."

They sat silently for a few moments enjoying the quiet and the sun.

Linscott asked Harry, "You got a wife or a girl back home?"

Harry immediately thought of Ellen Lowry. He imagined her soft skin, her auburn hair, and her musky smell that remained on the sheets after they lay together. Then he thought about Viktoria, the sophisticated charm, the blue-gray eyes, and how he felt one with her when they made love. He was suddenly conflicted. He snapped out of the daydream. "Not really."

Linscott shifted the conversation back to safer ground. "I have a pilot's license, and I tried to get into the Air Corps, but these held me back." He wiggled his glasses. "Sometimes I can't believe that I was cashing checks last winter in a small-town bank in Kansas. Now I'm on some island I never heard of, getting shot at by people I still haven't seen."

"Well, brother, I know it's hard to tell the difference between us and the Japs since Atabrine makes us all look so jaundiced, but the guys you want to avoid are wearing tan uniforms and mushroom helmets. Got it?"

Linscott chuckled. "Yeah, thanks for the advice." He stood up and brushed himself off. "I gotta shove off."

Harry reached his hand up as he said farewell. "I mean it, Linscott. Keep your head down. Be safe."

"Thanks. It was good talking with you."

Harry watched Linscott amble off down the bank and cut over into the coconut grove.

A few days later Harry sat in the bivouac near the Lunga with Swede and Ozzie. Ferdie showed up conspicuously carrying a large can of peaches. The four of them shared the treat, dipping their dirty fingers into the sweet nectar to fish out chunks of the fruit. "Got it from a guy in the 164th," Ferdie told them. "I traded a Jap banner for it."

Ozzie sucked the remaining juice off his fingers and asked, "Ferdie, you know the Navy was supposed to be bringing in a lot of supplies every week, but my men are still hungry. We're eating Nip rice, and we're limited to one C-ration and one K-ration per day. What gives?"

"Well, the Jap shelling got a lot of the supplies. But I'll let you in on a secret. There's a big supply dump down between the fighter strip and the Tenaru. It's guarded by Army MPs. I know Marines from the 1st and the 11th are going in there every night and coming away with crates of Spam and chocolate and cartons of cigarettes. They trade souvenirs and get their loot. Some of them don't bother trading; they just sneak in and take it."

"You gotta be kiddin' me!" Swede said incredulously, with a hint of anger.

Ferdie continued. "Now, if I had a platoon of men under me—or a company—I'd definitely tell them to *not* go down there and take supplies." He took a drag of his cigarette and winked at them.

"Anything else you have to report to us, Ferdie?" Harry asked.

"Well, some good news and some not-so-good news."

"Come on," grumbled Swede. "Spill the beans."

"The Army is definitely coming soon. The rest of the 164th is in New Caledonia right now. They should be here in November."

"November?!" Ozzie said. "That must be the not-so-good news. I thought you were going to tell us they're coming tomorrow. *That* would be good news."

"Oh, I can see it now," Swede chimed in. "They'll show up on November 30."

Harry looked at Ferdie and asked expectantly, "And the not-so-good news?"

"Well, it's between us, but you boys—the 5th—will be pushing west again. General Vandergrift wants to take Point Cruz, about five miles further down, to have a good observation post for the Tokyo Express." Ferdie took a puff from his cigarette. He cleared his throat, as if he wanted to say something else.

Before he could, Ozzie interjected, "Well, I suppose if we put the Tokyo Express out of order, the quicker we get to leave. Is it true about the Japs starving and all?"

"Yeah, I think they're in pretty bad shape, and most of them have malaria. But who knows, really?" Ferdie hesitated again and looked down.

Harry looked at him. "Ferdie, what are you not telling us?"

Ferdie threw down his cigarette. "Yeah, well, this is something you shouldn't tell your boys yet." He exhaled, rubbed his forehead, and continued. "They sunk another one of our carriers, the *Hornet*."

"Aw, Christ," Ozzie said.

"The *Enterprise* was also badly damaged. She's limping back to Pearl as we speak."

"Jesus," Swede said. "The *Hornet?* That's the flattop Jimmy Doolittle flew off of to bomb Tokyo, right?"

"Yeah," Ferdie answered.

Harry said, "Ferdie, my math may be off, but by my reckoning—"

"Yeah, that's right, Dutch, no more carriers."

Ozzie rubbed his face with both hands. "Aw, fuck. We're up shit creek now."

"Well, we *do* actually still have an operable carrier," Harry said. "Right there." He pointed toward the airfield.

Swede nodded. "Yeah, and *we* can actually have a say in whether we lose it or not. Let's make damn sure we don't." Then he looked at Ferdie, smiled, and said, quoting a popular song, "Pass the likker to me, John."

When the flask came to Ozzie, he paused and said, "Here's to the USS *Henderson Field*. Let's do our damnedest to keep her afloat." He took a swig and wiped his mouth.

"Amen," the others said in unison.

A few days later they began preparing for the push west. This time the 5th Marines would be alone. But the Cactus Air Force—what they had begun calling the Marine flyers on Guadalcanal—was back in business thanks to the Seabees and to the arrival of more planes that had relocated from the doomed *Hornet.* The Navy would also get in on the act, and three destroyers operating in what everyone was now calling Iron Bottom Sound would be able to exact a little revenge by lobbing shells against Japanese troop emplacements.

The offensive went off without a hitch in the beginning. The 2nd Battalion pushed easily across the ridges and reached the base of Point Cruz, a small peninsula jutting north into Iron Bottom Sound. The 1st Battalion met heavy resistance initially, however, and the Japanese forces almost pushed them all the way back to the river. The 3rd Battalion, Harry's unit, was called in to reinforce and push the Japanese back along the coast and trap them on the peninsula. Both I and K companies were to be in the lead, and they started out on the afternoon of November 1 in a skirmish line. They moved forward through a grove, moving perpendicular to the ridges overlooking the sound.

Suddenly they could hear the Japanese troops milling across the grove to the west. They began screaming threats in English. "Marine, you die today! Blood for the emperor!"

It was eerie, being unable to see the Japanese but listening to their calls coming from the other side of the grove. It put the men on edge. The Japanese understood psychological warfare well.

"Do you think they can see us?" Harry asked Bull.

He shrugged. "Insects in the bushes, Dutch."

Woody Woodring—now the CO of I Company—called the platoon leaders to conference.

As they huddled to look again at a map and get their bearings, Harry asked Woody, "You sure those companies from the 2nd Battalion are on that ridge?"

"Yeah, we can be sure. They'll hug that ridge tight because, if they don't, they'll be hit by our own planes. The Japs have to come through this grove."

The Japanese continued screaming, mocking the Americans. Pith, however, was undaunted. He yelled out angrily, "Hirohito eats shit!" He then said sheepishly, "Wish I knew some Japanese. I'd tell 'em to kiss my ass."

Harry laughed. "Yell *bakayaro*! They'll know what *that* means."

"Well, what *does* it mean?"

"Idiot, or dumbass."

"Can't you give me anything better than that, Lieutenant?" Pith scowled.

"Yeah, tell you what, Sarge. When you see 'em up close, growl and say *chikusho*!"

"What'd you say? Cheek show?"

"Yes. It sounds like cheek show. But you gotta growl it low, like a pissed-off dog."

Woody repeated it and laughed. "What's it mean?"

"Motherfucker, and every other bad word you can imagine. There aren't a lot of cuss words in Japanese. But that is as bad as you can get."

"Where'd you learn Japanese, Lieutenant?"

Harry winked at Woody and turned to Pith. "I picked it up from a prostitute in Shanghai."

Pith grinned. "Okay, now I *know* you're telling me the truth."

Haggard as they were from the daily grind of exhaustion, hunger, disease, and death, the Marines faced it all with gallows humor. It kept the camaraderie and a flame of life extant among them. Harry—like everyone else—was scared mostly by the anticipation of battle. Once the battle began, each man just wanted to be sure he wasn't going to let the guy next to him down. That responsibility carried even more weight among the officers, who felt the heavy burden of assuring the safety of their men. Harry was exhausted, and he just wanted to get it over with, whether through his own death or the ending of the battle—or one day the ending of the war. Just so long as everything ended. He felt as if he'd been on that island three years, not three months.

At exactly 1400, each platoon leader in I and K companies uncorked a red smoke grenade. Simultaneously, they could hear the buzz of planes coming low across the treetops. The gray undersides of the American planes swooped over the Marines, who were clearly marked by the smoke. The Avengers flew the first wave and unleashed their bombs over the grove to the west. Then the Wildcats began strafing the area. The Wildcats banked north and then east over the sound before coming back low over the treetops for another strafing run.

Once the planes had completed their run, the Marines could hear groaning and smell the cordite and burning flesh. They waited for a while until the smoke had dissipated. Then the momentary silence was shattered by a piercing scream.

"*Totsugeki!*"

"They're coming!" Harry yelled. The men had prepared defensive positions. They didn't have time to dig, but they lay behind logs, squatted behind trees, or found natural depressions in the ground. Then they saw the Japanese emerge. Their units had dissolved into small incoherent bands of wild-eyed men charging forward out of the grove. They looked even more shabby and skeletal than the Marines did. Harry noticed that many of them were not even discharging their weapons. Instead, they rushed headlong with swords and bayonets above their heads, screaming at the top of their lungs.

Harry could hear and see the mortars as the 2nd Battalion continued to shatter the grove behind the onrushing Japanese. He also heard the naval gunfire that was sweeping the command area even further to the Japanese soldiers' rear. The enemy was trapped and being funneled toward I and K companies. The Marines laid down a sheet of murderous fire. Harry fired off his first clip of twenty rounds in the first minute and then changed to a second clip. He raised his gun again to take aim at the onrushing mass of Japanese, which had become a tan blur. Once he ran through his second clip, he stopped firing. He had only one clip left. He moved among the men, assessing the situation. Harry called for corpsmen for the men who were wounded.

He then found Woody, and together they tried to keep the company from dispersing too widely. Some of the men had run forward into the grove in a mad, blind dash to find the enemy and kill him. Marines and Japanese exchanged fire at point-blank range. Harry saw one Marine sitting on top of a Japanese soldier, repeatedly stabbing his chest and torso with his Ka-Bar. With each knife thrust, blood spurted out of the dying soldier's mouth like a small geyser. He saw big Jefe smash the butt of his BAR into a Japanese soldier's face, swearing all the while in Spanish. One Japanese officer had come through the lines with an eight-millimeter pistol attached to his belt with a cord. He ran through the trees, dodging the bullets and shooting at the Marines. Bull Burns emerged from behind a tree and cut the officer in half with a fusillade from his BAR.

The battle was over in less than half an hour. I Company lost seven men killed and twenty-six wounded; K Company fared worse, losing a dozen men. *It really wasn't a fair fight*, Harry thought to himself as he walked among the scores of shattered Japanese corpses. Tenacious to a man, the Japanese had refused to give in, and they followed orders to the bitter end. Now, heeding the pure instinct of a soldier, the wounded among them tried crawling to cover. But having learned never to trust a dying enemy soldier, the Marines finished them off with pistol shots to their heads.

That evening I Company made a bivouac in the grove. The stench of the battle remnants kept the men awake. No one would have slept anyway, with the adrenaline surge they were all experiencing. Harry caught fitful catnaps, fifteen minutes at a time, seeing dreams all the while. He saw Sarah and Viktoria walking together hand in hand. He saw them in the park on Sleepy Hollow in Houston. They were looking at a statue of a woman and boy that had been toppled by a group of teenaged boys. All of it that was left of it were the boy's feet. Looking down, they saw that the feet were clad in Harry's grimy boots.

He awoke, startled and short of breath. He felt under his arm and touched the sore. He was still in the jungle. He thought about Henry. Tears came to his eyes. He looked up and saw the stars. They were beautiful. He sniffed the air and caught the smell of the burnt corpses. He pulled out a cigarette and then remembered the restrictions. He threw the cigarette away.

"Dutch, everything okay?" It was Bull.

Harry wiped his eyes and said, "Yeah. I just want to go home. I'm tired, Bull. I want to sleep. I feel like I'm drowning on this God-forsaken island."

Bull came over and eased his big frame down next to Harry. "Nothing that the finest in canned meat can't fix." He held out a can of Spam.

They finished it together.

"Thanks, Bull. Now I'm gonna be running off to the bushes all night."

"Oh, no, Dutch, you didn't hear? This stuff *cures* dysentery."

Harry laughed. "No, seriously. Thank you. I feel better now." Harry reached for his cigarettes, then stopped himself again. "You know, I think we've got to send a squad of men to pilfer those Army supply dumps we've been hearing about."

"I think you're right, Dutch. I'll detail some men when we go back." Bull paused a moment. "You know, I'm tired too. I've reached the point where this horse has been rode enough, and I'm ready to move on."

"Everybody's washed up," Harry agreed. "But we did well today. The men were ready for blood."

"Yeah, they were." Bull laughed. "I thought Jefe was gonna kill every last Jap on this island. He's a mean sumbitch. Glad he's on our side."

"You can say that again." Harry laughed. "Okay, Bull, go give your jungle ulcers a rest. We'll be pushing off in a few hours."

"Dutch?"

"Yeah?"

"You've been a good leader to the men."

"Considering I got you shot, you're laying it on a bit thick, don't you think?"

"I don't just say things, Dutch. You know that."

"Thanks, Bull."

Bull stood up. "Good breaking bread with you, Dutch."

He watched Burns move off to his foxhole, dragging his BAR beside him. Harry dozed off a few more times but awoke with a start each time. In his sleep he saw Japanese soldiers creeping up on him with knives. Each time he awoke he was short of breath. "I'm drowning in this damned jungle," he muttered to himself.

Harry and the rest of I Company remained in the Lunga perimeter for a week before there was another big firefight. The Japanese attempted a breakout from Point Cruz. That was when Harry killed a man face to face for the first time. A Japanese officer had run from a concealed hole and nearly bowled him over. They were both caught off guard. Harry turned his Reising gun on him. He heard a click. It was jammed. He hurled it like a baseball bat from his side, smashing the Japanese officer in the ribs. That slowed him down enough for Harry to pull out his Colt .45 and fire twice. "*Shoganai yatsu!*" Harry screamed. The man grabbed his midsection then looked straight at Harry with wide, curious eyes as he fell to the ground. Harry fired two more shots at his chest until he was sure he was dead. He stood over the dead man and yelled at him again. "*Aho!*" Harry was morose and moody for days afterward, trying to comprehend what had led him to take a life.

During the battle both Ozzie and Pith were wounded and evacuated by ship. Swede was unharmed. Harry put in a recommendation for a Navy Cross for Bull, who took out three Japanese machine-gun nests by himself. The Marines counted more than five hundred dead Japanese. There were no prisoners, only the echo of .45s being discharged.

After the battle the men sat quietly, eating cold rations and smoking cigarettes under ponchos in the rain. Harry's puffy eyes and drawn face couldn't do proper justice to the exhaustion he felt inside. He was tired beyond wanting to sleep. His ears rang constantly. His right eye ached. Most of all, he couldn't shake the thought of Henry and of the anguish his family must be going through. He looked over at the Japanese corpses in the rain about a hundred yards away. It was impossible to make out the individual bodies; it looked like a tan canvas tarp drapped over a pile of logs. The raindrops made the helmets of the dead men glisten. He thought of their families. No burial, just incense offered at a shrine in their hometowns. Probably farmers' sons, fishermen, laborers. Gullible and foolish perhaps, but no less innocent than the Marines were to the butchery being carried out in the name of the emperor.

The 8th Marine Regiment came ashore on November 8. They were a welcome sight. With them came more supplies. Men were eating better, there was plenty of ammunition, more artillery, and the Cactus Air Force now ruled the sky. One last convoy of Japanese transports was sent from Truk Atoll in late November in an attempt to relieve the emperor's starving troops. Every transport was either sunk or turned back. When several dozen night-capable P-38 fighter planes touched down at Henderson in late November, everyone knew that the game was up.

Word was given in early December that the 1st Marine Division was finally leaving. Shortly after they heard the news, Harry, Ferdie, and Swede visited the temporary cemetery that had been set up near Henderson Field. The Marines and soldiers called it Flanders Field. The three of them ambled among the hundreds of crosses, looking for men they had known. They found Country's cross. Harry took the flask from Ferdie and poured some Old Granddad onto the grave. "Be with God, Samuel."

Swede said, "I feel for his folks back on the farm. I know how it must be, in their isolation."

Ferdie added, "*Dulce et decorum est pro patria mori.*" Then he solemnly took a drink from his flask.

As they walked out of the cemetery, they passed the Army crosses. Harry happened to look up, and he saw a grave marked with the name Linscott. He stopped. It was the grave of the fellow from Kansas who had lent Harry his toothbrush. He looked at the date. It read October 28, 1942. Harry realized that was only a few days after he had spoken with the kind, gentle soul on the bank of the river. He hadn't been on the island much more than a week. Harry poured out some whiskey on Linscott's grave. From that day forward, Harry would think of Sidney Linscott every time he brushed his teeth.

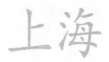

Chapter Fourteen

November 1, 1942

Dearest Harry,

Tanya has returned! She arrived yesterday out of the blue. Words cannot describe our joy at having her back home with us!!! She and Edward were detained in Hong Kong for almost a year, but they only recently were returned to Shanghai by the Japanese. They did not suffer, although with the food shortages it was difficult, as it is with everyone. Unfortunately, we didn't get to see Edward. He has been taken away to a camp somewhere northwest of the city. As the wife of a British subject, Tanya must now wait to hear what lies ahead for her. She has been issued an armband marked with a large B, which she'll be required to wear each time she leaves the house. But for now she remains with us. I am so happy!

The Japanese have started rounding up all the citizens of the nations they are at war with. Americans, British, Dutch, and even the French are being taken into camps. The husbands are being separated from their wives and their children. It is such a sad sight, seeing groups of people gathered at street corners here in the French Concession, waiting with their possessions for the Japanese trucks to take them away. The children hold their favorite toy close to their breast with one hand, and with their other they grip the hand of their father, as if they can somehow keep him there forever if they hold tight enough. Entire families have been dispossessed from their homes and have taken whatever belongings they can carry as they await imprisonment. Already the oncoming winter seems so cold!

The garden still sustains us, and Aunty Masha is a marvel at stretching carrots, beets, and potatoes and making do with whatever scraps we find. The citizens of other nations have set up their own relief organizations to help those less fortunate. But we Russians have nobody to rely own besides ourselves, and sometimes the Red Cross. The Church also does what it can, and Father Dmitry has been there for the entire community. But we are still a stateless people and have few options. Even the Soviet consulate has turned starving people away. They are so cruel and heartless, the Bolsheviks! Russian families come to us all the time, and we give them what we can spare.

I can imagine that our discomfort is but a fraction of what you and all the other young men in uniform are going through right now. We have heard the stories about British soldiers in Malaya and Singapore, and it is terrible. We know very little about the war in the West except that the British are fighting the Germans in North Africa, and that the Red Army is still holding out. We are able to listen in on some of the war news through the Russian radio station Voice of the Motherland. Uncle Grisha is also able to keep up with the news through his Chinese contacts. He has been allowed to keep his business open, but this forces him to deal with every assortment of greedy and wicked people—both Japanese and Chinese. Shanghai remains drab and grayish brown, just like the river flowing past us.

I confess to you, dear one, that I have been depressed and my spirits have been flagging, but Tanya's return has lifted me again. We will take each day together as a gift. We fear that she will be taken away soon to a camp, like Edward. Nothing is certain; the information we get changes all the time. For now, she stays with me in our room, and we are determined to spend every second together. She asks about you and wishes you nothing but the best. I told her everything about our parting last year. She expressed dismay when I told her I had refused to leave with you on account of her and Edward. She asked for my forgiveness, but I reassured her that I bear her no grudge. Sometimes fate intervenes and there is nothing we can do about it.

I think of you every moment, My Love. Although Tanya's return has given me new courage to face the coming months, my joy will not be complete until I once again see you. Please be safe and come back to me soon. I embrace you with all my heart and soul!

Yours, V

The day before she wrote her note to Harry in her diary, Viktoria was reading a book in the sunroom when she heard the maid, Natasha, shout out from the front hall, "Tatiana Grigorievna has returned!" Viktoria could not believe her ears. She ran into the hall and saw Tanya. For

a moment she stood still, wondering whether she was seeing an appa-
rition. They then rushed to one another, embraced, and then danced
arm in arm, screaming like two schoolgirls. "Tatiana Grigorievna has
returned!" Nata shouted as she went through the rest of the house. Tanya
was thin and haggard, and she arrived wet and weary, having walked all
the way from Hamilton House. But her beautiful smile lit up the Savin
household as all the family members and servants rushed out to hug
her. It had been more than a year since she had left home. Grigorii and
Maria—in spite of the harsh things they had said about their daughter
after her elopement—were absolutely overjoyed and could not contain
their glee.

They took her to the sitting room, and Nata quickly brought hot tea
with biscuits. They peppered her with questions and so many exclama-
tions that she barely had the chance to tell them what had happened to
her over the past sixteen months. Once she began to eat, they finally let
her be.

When the excitement had subsided, Maria urged Viktoria to take
Tanya to the room they had shared for so many years.

"Dear, we'll catch up after you rest. But meantime you'll find the
biggest surprise of your life," Maria said beaming and looking at Viktoria.

Tanya took Viktoria's arm, and as they walked up the stairs she asked,
"What is she talking about, Vika?"

"You'll see."

They walked upstairs and made their way to the bedroom at the
end of the hallway. Viktoria opened the door, and Henry—who had
been napping—was standing and looking through the slats of his crib,
awakened by the commotion downstairs. When he saw his mother, he
broke into a broad toothless smile. "Tanya, meet your nephew, Henry."
She walked over to the crib and gently picked up the boy. "Henry, this
is your aunt Tanya."

"Vika!" She gasped. "What? How in the world?"

"He is Harry's son. When you left last summer, I was pregnant, but I
didn't know it," she explained. "I was so lost. I didn't know what to do."
She shook her head. "You had gone, and I had no way of contacting you.
I felt so helpless. But Aunty Masha and Uncle Grisha have supported me
and helped me as any true mother and father would have. Your mother,
especially, has been a godsend. I couldn't have managed without her."

"Well, are you going to let me hold him?"

Viktoria smiled, "Of course." She handed the boy over to Tanya.

She held the boy tenderly. She sniffed his golden hair and kissed his head, gently rocking him as if she were his own mother. When she pulled him away to look him in the face, he appeared to be momentarily caught off guard at the similarity between this woman and his mother. He looked back and forth between the two of them. After a few moments he reached for his mother. Tanya playfully said, "No, you're mine now. You belong to me."

Viktoria laughed and reached for Henry. "I think this boy is hungry." She walked over to a rocking chair in the corner of the room and sat down. As she began breast-feeding him, Viktoria related all that had happened since Harry left, and how her heart ached because he didn't even know he had a son. Tanya listened patiently, adding comforting words now and then.

She looked lovingly at Viktoria and child. "He is a lucky boy to have this family. And I will spoil him rotten while I'm still here."

Viktoria looked up, "While you're still here?"

Tanya simply nodded and said she would tell her and Edward's story later, when her parents could hear it too.

Eventually the cousins rejoined the family in the parlor for an aperitif. Grigorii produced a bottle of good French wine that he had been saving for a special occasion. Tanya explained that after she and Edward were wed, they thought first of going to Singapore or back to England. But Edward was offered a position as bank manager, so they decided to stay in Hong Kong. When the war broke out, the Japanese arrested Edward, but he was released after just a few days. Several months later they were informed they could take part in a prisoner swap for Japanese diplomats stranded on British territory. She and Edward prepared to depart for England in the spring of 1942. At the last minute, however, the Japanese informed them they were no longer on the eligible list. A month later they were told they would be sent back to Shanghai as POWs. "You cannot imagine how crushed we were to hear this."

Now, eight months later, they had arrived in Shanghai by ship from Hong Kong, along with a group of about five hundred British subjects and their families. Edward and the other men were to be interned in a camp outside of Shanghai with other high-ranking British civilian officials from around China. By this time the general roundup of "bellig-erent" foreigners in Shanghai and the rest of China had begun. Many people met the news with relief, because they had been forced to fend for themselves amid widening food shortages. They hoped they would be fed regularly in the Japanese camps. Tanya explained that the wives and children of the British officials were to be placed in separate camps. Tanya was required to register at Hamilton House and was told she could rejoin her family in the French Concession until later in the month when the authorities had decided on her destination. The last Tanya saw of Edward was on the Bund, where he was loaded onto the bed of a large truck with the other men.

Tanya began to cry, and her mother and father clasped her in their arms. She was home now, so they would savor every moment they had together. The family's anger and disappointment about her having eloped evaporated in the joyous reunion. That night they feted her arrival with canned salmon, homemade jam, and Russian crepes made with Red Cross–supplied cracked wheat. Viktoria never left her side, except to care for Henry. Tanya, likewise, would barely let Viktoria out of her sight.

Viktoria didn't know that her moment of elation at seeing Tanya occurred at perhaps the nadir of Harry's existence on Guadalcanal. Natu-rally Viktoria couldn't know, and even if she had, it would not have taken away any of the joy at having Tanya back with her.

Three weeks later Tanya was ordered to report to an internment camp southwest of the city. The family saw her off.

Tanya offered her cousin words of comfort as she stood with her baby boy in her arms. "Vika, Harry'll come back to you and Henry one day, and he will be happy and proud. It all seems so far away and so hopeless now, but the Allies will win, and Harry will come back to China to find you." She leaned toward Viktoria, hugged her, and kissed the top of her head.

Viktoria was despondent in the days that followed, but the need to care for Henry forced her to carry on.

上海

Chapter Fifteen

On December 9, 1942, Harry and the other survivors of the 5th Marine Regiment re-embarked on transports. They were finally leaving Guadalcanal. It had been four months and two days since they had arrived. Too tired and too sick to show any emotion, they felt as if they had been released from a dark cell after a long internment. It would take time to get used to the brightness. For now, they were too spent from the effort of remaining alive to be able to enjoy the relief of leaving.

As they waited to board the Higgins boats the weary men formed columns on the beach, looking like a group of down-and-out bums standing in line at a soup kitchen. Harry stood and watched the men file onto the transports, and he thought of the beginning of the poem by Wilfred Owen that Ferdie had quoted in the cemetery.

Bent double, like old beggars under sacks,
Knock-kneed, coughing like hags, we cursed through sludge,
Till on the haunting flares we turned our backs,
And towards our distant rest began to trudge.

Of the original two hundred men in I Company, eighty-seven were able to depart the island under their own power. For the four days in transit, they slept, waking only to eat. They arrived at Brisbane, Australia, on the afternoon of December 13—the same day Tanya had to report to the internment camp outside Shanghai. They were not allowed to disembark until the following day. Once the men stepped ashore, they were trucked forty miles north of the city to Camp Cable, the new home of the 5th Marine Regiment. Meanwhile, both the 1st and the 7th Marine Regiments were sent to the temperate climes and comforts of Melbourne. The 5th Marines were bitter about being sent out into the boondocks. The mosquitoes flew in clouds around Camp Cable and were so prevalent that the men had to be issued nets. It was worse, everyone said, than on Guadalcanal. The entire area was home to malaria-carrying insects, yet the men weren't supplied with Atabrine, and they hadn't been since leaving combat. They grumbled incessantly and asked the officers why they were given the short end of the stick while the others got to stay in a city?

While at Camp Cable, Harry received a letter from Uncle Walter dated September 12. Aunt Jo had given birth to a baby boy on September 10. They named him Paul. Henry was still undergoing treatment for his leukemia. Harry penned a long letter to Henry, hoping to lift his spirits. In it he wrote as many funny stories as he could. He sent a captured Japanese banner in a package along with some other souvenirs to his ailing cousin. He also wrote to Jolyn and encouraged her to help her mother with the new baby.

Harry received good news in the form of a letter from Frenchy, who was now convalescing in a hospital outside Chicago. He was unsure whether he would be discharged from the service. Harry thought every day about the battle in which Frenchy was wounded. The bloodied image of his friend haunted him from time to time.

Harry and Swede were both informed that they had been promoted to first lieutenant. As the only two active-duty members of the League of Nations—since both Ozzie and Frenchy were *hors de combat*—they had grown especially close. To celebrate their promotion, they decided to attend the officers' Christmas party at the Brisbane Golf Club. On Christmas Day they hitched a ride into Brisbane. They were entranced by the tidy homes and manicured lawns they saw on the way. It was the closest they had felt to being home in a long, long time.

The celebration was held in a massive banquet room, replete with a brass band that played an endless selection of Christmas songs. Senior U.S. Army and Marine Corps officers fraternized with Australian dignitaries. Many of Brisbane's attractive young ladies attended the festivities, most of them on the arm of an American officer. Harry smiled to himself: The higher the officer's rank, the younger and prettier the girl. He and Swede walked over to the bar and ordered drinks. Swede—not having seen a woman since leaving New Zealand five months earlier—immediately went over to speak to a pretty brunette. Harry kept to himself on the fringe of the party and sipped sloe gin on crushed iced. When the band played a slow dance song, Harry thought about Viktoria at another Christmas ball.

On December 24, 1940, Harry was at the Christmas Eve ball at the British Shanghai Club with Viktoria, Tatiana, and Edward. Given the dire war situation in Europe, the gala was not as sumptuous as it had been in years past. The crowd was thinner, and the food was unremarkable. But that did not stop the assembled guests from noisily celebrating. The affair lasted well past midnight.

As they danced, Viktoria rested her head on Harry's shoulder. "Oh, *Lyubov Moy*, why did we have to meet during such an awful time?"

"I'd go through the gates of hell to meet you again."

"Sometimes I think that's where we are now. This city has become such an awful place."

"I'd do it all over again to be with you, Babe. I'd go anywhere, do anything, be anyone you want." Suddenly an idea came to Harry. "Say, why don't we get married?"

"*What*?!" Viktoria pulled away to look at Harry's face.

"I'm serious. Why not tomorrow? Christmas Day. Can you think of a better day than that? Listen, I don't know when I might have to go back. It could happen anytime. Why not be prepared? Let's get married so that when the time comes, all we have to do is pack our bags and leave for America."

"You're making a bold assumption, Harry Dietrichson. I never agreed to leave with you."

"Viktoria, I love you. I don't want to leave without you."

"What about my family?"

"What about them?"

"Harry, you don't understand. This isn't a lark. This isn't a decision we can take so lightly. I know that you Americans easily jump into things." She paused and smiled. "I've paid attention to the movies you take me to."

"Viktoria, you know that one day you and your whole family might need to get out of Shanghai. What better plan than to leave with the man you love?"

"But, leaving my family . . ."

"They'll be fine. Your uncle will see to that."

"But you know how attached to my family I am, Harry. We hope one day to return to Russia. That has always been our plan."

"I know, Love. But things change. People fall in love and marry all the time."

"Yes, but it's just that I haven't had time to digest all this. I mean, I've thought about having you as a husband, but . . ." She leaned forward and kissed him. "Oh, Harry, let's just agree on one thing: We do love each other. I'm not ready yet. But I *do* know that when I marry someone, it will be you."

"Then it's agreed. You'll be my wife."

She smiled demurely. "No promises right now, but perhaps, one day . . ."

"Dutch, are you gonna just stand here and drink, or are you gonna find a nice lady to dance with?" Swede pulled Harry along with him over to the bar where Swede ordered two whiskey sodas.

Harry shook his head. "It's surreal, Swede, don't you think? Each time I tried to imagine what it was like at home, when we were on Guadalcanal, I just couldn't square it. People going on with their lives like nothing's happened."

"Surreal, unreal, whatever. Hell, I don't care, Dutch. Either way, I'm gonna enjoy my Christmas with that lovely lady." He pointed to the petite brunette standing across the room with a group of her friends. "Her name is Emily, by the way. She's fine, isn't she?"

"Yeah, she certainly is."

"Come on, pardner, there's plenty of 'em!" He took the drinks from the bartender and started to leave.

"No, I'm not feeling like it right now, Swede. You go on."

Swede set down the drinks, put his hand on Harry's shoulder, and said softly, "Listen, Dutch, I understand what you're saying. It *does* seem strange. Three weeks ago we were walking around like scarecrows in shredded dungarees, picking at jungle rot, hoping to get a lukewarm cup of coffee, dreaming about a can of corned beef hash." He adjusted his necktie, which the Marines called a field scarf. "Now here we are, dressed in spanking clean uniforms, drinking fine liquor, and supping on roast lamb."

"I'm trying, Swede, I really am, but I just can't quit thinking about Frenchy, Ozzie, Pith, and the other guys."

"I know, but listen. We've been to Hell's Corner and back. I aim to have a lively Christmas. Sorry to spoil your sad party, chum, but I ain't in the mood to reminisce just now."

"No, Swede, I'm the one who's sorry. I didn't mean to be so glum. Go on. Go back to your girl." He good-naturedly pushed him toward the dance floor. Swede walked off with the two whiskeys toward a broadly smiling Emily.

Harry turned and walked out onto the verandah at the back of the hotel. The flowers in the garden gave off a lovely fragrance. He leaned on a railing at the top of a large staircase and looked up at the stars.

The previous week they had set up a big tent at Camp Cable so the men could watch movies. One of the movies was *Now, Voyager,* with Bette Davis. Harry thought of the final line the actress said just before the credits rolled. "Don't let's ask for the moon. We have the stars." Harry smiled thinking how much Viktoria would have loved hearing that.

A few minutes' later three young Australian women walked out onto the verandah and stood a short distance from Harry. They spoke for a bit, smoking cigarettes. One of them gave him a smile when he looked their way. She gestured to the others and they all walked over to him.

"We didn't want to see any of you Yanks feeling left out," said the one who had smiled. "So we've come to rescue you. My name is Miranda. This is Marion and this is Irma." They each offered Harry their hands.

"How do you do? My name's Harry." He shook their hands in turn. "I'm not feeling left out really, but thanks just the same."

Miranda was the leader, and the other two clearly deferred to her. She was probably twenty-one or twenty-two. She had gorgeous thick auburn hair. Harry thought she looked like Ellen Lowry. She even acted a bit like Ellen. Her radiance and confidence overshadowed Marion and Irma. Looking at Miranda, Harry suddenly became conflicted about Ellen and Viktoria.

"But you weren't dancing, and you haven't been talking to anyone."

"Oh, you noticed? Well, it's okay; I'm fine. I've just been thinking about my family, it being Christmas and all."

"Yes, it must be tough on you boys being so far from home. Were you on Guadalcanal?"

"Yes, I was just telling my friend how much I miss it."

They all laughed. Miranda said, "Oh, you Yanks have such a good sense of humor."

Marion asked expectantly, "Are you from California? Or New York?"

"No, I come from Texas."

"Texas!" they all exclaimed in unison.

"You know, some people say Texas most resembles Australia among the States. Is that true?" Miranda asked.

Harry paused a bit, as if reflecting. Then he nodded. "I can definitely say yes." He gestured upward with his hand. "Big sky, wide-open spaces, and most of all, beautiful . . ." he paused a moment, looking at each of them thoughtfully before finishing, "horses."

They all laughed together again. After a few more minutes of conversation, the four of them walked back inside. The band was playing Cole Porter's "Stardust." Couples danced slowly together. Harry wasn't feeling social anymore. Miranda asked him if he wanted to dance.

"I'm sorry, I'm not sure I'd be good company tonight. You see, I . . ."

"You're thinking about your girl back home?"

"Something like that. It's complicated."

"It's okay. I understand. I'm sure she's a lucky girl." She smiled and squeezed his hand.

Harry excused himself. He walked out of the hotel and hailed a ride back to Camp Cable in a jeep. As they drove through the dark night, Harry thought of Henry and what his family in Texas must be going through on this Christmas. He chided himself for selfishly thinking about Ellen and Viktoria and his own loneliness. He was ashamed.

Chapter Sixteen

January 1, 1943

Dearest Harry,

I pray in this New Year you are well and you are happy. As for us, we are well, though not necessarily happy. Tanya was taken off to an internment camp just before Christmas. We had nearly two months of her joyful company. But, as you can guess, her absence has dampened our spirits these past few days. We are all so worried. What will become of her? And will she be reunited with Edward?

We realize it could be so much worse, now that we have seen firsthand what is happening to the British and the Americans here in Shanghai. I'm so relieved you were not caught here along with us. Had you been here, you would have been taken into a camp, and we would still have been separated. So, you see, even though we are apart, at least neither of us is enduring that separation in Japanese captivity. At least we have that to be happy about.

Aunty Masha and Uncle Grisha keep us all fed and help us all feel secure. My uncle has been the foundation of stability for our family, and it is through him that we find strength. Unfortunately, the teahouse has been closed. But he keeps busy trying to maintain his contacts and find other means of doing business. He has also been reelected to the All-Russian Emigrants Committee. General Glebov is still the chairman. He and his wife come to our house occasionally for tea or a meager dinner. Aunty is a different kind of rock. In her wise words and her warm embraces we find love, solace, and comfort. We are all so reliant on both of them. We should feel blessed—though it's not easy to some days—that we are so much more fortunate than most people in this horrible time.

I pass the days by helping with the garden and doing chores around the home. Mundane things such as getting firewood or coal have become a big challenge for us. But we are getting by.

When I do have free time, which isn't often, I find myself thinking about you and all the adventures we shared. I watched an old Chinese lady walk by the front gate yesterday with a small group of ducks. I smiled to myself as I thought about the time your funny houseboy Willy cooked us wild duck. I could almost hear Willy calling wild ducks "flyaway ducks" and domesticated ducks "walkee-walkee ducks." When I saw the woman pass by, I called to them, "Here, walkee-walkee ducks." Remember, Harry, the evening when you tried to get Willy to understand that a group of ducks in flight is called a flock but on the water they are called a raft of ducks? Maybe you should have used Pidgin instead of Texas-accented English! He got so confused he ended up burning our dinner. I laughed to myself as I recalled that evening. For a short while—however briefly—I was able to escape this awful place, so empty without you. It felt good.

I leave you with this cherished memory. I trust and hope and pray we will share many more comic moments again in the near future. You are in my thoughts every day.

All my love,

Viktoria

Viktoria's primary occupation in the winter of 1943 in Shanghai was, of course, keeping Henry fed and healthy, something she didn't mention in her diary. It was an increasingly difficult order for a woman—even a woman relatively well off—to carry out in wartime China. Henry was prone to attacks of croup during the nights, especially in the colder, dryer months of the winter. It was terrifying for Viktoria, watching her one-year-old boy struggle to breathe. All she could do was run steam out of a teakettle under a blanket, huddle with him, and pray that he would recover from the attacks. Otherwise, he was a perfectly healthy boy, and though fussy at times, he was generally well behaved. His quick smile attracted every member of the Savin household, and at times Viktoria had to restrict others from taking him off and walking about with him in the garden, or for a short distance down the street. Viktoria didn't want to draw the attention of the Japanese and Chinese police patrols that wandered the streets of the French Concession like bandits. The sight of a white baby would only summon an unwanted curiosity.

She had made that mistake once.

One day she had decided to take Henry for a stroll along the embankment on the Bund. At one point a group of older Chinese women surrounded Viktoria and the pram, admiring the fair-haired boy. One of the ladies asked Viktoria if she could hold the boy. Viktoria, not understanding Chinese, nodded her head. As the woman reached down to take Henry, Viktoria shouted out and pushed her away, which drew the attention of bystanders. A larger group now gathered around Viktoria and the pram. She tried to correct the misunderstanding by taking Henry in her arms and showing him to the woman. The ladies took no offense, and they continued petting Henry and smiling, chattering away in Chinese.

A Japanese sentry, drawn by the crowd, stopped to look. When he saw Viktoria and Henry, his mouth dropped open. He came forth through the crowd and began asking Viktoria in broken English whether she was British or American. Viktoria explained that she was Russian. He didn't understand, so she showed him her papers. At that point, dozens of people were gawking at the awkward encounter. After some time, the soldier relented and let Viktoria pass. But as she pushed Henry back toward their home, Viktoria noticed a small group of curious Chinese following her. She grew uncomfortable and began moving faster. Eventually the group broke off, and she found herself alone again in the quiet streets of the French Concession.

It was impossible for Viktoria not to think of Harry each time she looked into the face of her son. Sometimes she tried to convince herself that Harry had moved on, that it was hopeless to wish that she would ever see him again, much less share any sort of future with him. It had been almost two years. She even went so far as to try to convince herself that he had been killed in the war (after a particularly vivid nightmare). But the sight of Henry brought Harry immediately back into her thoughts, and she would be convinced all over again that he was alive and that she would see him again one day. Instead, when she thought of Harry, she tried to remember the good things. Like their picnic lunches.

Harry and Viktoria loved to picnic when the weather permitted. One day in the fall of 1939 Harry chose a special place in the old walled Chinese town. Nantao was not the cleanest or safest place in Shanghai, but it was right on the border of the French Concession. Harry had managed to locate a spot with a small garden that was frequented by Chinese families on pleasant days. Besides, it featured a small pagoda, which felt as though he was bringing Reading, Pennsylvania, to the banks of the Whangpoo.

On summer weekends, Sarah would take her grandson Harry on a horse-drawn bus up to the Chinese pagoda for a picnic on the slopes of Mt. Penn overlooking Reading. A wealthy manufacturer had built the pagoda earlier in the century, hoping to turn it into a tourist destination. It was visible from almost anywhere in the town and had become a popular gathering spot. It was Reading's only true landmark. Sarah read aloud to Harry, often from the Bible or *The Pilgrim's Progress*. The boy dreamt of one day discovering the Celestial City. But being too young to entirely understand Bunyan's connotations of Heaven, he hoped to find it somewhere on earth. For Harry, the pagoda became synonymous with the Celestial City. Having seen prints of China, India, and Japan, Harry thought perhaps that region of the world would be the best place to begin his search for the Celestial City. Thus, Asia entered his consciousness at a young age.

That day Viktoria had packed a lunch with black bread, boiled eggs, dry salami, cold chicken, and some carrots from the Savin garden. Harry was able to acquire some peanut butter cookies from the American Club that he liked so much. He also brought along a thermos of coffee. They spread out a blanket to the curious stares of Chinese onlookers, but they were able to sit in peace and enjoy the nice fall weather. They lunched and spoke quietly.

Although Harry had arrived only six months before, they had come to know one another quite well. The spark between them was still in its early, most bright stages, when a blossoming romance retains its blissful excitement. Viktoria adored Harry's unaffected, candid nature. She was used to young Russian or English or French men of means in Shanghai, which meant they had usually been given everything and had never understood struggle or want. Viktoria confessed to herself that she had never really known privation either. But she had lost her parents at a young age and that was an experience that few people in her family's circle had undergone—even among the Russians. She felt she had developed a certain wisdom borne from heartbreak that few other people her age had—especially the groups of young women and men in

Shanghai that her family associated with. Of course, there were legions of poor Russians in Shanghai who knew nothing but want and hardship. Viktoria, however, did not personally know those people. She passed them in the street or saw them performing in clubs or theaters. But she rarely, if ever, spoke with them. Very few of those dispossessed Russians visited St. Nicholas, because seemingly they had given up on God and faith. One thing Viktoria knew for sure was that Harry's wisdom came from struggle and hardship. She knew practically from their first meeting. Once she had detected that, she knew only that she wanted to know him better and not only to learn from his wisdom but to convince him to let her into his life.

Harry had brought along his copy of *The Pilgrim's Progress*. He had discussed Bunyan with Viktoria before, but now for the first time he read to her. He chose excerpts from the Palace Beautiful and the Celestial City. "Now, upon the bank of the river," he began, reciting some of the passages from heart. Viktoria sat and listened. She drank in the sound of his voice and watched his clear eyes flit back and forth down the pages. At that moment, she decided she might be in love with him. But she wasn't sure; she had never been in love before. She did know, however, that she felt full and completely at peace when she was with him. When she saw him after an absence, no matter how short, her heart skipped a beat.

As he finished reading, they sat and finished their coffee. Viktoria asked him, "How did you choose Bunyan?"

"I didn't. He was chosen for me by my grandmother."

"Yes, of course, I remember, but what attracts you to him?" She leafed through the book as she spoke.

"I always aspired to find the Celestial City, I guess. Plus, the Epistles of Paul have always been my favorite writing in the Bible."

"I agree his letters are so beautiful."

"And you know he wrote them while he was in prison?"

"Yes, of course."

"Well, Bunyan wrote *The Pilgrim's Progress* while he was in prison. I find that coincidence fascinating."

"Why was he in prison?"

"He was so inspired to go out and preach the Gospel of Jesus that he did so, even though he wasn't ordained. He was charged for teaching without a proper license from the Anglican Church and sentenced to twelve years in prison."

"That long? For preaching?"

"They'd have released him sooner if he'd agreed to stop. But he wouldn't agree."

"Now, that's a beautiful faith."

"That's funny. I was just thinking that about you."

"Beautiful faith?"

"Well, mainly the beautiful part."

Viktoria smiled and pushed the open book toward Harry. "I think you've been reading too much Bunyan."

Harry looked down. She had opened the book to the section called The Flatterer. He threw his head back and laughed out loud.

Chapter Seventeen

After New Year's Day 1943, the 5th Marines packed up camp and moved to Melbourne. It was no cooler in Melbourne when they arrived in the midsummer of the Southern Hemisphere, but the air was less humid and, more importantly, the men were no longer pestered by clouds of mosquitoes. Melbourne made the Marines feel like they were one step closer to home and to normalcy. "It's like a little slice of America," Swede told Harry. The officers were billeted in hotels and in homes, where they slept on beds. They would be given a long and well-deserved rest.

Three weeks after arriving in Melbourne, however, Harry came down with malaria. As had many other Marines, he contracted it at Camp Cable. At first Harry thought he had caught a cold, but it quickly developed into a high fever. One morning he awoke, stood from his bed, swooned, and then collapsed. He was taken to the hospital. The diagnosis was a severe case of malaria. The periods of alternating fever spikes and bone-rattling chills were agony. The fevers were the worst. Harry was delirious and hardly knew what was going on around him. Nurses brought him cold compresses and administered a combination of water, glucose, and antimalarial drugs intravenously. His ears constantly rang, causing his head to throb and ache. When the first fever broke, after three days, Harry awoke under a pile of blankets. He was grateful for the chills. But when they persisted for several days, he longed again for the heat. And so it went, for more than a week.

In and out of his feverish nightmares, Harry continued to dream about Viktoria. She needed him. Whether she was surrounded by Japanese soldiers or drowning in the Whangpoo, Harry could not escape the image of Viktoria crying out to him. Sometimes he awoke calling out her name.

After the bout passed, Harry had a newfound admiration for the Marines he had known on Guadalcanal who had been struck with malaria. In spite of the debilitating effects of the disease, these men had carried on with their duties. Many walking malaria cases continued to patrol the jungles. Some of them continued to fly planes. Others crated ammunition and lugged it to the howitzers. Having passed through its extremes, Harry couldn't imagine being able to do any of that. The smallest of tasks, like getting dressed, seemed impossible.

By the time Harry left the hospital in March, he had lost all the weight he had gained in Australia. Though he was weak physically, he began to feel better. But he was still prone to bouts of depression. He spent much of his time playing cards and smoking cigarettes. He corresponded regularly with his family, keeping track of Henry's progress in the battle against leukemia. He worried constantly about him. He wrote him letters and sent him souvenirs to try to shore up his spirits. It was almost worse, Harry thought, that he was not in combat, because he often sat around thinking and worrying about his cousin. Harry and Ellen kept up a regular correspondence as well. But each time he wrote to her, he guiltily thought of Viktoria.

As replacements arrived in Australia over the course of the summer to take over for the dead and wounded, the Marine Corps reshuffled the individual units and companies. Harry was reassigned to the 2nd Battalion of the 5th Marines. He was to be the executive officer—the number-two ranked officer—for F Company. The commander of F Company was Captain Dave "Chap" Chappellet from Idaho Falls. Harry knew Chap from Guadalcanal and was happy to hear that he would be with him. The company first sergeant was Bill "Pinky" Dolworth, another westerner from Bakersfield, California.

Chap was a good leader. He had reddish-blond hair and a muscular athletic body. He had played baseball at the University of Colorado and joined the Marine reserves when the war in Europe broke out. He was known to be calm under fire and was respected by the leadership of the 5th Marines. Swede was the new executive officer for E Company. Ferdie Goff was still in B-2 with the 5th Marines, and he was also with the 2nd Battalion.

One day at an inter-regimental baseball game Swede and Harry ran into Ozzie, who was healthy and had recovered from his wounds. He was now assigned to the 1st Marine Regiment. Ozzie had recently received a letter from Frenchy, who was still in and out of hospitals around Chicago. Bull Burns had been awarded a Silver Star and a well-deserved battlefield commission after Guadalcanal, and he was now a second lieutenant in A Company in the 1st Battalion of the 1st Marines, where Ozzie was assigned to be the exec.

Besides a scattering of PFCs, the only familiar faces from Harry's old I Company of the 3rd Battalion were the corpsman Sully, Corporal (now Sergeant) Jefe Vargas, and the company sharpshooter Happy Hargrove (now a corporal). One night, Harry had to bail Happy out of the shore patrol brig for being drunk and disorderly. Harry was shocked to hear that of all the Marines he knew, Happy was the first that needed to be bailed out. On the drive back to quarters he lectured Happy like a stern father: "What would your mother and your sisters think about you?" Happy was the fifth child in his family. He had four older sisters. Harry tried to play on his conscience. Happy brushed it aside, saying that he didn't remember much but that he was sure it was simply a matter of falling in with bad company.

"I promise, sir, it won't happen again."

"Okay, Happy. Stick with Coca-Cola and Clark Bars."

From March 1943 onward the men drilled long and hard during the day and played hard at night in Melbourne. Many of the replacements were cocky and expected an easy war now that Japan was on its heels. But Harry knew once they saw the elephant their attitudes would change. New weapons were introduced, including the M1 Carbine and the M1 Garand. Harry chose the Garand. It was light and accurate, and you could fire eight rounds without the onerous bolt action of the Springfield. Most officers chose the Thompson submachine gun because of the power it afforded them in a jungle environment. But Harry chose the same weapon that was assigned to the lowliest of privates.

While he was in Melbourne, Harry found a used copy of *Lost Horizon*, by James Hilton. He had first read it in Shanghai. As he leafed through the pages, he thought of the conversation he and Edward Muncy had about the utopian novel.

In the fall of 1939 Harry ran into Edward in the Horse and Hounds Bar at the Cathay Hotel. They had recently been introduced to one another by Viktoria and Tanya, and they quickly became friends. Harry often picked Edward's brain about British policy in the Far East. One of Harry's main jobs as correspondent for United Press was to assess British intentions in China. Britain had in excess of a quarter of a billion U.S. dollars invested across China. Harry wanted to know whether the British would accommodate the Japanese or resist their aggression. It was an important question for the United States because American investment in China was not insubstantial and American businesses there had been relying in part on Britain to maintain order. Now with war having just broken out in Europe, Britain's staying power in the Orient was being questioned,

"*Lost Horizon*?" Edward walked up to Harry, who sat alone at a table, nursing a beer. "Hoping to find your own Shangri-La here in Shanghai?"

Harry looked up and smiled. "Nice to see you, Edward. Please, join me."

Edward sat down, reached into his pocket, and fished out a silver cigarette case. "You know, you'll find nothing like Shangri-La in China." He lit a cigarette. "Tibet, maybe."

"Yes, I'm aware of that."

A waiter came to the table, and Edward ordered a whiskey soda. "Lots of Westerners like yourself come into Shanghai with that book under their arm, all wide-eyed and full of wonder, hoping to find a piece of Paradise."

"I suppose I once had that same fascination with the Far East, the hope of finding something different. Only I called it the Celestial City." Harry took a sip of his beer. "But instead, I've found the same things that make all us humans alike: selfishness, greed, callousness, war."

"You're a bit of a pessimist, aren't you?"

"I've reason to be."

"So what do you think of Hilton's masterwork?"

"What strikes me more than the idea of Shangri-La is the defining *philosophy* of the place. The fact that it's not meant to be perfect. You remember how the fellow Chang explains that to Conway early on in the book? 'The people are moderately sober, moderately chaste, and moderately honest.' If a man can live his life in such a way, I figure he's doing okay."

Edward chuckled and shook his head. "Well, my boy, you won't find much moderation in Shanghai."

"No. I understand that." Harry paused and sipped his beer. "You know, it's interesting. The Japanese use that word a lot. 'Moderation.' I heard it all the time when I was living there. They call it '*setsudo*.' Also, you hear the word '*kenson*' a lot. It means modesty. And, for the most part, they practice it in their homes and among themselves. But now, with all this going on around us," he gestured toward the Japanese ships on the river, "they're anything but moderate."

Edward nodded and dropped cigarette ash into the tray. "Yes, this damned war might be the end of us all. Especially for us Westerners in the Far East."

Now Harry could see how spot-on Edward's prediction was. America, Britain, and Australia were losing some of their best young men in the maw of an Asian war.

At the end of October 1943, the 5th Marines again boarded transports. Where they were headed was a big mystery. The scuttlebutt was that it would be either New Guinea or Rabaul. The Japanese base at Rabaul on the island of New Britain was garrisoned by one hundred thousand of the best Japanese army and navy troops. It would be a bloody nut to crack. Meanwhile, General MacArthur's Army troops were fighting alongside the Australians on New Guinea. The transport sailed for a week before arriving at Milne Bay on the southeastern tip of New Guinea. F Company was told they were disembarking, not to fight the Japanese but for more training. The men newly arrived from the States groaned when they heard the news. "But we came to fight the Japs," they complained. The veterans, on the other hand, were relieved to know that combat was being put off a while longer.

The southeastern coast of New Guinea didn't look too different from Guadalcanal, except for fewer coconut groves and more jungle. As much as they tried, the Marine Corps could not easily bring the comforts of home onto the wild shores of New Guinea, where headhunters and cannibals had existed one generation before. But it was nature—not the people—that made New Guinea wild. The daily tropical deluge was disheartening. Any attempts to cook and eat hot food usually failed. The men found themselves once again eating cold food from C-ration cans or K-ration boxes. If they tried to eat out of the mess kit, the food turned into a soupy gruel in the rain. The steak and eggs of Melbourne were now a fond but distant memory.

Harry became depressed again. He shared a tent with Chap and two other junior officers. Most afternoons when the rain came the men gathered in their tents or the mess tent with officers from other companies. They read, played cards, wrote letters home, and smoked; when they got tired of all that, they reminisced—about their girls and their homes— and mused about careers they wanted to pursue when they got back.

One afternoon they got to talking about postwar plans. Chap said that he had no plans beyond kissing his wife and snow skiing in Idaho. Some of the others mentioned sweethearts and jobs too.

Then Chap grew serious. "I know we all left someone behind, but I was ready to serve for a larger calling."

They all nodded, acknowledging what he meant. After a moment of silence Chap continued. "In New River—I'll never forget it—one night we were sitting around like this, playing cards and drinking beer. It was a few weeks after Pearl." He cleared his throat and went on. "Anyway, someone turned up the volume on a radio. It was FDR, and he was making a fireside speech about the war and all the sacrifices we should expect to make."

Swede said, "Yeah, I remember the speech. The one where he asked everyone listening to pull out a globe or a world map and follow along."

"Exactly," Chap nodded. "I'll never forget what he said." He then repeated the president's words almost verbatim: "*There is something larger and more important than the life of any individual, something for which a man will sacrifice—and gladly sacrifice—not only his pleasures, not only his goods, not only his associations with those he loves, but his life itself.*"

Harry said, "I remember that too. It wasn't just idle talk about the war and buying bonds and all that. He was telling families to be ready to sacrifice a son, or a brother, or a husband for the cause."

After a moment of reflection, Chap said, "After I heard FDR's speech, I thought of my family and everything they had done for me. My community, the church that baptized me, the schools that educated me, the people who have been suffering around the world at the hands of the Fascists, and I was ready at that moment to give back to them—I mean give *everything* back. Suddenly my own problems didn't matter as much. If I die doing that, well, then that's what I'll have to do. It'll be worth it."

Everyone remained silent at the mention of death.

Chapter Eighteen

In mid-December 1943, the order came for the 5th Marines to embark again. It was announced at a briefing that the next landing would occur before January 1 on the island of New Britain. When everyone heard the news, a murmur rose in the crowd. The regimental intelligence officer, a major, sensed the disquiet and immediately said, "No, gentlemen, we are not landing at Rabaul." The men laughed nervously, but the sense of relief was palpable to Harry.

The 1st Marine Division, led by the 1st and the 7th Marine regiments, would be landing at Cape Gloucester on New Britain's westernmost coast. Rabaul, which served as the Japanese headquarters of the Southwest Pacific area, sat on the island's northeastern tip. Between them is more than two hundred miles of almost impenetrable jungle and ridges. The goal was to flank the main Japanese forces and draw them from Rabaul. The 5th Marine Regiment would remain afloat as the divisional reserve and would land later at a place and time of the leadership's choosing. That meant they wouldn't be among the first wave.

As the officers of the 5th Marines breakfasted on board the day after Christmas, Ferdie came into the galley and made an announcement. "The 1st and the 7th Marines landed this morning on Cape Gloucester. Initial reports indicate that there was no opposition. They're all safely ashore."

Everyone let out a cheer of relief.

Swede, who was sitting next to Harry, spoke up. "That don't mean a damned thing. Those Japs'll be coming out of the bush soon enough."

Ferdie said, "Yes, but better when we have all our equipment and supplies on the beach than to be met in the surf."

Just then someone said, "Shhh. Pipe down, fellas. We got Tokyo Rose on the radio."

A sultry, exotic voice filled the airwaves. "Hello, all you poor boys of the 1st Marine Division. You're fools to go to New Britain. Everyone knows that Americans can't fight in the jungle. The swamps are going to swallow you up. And when the soldiers of the Imperial Army find you slithering on the jungle floor, they are going to send you to your maker. What a silly way to spend Christmas, so far from home, and so far from your girls. This next song is for you, Marines. I'm sure you'll like it. Bing Crosby sings, 'It's Been a Long, Long Time.' It's been a long time since you've seen your wives and girlfriends. I'm sure they must be lonely. But don't worry, boys, they'll find comfort in the arms of a 4-F man. Sweet dreams. And Merry Christmas." Her voice fell off, and a soft guitar strummed on the air, followed shortly thereafter by the crooning voice of Bing Crosby: "*Kiss me once, then kiss me twice . . .*"

"Bitch," someone said.

"Yeah, but she sure plays good music," Swede said with a sigh.

Three days later, on December 29—a rainy, overcast morning—the 5th Marines disembarked from LCVPs and waded ashore onto the firm black beach at Cape Gloucester. Calling the shore's edge at Cape Gloucester a "beach" was being kind. Ten feet from the edge of the water an almost impenetrable low scrub jungle began. The thicket grew higher and denser as the jungle ascended the ridges and tall mountains further inland. The only places along the shoreline where no trees stood marked the location of mangrove swamps capable of swallowing up trucks and even tanks. The only consolation the men could take—and it was a big one—was that there was no opposition that morning. They were landing on a part of the coastline that had already been secured by the 1st and the 7th Marines. They would take part that morning in an operation to seize a small Japanese-built airfield.

As the company executive officer, Harry had no platoon to command. Instead he spent his time with Chap and Pinky Dolworth, helping to run F Company. Should something happen to Chap, F Company would become Harry's. In the meantime, he was given various tasks such as monitoring communications, leading patrols, and overseeing logistics. This last task would be the most challenging on Cape Gloucester. The incessant rain made the single coastal road almost impassable, and the overgrown tropical vegetation was a quagmire even for foot patrols, and especially for heavy weapons and equipment.

The 5th Marines were to flank the airfield in a southwesterly direction from the coast, through thick jungle and across several ridges. Then they were to move onto the southern edge of the airfield. It took them the entire morning and the early part of the afternoon to ascend the series of ridges rising over the airfield to the south. The going was slow through the wet and muddy jungle. Men would step into a bog and sink to their knees or sometimes to their mid-thighs. Others would have to pull them out, whereupon the man's boot or boots would be pulled off by the suction. The men hadn't been in combat conditions for more than a year, so they were especially careful to stop and check each sound or anomaly. No matter how quiet they tried to be, it's impossible for a group of several thousand men slogging through the jungle to maintain silence, and that unnerved Harry.

During the entire morning they saw no evidence of a Japanese presence. At one point, Chap whispered, "This is just like Guadal on the first day, Dutch, only no coconuts."

"Yeah, the suspense is awful."

Pinky whispered from behind, "Take it from me, brothers, they're out there alright. Probably watching us."

Just after noon, the sweaty and nervous men emerged from a steep climb onto a large open patch on the top of the first ridge between them and the airfield. At just that moment the sun briefly broke through the clouds. The men breathed easier. They halted to lunch on K-rations of canned cheese or beef loaf, crackers, and vanilla caramels. Harry urged the men to conserve their water.

They continued their march down into a ravine and up and down two more ridges. By mid-afternoon they were perched on the final ridge overlooking the southern approach to the airfield. As they came down the backside of the ridge, scouts noticed a series of fortified log-and-mud bunkers. The bunkers were facing north, toward the airfield and the coastline beyond it. F Company approached the bunkers warily from behind. Harry walked among the company, issuing last-minute instructions.

"Remember, fellas, we'll be coming in from the back, so we'll probably catch 'em by surprise. Try not to waste your ammunition. Use your grenades. We should be close enough." Harry paid special attention to the men who were in combat for the first time. "Stay alert and stay calm. You'll be fine," he reassured them.

At precisely 1500, E, F, and G companies leaped out of the thick cover and ran toward the bunkers. Men hurled their grenades. Harry spied a bunker to his left, and he climbed on top with several men. They located two openings—one in front and one in back—and poured fire into them with their weapons. Pinky dropped two grenades in the rear opening. They jumped down, seeking cover. After the explosions, Pinky came forward and kicked in the rear cover. He jumped into the bunker and let loose with a barrage of fire from his BAR. The men waited expectantly for ten seconds. When he reemerged he looked at Harry and said "Nuthin'."

Chap was standing on another bunker nearby. He yelled out to Harry, "Anything, Dutch?"

Harry signaled all clear.

Pinky shouted back, "Sir, it's abandoned. No equipment, no maps, nothing."

Chap called further down the line to his right. It was the same story with each bunker. He walked over to Harry and said, "I'll be damned, Dutch. Where are they?"

"Hell if I know, Chap. It's strange."

By 1600 they had linked up with the 1st Marine Regiment on the airfield, which was in a pitiful state. The installations were in shambles, the runway was cratered, and the wreckage of two seaplanes stood starkly. The Japanese seemed to have abandoned it months ago. As Chap walked along the airfield, he directed F Company to establish a bivouac and a defensive perimeter. He looked at Harry and said, "Got to give it to the flyboys, they really took the hammer to this place."

"Yeah, but you can be sure the Japanese'll try and retake it, just like Henderson."

They spent the night on the airfield. Around midnight a storm broke loose the likes of which Harry had never seen—far worse than anything on Guadalcanal. Lightning, thunder, and stinging rain pounded the men, who huddled without tents. There were no trees from which to sling their new waterproof hammocks. Sitting in his poncho in the downpour at the edge of the airfield, Harry took solace in the thought that he would rather be battling the elements than the guns of the Japanese.

The next morning, after the rain had stopped, the men wrung out their dungarees and their blankets. Just as they sat down to open their C-rations, the clouds promptly opened up and it started raining again. The men cursed. Word was passed from the battalion command post for the companies to send out patrols to establish contact with the 1st Battalion, which had spent the night on the first ridge south of the airfield. Chap sent Harry and Pinky to lead a squad of ten men. Harry didn't bother to bring a corpsman.

They set out at 0700 in the heavy downpour, which limited visibility to no more than fifty yards, even on the flat plain of the airdrome. They instinctively tensed up once they were back in the jungle, where visibility was no more than ten yards. As they ascended the low ridge, Pinky assumed point with an enlisted BAR man, Lance Corporal George Nadiradze from Providence, Rhode Island. Everyone called Nadiradze "Georgie." Happy Hargrove came along as the squad sharpshooter.

At their first halt Harry quietly cautioned them, "Remember, we might run into patrols from the 1st Battalion. Check your fire until you're sure."

"Aye, sir," they all whispered and nodded.

Suddenly the rain stopped. When as they reached a point about fifty yards in front of the empty Japanese bunkers an explosion sounded behind them. They instantly fell to the ground. Harry called out, "Was that a mine?" He looked back. "Is anyone hit?"

Another explosion sounded even closer behind them. Pinky looked at Harry with bulging eyes. "It's mortars, Dutch!"

Just then Georgie opened up with his BAR, shooting toward the bunkers. Harry looked up and noticed muzzle flashes coming from the Japanese gun pits. The bullets popped in the air around their heads, snapping like mini-thunderclaps. Pinky shouted, "They must've gone back into the bunkers last night!"

Harry motioned the men to pull back thirty yards to a position behind a barrier of fallen logs and coral outcroppings. Harry stayed with Georgie to cover the withdrawal. As they did so a squad of Japanese burst out of a bunker and ran down the trail toward them. Harry raised his M1 and fired at the leading soldiers. Georgie fired his BAR from the hip, releasing a torrent of thirty-caliber slugs into the onrushing Japanese. That stopped them momentarily, long enough for Harry to pull out two grenades in quick succession and fling them uphill toward the Japanese.

He and Georgie then fired off a few more rounds and rushed back down the ridge, shouting to Pinky that they were coming in. They jumped down behind the fallen logs, breathing hard.

"You okay, sir?" Pinky asked.

"Yeah, we stopped 'em for a minute, but there's a heap o' Japs up there." In spite of the damp and moisture, Harry's mouth felt full of cotton. "We need to send a runner down to alert battalion that the bunkers have been reoccupied, and that the Japs have mortars and heavy machine guns." He looked down at his shaking hands, gripping the M1, and hoped they were not too obvious to the men.

Pinky motioned to a private to come over, but Harry stopped him. "Wait, Pinky. Let's move back down the ridge a bit. We passed a stream bank about fifty yards back. It's better cover."

Just then another explosion rocked their position. The screams of onrushing Japanese could be heard above the booms of the mortars. Georgie and Pinky fired back up the ridge with their BARs. Happy was next to them, firing his Springfield. Harry motioned for the rest of the squad to move out quickly. As they did, mortars exploded to their right. Harry looked back and saw Pinky crouching over Happy. Harry raced over and saw that Happy was grasping his neck, blood steadily flowing through his fingers.

Harry shouted, "Pinky, grab your BAR and help Georgie cover our retreat. I'll get Happy down the ridge." Harry helped Happy slowly down the trail to the stream bank. The rest of the squad had established a defensive position, with their weapons at the ready.

Harry instructed a private to go back to the battalion command post and get a corpsman and stretcher-bearers. "Tell them we have a badly wounded man."

Pinky and Georgie arrived soon thereafter, plopping down onto their bellies next to Harry, out of breath.

Pinky looked over at Harry, who sat on the ground cradling Happy's head in his lap. Pinky gave him an inquisitive look, as if to ask what Happy's chances were. Harry shrugged and shook his head.

Happy held a yellow handkerchief tightly to his neck. He looked up at Harry and said, "I'm cold, sir."

"You'll be fine, Happy. You did a helluva job holding them off back there. I'll get you a citation for this."

Happy then smiled slightly through gritted teeth. "Better you get me a corpsman instead, sir." His face was white. Blood continued to seep through his fingers. The rain had begun again. He shivered uncontrollably.

"He'll be here soon. You'll be on a ship back to Australia in no time." Harry looked expectantly down the ridge, hoping to see the figure of a corpsman.

"Lieutenant," Happy gurgled with difficulty through the blood in his throat, "please don't let me die." There were tears in his eyes.

"It's okay, Happy. I see the corpsman. It's Sully. He'll patch you up just like that night on Guadal." Harry leaned down and put his face close to Happy's. He wanted to hold him close, to reassure him that all would be well, but Happy was slipping out of consciousness. His eyes went back into his head. Harry shook him slightly. "Happy."

Happy opened his eyes, looked at Harry, and said again, "I'm scared." He gurgled up some blood, and the last word he mumbled was, "They . . ."

He died right there on Harry's lap. Marion "Happy" Hargrove, who had celebrated his nineteenth birthday in Melbourne. Harry had seen men die on Guadalcanal, but he had never held them as they took their last breath. He felt a lump in his throat. He stared down at Happy's face, stroking his left cheek. He looked up to see Pinky standing over them. He stared down at Harry with a vacant look in his eyes, his jaw clamped.

Georgie maintained a vigilant watch up the ridge, but the Japanese seemed to have stayed near the bunkers. All firing had ceased. Five minutes later a corpsman and a stretcher detail arrived. Before they took Happy away, Harry took his billfold, the yellow handkerchief, and one of his dog tags. He would send them with a letter to Happy's family.

Harry thought of Happy's last word, "they," and wondered who "they" were. Were they the Japs? Were they his friends in F Company? Were they his parents? What were his four older sisters doing at that very moment? Were they laughing, playing, sleeping, listening to the radio? Maybe in a movie theater or a diner? Harry could imagine how the youngest child and the only boy must have been the most treasured family member. Had Happy's mother seen a premonition about her baby boy? She and her husband and their daughters would never see Happy again. He died on a ridge in a distant shrouded rain forest, on an island nobody had ever heard of.

Harry looked down the ridge and saw Captain Ray Loomis of G Company moving up. He had come with heavy weapons and two hundred men. Loomis looked at Harry and saw the blood on his dungarees and his hands. "You okay, Dutch?"

"I'm fine, sir, this isn't mine."

"Oh, the kid? Yeah, I saw them take him away. That's tough luck." He slapped Harry on the shoulder. "Now, let's go clear those bunkers and link up with 1st Battalion. We've called in some tanks, but for now, it's just us."

Harry, Pinky, and Georgie guided G Company back up the ridge. It took them two hours, but with tank support at the end, they wiped out the last of the Japanese resistance in the bunkers. By 1500, the 1st Battalion had come off of the ridge and onto the airfield to link up with the 2nd Battalion.

It never stopped raining that day after Happy died.

上海

Chapter Nineteen

Christmas Day, 1943

My Dearest Harry,

I hope and trust that you are well and that you are staying out of danger, wherever you are on this Christmas Day. I think of you daily, although I have little time and energy for keeping this diary.

We are struggling to get along here in Shanghai. Without Tanya and without you there is a huge hole in my life. I keep busy caring for family members, but the emptiness is almost unbearable for me.

Aunty Masha is occasionally able to visit Tanya at the camp, and she takes with her small parcels of food. Tanya seems to be doing fine, but we know it is tough for her to be away from the family and from her beloved Edward.

It is ever more dangerous to walk around the city. Bands of brigands rule the streets. Japanese and Chinese soldiers sometimes round up women walking about and force them into prostitution. This happens mainly to Chinese women, although sometimes Eurasians or even Russian women have been taken. Uncle Grisha insists that we go out only as a group, preferably with one of my male cousins. We try to go together to church at St. Nicholas Cathedral every Sunday. I try to go even more often. I find solace in my conversations with Father Dmitry. He is such a wise man, and he understands suffering. It's my attempt to keep the faith in these awful times. We women cover ourselves with scarves as best we can, but that does not always prevent the local thugs and Japanese soldiers from leering and shouting lewd words at us.

The food situation has worsened. Once local authorities discovered we had a garden, we were forced to give an allotment of food to Japanese offi-

cials. Almost all our chickens and ducks have been taken, leaving us a few puny specimens and some pigeons. Sometimes the boys catch fish and small freshwater crabs from the Whangpoo River, and Aunty barters with fishmongers to procure large carp. Along with vegetables, the garden also provides us with apricots, pears, and kumquats.

Aunty Masha has developed beriberi, and every one of us has suffered from some sickness or other at some point. Each of us is iron- and calcium-deficient, which makes us so lethargic. But at least all the Savins are together and we've avoided the detention centers. We are far luckier than Tanya and the other Westerners in the camps, or the Chinese we see on the streets. They live among the rubbish that is no longer collected, and among corpses that accumulate along the roads. The authorities send trucks weekly to collect them, which means that sometimes a corpse lies on the pavement for a full seven days. Horrible smells fill the air—more so even than before. It is a terrible spectacle and yet another reason why we hardly venture outside.

Uncle Grisha not only has had to give over most of the very little profits he makes, he also is forced to sometimes host Japanese officers, groveling before them like a sycophant. In the autumn the collaboration government of China was given full power over Shanghai. Now he must kowtow to the Chinese too, paying them taxes and hosting their officials, who are even more venal than the Japanese. Sometimes we receive packages from my Uncle Alexei in Japan. His good connections in the Japanese government keep the company from the tentacles of the Chinese—for now. How much longer this will last is anybody's guess. We hear from Boris in Tientsin only occasionally; he is also struggling to maintain a seminormal existence. Nobody can escape this nightmare.

That is why the war must come to an end soon, Harry. We hear from the Japanese that they are winning and that they will soon bring all of China to heel. But there are rumors that the Americans are moving closer to the Philippines and that the British have gone on the offensive in Burma. We have also heard on the Voice of the Motherland that the situation in Europe is going well for the Allies and that Germany is being bombed every day. They say the Germans have suffered major defeats in Russia. We are all cheered by this news, although any hopes Uncle Grisha had of returning to Russia are gone. If only all of this madness would come to an end! It seems like two lifetimes ago that you and I were forced to part. I miss you so much!

I pray that the coming New Year will bring peace and that you will

0

emerge from this horrible catastrophe unharmed. Though you have almost become a distant memory, I still see your face every night in my dreams. And I see it during the waking hours as well. I long to hold you in my arms again and pray that you may one day reappear to hold me in yours.

With all my love,

Your Viktoria

Viktoria glumly took stock of her life at the end of 1943. The Savin family remained together, except for Tanya, who for more than a year had been in a British camp for women and children southwest of the city. Although Viktoria tried putting Harry out of mind, she couldn't escape the random nature of thoughts coming and going. When she felt exceptionally lonely, she would write in her diary. She also penned notes to Tanya in her diary. Meanwhile, another horrible year had passed in Shanghai.

Grigorii Savin was reaching the end of his tether with the Japanese, but he was no fool; he was above all a survivor. So he did what he needed to do. Increasingly, the family relied on the support of Viktoria's uncle in Japan. Alexei and his wife sent what they could. Canned and consumer goods—though hard to procure in Japan—were at least easier to find than in occupied China.

Viktoria and the other ladies of the household tended to the immediately pressing need of getting food. All other duties were secondary, especially given the number of mouths to feed in the household. The boys and servants had a myriad of other chores, such as collecting firewood. That was becoming harder as the number of refugees in Shanghai swelled and the felling of the few remaining trees in the nearby countryside increased.

Shanghai—always a city on the edge—was becoming ever more dangerous, even as it sat under the weight of an occupation authority.

One day, Viktoria and Maria left the compound to go to the river to greet boats that had been out fishing. They took Maria's youngest daughter, Asya, who was thirteen, and her eldest son, Misha, who was now a strapping lad of seventeen. Maria and Viktoria wore scarves over their heads. Asya chose to wear a black beret, and she tucked her short hair inside. They walked down the embankment along the Whangpoo River, past the original border of the French Concession to the old walled Chinese section of town. They were able to find a fishmonger who had several large carp that had been caught that morning. Maria bartered with the man and managed to procure one fish in exchange for some eggs and some of Grigorii's beloved cigars.

After the transaction they walked north along the river and came upon a group of Chinese collaborationist soldiers, who stopped them. Maria showed them her papers. The leader of the group, a short man with a pockmarked face, leeringly looked at Asya. He asked her to remove her beret. When she did, the man stood and gawked at her fair skin and hair. His beady eyes seemed to undress her.

Maria beseeched him in English, "Please, our papers are in order. Let us proceed."

The leader turned and said something to the others in Chinese. He then pointed at Misha. "Me wanchee see papers."

Maria pointed out his papers. "He is my son, and as you can see, our residence permits were issued by the Japanese authorities."

The man shook his head. "No." He pointed to the permit. "This, no good. Must go station."

Maria protested. "But why? Everything is in order."

"No good. He must go this side," the man shook his head and gestured toward Misha.

Two of the soldiers stepped forward and each took hold of one of the lad's arms. He resisted and pushed one of the men away. The other man, bigger than Misha, went behind the boy and restrained his arms. The carp he had been carrying on a string went tumbling onto the pavement.

The leader shouted something in Chinese. Another soldier began searching Misha's pockets. Maria protested and tried to pull the boy to her.

Viktoria stepped forward and spoke to the leader. "Sir, we know the Japanese commandant of police very well. He is a friend of my uncle. He will not want to hear of any trouble. You must release the boy immediately."

The leader turned his attention to Viktoria, whom he now noticed for the first time. He sized her up. "Problem with paper. Someone must go station. You come this side, or her." He pointed at Asya. "Lady come this side, no problem boy. All plopah."

Viktoria understood what they wanted. She and Maria both shouted in unison, "No!" A crowd had now gathered to witness the unfolding spectacle of Russian women arguing with the soldiers on the streets. A Chinese lady said something harshly to the soldiers.

Viktoria boldly said to the leader, "If you want me to go to the station, fine. I will come with you." Maria objected, but Viktoria held her hand up at her aunt. She moved closer and fixed a set of angry eyes on the leader. She said harshly, "But if you want me to come, first we will go to the Japanese station. We will explain to them. We will show them that the papers *are* in order."

The leader looked back at the other soldiers. Then he turned and said something in Chinese. The large soldier released Misha. He turned back to Viktoria. "You want go Japanese side?"

"Yes, we insist. All of us."

"Okay, all plopah." He looked at her and gestured with his head. "You go home."

Relieved, the Savins gathered themselves and made their way hurriedly through the crowd and continued north along the river.

Maria gasped. "Misha, the fish!" The boy ran back and looked, but someone had already taken the carp.

He returned to the women, his head down. "I'm sorry, Mama."

"It's okay, son. We got away with something more important. We can have eggs tonight for supper. I'll cook them with leeks."

As they walked on, Maria turned to Viktoria. "That was good thinking, Vika dearest. You saved us."

Viktoria shook her head and said with disdain, "I'd rather die than submit to them. But most of all, we have to keep the children safe. We should never bring Asya anymore. We can bring the boys, but never the girls."

"You're right." They walked a few more paces, then Maria said, "Oh, the shame!"

"We must get used to demeaning ourselves, Aunt Maria. Things will only get worse. We must use all of our wits to stay alive."

上海

Chapter Twenty

On Cape Gloucester the 5th Marines were engaged in a game of hide-and-seek with the Japanese. They could never quite get to the main body of the two separate Japanese army elements that were present in western New Britain. For now, the biggest enemy was the island itself.

The rain was unceasing. The ground was a sea of mud. Week after week the men had to live, eat, and sleep in wet dungarees and sodden boots. They stopped shaving and brushing their teeth. They couldn't dig latrines in the muck, so the men emptied their bladders and bowels where they were. Jungle rot took its toll, especially on their feet. Some Marines had to be evacuated because they could no longer walk.

Letters from home could be read only once or twice before the paper fell apart and melted away. Writing letters was out of the question since there was no dry paper.

Even when they got hot chow, it turned into a lukewarm mush before they were halfway through eating it. The only reliable comforts were hot coffee and cigarettes, kept dry under their helmets. The climate was utterly depressing.

To add to their discomfort, the island was home to spiders as large as dinner plates, poisonous snakes, and crocodiles. Men were often sucked down into boggy swamps up to their waists. If nobody was there to help them, they could drown. Although Harry knew of no cases of death by drowning, men did go missing. But an even bigger threat to the physical safety of the men came from falling trees. Due to the incessant shelling and the constant rain, giant but fragile trees would sometimes come crashing down on unsuspecting or sleeping Marines. These falling trees became known as "widow makers," and they killed twenty men in the four months the 5th Marines were deployed in the Cape Gloucester area.

One day Harry witnessed the dominance of nature and the elements when a squad he was patrolling with discovered the grimacing head of a Japanese soldier in the mud. The man had been in a foxhole that had caved in on him. He was buried from the neck down, utterly helpless and unable to move anything but his head. The solitary head, alive and moving, scared the life out of the Marine who came upon him first. After he regained his wits, the Marine leveled his M1 to shoot him. Another Marine stepped in and suggested they run a bayonet through his eye socket instead, saying, "Don't waste your ammunition on him." When Harry came upon them, he ordered his men to dig out the soldier.

Harry squatted next to him and quietly spoke to him in Japanese. The soldier told Harry his name was Shigeta, and he had been wounded in the hip and was in great pain. He had been there for more than twenty-four hours and was exhausted and thirsty. Harry let him drink from his canteen and then lit a cigarette for him. Shigeta shook uncontrollably as he took the cigarette and thanked Harry profusely.

Harry explained that he viewed the two of them as human beings first and different nationalities second. They should stick by one another against their common enemy, the jungle. Then he sent Shigeta to the rear with a corpsman and a guard.

As they marched off, one of the young Marines stopped and asked Harry, "Sir, why did you bother? They're just gonna waste food and water on him. Might as well just have left him buried there."

Harry turned to look at the private and said, quietly, "Move out, Marine." He felt it pointless to explain to an enlisted man the possible value of any intelligence they could extract from the prisoner.

On patrol they often came upon abandoned Japanese encampments, but rarely did they find live Japanese soldiers. Those they came across were often stragglers left behind by their comrades. Emaciated from hunger and disease, they slithered across the jungle floor, exactly as Tokyo Rose predicted the Americans would be doing. Harry had grown to pity these men, who—with sunken eyes and bony bodies—looked more reptilian than human. The Japanese were not the jungle supermen they had once been made out to be.

In mid-January 1944, Harry and the rest of the 2nd Battalion were moved southeast from the cape to relieve the 7th Marines, who had recently fought one of the larger battles around Gloucester. F Company was to occupy Hill 660. It was here that Harry confronted another enemy of the Marines on Cape Gloucester: disease. Malaria, dengue fever, and dysentery were rampant, but on New Britain, scrub typhus was a particularly insidious disease. It was fatal if not treated properly. By now the men understood the importance of taking Atabrine, but sometimes they still forgot. The officers—including Harry—were not immune to forgetfulness. In fact, because the officers had more to think and worry about, they were even more prone to neglect to take their medication.

The day F Company set up their bivouac on the slopes of Hill 660, Harry started to feel feverish. The shakes began several days later. He continued to patrol and help run the company, but he felt miserably weak. He suspected that he might have malaria again, but, remembering the men who had endured it on Guadalcanal, he pushed on. He found himself frequently slipping and falling. Chap asked him if he wanted to be evacuated, but Harry refused. He had been through two campaigns with nary a wound, except splinters in his eyes. To be evacuated in front of the men because of malaria would be disgraceful, he felt.

On the last day of January, during a patrol south of Hill 660, F Company came upon a small group of well-armed Japanese. The skirmish was brief. The Marines killed four Japanese and captured one who was badly wounded. Only one Marine was wounded. But during the firefight, Harry had been unable to raise his Garand. He tried to pull out his .45, but as he did so, he pointed it directly into the back of a fellow Marine. Fortunately, the pistol didn't go off, but Chap had seen enough. He ordered some men to take turns helping Harry walk back to Hill 660. By the time they reached the bivouac, Harry was delirious. He was evacuated the next morning.

Harry was carried out by stretcher and placed on an LCVP that transported him to a hospital ship. The delirium continued for several days. He babbled nonsense out loud. Then the fever broke, and the chills commenced. The malaria seemed more severe than the case he had contracted in Australia, but after a week or so he had passed through the worst part.

One day as he lay on his bunk on the ship, a corpsman came into the room and checked on everyone. He stopped and asked Harry how he felt. Then he asked about his girl.

"My girl?"

"Yeah, Victoria." The corpsman smiled. "You shout her name out all the time. That's what the fellows call you. When someone says, 'Victoria needs the sheets changed,' they know exactly which rack to attend to. She must be your girl, right?"

"Yeah," Harry answered dully.

"I also heard you calling out for Henry a time or two, but you never cried out for your mom like most of the other Marines do."

An orderly brought Harry a cup of beef bouillon. When he'd finished drinking it, he handed the cup to the garrulous corpsman. "It also sounded like you were speaking some Nip gibberish at one point. You were saying something like '*shogun*' and '*baka*.' You speak Japanese?"

"No," Harry answered curtly.

"Well, Lieutenant, you've got falciparum malaria. It's the worst type. You probably had it in Australia as well. We aren't sure whether this is a new infection or a recrudescence."

Harry furrowed his brows and looked quizzically at the corpsman.

"The doc says he isn't sure if you caught a new case or if this was a recurrence of the malaria you had in Australia. According to your records they didn't diagnose falciparum malaria in Melbourne, but that doesn't mean you didn't have it. Were you regular with your Atabrine tablets?"

"Sometimes." Harry sat up from his pillow. There were seven other men in bunks around him. All of them except for one were heavily bandaged.

"Well, Lieutenant, you're grounded—or rather ship-boarded—for a while. You lost a lot of weight, and we need to keep getting fluids into you. You'll continue on medication for another week."

"What day is it?"

"February 8."

Harry shook his head and rubbed his face. It was his birthday. He was twenty-seven. He said out loud, "Oh, brother, I gotta get back to my company."

"Well, Lieutenant, unless you've got a good bribe for the doc, you won't be going back anytime soon. Besides, they say it's been pretty quiet out there."

Later that day the doctor came around on calls. He was a stocky, balding man who sported a red moustache. After he examined Harry, he asked, "How does Australia sound, Lieutenant?"

Harry smiled wanly. "Well, I *am* tired of the rain and the wet, Doc, but I'd like to get back to my company."

The doctor smiled sympathetically. "I understand you want to get back to your men. But you must understand this: The type of malaria you had can be fatal. You could use a long rest. The good news is that if you did have falciparum malaria before, by now you'll have developed immunity. You'll be less prone to catching it again. Get rested and get better. I also want you to start walking around topside in the next couple of days. The air will do you good."

"Before you go, Doc, I've got a question for you. When I dream, sometimes I get the sensation that I'm drowning. I wake up and I can't move or breathe. What does that mean?"

"They call that type of dream 'incubus.' People get the sensation that they can't breathe or move, and they feel like someone is lying on top of them. But what it *really* means is that you're a tired Marine. So get some rest, Lieutenant. It'll also be a good time to catch up on your letter writing." He stood to leave. "You can write to Victoria."

"Thank you, sir."

"You're welcome, and Happy Birthday."

Viktoria. Harry could think of nothing else for the next few days. Why hadn't she come with him? He agonized over it. Again, he grew angry. He was vexed by the fact that he might have planted the idea for Edward and Tanya to elope. His mind wandered to a conversation he had had one evening with Edward in late 1940.

Harry and Edward often escorted Viktoria and Tanya to evening galas, dances at nightclubs, or picnics at parks in the International Settlement. One evening at a soirée, while all of Shanghai was gripped by news of the London Blitz, Harry asked Edward about Tanya, and whether he hoped to marry her someday.

"You know, you Americans are different in your attitudes about social status and marriage. Even the French are." He took a puff of his cigarette. "You'd never see them keeping their own countrymen out of the Cercle Sportif because they took up with a Russian or a Eurasian woman. But with us British, it's a whole different story. Social life and careers depend on following the societal norms. You know: 'Keep it in the family, Old Boy.'"

"Sure, Edward, but come on, Tanya's not just *any* woman. She's one of the most cultured, beautiful, and intelligent women I've ever met. She'd walk on fire for you. Tanya's the type of woman you should go to the ends of the earth for."

"I'm madly in love with her, Harry, and I so desperately want to marry her, but my family . . ."

"Don't be a damned fool. Take her. Never let her go."

"What about you and Viktoria?"

"I'm not on such a tight timeline as you are. We're sitting out the war for now. Of course, should we get into the act, I'd have to decide. But if I had to leave tomorrow, I'd take Viktoria with me in a heartbeat. I'd give everything up for her."

At that moment Viktoria and Tanya returned to the table, and soon they all moved onto the dance floor. Harry took Viktoria in his arms and they danced slowly to the Glen Miller tune "At Last." She looked up at him and asked, "What did you two talk about while we were gone, *Dorogoi*?"

"Oh, nothing much. Just how we're the two luckiest fellows on earth."

"Did Edward say he was in love with Tanya?"

Harry looked over at Tanya, who was dancing in Edward's warm embrace. "Look at them. Can't you tell?"

Viktoria looked Harry in the eyes and asked, "Do you think people watching us dance say the same thing?"

Harry shook his head. "I don't care, Love. The opinion of others never meant much to me. But I'll tell you this: I'm in heaven when I hold you close."

"I feel the same way." She put her head back on Harry's shoulder, and they danced on.

Three days later Harry was transferred to a field hospital on Good-enough Island, off the northeastern coast of New Guinea. During his time there Harry wrote a few letters, including one to the family of Happy Hargrove. He relayed all the details about Happy and the fondness the entire company felt for him, and the bravery he had displayed on Guadalcanal and New Britain. Harry told the family that he prayed for them and hoped they would find peace. That, eventually, the pain from Happy's passing would heal to a simple dull ache.

The very day Harry posted the letter at the mail tent, a corporal in the mailroom handed him an envelope. It was a cable from Uncle Walter dated January 10. Harry opened it with shaking hands. Henry had died of leukemia just after the New Year. He was twelve years old.

Harry sought out a quiet corner in the encampment at the edge of the jungle. He sat on the ground, placed his head in his hands, and wept.

Chapter Twenty-One

On March 3, Harry rejoined F Company on Cape Gloucester. He hardly recognized the group of men he had left one month before. They had looked grimy and tired then; they looked apathetic and exhausted now. The combination of the rain, the mud, and the fatigue of chasing after Japanese ghosts left them despondent. Chap hardly showed any emotion when he saw Harry. He simply said, "Good to see you back, Dutch." Harry felt guilty standing in front of him with a smoothly shaven face, a belly full of meat and potatoes, and clean dungarees. But he knew it was a matter of hours before his garb would be as black as the next man's.

By now the fighting on New Britain had become a rout. Japanese troops were on the run. The U.S. Navy had interdicted Japanese supply lines throughout the Pacific theater and was slowing starving its citizens. Emperor Hirohito's once-proud soldiers were scrounging to find taro roots or perhaps to luck onto a jungle rodent. Marines who came upon unarmed Japanese stragglers often simply let them crawl off into the jungle rather than kill them. In the eyes of the Marines, letting them suffer and rot in the jungle was a far better way to exact revenge. "Living is worse than dying out here" was the saying.

On the afternoon of March 5, Harry's battalion boarded several LCM transports and traveled 60 miles from the Iboki Plantation—where they had been based since February—to the Willaumez Peninsula, which juts northward from central New Britain, roughly 120 miles from Cape Gloucester and almost halfway to Rabaul. They landed at a place called the Volupai Plantation. Initially, the opposition was light. But further inland, E Company of the 2nd Battalion—Swede's company—encountered a heavily fortified network of bunkers. During the ensuing firefight to clear the Japanese hideouts, they lost their company commander, Captain "Babe" Babashanian. The enraged Marines of E Company quickly overran the Japanese positions and killed the Japanese to the last man, bayoneting two privates who tried to surrender. If the men had felt any pity for the Japanese earlier in the campaign, by now it was all gone. The memory of dead friends and the misery of life on New Britain had turned the men into berserk killers. This attitude—combined with the inhuman, reptilian form many of the enemy had assumed—made the thought of killing Japanese no more distasteful than smashing an insect.

The next evening F Company set up a bivouac in a grove next to E Company. It was growing dark and the rain was pouring down. Harry walked around checking on the men. He stopped in his tracks when he saw what he thought was a solitary figure standing under a coconut palm at the edge of the bivouac. The shape detached itself like a ghost from the dark background and came forward. Harry relaxed his grip on his .45 when he saw that it was Swede. They exchanged a handshake. His friend was so gaunt Harry hardly recognized him. Swede had grown a full beard that was streaked red and blond. He hunched under his poncho, water pouring off his helmet.

"Feeling better, Dutch?"

"Yeah, I didn't want to miss the fun."

"You heard about Babe?"

"Yeah, I'm sorry." Harry sighed. "It seems like the Japs want to kill only the good ones."

"Babe was a great man. Everyone just gravitated toward him," Swede said. "He didn't just teach me how to lead, he *showed* me how to be a leader. He remembered each Marine's name, where he came from, and what his family did. He once said to me, 'Swede, a good leader takes a little more than his share of the blame and a little less than his share of the credit.'" He continued, in a low voice choked with emotion, "They broke the mold when they made him."

"I understand why they ran those prisoners through." Harry paused, and then he confided, "My cousin Henry died."

"Damn, Dutch! I'm so sorry. I know you felt he was like your kid brother." He looked down and shook his head. "It just ain't fair. Poor kid."

"Seems like everyone I've ever loved goes and dies on me." Harry thought of Viktoria. She was probably dead too. If not, then she would be soon, through association with Harry. He sensed the black cloud lingering above him. Then he felt Swede's hand on his shoulder. With that touch, Harry felt an instant gratifying kinship. Suddenly, in the blink of an eye, he was reconnected. He felt tremendous affection at that moment for his friend.

"Get back to your men, Swede. Try to get a few winks tonight."

"Sure, Dutch, but I've kind of given up on sleeping."

"Yeah, I know. It's like sleeping's too much of an effort." He patted Swede on the back. "Go on, now." As Swede turned away, Harry called out to him, "Hey, Swede. E Company is your company now."

Swede shrugged. "I can never be like Babe." He turned again to walk off.

Harry stood and watched him for a second. Then he called out once more, "Swede, you're a good leader. Keep your head down, and you'll be okay."

Swede stopped, looked at Harry, and nodded.

"I mean it. We'll get through this. No one will speak about us like we just spoke about Babe. I want to meet your kids one day and tell them what a good friend you've been to me." Harry felt his throat tightening.

"You keep your head down too, Dutch." Swede turned and disappeared into the dark evening.

The 5th Marines continued their trek through the mud, chasing the vanishing Japanese. And so it went for another month: rain, jungle, swamps, more rain, and an occasional skirmish with the enemy. The last big battle took place on April 9, 1944, when the Marines wiped out the remaining 500 Japanese troops on the headland. Over the course of four months, they had killed more than 5,000 Japanese and had lost 310 of their own dead, including Babe Babashanian and Happy Hargrove. In Harry's mind, Henry was also a casualty on Cape Gloucester.

As Harry walked to the battalion command post the morning after the fighting stopped, someone said to him, "Happy Easter, Dutch. He is risen!" At that moment, Harry was transported back to Shanghai.

On Easter Sunday, April 9, 1939 Harry visited the Savin home for the first time. Shanghai was still new and fresh to him, his having arrived just the month before. His invitation to the Easter luncheon was an unexpected surprise. He received a note from Viktoria the day after their first meeting at the Savin teahouse. The Savin house and its grounds were in the western section of the French Concession, where all the large residences were located. The house was built in the English country style. High walls and a wrought iron gate surrounded the property, which covered about an acre. A bevy of Chinese servants greeted cars at the head of the circular driveway and pointed the guests toward the entranceway, which was flanked by two large Russian men dressed in traditional white shirts that were untucked and buttoned across the bottom. The men wore Cossack wool hats, and although they were not armed, they looked menacing.

Guests waited inside the front hallway in a receiving line, which wound into the hunting room, where Grigorii and Maria Savin greeted each guest. The hunting room was decorated with stuffed partridges, pheasant, and game hens, and mounted along the walls were the heads of boar, deer, rams, and other game that Savin had shot in China, Korea, and Mongolia. Maria wore her black hair pinned up in a fashion like the daughters of the Tsar that Harry had seen in photographs. The two greeted their Russian guests with the saying "*Khristos voskres*" as well as three kisses on alternate cheeks. To others they said the same greeting in English, "He is risen," and gave each a handshake. Once the guests moved beyond the hosts, the servant Natasha handed each person a red Easter egg, dyed in the traditional Russian way with beets and onionskins.

Viktoria had been monitoring the arrivals, and when she saw Harry, she approached him just as he was preparing to meet her uncle. She stayed back a few moments and watched as Harry extended his hand to the bear of a man at the head of the line.

Savin smiled as he recognized Harry and shook his hand. "Ah, yes, Mr. Dietrichson. My traveling companion from Yokohama. I'm glad you could make it. I look forward to speaking with you this afternoon."

After Savin released him, Harry greeted Maria Savina.

"Mr. Dietrichson, welcome! My husband told me that you were acquainted on the boat. We are so happy to have you."

"Thank you, Madame Savina. I'm honored."

Just then Viktoria stepped forward. She smiled and handed him an egg. "He is risen."

"He is risen, indeed," Harry replied and kissed her on alternate cheeks.

"Welcome to our home."

"Thank you. I must say I was pleasantly surprised to receive your invitation."

Viktoria smiled. "It's my pleasure. I wanted you to see another part of Russian culture."

There were well over two hundred guests at the celebration, many of them Russian, but there were also American, British, and French, as well as other scattered nationalities. A typical Shanghai hodgepodge of peoples. In the dining room the table was heaped with roast beef, boiled ham, roasted chicken, poached whitefish, smoked herring, pickled vegetables, and salads made from beets, potatoes, and cabbage, as well as various other dishes.

Viktoria asked Harry to follow her to the sunroom, which let out onto a covered verandah. He didn't know what to do with the egg, so he carried it in his left hand. There on the verandah she introduced Harry to a tall, stunning Russian woman. Although she had dark hair and dark eyes, the resemblance to Viktoria was remarkable. "This is my cousin and my best friend, Tatiana Grigorievna. Her father and my father were brothers."

Tatiana smiled. "I am pleased to make your acquaintance," she said in flawless English. "He is risen." She leaned forward and kissed Harry three times, alternating cheeks. "You may call me Tanya."

"Actually, we met last month at the quay when your father was returning from Japan. I was on the boat with him."

"Ah, yes. I remember now. You're the one who rescued my scarf too, correct?"

"Yes, that's right."

"Well, thank you. Viktoria Sergeyevna tells me that you are from Texas."

"Most recently, but I guess now you could just say that I'm an American."

"No, being from Texas is so much more interesting for us to hear." She leaned toward him and asked, "Do you have oil wells and horses on your ranch?"

Harry furrowed his brows and assumed a serious demeanor. "No, but there are plenty of snakes and scorpions."

Tanya smiled. "You must feel safer here, then."

"In your house, yes. In Shanghai, not necessarily."

"Yes, the Japanese are making us all uncomfortable."

Eager to change the subject, Harry said, "I must say, the family resemblance between you two is strong."

"We have grown up and have seen the world through the same eyes. You see, we have a loving family, and yet we have no real home."

"This seems like a nice home to me."

"Yes, but we have no homeland, no government, and no allegiances apart from Tsar and family." When she said "Tsar and family," she crossed herself. "We have a nice existence, but all of this can be distressing while the world around you crumbles and you can only watch helplessly."

Harry nodded, and let her go on.

"You, for example, have Texas and family—I presume—to go back to eventually. Our dear British friends, even though they may soon be returning to a country at war, have their country manors and villages to return to. The Savins have . . . Shanghai? And how long does Shanghai have?"

"Well," Harry paused momentarily, "admittedly you paint a dire picture. But there is room for optimism, I should hope."

"Oh, I'm sorry. I'm probably boring you or scaring you. Either way, please forgive me. I know Viktoria would prefer to monopolize the conversation with you. Please, enjoy our hospitality. We shall chat again soon, I hope."

With that Tanya moved on to engage in conversation with an elderly Russian couple.

Viktoria took his arm. "The times we live in . . . I'll introduce you to more family members. But first, let's get something to eat, shall we?"

Harry realized he still had the egg in his left hand. He placed it in his jacket pocket.

"Have you had much Russian food before?"

"Not a lot, but what I have had I really liked, especially the pastries we had at your teahouse."

She laughed. "Well, this will be much more substantial. Traditionally we eat an Easter cake known as *kulich*. You should try some after you have had dinner."

Harry and Viktoria took their plates out into the garden to a quiet table under a tree. They slipped easily into a long conversation. They never spoke of the war, or really even of Shanghai. Mainly they talked about family and life and, of course, music. Viktoria seemed at ease in Harry's presence. Although he acted as casually as he could, he couldn't help escaping the feeling that his fondness for her was far too obvious. But he sensed the feeling was mutual, and they spoke with a candid frankness. It was clear that a mutual affection bound them together.

Viktoria offered to show Harry around the gardens. Harry noticed Viktoria's aunt glancing sideways at them from afar as she spoke to a guest. It made him self-conscious, but he also realized that the aunt sensed her niece's affection for Harry. He took her curiosity as a good sign.

Viktoria explained that the garden was her aunt's pride and joy. The blossoms were out in profusion, and they included a wide variety of indigenous and nonnative plants. Harry noticed some trees that looked like dogwoods, and there were magnolias already giving off their fragrance, two full months before they would bloom in Houston. "My aunt spends hours out here. You see the vegetable garden in the back there? She won't admit it, but she is fondest of that patch. All Russians think of themselves as gardeners. She grows much of the food that we eat: potatoes, leeks, beets, turnips, carrots."

Sparrows flew from the branches of the fruit trees, chirping among themselves. Several electric-blue butterflies fluttered in front of them, landing on flowering bushes nearby.

"It's magnificent," Harry said. One can really feel at peace just being in a garden like this."

"It's true, isn't it? I love to read out here."

"There was a great American naturalist named John Muir. He once wrote, 'In every walk with nature one receives far more than he seeks.'"

"Claude Monet once said, 'When my eyes were opened, and I really understood nature, I learned to love at the same time.'" Viktoria blushed once she had repeated the quote.

Harry smiled at her. To defuse her embarrassment, he quickly added, "This is a garden that Monet would want to paint."

"Have you been to his home in Giverny?"

"No, I've never been to Europe."

"I hear that it is heaven on earth during the springtime in his gardens."

"Well, I must say, your family has a beautiful house. It doesn't take second place to many homes; nor does your garden." He paused and then said with a sly smile, "Although the hunting room can be a little intimidating."

Viktoria laughed. "Yes, my uncle has certain passions. Anyway, I hope you can come another time, perhaps for supper one evening."

"Swell," was all Harry could think to say.

They went back to the house and mingled with other guests for a while. Soon Viktoria was called away by her aunt.

"Don't leave without saying good-bye," she said.

"I wouldn't think of it."

Later as he prepared to leave the party, he located Viktoria. As they spoke, she took his hand and squeezed it. "I hope you enjoyed yourself."

"Immensely. And I look forward to seeing you soon. I would like to be able to call on you here, if that's okay."

"Of course, you may call on me anytime."

"Then, good-bye. Happy Easter." He gave her three alternating kisses on the cheek and turned for the door.

Harry decided to walk back toward the river. The spring day seemed softer and milder than any other day since he had arrived. He was ecstatic. Although the world around him may have been crumbling, he could not have been happier. The air seemed fresher, the birds chirped more loudly, and the city looked clean for once. Harry hummed some sappy lyrics to himself as he walked.

When he reached the Bund, he fished in his jacket pocket and found the red boiled egg. He had meant to leave it on a table at the Savin's home, but now as he looked around him and was suddenly reminded of Shanghai's squalor, he was glad he kept it. He handed the egg to a child beggar.

上海

Chapter Twenty-Two

The 5th Marines were hoping to return to Australia, but instead they were sent to a newly established rear area camp on the small island of Pavuvu, fifty miles northwest of Guadalcanal. The island had once been a copra plantation. But now the trees were falling down, and the place reeked of rotting vegetation. Instead of sharing the island with fanatical Japanese troops, the Marines shared the island with rats and land crabs. The men complained at first about their new accommodations, but they knew Pavuvu was preferable to Rabaul.

For the next few months the 5th Marines recuperated from their ordeal on Cape Gloucester. When Harry thought of Gloucester, he envisioned the Slough of Despond—the "swamp of despair"—described in *The Pilgrim's Progress.* "This miry Slough is such a place as cannot be mended; it is the descent whither the scum and filth that attends conviction for sin doth continually run . . . there ariseth in [the sinner's] soul many fears, and doubts, and discouraging apprehensions, which all of them get together, and settle in this place; and this is the reason of the badness of this ground."

Many of the men had reached a breaking point on Gloucester. Physically and mentally, every man was exhausted. On Pavuvu, jungle sores dried out, malaria was tamped down, and the psyche of the men—so long exposed to rain, mud, fear, and Japanese troops—regained a balance that, though certainly far from normal, was at least better than it had been under combat conditions. They were served hot meals and canned fruit regularly. For the first few weeks on Pavuvu the men slept, read, watched an occasional movie, and wrote letters home. Harry wrote his first letter to Uncle Walter, Aunt Jo, and Jolyn since he had found out about Henry's death. He knew they were all relieved to hear he was unhurt; the long the periods of silence no doubt weighed heavily on them. He didn't know how to address their unbearable loss in his letter beyond a mere acknowledgment of it. He worried mostly about Aunt Jo.

Harry received a letter from Frenchy, who had been medically relieved of combat duties and was now in Virginia, helping to train officers for combat. Harry wanted to write to Jingu-sensei. He felt guilty about all the dead Japanese soldiers he had seen and how they had been left in the open to rot. He thought about their families, how they would never be buried properly. He also thought about the men he had personally killed. He might have asked Jingu to offer a prayer for them, but he just couldn't bring himself to write the letter, which would have been more of a confessional than anything.

One day he looked in his wallet and found that the photo of the kids and Popeye had disintegrated beyond repair, a victim of the rain of Cape Gloucester, as was the photo of Ellen. Viktoria's photo, which had been kept between them, however, was still intact. He dried it out. Since he knew it probably wouldn't last through one more campaign, he decided to send the photo to Jolyn and ask her to keep it for him.

On Pavuvu, Harry, Swede, Ferdie, and Chap spent hours lolling around their tents in bull sessions. Ozzie was also on Pavuvu, with the 1st Regiment. He would come around when he could to engage in the banter. They had all become Harry's family now; they were the brothers he never had. Harry was still the executive officer for F Company, 2nd Battalion, under Chap. Ferdie was promoted to captain and was the B-2 executive officer on the battalion staff. Other companies of 2nd Battalion picked up replacements during their stay on Pavuvu. One Marine, Captain Tim Staley from St. Paul, Minnesota, had been transferred from the 1st Marine Regiment to the 5th. He would be in command of E Company. Swede would be his exec. Tim had lost the top part of his left thumb to a grenade fragment on Tarawa. Everyone called him Stubby, and he quickly endeared himself to Harry and the others because of his affability, his bawdy sense of humor, and his skill at poker.

One day as they assembled over a card game, the men talked about where they would be sent next. Ferdie assured them that Rabaul would be bypassed because islands that had already been captured, like Guam and Saipan, were much farther north of Rabaul and closer to Japan. "Just expect the unexpected. It's probably going to be some place we've never even heard of, like Guadalcanal or Cape Gloucester. And it'll be rugged."

"I'm hoping for Melbourne again," Ozzie said.

"Either way, we're gonna end up in Japan," Swede explained resignedly.

Stubby, without taking his eyes off his cards, joined in the conversation. "I just hope they get it over with quickly in Europe so that we can get more replacements out here."

Ferdie said, "I hear it could be over there by Christmas."

"Yeah, well, that's what they told my pop when they sent him over to France in the fall of '17," Stubby said. "He came back instead in the summer of '18 with a lung full of mustard gas."

"Gee, thanks for the encouraging words, Stubby," Ozzie said.

"It's all good." Stubby winked as he laid down his hand. "Full house. Dames and deuces."

"Stubby, if I didn't like you so much, I'd accuse you of cheating," Swede said as he threw down his hand in disgust.

Ozzie put his cards down face up and said, "So much for my three eights."

Ferdie quipped, "And so much for our understanding of war strategy." He took a drink from his flask and handed it around.

Harry put down his losing hand and took a drink. He handed the flask to Ozzie. Ozzie swished the liquid around in his mouth, swallowed, and then said, gesturing to Ferdie, "This guy still manages to get Old Grandad even on Pavuvu. Ferdie, tell us, do you have compromising photos of the general or something?"

"No. It's just that he knows quality when he sees it, and he rewards it." Ferdie took the flask from Ozzie and screwed the top back on. Stubby never drank, which was probably why he was so good at cards.

In a nearby tent a major on battalion staff had a portable Victrola. He always played it loud enough for the neighboring tents to hear. The men had been listening off and on to the records during their card game. It was a hot afternoon and hardly anybody on the island was stirring. Just then the major put on the Harry James tune "By the Sleepy Lagoon."

As the men listened to the slow flute riff in the beginning, Ferdie said, "Lucky we found our own sleepy lagoon right here on Pavuvu. No Japs."

"Yeah," Stubby added, "and Harry James found his own with Betty Grable."

"That guy's a heel, after what he did to Louise Tobin," Harry interjected.

Swede almost leapt off the trunk he was sitting on. "What? Are you nuts, Dutch? Comparing Louise Tobin to Betty Grable?"

"Sure, as a musician; she has a lot better voice than Betty Grable. Plus, she's cute. But mainly I just can't get over the fact that he abandoned her and two kids to run off with a starlet."

Stubby put his hands up for emphasis. "Yeah, Dutch, but not just any starlet, you understand? He left her for *Betty Grable*."

Harry just shook his head. "Still, the man has no class and no morals."

Ferdie pulled out a cigarette and said, "Dutch is a romantic. He's not like the rest of us. Besides, Louise Tobin ain't so bad looking. And you got to feel for her."

They listened quietly for a few minutes. Then the next song came on. It was the Glen Miller Band's "I Know Why, and So Do You."

They started talking about the merits of Paula Kelly, who sang the lyrics so beautifully. After the song finished, Stubby said, "A guy can go nuts listening to all these gorgeous dames singing these songs. Wish the major would put on Gene Autry or Tex Williams. Of all places to be right now, we're stuck on Pavuvu. Not even any hula girls around."

Ferdie smiled and said, "Stubby's been reading *Forever Amber*."

Swede added, "Yeah, Stubby, is this the third or fourth time you've read it?"

"Second, and it's okay if a country bumpkin like you, Swede, can't recognize fine literature."

Ferdie laughed out loud. "Fine literature? More like a masturbation manual."

"Hey, he who casts stones lives in a glass house, you know . . . Who among us isn't guilty on this scrub-shit island?" Stubby said as he shook his finger at Ferdie. The next song up was Billie Holiday, singing "Embraceable You." Stubby slapped his leg. "Not again!?"

Ozzie smiled, winked at the others, and said, "So, Stubby, you got the hots for Billie Holiday?"

They all laughed out loud.

Stubby frowned and said, "No, but the song makes me think about Frances Langford."

Swede shook his head. "Stubby, you're hopeless. Deal the cards already."

"Hey, Dutch, what's eating you? Cat got your tongue?" Ozzie asked.

During all this banter, Harry was a thousand miles away in his thoughts. He found himself imagining all the people he was close to back home at that very moment. What might they be doing? Were they awaking to the aroma of a good cup of coffee and a fresh newspaper? Were they at work or at school? Were they listening to the radio? As he thought about Ellen, Viktoria's face flashed in his mind. He was shaken from his thoughts by Stubby's gruff voice.

"Dutch, are you in or out?"

Harry looked at his cards; he held a single ten. He threw them down and said, "Deal me out, Stubby. I'm going for a walk on the beach." Stubby shook his head and grumbled. The others chuckled, knowing that Stubby was put out only because he would have less money to win.

Harry took his chips and stood up from the table. He sensed dark thoughts coming over him, and he didn't care to share them with the others. They ignored Harry as he walked out of the tent. As he headed down the sandy pathway toward the beach, Harry heard Stubby call the others, and when they laid down their cards, he had won yet again.

Harry never mentioned his depression to Viktoria, but she sensed it after they had been seeing one another for several months. "I know what losing your parents at a young age is like. I was lucky I had a loving family to take me in," she said.

Harry nodded. "My aunt and uncle were good to me. But when they took me in . . . I don't know." He shook his head and paused for a moment. "I missed my grandmother more than I missed my mother. So, when she sent me away to live with my uncle after my mom died, I just couldn't understand it."

"She understood it was best for you to be with a family, with children and parents."

"After I was sent to my uncle's house, I used to go off by myself for hours at a time. I'd find a sheltered spot in the woods and read or daydream. I craved the cool, green hills of Pennsylvania and the warm fire in my grandmother's house. My aunt and uncle hardly ever knew I was gone, they were so busy with their own kids."

"I'm sure they love you. Some people just can't express their love openly."

"They tried to be inclusive—especially Aunt Jo." Harry shook his head again. "But, by that time, I guess I had already built a wall around myself. I preferred to maintain my distance emotionally. I was tired of losing people who were close to me. So I built this protection mechanism—as a safeguard. I got really reckless too, at the same time."

"What did you do?"

"Oh, you know, stupid things. Taking cars on dangerous joyrides. One time when I was fifteen, I decided I was going to swim to Mexico. I just swam out from the shore at Galveston and swam and swam until I couldn't see the beach anymore. I got caught in an undertow and was dragged miles out to sea. I was picked up by a shrimper after two hours. I could hardly stay afloat anymore; I nearly drowned." He shook his head. "Another time I jumped off a high bridge into a river. I hit the bottom of the river and broke my leg and my nose. Then, I went off to college in the east, but I got even more depressed. Sometimes I thought about killing myself. My uncle put me in a hospital for a few weeks. It wasn't a real hospital, if you know what I mean. It was for loonies. You know, for psychological cases? That's when I decided to join the Navy. They offered to pay for college. So I went to Austin to study at the univeristy. I couldn't wait to put my childhood behind me."

"Harry, I'm sorry. I had no idea."

"How could you know? Anyway, it's good for me to talk about it; at least that's what the doctors told me. I've never opened up to anyone about this. But I'm not afraid to tell you." He stopped and looked at her. "I'm sorry. This must be difficult to hear."

"No, Harry. I want you to tell me everything. I care for you very much."

"You see, Viktoria, that's what scares me most. When I start to feel close to somebody, I get scared they'll be taken away. The only two people in the world that I felt completely free and uninhibited around—my mother and my grandmother—left me. I've never really been close to anyone since then."

She took his hand. "Harry, no matter what you think, or however your uncle feels, you two have a special bond. It's in your blood; you are family. When you have nowhere else to turn, you can always count on your family. We had to learn this after we left Russia. I felt the same anger that you did, when I lost my mother. But I knew that I had a place here with my uncle's family. You can find that too."

Harry shrugged. "I don't know. But I didn't want to stick around long enough to find out. As soon as I finished college, I went as far away as I could."

"I have never been away from my home or family. Sometimes I wonder whether it is a blessing or a curse."

Harry smiled. "Well, I suppose Shanghai is such a cosmopolitan city that you don't need to travel to find the exotic. You can have English high tea, attend a French soirée, see a Russian ballet, and experience Japanese kabuki all on the banks of a scenic Chinese river."

She laughed and put her hand on his cheek. "You have no idea how much I treasure our time together."

He took her hand and kissed it. "You make me feel like I'm a part of something, Viktoria."

That evening they made love for the first time. It was as if they had been together all their lives. There was no awkwardness, no guilt. Only simple pleasure and pure love.

At chow that evening on Pavuvu the men were told that Bob Hope would be flying in the following day for a ninety-minute show with a USO troupe. That he would come to such a godforsaken place as this island made the men feel that much closer to home. Harry overheard one young Marine in his company ask another, "You think he's coming here just for us?"

His counterpart answered sarcastically, "No, he's on his way to France, I hear. This was the most direct route."

"Gosh, I didn't know we were so close to Europe," said the young Marine earnestly.

The show that Hope and the other entertainers put on the next day was the best Harry had ever seen. The jokes seemed funnier and less corny. But the true highlight was the dance routine of Patty Thomas, who was outfitted in a dazzling one-piece leotard and fishnet stockings. The men were awed by her beauty and her grace. As they watched her wiggle and shake, Stubby grumbled, "God Almighty, I'm gonna go crazy, sure as hell."

Bob Hope wrapped up the show with his trademark song "Thanks for the Memory." When he finished singing, the men were quiet for a moment, caught up in their own memories of loved ones. Bob, Patty, and the others were then given a rousing send-off as they flew off in Piper Cubs to return to the naval base on nearby Banika Island.

Walking back to their tent, Chap said to Harry, "The only way that could have been any better was if Shirley Ross had been there to sing with him at the end. My wife loves that song. I'm going to go write her now to tell her about the show."

Before they left Pavuvu for the next landing the men were given several days of downtime to get their affairs in order and write letters home, since they would be unable to send mail from the transports. For the newly enlisted men, the biggest shock was being presented with a $10,000 life insurance policy, which they were asked to sign and send home to wives, parents, or next of kin. The weight of their pending journey seemed to press down that much heavier upon them.

The embarkation date was September 4, 1944. Only a select few of the officers had been told that their destination was a small atoll called Peleliu in the Palau group of islands, roughly five hundred miles southeast of the Philippines.

上海

Chapter Twenty-Three

September 4, 1944

My Dearest Love,

It's funny that I'm writing to you to describe my happiness that Shanghai has been bombed. We are fine. The city suffers, as ever. But the joy I feel is in knowing that <u>American</u> aeroplanes are doing the bombing. If American aeroplanes can fly to Shanghai, the American Army and Navy must be near. This also means that perhaps you are close.

Life is still a struggle in Shanghai, but as you know, the entire world is in shambles. I constantly think of you and pray that you are safe in whatever endeavor you are undertaking for your country—and for the world. The Americans are the great hope for everybody in China. Nobody wonders about the British or the French, or even the Chinese. Everyone asks: "When will the Americans be here?" We are hearing that your armed forces are near the Philippines. Perhaps after that, you will be in Formosa, then maybe China, and Shanghai…

We have also heard that the Allies have landed in France, taken Paris, and that the Nazis are near defeat in Europe. Hopefully once that happens the Allies can concentrate on the Japanese. My uncle is torn about the news from the Eastern Front. He wishes for Stalin to be pushed out of power. But at the same time, he wishes nothing but the best for the Russian people, and he agonizes when he hears how greatly they have suffered under the Nazis. The rest of us all quietly rejoice at the news that the Red Army has driven the Germans back into Poland.

Since the Japanese are more and more distracted by the war with America and now by the bombing raids, the Nationalists have been sending resistance fighters into Shanghai and they have attacked many Japanese installations.

As a result, the Japanese and their Chinese collaborators are on edge and have become angry and desperate. My uncle worries that they will confiscate every last thing we have and then evict us from our home. Fortunately, we have been able to stay here unmolested, but we do not know how much longer this will last. So many other Russian families have suffered under the Japanese, and their desperation is difficult for us to witness. We help out what people we can, but in the end, as my uncle always says, we have only one another. We must look out for the family first.

When we can, we listen to records, mostly classical music. When I get the chance, I sneak on a jazz record. I still have the record by Billie Holiday that you gave me. Her voice is so beautiful. It takes me away. I listen often to the song "Easy Living." When I hear Ben Webster on the saxophone, I think of you. So you see? I was paying attention to what you were saying all that time we listened to jazz records together. Otherwise at the house, we have little other to distract us but books, so we have been reading constantly since the war broke out. I try to read detective books. My uncle has a collection of Sherlock Holmes mysteries in English, so I'm able to continue thinking in English and using the language, even though you are not here. In fact, I have been giving my cousins English lessons, since they have been deprived of someone to teach them proper English. It helps me to pass the time and helps me to keep up with the language.

We continue to subsist on our meager diet—mostly vegetarian—from our garden, supplemented by cracked wheat supplied by the Red Cross. However, last week some Chinese friends were able to get us two ducks, and we had quite a feast! They were flyaway ducks! The meat was so rich that we all had upset stomachs for a few days afterwards—but it was worth it. We hardly ever see sugar, and whatever sweet craving we get we have to satisfy with fruit from the trees in our garden. Oh, how we crave cakes and pies! Coffee is a distant memory, but we do have plenty of tea, as you can imagine.

My Aunt Maria saw Tanya recently at the camp. She said that the poor girl is skin and bones. And she is also, of course, rather sad and depressed. But the British women in the camp have taken her in as one of their own, and they look after her. They are all suffering in those camps, and Maria takes parcels of food and medicine to help them when there is something extra available. We miss her so very much.

I'm starting to become hopeful that this horrible time is coming to an end. I pray for your deliverance and dream of the day when we may be

reunited. Until then, I can only dream about you and your kind face.
A strong, loving embrace to you, my dear.
All of my love, V

Several weeks prior to Viktoria's penning the note to Harry in her diary, the Savin household had been awakened by the sound of droning motors followed by explosions. All of the windows were open because of the hot weather that night. The explosions grew louder but never loud enough to drown out the noise of the engines of what were obviously large planes above the city. The family ran together to the garden house, a small concrete structure where the gardening tools and wheelbarrows were stored. It was as solid a structure as they were likely to find with no windows. The adults were terrified, but the younger members of the family were highly amused by the nighttime evacuation. Fortunately, the bombs never fell anywhere near the house. When the noise of the explosions abated, the family emerged and saw thick smoke and flames on the northern horizon. A formation of large planes was flying off to the southwest. They were gigantic four-engine bombers, and the reflected glare of the burning fires glowed red along the silver underwings of the aircraft.

Watching the planes fly off, Grigorii Savin remarked, "My God, it must be the Americans. How can they have flown bombers all the way here?" He turned to his wife and said, "They must be quite close now."

Viktoria's heart skipped a beat when she heard her uncle mention the word "Americans."

Maria asked her husband, as they walked back into the house, "What news are you hearing, dearest?"

Savin looked around furtively and said, "I heard that the Americans have taken Saipan. It was a major naval base for the Japanese, only two thousand kilometers from Tokyo. It is now no longer a question of *if* but *when*. I've also heard that the Americans have airbases in Chengtu and Kunming. Maybe these bombers came from there. Or someplace closer."

"Chengtu? That's near Chungking." Maria observed.

Viktoria lay awake in bed the rest of the night, wondering whether the war might actually soon come to an end. For her the progress of the war had provided an emotional context for her relationship with Harry. The better the war news, the closer he was. The next day they listened intently to the radio broadcast on *Voice of the Motherland*. The announcer said that Allied forces were closing in on Paris, and that British Commonwealth troops had liberated Florence. Meanwhile, the Red Army was slicing through Poland and the Baltic republics. No mention, however, was made of the Pacific campaign or of the previous night's bombing raid. Over the next two nights, the planes reappeared and bombed Japanese facilities around Hongkew. By the end of the summer American planes had made several more appearances in the skies over Shanghai, which brought great optimism as the summer of 1944 came to a close.

Viktoria could now start to think of the future and a world in which her son might grow up in peace. Henry was growing into a fine, handsome boy. He began speaking, and the words—all Russian—came out in a torrent. He was precocious, and he spoke endlessly with each member of the family, even though most of the time they couldn't fully understand him. By his third year, Viktoria began speaking to him in English. He still suffered from croup, but not nearly as badly or as often as when he was an infant.

The Savins hung on with grim determination, praying for a rapid end to the war. They suffered from various ailments, because of the lack of vitamins and a meager diet. The Russians were still given freedom to move about Shanghai and to live their lives as best they could, but that did little to alleviate the suffering. Most of them were destitute. Every day newly deceased people lay in the streets and alleyways of Shanghai; increasingly they wore the exotic clothes of Russians. The Japanese used the Russians when they could, whether for political purposes or more nefarious activities, but when they no longer served a useful purpose, they were cast aside. Grigorii Savin strived to maintain his usefulness and to continue supporting his family. It was becoming increasingly difficult each day. But the family continued to hope. The appearance of American bombers had bolstered that hope.

After Viktoria finished writing to Harry, she put down her pen and sighed. She looked over at Henry, who was peacefully napping, and tried to envision the meeting of father and son. She smiled for a moment to herself. It could be soon, she thought. She closed her eyes and remembered the first time Harry came on his own as a dinner guest to the Savin house, shortly after the Easter celebration.

War and religion were the themes that night at the Savin house in the late spring of 1939. Before dinner Grigorii Savin and Harry had a quiet conversation alone in the study, which Harry later recounted to Viktoria.

Harry surveyed the large study and noticed the vast collection of books and volumes in Russian, English, French, German, and even some in Japanese and Chinese. Several Japanese wood-block prints hung along the walls, along with Chinese scroll hangings. Icons also dotted each wall, and they were prevalent throughout the house. Old maps of Asia and Russia hung in frames, and in the corner of the study stood a large globe on a movable wooden stand. The main spaces on the wall were reserved, however, for portraits of individual family members. The eclectic study spoke volumes as to the complex nature of the man who sat behind the desk.

"My wife tells me we have several things in common," Savin started off.

Before he let Savin go on about Japan or China or the war in Europe—or their mutual interest in world politics—Harry started in himself. "Well, yes, sir. Having seen the hunting room, I can tell you that we both have a passion for shooting."

Savin, expressing surprise, raised his eyebrows and smiled, "Is this so?"

"Yes, sir. I have nothing like your trophies, but I've done some hunting myself in Texas. We hunt duck, quail, and dove. We also go for mule deer and javelina—that's the Spanish word for wild boar. I would love to hear the stories, one day, about the mounts and skins you have around the house."

Savin explained how he had picked up the passion for hunting once he moved to the Far East before the First World War. As he spoke, he warmed to the topic. He and Harry discussed rifles, shotguns, bird hunting, and preferred terrains before Savin showed him out to the sitting room, where the rest of the family was gathered.

Harry greeted Viktoria's aunt Maria, who thanked him for the flowers he had brought. A servant approached, carrying a tray of aperitif glasses filled with Dubonnet. Another servant arrived with a tray of beluga caviar. Harry had tried caviar once and didn't like it. But he took the caviar on toast when offered, generously topping it with chopped onions and eggs. He polished it off with a swallow of Dubonnet.

"Tell us, Mr. Dietrichson," Maria began, "how are you finding life in Shanghai?"

"It has been a great professional opportunity for me. Every American correspondent dreams of being assigned to China or to Europe. History is unfolding before our eyes. As for Shanghai itself, the city's a fascinating contrast. Opulence surrounded by misery."

He hoped he had not offended anyone with the last comment. The guests all looked at him expectantly. He took a sip of the Dubonnet and continued. "Anyway, I'm glad to be here, and it beats being in Tokyo. I've had the good fortune to meet some wonderful people here." He made an effort to not look at Viktoria.

"And how long do you plan on staying in Shanghai?" Maria asked.

"Well," he started in, before she interrupted him.

"With all the British and French citizens leaving, does your family want you to stay?"

"My family is concerned for me, but I reassure them that I'm keeping myself safe. They understand the opportunity that's been afforded me."

Grigorii Savin spoke up. "You are right, Mr. Dietrichson, an opportunity like this doesn't come along often for a man your age. But I trust you are not—how should I say?—whistling in the dark about the situation in Shanghai."

"I understand how dangerous life can be here." Harry found it ironic that the Savins seemed to feel so at ease in the city. Of all the various peoples in Shanghai, the Russians, it would seem, would have the most to fear. Yet they were asking an American whether he felt safe.

"How do you feel about the situation between America and Japan? Will it get worse?" asked Maria.

"With war imminent in Europe, I don't see how our government can allow relations with Japan to deteriorate."

Savin added, "As long as Chiang maintains his position at Chungking, he will bleed the Japanese, and America won't need to lift a finger. Just like we Russians did with Napoleon. But come," he clapped and rubbed his hands together, "let us not spend the entire evening discussing politics." He picked up a bell and rang it, indicating to the servants that it was time for supper.

They moved to the dining room. Viktoria sat to Harry's left. After they had all been seated, the Savins crossed themselves in the Orthodox fashion. The supper was a multicourse affair, which started with cold potato and leek soup. The main courses were roasted goose and poached salmon. The food was excellent. A different French wine accompanied each course. The conversation flowed, and although the family members occasionally whispered Russian or French among themselves, they spoke primarily in English for Harry's benefit. Harry and Viktoria engaged in small talk, but whenever she looked up and saw family members watching the two of them, she stopped and looked down. At one point the question of religion came up. Maria asked Harry about his beliefs. He answered merely that he had been baptized and confirmed as a Lutheran. When pressed to go on, he hesitated.

"Well, I've read the Bible and believe that Jesus existed, and was a great man," he said. "As to his divinity, I've still not formed an opinion on the matter. And as to an afterlife, I believe that souls exist to the extent that we think back on the ones we love. But existence in paradise—I'm not so sure." Harry thought how disappointed his grandmother would be to hear him speak like this.

"What *do* you believe in then, Mr. Dietrichson?" Maria queried.

"I believe in family," Harry responded at once, though, frankly, he was unconvinced by his own answer. So, he added, "And in oneself."

"Bravo, young man." Savin slapped his hand once on the table. "This is the only thing we can rely on. Without a family, there is nothing—besides, of course, God." He looked at his wife. "You can count on a good friend, but once his family becomes involved, all bets are off. Naturally, a family holds precedence over everything else."

Maria looked at Harry. "It sounds, Mr. Dietrichson, like your family has loved you and supported you."

"I have been luckier than most." He went on to tell them the story of his youth, and how his grandmother had had such a formative influence on him.

"Aha!" Maria interjected. "I *knew* a woman had to have influenced you for you to be so sensible and much wiser than your years."

Viktoria squeezed his hand under the table.

Maria continued, less assuredly. "Family will be all we have if the Japanese do come and take Shanghai. They seem so patient—just watching and waiting."

"The Chinese will prove even more patient," Savin opined. "The Japanese may take Shanghai, but it will be only a matter of time before they will be run out again by the Chinese. You'll see."

At the moment Viktoria was writing to him, Harry was on board a transport steaming to the island of Peleliu. Although she was praying for him, she couldn't imagine the cauldron Harry was about to be cast into.

Chapter Twenty-Four

Ferdie was right. Nobody had ever heard of Peleliu, a small coral atoll that was part of the Palau Islands. The colonel conducting the intelligence briefing explained that once the Marines captured the airfield on Peleliu, MacArthur's flank would be protected for the upcoming Philippine invasion. He told the men bluntly that the operation would be "very rough but very short." He quickly added, "it'll probably be over in three days." Swede, who sat next to Harry, grumbled in a low voice, "So we're taking this for MacArthur's sake?" The island itself was only seven square miles. They were told that the Japanese had built a series of strong fortifications, including bunkers and numerous reinforced pillboxes. The colonel assured them that the Navy and the Air Corps would unleash one of the greatest sea-to-shore and aerial preinvasion bombardments in history, in his own words, "rivaling D-Day on Normandy." They weren't even going to issue Atabrine to the men because their stay would be too short.

The word in everyone's mind as they filed out of the briefing room was "Tarawa." The previous year the Marines of the 2nd Division had been told that tiny Tarawa Atoll in the Gilbert Islands would be taken in a mere two to three days, and that it *might* be rough. In fact, as Stubby pointed out, taking the Japanese stronghold cost more than three thousand Marine casualties in three days. Thus far the 1st Marine Division had been fortunate. The Japanese hadn't expected them to land on either Guadalcanal or Gloucester. But the Japanese had been expecting the Marines on Guam and Saipan, and consequently the casualties had been heavier. Now they would be expecting the Marines on Peleliu.

The day after the briefing, Harry stood at the railing of the transport by himself. He was empty of feeling. The night before, he had had a premonition of his own death. Once again, he realized he didn't even care whether he survived the war. He just wanted it to be over.

A private from the company came up to him. "Sir, may I have a word with you?"

Harry turned around. "Of course." Harry recognized the face of this newly enlisted Marine, but he couldn't recall his name. A thought flashed through his mind: *Babe Babashanian would have remembered it.* The young man had acne on both cheeks. He looked no more than sixteen years old. "What's on your mind, Marine?"

"Sir, they say it should be short but pretty rugged." He paused uncomfortably then looked earnestly at Harry. "Well, sir, what do *you* think?"

"Duck soup," Harry said nonchalantly. "It won't be that bad, Private. Keep your head down, listen to your platoon sergeant, and you'll do fine." He dismissed the lad with a kindly pat on the back.

As the private started to walk away, however, Harry called him back. He remembered now the youth's name and that he had joined up in Times Square the day he graduated from high school, only five months previous. Normally he spent his summers on Nantucket Island. Instead, here he was in the South Pacific, about to visit a much less picturesque island.

"Listen, Benjie, I know that's what we've been told time and again by everyone. And, honest to God, I hope it's short and *not* rough. But just remember: Whatever happens, don't try to be a hero. You've got nothing to prove. We have a great material advantage over the Japanese. Trust in your officers, especially the noncoms. They've seen a lot of action, so if you're given an order, follow it explicitly. You're gonna see some horrible things but try to put them out of mind as quickly as you can and get on with your work. When the action is hottest and loudest, try to find an inner calm."

"Thanks for shooting straight with me, Lieutenant."

"We owe you boys that much."

The landing was set for September 15, 1944. The transports arrived and positioned themselves off the southwestern coast of Peleliu at dusk the evening before. The preinvasion bombardment had been going on for three days. The enlisted men stood on the deck and watched in awe as orange fireballs streaked toward the island in arcs, like giant flaming arrows being shot over miles of ocean. The island was illuminated in an orange glow, juxtaposed against the dark eastern sky. To their rear, the setting sun was also creating a burnt-orange panorama. It was like watching two simultaneous sunsets.

On the morning of the landing, Ferdie came by at 0400 to wake Harry and the other officers of E and F companies, who racked together in a cramped gray room lined with two-tiered bunks to accommodate twelve men. They could hear Navy dive-bombers zooming past overhead. The planes were the last to have a crack at the island defenses.

"We got a good draw on this one, gents." Ferdie explained that the 1st and the 3rd battalions would be landing at 0800. But Harry, Swede, Chap, Stubby, and the men of the 2nd Battalion would be landing in the second wave two hours later. Their objective was to capture the airfield that abutted the beaches on the southwest coast of the long, thin island, which ran southwest to northeast.

"Well, that's good news," Chap said as he rubbed his eyes with the butts of his palms.

Stubby stretched and yawned out loud. He shook his head briskly and snorted like a horse. He started to say something, but Swede stopped him.

"Alright, Stubby, we don't want to hear any of your dire prognostications." He looked at Ferdie and asked, "Did I say that right?"

Ferdie nodded and said, "Yes, Swede, you said it *correctly*."

"Okay, professor, thanks for teaching me to say it the *correct* way."

Harry said, "Sounds like our friends in the Navy are drawing their pay."

Stubby laughed and then said sarcastically, "Duck soup, eh, Dutch?"

"Stubby's just sore because he lost last night at cards," Swede said.

Chap stood up and said, "Okay, fellas, get your dungarees on. Time for chow."

The ship's speakers blared the Andrews Sisters' "Rum and Coca-Cola" as the men walked toward the officers' mess. Stubby playfully swayed to the music. Harry and Chap split off from the group to visit F Company.

Chap walked among the men and spoke quietly but confidently. "Fellows, some of you have done this before. For those that haven't, trust your training and trust your noncoms. Keep your heads down and do your jobs. The sooner we get this done, the sooner we can all go home. No John Waynes out there. Understood?"

"Aye, Skipper," they said in unison.

Harry came upon the youth he had encountered on deck several days before. "Get some of that hot chow in you, Benjie. It could be the last you'll get for a few days."

"I'm too nervous to eat, sir."

"We're all nervous. Hell, I remember my first night patrols on Guadalcanal. I'd jump at every damned sound. One time I got a nasty ant bite on the back of the neck. I 'bout leapt out of my trousers; I thought a Jap had stuck his bayonet in me." He chuckled and gave Benjie a pat on the shoulder. "Just keep close to your squad sergeant and follow orders."

On this morning Harry's nerves weren't gnawing at him as much as they had before prior landings. He felt more relaxed than ever before going in, almost indifferent. *At least my depression serves some useful purpose,* he mused to himself.

After a breakfast of hamburger steak and powdered eggs, the men of the 2nd Battalion waited nervously for their appointed hour. Finally, the claxon sounded. The men went below to the belly of the transport to be loaded onto the LVTs, the amphibious tractors—or amtracs—that held twenty-one men each. They cinched the straps of their packs. In their haversacks each man carried a poncho, a blanket roll, a mess kit, a small first aid kit, a change of socks, a dungaree cap, three boxes of K-rations, and a waterproof bag that contained his personal items. Those included a toothbrush, a razor, a wallet, a Bible, or anything else he wanted to carry. Each man also wore a helmet and toted "782 gear"—a web belt with straps that held an assortment of equipment, such as an entrenching tool, a gas mask, a Ka-Bar knife, two canteens filled with water, and two grenades.

Lastly, they shouldered their rifles. Those with a Thompson or a BAR carried 240 rounds of 30.06 ammunition in cartridges placed inside magazine pouches, which numbered three to each side of their cartridge belt. This was double the amount of ammunition carried by men like Harry, who had a Garand rifle, or those who preferred a Carbine. Like every officer, Harry carried a .45 sidearm.

The officers began receiving ominous reports of heavy resistance on the beach. A good number of LVTs had been knocked out in the first wave, and the Japanese were pulverizing the beaches with artillery and mortar fire. Harry and Chap moved among the men, dispensing

last-minute encouragement and instructions. They told the men the
same thing they had been hearing all morning from their squad sergeants
and platoon lieutenants. "Move quickly off the beach." Or, "Conserve
your water. It'll be hot out there."

Harry saw Swede in the assembly area and walked over to him. They
looked at one another and shook hands without a word. After a short
silence, Swede said, "May the Lord be with you, brother."

"And with you."

Swede took a big breath, "Dutch, my old man ain't sentimental, but
he'd be mighty pleased if you stopped by the ranch in Texas to see him."

"I look forward to seeing you there as well, Swede. We'll get home
leave after this. Come on down to Houston, and I'll come up to Stamford."

"I'll get you the best damned steak you ever ate. Helluva lot better
than the one you got this morning."

"And when you come down, we'll go to Galveston and do some fishing. We'll eat lots of fried shrimp."

The lump in Swede's throat was working up and down. "I think
about Babe all the time."

"Think about yourself today, Swede. Stay low and keep Stubby out
of trouble. Don't think about anything else. I'll see you and the others at
the battalion command post." They shook hands again, and Harry went
back to join the other men in his group.

Harry was on the same amtrac as Chap, Pinky, Sully, a second corpsman, the communications unit, and various individuals who were carved
off battalion or regiment. One of them was a Navy chaplain. Harry smiled
at him. The chaplains were there for comfort, but for many Marines, the
chaplains were anything but comforting. They were a reminder of each
man's mortality. Harry didn't feel this way, and so he sat next to him.
They introduced themselves. The chaplain was a pleasant Catholic priest
from New Orleans named Father Byron. Harry had heard Father Byron
earlier, walking among the troops and speaking Psalm 23 aloud. "Yea,
though I walk through the valley of the shadow of death, I will fear
no evil: for thou art with me; thy rod and thy staff they comfort me.
Thou preparest a table before me in the presence of mine enemies: thou
anointest my head with oil; my cup runneth over."

Harry told Father Byron that this upcoming day would be such as
The Trial of Faithful, alluding to a chapter from *The Pilgrim's Progress*.

Without missing a beat, Father Byron quoted Bunyan, "About the midst of the valley, I perceived the mouth of hell to be, and it stood also hard by the way-side."

"And ever and anon the flame and smoke would come out in such abundance, with sparks and hideous noises," Harry answered with some surprise.

"Lieutenant Dietrichson, I think maybe you chose the wrong profession."

"No, Father. I'm too much the cynic."

Just then the roar of the motors and the clanking of the huge steel doors opening up the belly of the LVT drowned out all attempts at conversation. Harry sat back and closed his eyes as the intensely bright morning sun shot into the hold of the ship. The amtrac began to shake as it rolled forward slowly and bounced onto the blue water of the Philippine Sea.

Their amtrac circled for half an hour, waiting for the other amtracs of the 2nd Battalion. The glare from the sky was intense, but the sun was shielded behind a haze of smoke and fog. Once the signal was given, the coxswain gunned the engine and vibrations shook their helmets. Each man seemed to draw into himself as they moved closer to the shore.

Halfway to the island the LVT rocked suddenly and violently. Thinking they had been hit, the men looked around in alarm. They had merely bumped onto the coral reef two hundred yards from shore. The coxswain calmly took the amtrac over the reef. Soon they were bobbing in the calmer lagoon waters. At the approach, they passed several disabled LVTs from the first wave that were dead in the water. Machine-gun fire was popping off of the front steel plate, and the men instinctively hunched down lower. Harry snuck a peak over the side and could see black bodies bobbing in the surf behind an LVT that was still on fire.

Finally, after what seemed an eternity, they bumped onto the shore. There was a momentary pause as the men waited for the ramp to go clanking down. The newer amtracs were designed with backward-facing ramps, so the men sat with their backs to the beach, waiting to exit and disperse from either side of the rear. Harry's heart was thumping and his mouth was dry. *It never gets easier*, he thought.

The ramp banged down, and Harry saw the white sand below the turquoise water. He was near the front of the LVT, which meant he would be one of the last to disembark. Pinky was the first to go pounding down the ramp. He turned to the right and disappeared. Next Chap bounded down the ramp and turned to the left. Harry saw geysers erupting in the surf as other LVTs approached. He grabbed Father Byron's arm and the two of them ran down the short ramp and plunged into knee-deep water. No sooner had they cleared the LVT than Harry heard the coxswain gun the engines and pull the craft back out into the surf.

They sprinted up onto land and fell on their bellies in a prone position. The beach was a veritable hailstorm. Bullets snapped the air and kicked up the fine sand; explosions ripped the palm trees. Harry yelled to some Marines lying on the sand, "Off the beach!" He motioned forward. They looked at him wide-eyed. Several of them then sprinted forward; others remained motionless, too terrified to move. One man crawled off the beach and back into the surf. Harry nudged Father Byron and indicated it was time to move on. The two of them rushed up toward the edge of the scrub jungle. The din of the fire all around was deafening. They found a small depression in the thick scrub where two other Marines were ducking.

"Are you two from 2nd Battalion?" Harry asked.

"No, sir," one of them said, with a terrified look. "A Company, 1st Battalion."

"You mean you've been here for two hours?"

"Sir, we haven't been able to move forward."

Harry looked back over the water at the departing LVTs. Then he peeked over the edge of the hole, searching for Chap. He spotted a radioman thirty yards to his right, toward the southern promontory of the island. He turned to Father Byron. "Father, thank you for being here and giving us all comfort and support." He extended his hand which Father Byron shook warmly.

Harry prepared to jump out, but then a mortar landed between the two positions and he fell back down into the hole. Harry smiled and said, "Had I not shaken your hand, I'd've been hit. Thank you." He jumped back up and ran toward the Marine with the field telephone. He dropped into the hole next to the radioman, panting. As he expected, Chap and Pinky were there. Chap was on the phone.

He put the receiver down and looked at Harry. "I can't get through to battalion, but we'll have to move forward through here. This jungle continues about three hundred yards, then gives way to the airfield."

It had to be more than 100 degrees. Mortars continued to *whoosh* down and each explosion seemed to be followed by a cry for a corpsman. Every so often a larger whistling sound would come in from the right and cause a great crash that shook the ground and caved in the foxholes. The Japanese had placed a seventy-five-millimeter howitzer on the promontory to the south. Harry watched several Marine dive-bombers swoop in and drop ordnance on the area. He looked over the edge of the hole and noticed flashes in the scrub jungle one hundred yards ahead to the right, southeast of their position.

While Chap tried the field telephone again, Harry moved next to Pinky. He shouted into his ear, even though his face was only six inches away. "Pinky, there's a Nambu nest about a hundred yards southeast of here." They crawled up and peered over the lip of their hole. Harry pointed again. "You see it there on the right? Two o'clock?" Machine gun emplacements were the key to any defense. They protected the mortars and artillery, and they kept the enemy pinned down. Knock them out, and the Marines could move forward to eliminate the larger threats.

They crouched back down into the hole. Chap put the phone down and looked at them. He shrugged and held up his right palm as if to ask them, *What do you see?*

Harry shouted, "Skipper, there's a machine-gun nest about a hundred yards to the southeast."

Just then another dive-bomber swooped down and dropped a round with napalm on the promontory to the south. A huge explosion followed. The bomb had ignited the ammunition, and with it the seventy-five-millimeter gun.

"Hallelujah," Pinky said in a flat voice.

A stringer from the communications team jumped down into the hole out of nowhere, startling everyone. He pulled his spool of wire into the bottom of the foxhole. He was a thin fellow who looked like he was forty years old, though he was probably no older than twenty-five. He was very cool under the circumstances.

"Captain," he panted and spoke to Chap. "I managed to bring a wire from Major Gant at battalion CP." The man took the phone set and finalized the connection. "The first connection was blown to smithereens." He then looked around at the others in the hole. "It's hell out there, Sirs. I was on Tulagi and New Georgia, but I ain't ever seen anything like this." He leaned back, and closed his eyes, trying to get his breath back. He then sat up and pulled out a salt tablet. He popped it into his mouth and took a long swig of water. Then he darted out of the hole, pulling the spool.

"Dutch, I'm gonna send you out to establish contact with the platoon leaders. Tell them to rally and start moving toward the airfield. Then report back here." Chap removed his helmet as he spoke and wiped his brow. "Pinky, you go with him. You may have to split up. The platoons should be dispersed down the beach." A large round exploded on the edge of the hole, collapsing a wall of sand over the men. When they had brushed themselves off, they looked down to see a smoking shard of metal in the bottom of the foxhole. It was slightly larger than a silver dollar and flat like a pancake.

"Chap, should we try to take out the Nambu first? We won't get very far until he's eliminated."

"Dutch, I won't order you *not* to do it. But we *need* to establish contact with the platoons. So do that first. Those lieutenants are all green."

"Aye, Skipper."

Chap tried the phone again. After a few moments he was connected with the battalion command post. Harry took a drink from his canteen and offered it to Pinky. They both watched as Sully scrambled out of the hole following a cry of "Corpsman!" from the left.

"God bless those boys," Pinky said as he handed the canteen back to Harry.

By now the sun had burned through the haze, and it bore relentlessly down upon them. Scarcely thirty minutes had passed, but it felt like they had been on that beach for six hours. Harry leaned toward Pinky and said, "We're going to be advancing right in the line of fire of that goddamned machine-gun nest. Let's skirt along the edge of the water."

Just then Chap took the receiver from his ear and shouted, "Move out, you two!"

They waited until there was a slight lull in the mortars and then ran back toward the beach, heading south, toward the promontory. Along the way, Harry did a double take as they ran by a group of black Marines. They were all carrying firearms, some of them angrily shooting toward the Japanese nests. Normally, black Marines served as ammunition bearers. But the losses on Peleliu that first morning forced the leadership to insert them into the lines. Harry noticed that they appeared to be acquitting themselves well.

After about a hundred yards, Harry and Pinky came across a large shell crater, where several corpsmen had established an aid station. There were twenty or so men there. Some were bandaged and sitting; some were lying on stretchers. Harry saw a pool of blood near one of the stretchers. He noticed the sharp contrast between the deep red of the blood and the bright white sand. Two of the men sat on the bottom, helmets off and heads in their hands. Three corpsmen and a doctor were moving from patient to patient. As he ran by, Harry caught a glimpse of Father Byron, hunched over a man on a stretcher with a bandage on his face.

He and Pinky moved on from hole to hole. In each foxhole they found wounded or frightened Marines. Harry gave each man whatever words of encouragement he could summon. "Did you see that flyboy take out the seventy-five?" Or, "Look at that: waves and waves of amtracs. The Japs'll never hold out." Sometimes he was blunter: "Marine, grab your weapon and get in the war."

Soon they located Lieutenant Sidney "Sid" Morant, who led the first platoon. First platoon had advanced a good way into the jungle, but two machine-gun nests were holding them up. As Morant spoke, Harry saw that he was in control and showed little fear. He was born in England but had immigrated to California as a teenager during the Depression to work as a ranch hand. He was a good officer.

"We just can't get past these Nambu nests," he explained to them.

"Those guns are protecting the Jap mortar squads that are knocking us around," Harry said. "Sid, I want you to locate the other platoons. Witten and Hancock should be deployed in that direction." He motioned to the south. "When you reach them, rally the platoons and drive them forward to the edge of the airfield to the east. Pinky and I are going to try to eliminate the Nambus and clear a path."

"Just the two of you? Don't you want to take a squad?"

"No, that would just attract attention. If two of us go, we're more likely to get around them unnoticed."

"Aye, sir. But careful with those Nambus. They shoot well."

Harry smiled, "Hell, I'm just the exec, Sid. I'm expendable."

Pinky growled, "Speak for yourself, Dutch."

Harry and Pinky sprinted out of the hole and moved into the jungle, angling slightly to the north. They stopped and crouched in a small hole behind a shattered palm tree. Harry took a drink from his second canteen, which was now almost empty. "If there's another nest, it should be about right there." He pointed to an area to the left, where shattered palm trees formed a natural hideaway. He pulled one of the grenades from his belt, yanked out the pin, and threw it in that direction. The explosion got no response. They moved to the area of shattered trees, where they found a large crater that contained an eviscerated Japanese corpse and a machine-gun belt.

Pinky reached down and picked up a stick of metal. It was part of a tripod. "Hurrah for the flyboys."

After they had run another thirty yards, an incoming mortar caused them to fall to the jungle floor. Harry jumped toward the base of a shattered palm tree and fell right onto a helmet. He moved to the side, and he saw that he was six inches from one half of a severed head. The brown eye was looking directly at Harry. It was a Japanese soldier. He crawled backward several feet and vomited.

Pinky came and crouched beside him. "Dutch, you okay?"

Harry nodded and wiped his mouth. "Let's go."

Move, move, move, was all Harry could think. *Keep moving.* The firing of the other Nambu continued unceasingly. A shot rang out from farther in the jungle. They ducked behind a natural barrier of coral that stood bare and obtrusive in the jungle.

Pinky looked out and saw a puff of smoke as a rifle discharged. "It's a sniper. He's in a tree."

Harry motioned for Pinky to follow him. They crawled through the scrub, damning the coral sand that was rubbing their skin raw under their dungarees. Harry stopped and retched again. He finished his canteen. From behind them the *whoosh* of an American mortar sounded, and a projectile came crashing through the foliage, hitting several trees, including the one where the sniper had been. They both saw the body fall into the brush. The Arisaka rifle remained hanging by its strap from the top of the denuded palm.

As they drew closer to the machine gun nest, Harry made a sign for Pinky to stay put while he flanked behind from the left. Pinky would wait until Harry threw his grenade, then he would approach the nest from the front.

Harry slowly crawled through the brush with his Garand strapped across his back. He kept his .45 in his right hand, ready to fire. The battle raged around them, but Harry was shut off in his own mini war and the din around him seemed temporarily muted. He could feel his heart thumping. He thought to himself that he had never been thirstier. As he approached the back of the nest, Harry found a slight depression on the jungle floor and crawled along it. He noticed a sudden movement directly in front and saw a Japanese soldier dart out from the opening at the rear of the concealed nest. It was a runner probably going for ammunition.

Harry waited until the soldier had disappeared before resuming his crawl forward. As he did so, another Japanese soldier darted out and nearly stepped on Harry's right arm. Surprised, the soldier fell to the jungle floor, rolled away, and sat up, awkwardly trying to level his Arisaka at Harry. Harry shot at him three times with the .45, aiming toward the head and chest. The first two bullets went into the man's upper arm and shoulder; the last hit him in the neck. He fell backward. Blood spewed from the prone body. The bullet had severed his jugular vein, just like Happy Hargrove. The man writhed in the brush, his hands around his neck. Harry could hear gurgling as the life wheezed out of him.

When all movement had ceased, Harry crawled forward. He noted that his enemy was a squat man whose markings indicated he was in the Imperial Japanese Navy. Harry pulled the pin from a grenade, waited for two seconds, and then tossed it into the back of the nest. He rolled away as the explosion sounded, waiting for Pinky's grenade. It came and exploded within five seconds, followed by a scream.

Harry leapt up, took his Garand, and fired it into the back of the nest until the clip pinged empty. At the same moment, Pinky rushed forward to the front of the nest, put his Thompson into the opening, and fired away. Harry waved his hand, and Pinky stopped. They pulled away the cover of palm fronds and sandbags. They found two Japanese soldiers in a hole that was four feet deep. Their bodies were bloody pulps. Smoked poured out of their shirts, as if they had been smoking cigars around a card table. Harry noticed a canteen at the edge of the hole. He grabbed it and greedily drank from it. He poked around, found another, but it had been blown in half. He handed the intact canteen to Pinky, who took a long drink.

They rested a few moments before making their way back north and then west toward the edge of the beach, dodging mortars and American gunfire and Japanese artillery along the way. Soon they came to a foxhole. Inside, two black Marines were manning a Browning fifty-caliber. They stopped firing when Harry and Pinky jumped down next to them. Harry calmly said, "Carry on, Marines."

They remained in the hole long enough to collect themselves and determine their next move. Harry said to Pinky, "Gather a squad of men and make your way south along the beach and help Sid rally the other platoons. Then bring them through this gap and move east toward the airfield. With these two nests gone it should be a hole big enough to put the entire battalion through. I'm going to find the CP and let Chap know about this."

Pinky nodded. His chest heaved. "Dutch," he said, "that was textbook out there. You couldn't draw it up any better in the sand."

Harry nodded, patted Pinky on the shoulder, and then ran out toward the beach. He stepped in a hole and fell. Intense pain shot through his ankle. He lay there in pain for a few seconds, cursing. He got up and limped through the sand. He asked several men the whereabouts of the 2nd Battalion CP. It took him fifteen minutes, but he located it in a large trench along the edge of the beach. He ran in and plopped down on the soft sand.

Ferdie saw Harry and came to him. "Dutch! Good to see you."

Harry sat on the bottom of the trench, gasping. "Is there any water?"

Ferdie pulled out his canteen, which was nearly empty. Harry drank from it, making sure not to take it all. He caught his breath and said, "We took out a Nambu nest about two hundred yards southeast of here. The one next to it was also knocked out. There's a big gap there. Major Gant should know about it."

Ferdie took Harry by the arm and helped him to his feet. At the other end of the trench on the phone was the battalion commander, Major James Gant. He was a thin man with a receding hairline and glasses. He was from Arkadelphia, Arkansas, and had participated in the Tarawa landing. His professorial demeanor belied a ferocious, combative disposition. The men called him Cannonball. Gant put the receiver down and looked at Harry.

"How are you, Dutch?"

"Fine, sir. I came to report that we've opened a gap two hundred yards to the southeast. We can exploit it. If we call in armor, we can be at the airfield in no time."

Gant pushed his glasses up on his nose and looked at Harry. "That's excellent news. We think we may have another opening here on the left. But the 1st Marines are catching hell up near the point." He indicated the promontory to the north with his thumb. "1st Battalion has been asked to roll onto their flank in support, so we're a bit shorthanded." He took out a pack of cigarettes and offered one to Harry.

"No thank you, sir."

Gant put the pack away and gestured toward a map lying on a crate. They squatted down to get a closer look. The major pointed with a pencil and said, "Show me exactly where the gap is."

Harry indicated the approximate location. "F Company is pushing through right now. The Jap mortars are still coming in thick, but they'll have no protection once we get under their range."

They stood up again, and Harry took off his helmet to wipe his brow. Gant said, "Great work, Dutch. I can't call in armor right now, but I want you and your men to exploit that gap. It's your company now. Go and lead them through to the airfield."

Harry regarded Ferdie questioningly. The look on his friend's face confirmed Harry's suspicion. "Chap's dead, Dutch"

Harry felt a thousand-ton weight fall on his shoulders. His face blanched, and he staggered back, mumbling, "I beg your pardon, sir." He collapsed onto the sand. The sky went black for a few moments. He saw stars. Ferdie crouched down beside him and offered his canteen one more time. This time Harry finished it.

Chapter Twenty-Five

That afternoon, around 1600, F Company and the rest of the 2nd Battalion fought through the jungle and arrived on the edge of the airfield. Remnants of the fighting to the north and south were still audible. After the green and brown of the scrub jungle, the white coral runway and the open skies were almost too much for the eyes of the exhausted men. They held their hands flat over their brows and squinted. In the distance north of the airfield was a hulking, whelked ridge, green in some areas and white in other areas where the Navy's shells had denuded the vegetation. In actuality the coral "ridge" was the Umurbrogol Mountains, where the Japanese had set up their largest artillery pieces in a series of caves. Aerial photography prior to the invasion indicated only one major ridgeline on the northern part of the island. Now that much of the vegetation had been blown and burned away, a series of ridges was exposed in parallel rows that any geologist would recognize as limestone and coral, prone to natural cave networks. "Perfect Jap territory," said Pinky.

Harry sat on the ground at the southwestern edge of the airfield. He couldn't stop thinking about Chap. His ankle throbbed, but he was loath to take off his boot to check it for fear that the ankle would swell. His right eye—damaged on Guadalcanal—ached due to the bright sun and the coral dust. As they waited at the airfield, the men nervously smoked cigarettes, keeping their eyes peeled on the distant ridges. Some of the men tried to eat K-rations but found it hard to do so without water. Almost everyone had emptied his canteen. Harry stood and began to walk around, checking on the men. He tried to encourage them. He told them they were bound to get water soon. Chap's death had plainly put a strain on everyone. The men loved Chap, and several of the younger, more impressionable wept openly for their captain. The tears left streaks in the white dust that covered their faces.

After more than an hour of waiting, Harry heard his name called. He stood up and saw Stubby walking toward him in the company of a radioman. Stubby's uniform was now light gray except in the patches where sweat stained it back to its original olive drab. Harry watched as the other men from G Company emerged like ghosts from the scrub jungle onto the airfield. Harry craned his neck, searching for Swede. Stubby knew who he was looking for. "Don't worry, Dutch. Swede got himself a Hollywood wound."

Harry exhaled in relief and got down on one knee. He stared at the ground so that nobody could see the emotion on his face.

Stubby walked up to Harry and kneeled down beside him. He put his hand on his shoulder. "He got shot clear through the thigh, and it broke his leg bone. It happened right outside the LVT in the water, before he even stepped onto dry land. I pulled him onto the beach. I saw him get carried off on a stretcher; he went right back onto the same LVT that brought us in. He was in a lot of pain, but he was okay. It's his ticket home." Stubby took off his helmet and wiped his sleeve across his forehead. He looked off at the looming ridges in the distance and then said quietly, "I heard about Chap."

Harry didn't reply, afraid that he would choke up. They stared off across the airfield. It had been badly cratered during the shelling. The skeletons of several Japanese planes were heaped together like a pile of dinosaur bones. The airfield installations on the far side of the runway were similarly wrecked.

A corporal by the name of Dietert came over with a field telephone. He was a well-built, fair youth who wore wire glasses. He had been Chap's radioman. Now he was Harry's. He handed the receiver to Harry. "Sir, it's Battalion." At the same moment, Stubby's field telephone rang.

Harry took the receiver and spoke. "Pine Tree, this is Flashlight Leader, go ahead."

He listened in silence for less than a minute then put down the phone. He looked at Stubby and said, "Major Gant?"

"Yep. Cannonball's calling us."

The meeting with Gant in the jungle west of the airfield was brief. They were told to hold their positions through the night and that they should expect counterattacks. In the morning they would advance in a northeastern direction past the airfield, across more than several hundred yards of open ground. The only protection would be the craters in the hard coral, left by the shelling. As he listened numbly to the major, Harry could think only about Chap's wife, Carolyn. Harry had seen her photo. She was pretty and had wavy brown hair. Chap spoke about her all the time. Harry knew he would write a letter to her, and he'd be able to pour some of his grief onto the paper. But at least Swede was safe. That was the only consolation from one of the worst days of his life. For Harry, one of the saddest parts of it all was that he had become inured to killing people. The Marine Corps had been successful in creating an automaton that could kill without remorse. Why couldn't they train him to be numb about his own men?

2nd Battalion was ordered to make a bivouac southwest of the airfield that night—on open ground where two of the runways crossed. Because they expected a counterattack, nobody slept. Just after dark an LVT brought forward two fifty-gallon barrels full of drinking water. The drums had not been given a proper cleansing, so the water was fouled with aviation fuel. The men spat it out when they first drank. They were forced to suffer through the night with no fresh water. Some of the Marines found water at the bottom of a shell crater. It was filthy with greasy mud and gritty with blasted coral. Flies flew all around it. Harry watched as some of the men drank the gray water, lying prone. They professed that it was the best drink they'd ever had. The rest of the thousands of Marines on Peleliu, however, chose to hold on until more fresh water was brought forward. The men that still had water shared it.

At night, weapons platoons fired flares sporadically to illuminate the northern portion of the airfield where the Japanese had last been seen. The rounds gave off an eerie glow. The pockmarked field was a moonscape.

Pinky stayed the night in a shallow crater with Harry. He pulled out a ration-D bar—a chocolate bar made with flour, powdered milk, and vitamin B1. They were as hard as bricks, and difficult to digest, but they were packed with protein. He offered a square to Harry. "Here you go, Dutch. Break your teeth on that."

"Thanks, but I can't."

"Come on, join me, Dutch. You need it." He extended a square to Harry, who reluctantly took it. He put it on his tongue to try to soften it up a bit.

A flare shot up into the sky. Harry looked north toward the ridges, which seemed to undulate under the waving light of the flare like a giant serpent. The twisted debris of the airfield gave off shadows. Bloated Japanese corpses were visible on the runway, and they too appeared to give off big shadows. But they weren't actually shadows. Harry knew that they were pools of dried blood. The fetor of the dead bodies wafted over the airfield in the still night air, along with the smell of diesel and cordite. Harry drifted off into his thoughts and tried to imagine that he was anywhere on earth besides this island. The luminescent green lights of the flare made him think of absinthe. "Those green distorting pools . . ." *God*, he thought, *I could use a drink.*

Harry had arranged to meet Edward Muncy one spring afternoon in 1940 at the Cercle Sportif Français on Rue Cardinal Mercier. They were joining the French regulars at five o'clock for what was called *l'heure verte,* or the green hour. Edward was about to introduce Harry to the rite of drinking absinthe.

Harry had never tried absinthe. It was known among aficionados as the "green fairy," due to its translucent green color. He had seen Edgar Degas' painting "The Absinthe Drinker" and read enough Oscar Wilde to know about it. He was also well aware that it had been banned in the United States at the turn of the century, long before Prohibition.

He sat with Edward on the club's enclosed verandah, listening to a Filipino orchestra with a slender mustachioed crooner doing a passable imitation of Bunny Berigan's "I Can't Get Started." The drinking process is a ritual, and Edward demonstrated. He poured the green spirit into a clear sherry glass. Next, he placed a silver slotted spoon, resembling a small spatula with holes in it, over the glass, with a sugar cube perched on top. An attendant brought an urn of ice water to the table. Edward then placed Harry's glass under the urn's brass spigot, turned the handle, and let the water slowly drip through the sugar cube into the glass of absinthe. The green spirit began clouding up into a pale milky-white liquid. As Harry brought the glass of absinthe to his lips, Edward explained that the taste was that of aniseed.

Harry took a sip and knitted his brows. "Licorice."

"That's right." As Edward prepared his own glass, he began to recite poetry. "My dreams throng to drink at those green distorting pools."

Harry looked at him strangely.

"Baudelaire. *Les Fleurs du Mal.*"

Harry took another sip, and the strong spirit burned in his chest. "A flower of evil indeed."

"I figured you'd like it, a kindred spirit such as yourself." Edward smiled.

The sounds of firing on the ridges continued intermittently through the night, and occasionally bright flashes lit up the southern portion of the island. But when there were no flares or flashes, the island was pitch black. They had landed in a new moon. The darkness put everybody on edge. The Japanese preferred not to fire at night and give away their positions. Instead, they chose to terrorize the Marines by sneaking into the lines and stabbing men to death before sneaking back out. The Marines issued strict passwords, which always contained a combination of the letters "r" and "l," since the Japanese had a hard time pronouncing those sounds. Tonight the password was "Phil Rizzuto."

The password prompted many of the men to pass the time in their foxholes talking about baseball. It looked like the upcoming World Series might be an all–St. Louis affair. Back home both the Browns and the Cardinals were closing in on the pennant. "Go figure," Harry heard a Marine muse, "the Browns in the Series? I wouldn't have believed it in a thousand years. With this war on, they must be hurting for ballplayers in the big leagues."

Someone—no doubt a Detroit native—answered, "The Tigers still may have something to say about that."

Harry thought about Henry and the ballgames they saw at Clark Field in Austin. He could hear Henry's sweet, innocent voice. "It just doesn't seem fair, Harry . . ."

The night seemed to go on forever. The eternal primordial fear of dark that humans have carried for millennia is magnified in the tropics, with all its strange noises and—in times of war—the expectation that at any moment a brutal enemy could sneak up and slit your throat.

Chapter Twenty-Six

September 18, 1944

My Dearest Love,

I find myself writing you again after only two weeks because, although we had been so optimistic this summer, watching American aeroplanes bomb Japanese facilities around Shanghai, we are again worried. This time we are terrorized by a new, unseen enemy—cholera. We have been told that we can no longer use the water from our taps, because it is drawn from the Whangpoo, which is now contaminated, along with Soochow Creek. A natural spring lies beneath the International Settlement. We can draw water from a nearby well for drinking and cooking purposes, but we are limited to two buckets per family per day. We can use the tap water at home for cleaning and watering the garden, but nothing else. Not even for bathing. In fact, when we use the tap water to clean, we have to use gloves, or soap—a very scarce commodity—to ward off any bacteria. Someone has to go each morning and draw our portion. The walk from the house to the well and back takes more than an hour. Usually we send Misha or one of the boys. Unfortunately, we had to let go our two faithful valets long ago, because we could no longer pay them.

For now, we are trying to remain healthy and to be vigilant against the dreadful disease that has afflicted the city. Each day the authorities burn the corpses of the cholera victims in large bonfires all over the city. It is too awful to even think about.

I shall switch to another topic to avoid this gloomy theme. We saw the Japanese bringing a herd of horses through the city one afternoon. They are being kept at the Recreation Ground. They are scrawny, dirty specimens, but they brought a flood of memories back to me. I thought of the many times we went with Tanya and Edward to see the horses run at the Race Club. Edward would get so excited, even though he never seemed to be able to pick a winning horse. And yet you, Harry, always seemed to have the luck when it came to picking a winner. Oh, how I miss those days!

Anyway, for now we are as well as can be expected. Uncle Grisha continues to work hard, and he keeps us afloat. Aunty Masha is my emotional rock. The funny thing is, she now says the same thing about me. I can't imagine why. I'm nothing but a burden to them. But I try to remain useful, and I share in the daily chores—the struggle to stay alive. I'm thinking of going on one of her visits to see Tanya in the camp, if my uncle will allow it. It is dangerous, but I feel that I need to see her. Doing so would give us all reassurance that we will make it out of here one day, and that this awful war will come to an end.

In the night, when I'm alone, I dream about you, Harry. When I see you, you carry that wonderful unaffected smile, and that earnest look in your eyes. I miss the way you patiently listen to me. Sometimes it seems as if it was so long ago, that it never even happened, but then I'll look at your photo—you know the one when we were at the Race Club? When I see that photo, I remember that it was real. It gives me the strength to go on, in hopes that we can relive all of it again.

Maria is calling me. I shall leave you here.

Until I take up the pen again, I leave you with these thoughts, my dearest. I love you with all of my heart,

Vika

When Misha came down with a fever one day at the height of the cholera epidemic, Viktoria decided she would go collect the water for the family. She wanted to get away from the compound for a spell. Maria felt comfortable letting Viktoria leave alone, remembering how she had dealt with the collaborationist soldiers when they visited the fishmonger and knowing that the streets were largely deserted due to the epidemic.

The morning she set out was hazy and humid. She carried only one bucket because they had water in reserve that they had not used, and two would have been too much for her to carry alone. The well was near the confluence of the International Settlement, the French Concession, and the Badlands. Viktoria walked north toward Bubbling Well Road, which ran east to west and turned into the Great Western Road. It was at that intersection that she would find the well. At the well, people were generally able to peacefully carry out their chore due to the Japanese police presence. The toll of victims mounted with inexorable certainty each day in a terrible reaping that added to the misery of a populace already reeling from the war and hunger.

Viktoria wore a scarf and a beret as well as dirty work clothes to hide her figure. She tried to stay on larger thoroughfares, where there would be more people. She walked up Route Père Robert, which led to Avenue Foch, the boundary between Frenchtown and the International Settlement. Along the way, boarded up mansions and gated compounds stood eerily quiet. She passed an old Chinese couple. When they realized she was a Westerner, they held out their hands, beseeching in Chinese for a morsel of food—or perhaps they wanted water. Viktoria walked by, pitying the couple, but she kept her gaze forward.

Just after she'd crossed Avenue Foch an acrid smell wafted past her. She pulled her scarf up over her nose. As she continued north, she saw a cordon of officials, some in uniform, others in white garb. Beyond them was a mass of bodies—cholera victims—being incinerated on the road. The flames licked the corpses, sending a plume of black smoke twisting into the hazy sky, soot falling everywhere. Viktoria crossed herself and quickly turned back toward Avenue Foch. She walked west a few blocks to avoid the soot, looking for another major crossroad to take her north again. She passed two streets that appeared to hit dead ends after about one hundred meters. At the third street, she saw a car coming toward her from the north. As it passed by, the driver—a man—looked at Viktoria with a surprised expression. She thought he looked almost Western. Probably a Eurasian. He didn't stop. She watched as the car turned left onto Avenue Foch. Viktoria surmised it was a through street that would take her to Bubbling Well Road. After a short while, however, she saw that the road headed west, so it might not intersect Bubbling Well Road.

Nevertheless, Viktoria walked on rather than doubling back, eager to get the water and return home as quickly as possible. The road narrowed and the buildings closed in on the street. She heard shouts and other noises coming from several open windows and doors. A black cat ran out into the road, and she crossed herself. She warily kept on, chiding herself for being superstitious. She looked behind her to see where the cat had gone. From a doorway nearby, two teenaged Chinese boys emerged onto the street. They began to walk toward her. She accelerated her pace, eager to find a crossroad. When she looked back again, she had gained distance on the youths, but just then another young man joined up with them. One of them shouted to Viktoria in Chinese. She walked faster. When she looked back, she saw that they were roughly thirty meters behind her. They called to her again. This time they used Pidgin.

"This side!"

She began running. The bucket was impeding her, but she clung steadfastly to it.

"Miss!"

They gained on her, and when they came within a stone's throw, she stopped and turned to them.

The oldest one walked toward her slowly. "Miss, no can find way?" Over his shoulder she could see the other two leering at her.

"Leave me, right now!" she yelled out loudly in English.

"Please go this side, Miss."

"No! Stay away from me!"

"Why fashion no can, Miss?"

Viktoria turned to run again. They followed, easily gaining on her. She began yelling for help. The calls were for naught. Nobody was in the streets, and if anybody could hear her, they would be unlikely to come to her aid.

They had surrounded her by now. The oldest one tried to coax her again. "No hurt, Miss. Go this side."

She swung the bucket awkwardly at him but missed. She yelled again. "No! Leave me alone!" She ran toward the smallest boy and swung the bucket at him. Again she missed, and the bucket flew out of her hand. The boy grabbed her around the waist, and they fell together to the pavement. The other two came and grabbed her arms and lifted her. She screamed as they dragged her back down the street where they had come from. Her beret was knocked off. She lashed out at them, kicking and screaming. She scratched the face of one of the youths, drawing blood from his cheek. The oldest one punched her square in the nose. She felt a sharp pain and saw stars. She tasted the blood as it ran from her nose. Tears of pain filled her eyes.

They continued dragging her toward the building the two teenagers had come from. As they neared the doorway, Viktoria grew limp. They relaxed their grip. She tried to run away from them, back toward Avenue Foch. They were on her within seconds. She hit at them again and kicked one of them in the knee from the front. He let out a cry of pain. They wrestled with her and finally got her back in a firm grip.

Just then a car turned the corner and drove toward them. Viktoria recognized it as the one that had passed by earlier. She yelled again, "Help! Help me!"

The car screeched to a halt several meters away. The driver—a tall man, dressed in a suit—stepped out and yelled something in Chinese at the boys. They released Viktoria and ran off, vanishing into a nearby building.

The driver turned toward Viktoria and asked her in French, "*Tout va bien, mademoiselle? Ils n'ont rien fait du mal?*"

She shook her head and instinctively answered in Russian, "*Nyet. Spasibo.*"

The man repeated his question in English. "Are you hurt, mademoiselle?"

Viktoria said, "Thank you, I'm fine."

He walked toward her and offered her his handkerchief. "For your nose," he said.

She took it from the man. It was monogrammed and made of fine linen. It was scented. She began to cry.

He came to her side and held her arm in support. "You've had quite a turn. Please let me help. Can I take you to your home?"

Viktoria looked closely at him for the first time. He was an attractive Chinese man in his thirties. He wore his hair slicked back and had light-colored, almost hazel eyes. She hesitated at the offer.

"Mademoiselle, you shouldn't be walking in these streets by yourself. It's very dangerous." He spoke with an American accent. "Please, let me take you home. I can drive you there." He gestured to his car, a French make. It was rare to see someone driving a car in Shanghai. Only high-ranking Japanese officials or Chinese collaborationists were allowed to drive private cars.

"Monsieur, thank you for your kind offer. If you could just escort me to Avenue Foch, I'm sure I will be fine and can walk home from there."

"Don't be silly. Let me drive you to your home. Somebody should tend to your nose. Are you hurt anywhere else?"

She numbly looked down at her arms and her body and said, "No, I don't think so."

"Mademoiselle, you have nothing to fear from me. I can take you to your home or your building. Where do you live?"

"I live in the French Concession, off of Avenue Du Roi Albert."

"Please, come get in the car." He escorted her to the passenger side and held the door open. She hesitated a moment but then got in, still badly shaken. He came around to the driver's side. He backed up the car, turned around, and drove toward Avenue Foch.

"Can you give me your exact address?" When she told him, he looked at her and asked, "Are you Grigorii Savin's daughter?"

Viktoria, surprised, looked at him. "I am his niece. Do you know my uncle?"

"I do. What a coincidence! But why are you walking alone around *here*?"

"I came for water at the well."

"Without a bucket?"

"I lost it back there."

"I see." Then he asked, "Your uncle couldn't have asked someone else to fetch the water?"

"Many of us in the household are sick."

"Cholera?"

"No, thank goodness. Just the grippe; fever, but nothing else."

He stopped at an intersection, where the black smoke from the funeral pyre was visible. "I know Grigorii Borisovich quite well. We have done business together." He smiled and looked at her. "Forgive me. My name is Samuel Gu."

"I am Viktoria Savina."

"It is a pleasure to meet you. I'll get you home in no time, and you can get cleaned up. After I drop you off, I'll go get water and bring it back to your home."

"You are very kind, Monsieur Gu."

"Think nothing of it."

When she arrived home, the family all expressed surprise and consternation when she walked in with a bloody blouse. They gave her a compress and made her lie on a chaise longue. She recounted the story. By the time she had finished, Gu had returned. He greeted Maria, who recognized him and spoke to him warmly. He inquired after Grigorii.

"He is away at the moment."

"Of course, always doing business." Gu smiled cordially. He looked at Viktoria. "Is everything okay?"

"Yes, thank you, monsieur."

"Please don't try to go out alone again." He turned to Maria. "Madame, I have arranged for a barrel of clean water to be delivered to your home. It should be here later this afternoon."

"You are too kind, Monsieur Gu. How can we repay you for this?" She looked at Viktoria. "And for rescuing our niece?"

"Madame, you know perfectly well there is no need to repay me. Grigorii has done me so many favors." He smiled and looked again at Viktoria. "I only ask that you take care of your charming niece." He took his leave.

That afternoon, a barrel of water was delivered. They heated several buckets' worth and each took a turn bathing in the luxurious hot water.

As Viktoria lay soaking in the tub, she remembered seeing Gu at the teahouse one day several years before. At the time, she remembered thinking how attractive he was. But she was distracted that day because it was the first time she and Harry had sat down together over tea.

Soon thereafter the cholera epidemic ran its course, leaving a terrible toll in Shanghai but sparing the Savin household. Gu continued to visit the house and check up on the family throughout the fall months. If they lacked for something, he was quick to offer his assistance.

上海

Chapter Twenty-Seven

Harry could scarcely remember the second day on Peleliu. It was a blur. 2nd Battalion was ordered to capture the remaining portion of the airfield to the north, below the deadly Umurbrogol Mountains. Although the airfield installations had been destroyed by American airstrikes and shelling, the Japanese managed to make almost impenetrable bunkers in the wreckage. Spotters in those shelters were able to call in Japanese artillery strikes onto the Marines from the ridges.

Before they moved out to attack the installations, Harry noticed that some of the men of his company were lying on the ground, their skin patchy gray, indicating heat exhaustion. He helped move some of them into the scant shade of the scrub jungle. But that was all he could do to comfort them. They needed water desperately, or they would die. Harry selected men who were still fit and left the others behind. He tried to restore some of the morale that had been shattered during the morning, when the battalion was shelled from the ridges. He told them: "The Japanese draw their water from underground cisterns. Even if we don't find faucets in their bunkers, kill yourself a Jap and take his canteen."

The battalion suffered serious casualties that afternoon. Harry acted recklessly, though he never asked any of his men to do so. He needlessly exposed himself to fire on several occasions. He was slightly wounded by a small grenade fragment in his left shoulder blade. In addition, he reinjured his twisted ankle. Late in the day, however, the 2nd Battalion finally secured the bunkers and cleared all Japanese opposition from the shelters. Afterward, F Company was deployed to the edge of a mangrove swamp east of the airfield, where they awaited orders. For the first time since they landed on Peleliu, no one was shooting at them. But for the men of F Company, the best news came in the form of an LVT bringing fresh water. Porters also distributed cans of tomato juice. Harry hungrily drank the warm, thick liquid, which tasted metallic and salty. He could feel it flowing down into his stomach, delivering well-needed nourishment to his battered body. Pinky made a fire from some Composition C for a pot of instant coffee, which he shared with Harry and Sid Morant. That evening a corpsman patched Harry's shoulder, wrapped his ankle, and pronounced him fit for combat.

The second night was even more terrifying than the first. Beyond their bivouac sat the mangrove swamp in all its blackness. Japanese infiltrators managed to sneak in through the darkness and kill several Marines in another company. Nobody slept. Harry crept from foxhole to foxhole, distributing dextrose tablets to the men. His ankle and shoulder throbbed, but he could take solace from the pain because it distracted his mind from dark thoughts.

Just before 0600 on the third day, the sky over Peleliu turned purple and then maroon. Within minutes the sun shot quickly over the horizon. The separation between pure dark and bright light was unmercifully short. The morning sun began to bake the coral. Within an hour the temperature was already in the nineties. Harry tried to eat a K-ration, but he couldn't swallow the dry crackers. Next to him Pinky ate from a C-ration can. The smell of the lima beans and ham made Harry's stomach turn. Stubby came to the bivouac with some tea he had brewed. They sat in silence and drank their cups.

A few minutes before 0800 Harry put Sid in charge of the company and left with Stubby to visit the battalion CP. On the way they passed a number of DUKWs—the six-wheeled amphibious trucks that the men affectionately called Ducks. They were headed across the airfield in the direction of the mangrove swamp. One of the drivers shouted down to Harry and Stubby, "Hot chow on the way!" Some of the DUKWs were also bringing replacements forward. Cooks, signalmen, clerks, and ammunition bearers had been drafted out of line duty to fill huge gaps that had been opened in the regiment.

Ferdie greeted Harry and Stubby at the battalion CP with hot coffee and ham sandwiches. Harry felt self-conscious as he held the white bread in his grimy black hand. He slowly chewed each bite. The soft bread melted into his gums. He savored the brewed coffee. He took a cigarette, lit it, and inhaled deeply.

That very morning a shell had landed in the CP. Several men had been wounded, including Major Gant, who took a fragment in the knee. But the indefatigable ball of energy limped around giving orders and exhorting the men.

Stubby asked Gant, "You okay, sir? I heard they threw a big one in here."

"They'll have to evacuate me feet first, Captain." He clapped Stubby on the shoulder. "I'm not going anywhere!"

At one end of the CP was an aid station. Harry saw a young man lying on a stretcher. He was talking out loud to himself. He looked to be about twenty-one years old. He had a terrible wound in his midsection and was breathing with difficulty. A corpsman with bloody hands tended to him. Clearly under the influence of morphine, the wounded youth kept up a stream of insensate gibberish, but occasionally he would shout: "Donovan! Where are you? Donovan! Where are you?" He had bright orange hair and a badly sunburned face. He reminded Harry of Happy Hargrove.

At the briefing, Major Gant explained that the 5th Marines were going to cross an isthmus east of the airfield to secure a small peninsula. 2nd Battalion would lead. Gant told them that the 1st Marine regiment had been pulled back and that the ridges were more heavily fortified than preinvasion intelligence had indicated. It was obviously not going to be a three-day fight.

Stubby looked over at Harry and winked. He silently mouthed the words, "Duck soup."

When the briefing was finished, Gant handed each officer a red apple. When he came to Harry, he said quietly, "Outstanding work yesterday at the airfield, Dutch. Effective immediately you have been promoted. Congratulations, Captain Dietrichson. F Company is now officially yours."

"Thank you kindly, sir," Harry said self-effacingly. "But we lost some good men."

"We are all taking heavy losses, Dutch. But you've earned this."

Back at the bivouac, the men silently ate their hot chow. Afterward, doughnuts were passed around with coffee. The DUKWs left with the wounded as well as the victims of heat exhaustion and combat fatigue. Harry looked around and recognized only about half of his company.

They were probably at no more than sixty percent strength compared to the first day, even with the replacements. Many other companies had suffered worse.

Harry briefed the officers and non-coms on the day's assignment. "It'll be rugged, but at least we aren't being asked to take the ridges." He regretted saying it once the words left his mouth, because they might be asked to take the ridges next.

At 1000, 2nd Battalion moved out to occupy the remainder of the Ngardololok Peninsula. Unable to pronounce the Micronesian name, the men took to calling it the "crab claw," or just "that damn peninsula." The Japanese had constructed a narrow causeway across the isthmus that was flanked on both sides by the mangrove swamp. Harry was ordered to lead F Company across the causeway first.

Harry and Pinky discussed how best to go about it. They decided they would have a Sherman tank cross with a small squad in support, using the armor as a shield. The causeway was in the direct line of the Japanese artillery on the ridges that flanked the peninsula to the north-west. Harry knew that he shouldn't be in the first group. He didn't want to send Pinky, because it would probably be a death sentence. But someone with experience had to be in the lead. He considered Sid Morant, but it was only his third day in combat. He shook his head at the realization that he had no choice but to send Pinky and nine men across the causeway. Harry had seen Chap grapple with similar decisions. Every commander struggles when he is forced to order men forward, knowing there's a good chance they'll be killed.

Pinky seemed to read his mind, and without prompting he said, "Skipper, I'd like to lead the first squad across." Harry nodded but didn't say anything.

They sat in silence, smoking cigarettes as they waited for the armor. Two Sherman tanks came forward fifteen minutes later. The driver from the first tank climbed out to consult with Pinky. They looked at a map and spoke quietly. The driver climbed back into his tank, gunned the engines, put it into gear, and drove slowly onto the causeway. The ten-man squad followed slowly behind it. The causeway was two hundred yards long. At the end it skirted a steep ridge. It was perfect ambush territory.

Stubby came and joined Harry to observe from the side of a small coral ridge above the beginning of the causeway. He loaned Harry his binoculars. They held their breath as they watched the group move cautiously. Harry could hear his heart pounding as he watched Pinky cross the causeway behind the tank. Halfway across, the tank suddenly came to a halt. Pinky grasped the field telephone suspended from the rear of the tank and spoke with the driver. After a moment he hung the receiver back on the tank. The tank moved forward again.

A section of the causeway on the right side began to cave in. The tank lurched to the right, and the driver gunned the engines, trying to reverse the vehicle. But it slid sideways and then turned over on its right side, precariously balanced on the ledge. It finally stopped, suspended halfway over the swamp. The tank lay there awkwardly, like a turtle turned onto its back. The driver stopped the engines and the crew began climbing out through the bottom escape hatch.

"Dammit!" Harry said aloud. He handed the binoculars to Stubby and went down to speak with the other tank driver standing below them. The driver followed Harry back up the ridge. Harry pointed and asked him whether he could push the other tank out of the way, into the swamp.

"Sure, that shouldn't be a problem, sir. But he's not gonna be happy about it," he said, indicating the driver of the first tank.

Harry looked at Stubby, who was chewing his lip. He thought a moment and then said, "I'm gonna go with this tank, Stubby."

"I figured as much, Dutch."

"Hopefully the Japs haven't fired yet because they can't for some reason. Hell, maybe they don't see us." Harry descended the ridge. As he slipped down the last few feet, he landed hard and flinched as pain shot through his ankle.

The second tank set out, and Harry went with five men. They proceeded slowly. At this point Harry was more worried about the integrity of the causeway than Japanese fire. They reached the first tank, and the second driver dismounted. He spoke with the first tank driver for a minute, each suggesting to one another how to proceed without causing the second tank to also slip off the causeway.

The second squad joined the first, taking cover on the embankment. Harry crouched next to Pinky and offered him a cigarette. Pinky took it and thanked him. The two tank drivers broke apart, and the second driver climbed onto his tank. Harry stood and walked over to the first driver. That's when he heard the scream of an incoming shell pierce the clear morning. Harry had no time to move to the embankment. The explosion threw him up and forward. He landed on the edge of the causeway and then rolled off to the hard bank just above the swamp. He lost his breath . . . and then his consciousness.

Harry came to and saw a corpsman leaning over him. He closed his eyes and opened them again. He saw Pinky's face looking at him from behind the corpsman. Harry could hardly breathe. He tasted blood in his mouth. He tried to say, "I can't breathe," but he could only gurgle. He felt as if he were drowning—just like in his dreams. *Incubus*, he thought to himself.

The next thing he knew, he was being carried on a stretcher. They were near the end of the causeway. He knew because he could see the coral ridge where he had been standing moments before. He could hear the sound of explosions. Men were yelling and running. Harry looked up and saw a Navy plane banking in the sky. He thought to himself: *What a beautiful contrast in colors, the dark navy blue of the aircraft against the clear light cornflower blue of the sky.* The sky disappeared as two men carried him into the back of an LVT. After the ramp closed, the amtrac bounced roughly over the pockmarked coral runway, jostling Harry as he lay on the stretcher. Two other men on stretchers were in the vehicle. Harry lost consciousness again as the calming sedation of the morphine flowed through his veins.

He saw his grandmother Sarah's face. She smiled at him from under the eaves of the Chinese pagoda. Then her face became Viktoria's face, and she smiled at him from a Chinese temple in the old walled city of Shanghai. He reached out to her, but she walked away, toward the brown river. He followed her. Then Harry felt as if he were gurgling water, and he had trouble breathing. He tried to swim, and again he saw Viktoria's face. Soon it became Sarah's face again.

Harry regained consciousness in a bright room that smelled of antiseptic. A surgeon was speaking to him in short, clear sentences. "Captain. Can you hear me? We're going to operate. You've lost blood. We'll fix you up."

Harry could barely make out the man's face. Other people in the room were speaking and Harry sensed busy motion in the background, but he tried to focus on the doctor's face and his words. He wheezed, trying to gain his breath.

The doctor continued. "You'll be okay. Be strong. Stay with us."

Harry looked at the man and nodded weakly. He noticed for the first time that the doctor had a pencil-thin black mustache that seemed to shine with wax or sweat. Douglas Fairbanks Jr. Harry thought of Edward Muncy. Behind the doctor Harry saw a nurse. Before fading out again, he thought how funny it was that she was the only woman he had seen during the past year, apart from Patty Thomas dancing on Pavuvu in fishnet stockings. He thought again of Viktoria before losing consciousness.

When Harry came to, he noticed that he was on a lower bunk. He was heavily bandaged and still sedated. A plastic tube had been placed in his right nostril. The tube led to a green canister next to the bunk. His head was elevated on two pillows. An attractive nurse, slighty pudgy, with a warm smile and a dimple on her chin, appeared at his bedside. She wore bright red lipstick. Her perfume smelled like a magnolia blossom. She leaned over Harry and asked how he was feeling. Harry just nodded his head and blinked. His chest felt sore and heavy with each breath he drew.

She stood by the bed and spoke to him quietly for a few minutes. "You're doing well, Captain. You have been sedated and unconscious for forty-eight hours. You are on the hospital ship *Tryon,* and we're sailing to Banika Island. The doctor operated on you the first day you came aboard. Your lung was punctured. That's why you have the tube in your nose. Please don't try to take it out. We need to get oxygen into your lungs. Also, your left hand had to be stitched up. But everything will be normal soon. The doctor said you'll be okay. If you like—when you're up to it, I mean—I'd be happy to write a letter for you to your folks or your sweetheart." She looked at him tenderly with big brown eyes. He read her nametag: LTJG MacMahon. He nodded. He thought about the letter to Chap's wife. Tears pooled in his eyes.

"It's okay, Captain. I'll leave you for now. If you need anything, just call for Nurse Mac. That's me. I'll be bringing you some bouillon shortly. Does that sound good?"

Harry nodded and blinked his eyes. A tear rolled down his cheek. Mac took a handkerchief and gently wiped it off. He closed his eyes and began thinking about the events of the past few days: the landing, Chap, the airfield, the corpses, the stench, the intense heat, the constant thirst, and that damned artillery. He gazed around the room. Everyone had bandages and was hooked to plasma or oxygen. The reaping from Peleliu. He nodded off to sleep, trying not to focus on the dull pain that nagged him each time he drew a breath.

That evening the surgeon visited him. It was the man with the thin mustache who had operated on him. He pulled up a chair alongside Harry's bunk. "Hello, Captain Dietrichson. I'm Lieutenant Commander Lyman Jordan. You can call me Doc." He explained, "You took a fragment of shrapnel in your chest. Directly below your right nipple." He indicated the spot on his own chest. "It punctured your left lung and exited below your left shoulder blade. It looks like you had a small wound back there from before. We removed a few other small splinters. It was a clean wound. Two of your ribs were broken. We had to break two more to operate and fix up your lung. The good news is that the fragments missed your heart and your spine. You have a tube inserted between your ribs on the left side. It is bringing air out of the cavity around your lung. We will remove it in a few days. Your left hand was also hit. We patched that up. Try not to use that hand. Let it lie there. And please don't try to remove the oxygen tube from your nose." The doctor paused for a moment. "Oh, and your ankle also appears to have been fractured, but I guess you already knew that. How long had you been running around on that ankle?"

Harry shrugged.

"Get some rest, Captain. More than anything, it's what you need. And eat what you can. For your strength." He paused and smiled. "I think you'll find our food better than the Marine chow." The doctor stood, took the chair, and moved on to the next bunk.

The next morning Nurse Mac brought Harry breakfast. She fed him scrambled eggs and oatmeal. It was the first solid food he had eaten since the ham sandwich on Peleliu. He gladly took each spoonful from her. She fed him slowly, occasionally whispering soothing words as he ate. At the end of the meal, after she wiped his mouth with a cloth napkin, Harry said hoarsely, "Thank you."

"You're welcome, Captain."

"You can call me Dutch."

She smiled and said, "Okay, Dutch. You just let me know if I can do anything for you."

He nodded and said weakly, "I'd like you to write two letters for me, please."

"Let me get things cleared up here, and I'll come back in a few minutes with stationery and a pencil."

About fifteen minutes later Nurse Mac returned and pulled up a chair. She straightened her skirt and sat down. She readied the pad and pencil. "Who is this for?"

"My Uncle Walter. He lives in Houston, Texas. 1923 Olympia Drive." Harry started to think about the letter and what he might say.

Nurse Mac said, "Anytime you're ready, I'm ready to write."

Harry started dictating in a low voice, pausing every few seconds to catch his breath. *"Dear Uncle Walter: By the time you read this letter, you may have already received a telegram from the War Department about my wounds. Please rest assured that I'm okay and receiving wonderful attention. I'm on a hospital ship and we're headed for a quiet, peaceful island in the South Pacific. Please tell Aunt Jo . . ."* he paused. He tried to catch his breath. His voice was weak and hoarse. He thought about Henry. He tried to go on several more times, but each time, his voice became choked with emotion. He stopped and pursed his lips. He closed his eyes and exhaled through his nose. There was a long silence.

Nurse Mac looked at him expectantly. When she realized his torment, she put the pencil down. "Don't worry, Captain. Why don't I come back and we'll finish the letter another time, okay?"

Harry looked at her and nodded.

She reached over and stroked his hair. "It'll be okay. You're just tired. You need to rest and eat." She stood up, moved the chair, and then walked to the door of the room. She paused and looked around at the other bunks. Nobody else called for her. She looked again at Harry and gave him a sympathetic smile before leaving.

Two days later, the day before the ship was due to arrive at Banika, Harry looked up from his bunk and saw a familiar grinning face come into the room. It was Ozzie. He was wearing a robe and was on crutches. Harry's face shone with the first genuine, unaffected smile he'd worn since he had landed on Peleliu.

"Ozzie!" Harry cried hoarsely. Curious, the other men in the room looked over at Harry and the stranger on crutches.

"Hullo, Dutch." Ozzie beamed. "So you *are* here?" He pulled up a chair and took Harry's right hand in both of his. They smiled and looked at one another wordlessly for over a minute, gripping hands, taking each other in. Finally, Ozzie broke the silence. "They clipped my shoulder last time; this time they clipped my leg." He looked down at the long cast that encased his leg from mid-thigh down.

"How'd you know I was here?"

"It was the damnedest thing. I was out topside having a smoke last night, just minding my own business. Then I overhear this nurse talking about a wounded officer named Dutch. I knew it had to be you." He leaned forward and said with a wink, "I think she's sweet on you."

"You know, normally I tell people to call me Harry. For some reason, I told this gal, Nurse Mac, to call me Dutch. You'd never have known I was here if I hadn't told her that."

"Well, I suppose I would've seen you on Banika anyway. I've been going around this ship trying to see if anyone we know made it off that damned island alive." He looked over Harry's body. "What happened to you?"

"Artillery from that goddamned ridge. It was on the third day. You?"

"Yeah. Same. Bloody Nose Ridge. Artillery. Third day. They just poured it onto us. They withdrew the entire regiment we lost so many fellas. The 1st Marines doesn't exist anymore . . . except on paper."

Harry bowed his head in reflection. Then he asked, "You heard about Chap?"

"No."

"He was killed on the first morning."

"Damn, Dutch. I didn't know."

"Yeah."

"Didn't he have a kid?"

"A little girl. Four years old."

"Damnation. That's what she must have been talking about."

Harry looked at Ozzie quizzically. "Who?"

Ozzie explained. "This nurse—Mac, was it? I overheard her talking to some other nurses about a letter she wrote down for an officer named Dutch to the wife of a friend. That's when I thought it might be you." He paused and put his hand on Harry's shoulder. "She said it was a beautiful letter, Dutch. She said you poured out your heart and soul. She was crying when she told the others about your letter."

Harry closed his eyes and lay his head back onto the pillows.

Ozzie gripped Harry's shoulder. "You did Chap good, Dutch. I'm sure his wife will take consolation from the letter. You know, coming from a close friend and all."

Harry reached behind his pillow for a book. He opened it and pulled out some leaves of paper. He handed them to Ozzie. "I haven't sent it yet." Ozzie read it quietly for a few minutes without commentary. He nodded, sighed, and handed it back. Harry took the letter and put it back in the book. "I don't even know his address."

"There can't be too many Chappellets in Idaho Falls."

They sat in silence and reflected for a few moments.

Ozzie then said, "Terrible about what happened to Swede."

"Yeah, but he'll recover fine. 'Hollywood wound.' That's what Stubby said. Shot clear through the leg."

Ozzie rubbed his forehead. He exhaled and looked away for a moment and then turned back to Harry. "You didn't hear what happened, did you?"

Harry said weakly, without conviction, "Yeah, Stubby saw him and said he was in a lot of pain, but he helped load him onto an LVT."

"Dutch, the LVT took a direct hit as it was going back out to the ship."

"What?"

Ozzie nodded and bit his lip.

Harry put his head back on his pillow and started seeing black spots. He began to wonder whether this was a bad dream. He looked up at Ozzie and said hoarsely, "How . . . how do you . . . how . . . how can you be sure?"

"Sully told me. Sully's friend—another corpsman—was wounded and taken onto the same LVT. Sully saw it all happen. He said they heard a loud explosion from the beach. They turned to look back and saw the LVT in flames about a hundred yards out. It hadn't even made it back to the reef. There were four other wounded guys and three corpsmen, plus the coxswain. No survivors." Ozzie exhaled and then went on. "Sully was wounded on the third day too. He's on board now. I saw him yesterday."

Harry started breathing heavily. His mouth remained open and he heaved with each breath, as if he had just run a hundred-yard dash. His right side ached. Ozzie leaned toward him and put a hand on his thigh. "You okay, Dutch?" He looked around. "Lemme get you some water."

Ozzie struggled to get up, and then he went over to a table near the door and poured water from a pitcher into a glass. He returned, spilling half the water as he tried to balance it while using his crutches.

"Here, drink this."

Harry leaned forward and took a sip. His head was spinning. "My God," he gasped.

"It's okay, Dutch." Ozzie tried to soothe him. "We made it. It was hell on that island. But we *made* it, you and me."

Harry regained his breath. He stared vacantly ahead and said in a low voice, "It makes sense now."

"What do you mean?"

"Swede told me that his father would be happy if I visited the ranch." He paused and drank more water. "It was like he knew he wasn't gonna be there. Like he knew his number was up."

Ozzie looked at Harry for a few moments and then said, "I guess you'll be going there after all. To see his father, I mean."

"I guess I will."

Ozzie stayed another few minutes, but neither of them really had anything more to say. Ozzie got up and balanced himself on his crutches. "Okay, Dutch. I better move on. We'll see you on Banika. I hear the nurses are pretty and the chow is good. They show movies every Wednesday and Saturday, and you can get popcorn. They also say you can get as many bottles of cold Coca-Cola as you want, anytime. Sure sounds good, huh?"

"Sure, Ozzie," Harry said numbly. "That sounds swell."

"Listen, buddy, it's over for us. Now's the time for you and me to concentrate on living. That's what we're gonna do. We owe it to ourselves. And we owe it to Swede and Chap, and the others that bought it."

"You're right, Ozzie." Harry nodded and reached out his hand. They shook hands. Ozzie stood quietly for a moment. Then he turned and made his way slowly out of the room.

Harry lay there taking it all in. He had just gotten over the torment of writing the letter to Chap's wife; now he pondered the loss of his best friend, Swede. He'd never see either of them again.

Just then a faceless voice from somewhere in the room spoke. "Hey, Cap'n." Then a pause. The voice spoke again. It was a deep, gruff voice, and Harry understood it came from the bunk directly above him. "Damn shame about your buddies. I lost my two best friends. The three of us were platoon lieutenants from the same company. We were together in New River, Melbourne, and then Gloucester. We spent every minute of every day together for two years. Then, on the first day—*poof*—just like that, they're both gone." He snapped his fingers loudly to punctuate the sentence.

The voice went on. "We had five men fit for combat in my platoon by the end of the second day. Like your friend said, the 1st Marines don't exist anymore." The voice was silent for a few moments. Then it went on in a softer tone. "But your friend's right. Time for us to start living. Don't you agree, Cap'n?"

"Yeah, I guess." Harry closed his eyes and laid his head back on the pillow.

After a long moment of silence, the deep voice started again. "You know, Cap'n? We found lots of Japs on Gloucester, crawling around the jungle like skeletons. They were starvin' to death. We just left 'em to rot. Didn't even bother to kill 'em. Figured they'd be worse off havin' to live like that. Dying woulda been the easy way out. I kinda felt sorry for 'em at the time." He took a deep breath. "But I'll tell you what, Cap'n. I ain't ever gonna forgive the Japs for what they did to us. Making us come ten thousand miles out here, leaving our homes, our families. Living on these awful islands; piling onto transports, landing on some muddy snake-infested shithole; eating that awful chow outta cans; seeing the best men I ever knew die." He paused again and then finished. "No, sir, Cap'n. I'll never forgive those bastards as long as I live."

Harry didn't answer. He stared at the bottom of the bunk above him, and though he couldn't see the man, he could feel the hatred. He lay awake all that night, thinking about Swede and Chap. He wished Nurse Mac could give him more sedation so he could sleep. He had asked her when she came in on her rounds, but she wouldn't authorize it. He supposed it didn't matter. He'd just see them in his dreams anyway if he slept.

He never saw the face of the man in the top bunk. When they carried Harry out of the room the next day, he glanced up to see that the head of the disembodied voice was entirely wrapped in bandages.

Chapter Twenty-Eight

December 25, 1944

My dearest Harry,

I wanted to write down a few thoughts, and to wish you and your family a Merry Christmas wherever you may be. I hope this New Year's holiday brings you good tidings of peace and that you are safe. And I'm not alone in sending these greetings. Aunty Masha and Uncle Grisha sometimes wonder out loud how you might be doing and where you are. Maybe you have even been able to return to celebrate the holidays with your family in Texas? I do hope this is the case.

We know that the war has turned favorably for the Americans and the British. We still see American planes regularly. Sometimes they bomb Hongkew, and sometimes they fly over Shanghai on their way to bomb another city. The Japanese are nervous and angry, but we all know that it is a good sign.

My family and I are still okay. We live in a dreary monotony in which getting food is our primary chore, and it occupies the time and energy of all the adults in the home each day. I'm sad to say our dog Lev has disappeared. We assume he was stolen and probably sold for food. It saddens me because he was a direct link to you, and we all loved him so. We are having to pay more and more to keep the teashop and warehouse out of Chinese hands. The business in Japan so far has not been touched, so we can still count on Uncle Alexei's support. But it is our only source of income. We are selling off what household goods we can spare, but even our jewelry returns a pittance. The situation in Japan is steadily worsening, we hear, so we don't know how much longer our uncle's shop in Kobe will be left alone. Apparently, the American planes have started bombing Japanese cities, so we worry about his family.

Oh, Harry, I'm so concerned for Uncle Grisha too. Remember how we admired him for being, first and foremost, an opportunist? He reminded me often of the famous Chinese proverb that it is better to "bend like the bamboo whichever way the wind was blowing." He prided himself on having an innate sense of understanding where the politics were going—and we believed he was always right.

But Uncle Grigorii has been taken into custody twice already and questioned by both the Japanese and the Chinese authorities. They are more and more suspicious of Russians. When he's returned from such interrogations, his mind has been preoccupied and peculiar. He even calls me Tanya now and again! He has also had a falling out with General Glebov, who as you know is chairman of the All-Russian Emigrants Committee.

Sometimes he is also called away on business to Tientsin and we don't hear from him for long periods thereafter. Aunt Maria worries when he is gone for more than two or three days. Though he won't admit it, we hear he's been involved in deals with that mad Cossack Pastukhin in Tientsin. You may or may not remember, but Pastukhin is an associate of Ataman Semyonov, who rules the Russian underworld in Harbin and Dalian, in league with the Japanese. He committed all sorts of atrocities during the civil war, mostly against innocent civilians. This is what Uncle Grisha's dispute—we assume—with General Glebov is about. My brother, Boris, and his family are hanging on in Tientsin, but they too are at the mercy of the Japanese and the vile Pastukhin. I pray for them every day.

The situation in China is so dangerous, even if you work and travel with the Japanese. There are so many small skirmishes around Shanghai between the Japanese and the Chinese Nationalists, and also between groups of Chinese. You remember what it was like before the war? It is far worse now. We pray that we can continue living in our home and that the war will soon come to an end. It has gone on for so long! Everyone expects the end to come soon, but we are all dreading what may come to pass before it ends. Before it gets better, we know it will probably get worse. We can only hope that the worst is still survivable.

I hate to end this letter on such a gloomy note, but it has come to this. I hope you have fared better, My Love, and I truly hope you have returned safely to Texas and will have a Merry Christmas with your family.

I understand—should you one day read this—if you have already moved on with your life. Maybe you have even found another woman and have married her. If this is the case, I fully understand. If you do meet someone you love, I would expect you to not worry about me. It is okay if you have moved on with your life. This happens, and we cannot expect the world to stop for us. But I, for one, cannot keep you out of my mind. I love you, perhaps more than you will ever know.

Yours,

Viktoria

Grigorii Savin was a changed man. The rock of stability that stood unfalteringly and bound the extended family together for so long now seemed vulnerable. The stress of trying to hold things together and the strain of maintaining an optimistic face for the family were catching up with him. Oftentimes Viktoria found him alone in his study, speaking to himself while leaning over a map of Russia. Viktoria tried to reach out to him, but she found it increasingly hard to do so. He would look distractedly at her and brush away any concerns she voiced. When she brought up the topic with Maria, her aunt was quick to change the subject.

Viktoria approached her uncle one day about acquiring medicine for the children. After the cholera epidemic and the flu that had gone around, she hoped to keep more medication on hand for emergencies, especially aspirin.

Grigorii waved her off. "Don't you worry about that, dear. We can get the medicine when we need it. The sisters at the hospital will provide it if we need it," he said referring to the Catholic mission hospital.

"I know, Uncle Grisha, but when the children awake at night in a feverish sweat, it would be nice to have aspirin on hand. Is there some way we could acquire a bottle? Perhaps the Japanese could help us out. Is there someone you can speak with?"

"Dear, as I said, everything is under control. No need to worry about the details."

"Are you listening to me, Uncle Grisha? We should keep aspirin in the house. Can we get some? As I said, maybe the Japanese . . ."

"You never know with the Japanese. They may smile at you one day, then the next day they might come to interrogate you about some imaginary crime."

"But surely we could try . . ." She waited for him to answer.

Savin stopped and pondered a piece of paper on his desk. He then picked it up to study it further. Finally, he looked up at his niece. "Did you know that the Red Army has halted on the outskirts of Warsaw? I think the Germans have finally made their stand and will begin a counteroffensive soon." He pulled out a map of the Russian Far Eastern Pacific coast. "And perhaps the Japanese will launch an offensive from the east. It would be the end of Stalin, that dirty Georgian thug."

Viktoria sighed to cover her frustration with her uncle in that moment. And she realized his comments reminded her of the discussion the family had over supper one night with Harry, not long before he was suddenly called back to America. An evening several weeks before Hitler's invasion of the Soviet Union, in June 1941. Harry unexpectedly broached the topic of marriage to her aunt and uncle at the table. At the time, Grigorii Savin seemed so confident and sure about himself and about their eventual return to Russia.

The entire family—including Viktoria—was clearly shocked at Harry's open pronouncement of his desire to marry their niece. After he recovered from the initial surprise, Savin tried to explain himself. "I speak for my entire family in saying that we are all fond of you, Harry. But you must understand, Viktoria is still a young lady. She is also a Russian, and what we would hope is to one day see her married to a Russian man. I have no control over her actions, ultimately, but my wife also feels very strongly about this. Our world is uncertain, but the community of Russians who have chosen to escape the Bolshevik terror is tight knit. We have strong beliefs and a strong faith. One of these is the belief that we will return to a Russia that is free of Bolshevism. It is important that we stay together and that we one day return together."

Viktoria took Harry's hand, a defiant look on her face.

Maria added her voice in support of her husband. "Our primary concern, Harry, is that Viktoria not be hurt. We have great affection for you, but we must think of Viktoria's future. You will return to the United States at some point, this is clear, and when you do, what would there be for a cultured woman like Viktoria? Could she live the life of a correspondent's wife? In Texas? Her destiny is to carry on as a Russian. We stay together, we fight together, we pray together. And one day, God willing, we will return to Russia together." She crossed herself.

Harry was moved by the Savins' impassioned explanation of family

JODY FERGUSON

and motherland. But with Viktoria's silent support he gathered himself and offered his own passionate beliefs. "I understand your protective attitude toward Viktoria and your family. I also love Viktoria, and I know she feels the same about me. And as much as we would all like to see the tyranny in Russia overthrown, let's be honest with ourselves. There is no evidence to suggest that the Soviet Union is weakening. In fact, now that Stalin has a free hand in Eastern Europe, and since Japan seems to be preoccupied elsewhere, how many years do you think it will be before a return to Russia is possible? I could think of worse places than America to live and raise a family."

Savin countered, "I grant you that Stalin and his band of criminals are strong for now. But things can change quickly. I feel—and many other people agree with me—that it is a matter of time before the Germans and the Bolsheviks come to blows. And, assuming that you are correct and the Bolsheviks do remain in power for a long time into the foreseeable future, then it's all the more important that we Russians abroad maintain cohesiveness, and that the younger generation continues to carry the fight into the future."

As Savin grew more zealous, Harry became even more determined to challenge him. "Grigorii Borisovich, I respect your cause and your devotion to family. But, at some point, the younger generation needs to decide for themselves what interests them more: a cause or actually surviving and being able to live a normal life? When the Japanese come and take Shanghai, then what? You have no homeland. China's not your home. The Japanese will do what they please. Given the alternatives, America might not be such a bad place to settle down."

Savin waved off a servant who had come at this inopportune moment to inquire about serving the meal. "We will have to manage our struggle from China together; we have no alternative," he said with implacable stubbornness.

"Uncle Grisha, before we start planning our return to Russia, let's focus on getting some medicine. For the children. I know the Japanese keep aspirin in the medical dispensary on Nanking Road. Maybe you could speak with someone in the Japanese administration. We still have jewels. We can still buy things."

"You know, dear, you are right. I *should* speak to the Japanese. If I

247

can only convince them that the time for an offensive against the Soviet Union is *now*."

Viktoria shook her head, flummoxed at the absurdity of their conversation. She saw that her uncle was once again engrossed in studying the map. "Uncle Grisha, do you wish to have some tea?"

He looked up at her. "Yes, that would be wonderful, Vika, dear."

Later that evening she had an equally dissatisfying conversation with her aunt on the subject of Uncle Grigorii's state of mind.

Maria agreed. "Yes, I see it too. It's all this stress of having to grovel in front of all these baboons in uniform. But he'll come around. He needs to rest more. I tell him that he's wearing himself out with worry and with his travel."

"I think he may need more than rest, Aunty Masha. Who can rest these days anyway? You need to keep a close eye on him."

"Of course, dear. He'll be fine. I will see to it that he stays away from his business for a while. Perhaps he can find time for a break."

"Aunt Maria, *somebody* needs to be the leader of this family. Somebody needs to protect us and keep the business going."

Maria tried to end the conversation. "Well, at least we have Uncle Alexei in Japan. I don't know what we would do without him. The company would probably no longer be afloat." She distractedly asked Viktoria something about Henry.

"Aunt Maria, please listen to me. I'm talking about affairs here in Shanghai. We need the business here to remain solvent. If Uncle can't handle the business, then someone will have to."

"Vika, dear, you needn't worry about business affairs."

"Well, *someone* needs to worry about them."

"And your uncle is. That's why he has come under so much stress recently. He thinks of nothing but the business."

"Well, it won't do us any good if he goes out of his mind."

"Dear! How can you say such a thing?! Don't ever speak such nonsense again. Your uncle is fine; he just needs some rest." She began folding some napkins and looked down as she spoke. "Anyway, hopefully this war will come to an end soon. He tells me the Americans are getting closer. And the Red Army is—"

"I know, the Red Army is on its knees," Vika interrupted. "He repeats the same drivel almost every day. Only, we know that they are *not* on their knees. They are closing in on Germany. And with his judgment so clouded against the facts, I begin to wonder whether the Allies are actually close to ending the war out here. In fact, until Hitler is beaten, they won't be able to concentrate on the Japanese."

"But Vika, you've seen the American planes . . ."

"Yes, big planes that can fly long distances. That means they are flying from bases far away."

Maria took Viktoria's hand. "Dear Vika, please don't be so pessimistic. I know that the end is near. Your uncle and I sense it each time we speak with the Japanese."

Viktoria looked down. "Aunty Masha, that doesn't change the fact that Uncle is getting sick. How will we survive to the end if we can't feed ourselves and feed the children?"

Maria put her hand on Viktoria's cheek. "My child, you need to focus on Henry. We only just missed the cholera. We need to stay vigilant. You worry about the children. Grigorii will take care of the business."

Viktoria turned and walked out of the room. She went upstairs to Henry, who was napping. She rocked herself in the chair and looked out the window. She could see the tops of the fruit trees in the garden. She stayed in the chair and fell asleep. She saw vivid dreams. Harry was wounded and lying on the deck of a ship. A man—a medical officer—came to him and inspected him. He shrugged and rolled Harry off the deck into the deep waters of the ocean. She startled awake.

In early January the family was paid a visit by Viktoria's rescuer, Samuel Gu. He wore a checkered wool suit. He brought a carton of eggs and some fish for the family. Maria expressed her gratitude and offered him tea.

The four adults settled in the hunting room. Gu and Grigorii took up a discussion of the war.

"What have you heard about the Americans? Is it true they have retaken the Philippines?"

Gu kept his voice low as he spoke. "Yes. American forces are now on Luzon, just north of Manila. But, more importantly, they've retaken Guam and Saipan. They have started bombing Japan from bases in the Marianas. Some say they will take Formosa next."

"How much longer can the Japanese hold out?"

"It's hard to say. They're fanatical, as you know. It could last for years. They still have more than a million troops in China."

Maria poured Gu some more tea. He thanked her. "Oh, yes, one more thing." He produced a jar from his valise. It was honey. "Please, keep this for your tea. It has many natural vitamins and nutrients."

"Oh, thank you!" Maria exclaimed. "Would you care for some now?"

"No, no." Gu shook his head. "Thank you, madame, but I prefer my tea unsweetened." He glanced at Viktoria and smiled.

She looked down.

Grigorii then asked him about business affairs. Gu spoke in a louder voice about some deals that he had going on in Manchuria. He unaffect-edly explained that the cholera epidemic had carried off a few business rivals.

"Do you think, Monsieur Gu, that you could procure for us a supply of aspirin?" Everyone looked up in surprise at Viktoria.

Maria chided her. "Vika, please do not inconvenience Monsieur Gu. He has done so much for us already."

"I am not inconveniencing him by simply asking a question. It is perfectly within his right to say no if it is an inconvenience."

Maria started to protest, but Gu held up his hand. "Madame, please allow me. She is not inconveniencing me." He turned and looked at Viktoria. "If you are in need of aspirin, then I am at your service. It is not easy to come by, but it can be acquired."

Grigorii started to explain. "My niece—"

"I have the means to pay," Viktoria interjected.

Grigorii and Maria were taken aback. But Gu answered, speaking directly to Viktoria. "For now, do not concern yourself with money. Let me get what I can, and we can arrange the payment later."

Viktoria nodded once and said, "We are much obliged, monsieur."

He bowed toward her. "It is my pleasure, mademoiselle."

The next day Gu arrived at the house and presented Viktoria with a bottle of fifty doses of aspirin. He also gave her a glass tube of Bro-mo-Seltzer tablets. "In case the children have upset stomachs."

"Thank you so much, monsieur. How can we repay you?"

"There is no need."

From that moment on, if the Savin household lacked for anything, Viktoria knew to whom she should turn.

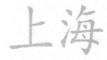

Chapter Twenty-Nine

Harry was confined to his bed for the first two weeks at the hospital on Banika Island. Ozzie came by to see him often, bringing him treats like candy bars or an occasional can of warm beer. The Navy screened movies in the ward, and each man looked on with a mixture of fascination and revulsion at the scenes from the home front, finding it hard to believe that normalcy still existed somewhere in the world.

But mail call was the highlight of each day. Ellen Lowry wrote Harry several letters, pouring out her longing to see him when he returned to Houston, and he convinced himself that he longed for her. Two letters arrived from Aunt Jo. They had been written prior to Peleliu, the first as far back as early August. Jolyn was at a summer camp, and toddler Paul was growing into a rambunctious boy. Jo never made reference to Henry's passing. This omission made Harry sad. He had gained a tremendous appreciation for family during his time among the Marines. He vowed to rebuild his relationship with Walter and Jo. He wrote them both a long letter, explaining that his recovery was going well and that he would probably be coming to Houston after the New Year. He finished the letter with a tender message to them.

I know how lucky I have been to be taken in by you two. Walter: you have been a great uncle and a father figure for me. Aunt Jo: you have given me so much love, affection, and wonderful companionship. I will never be able to repay you. I wasn't always warm or receptive, but please do know how I feel. I've been able to become the man I am in part thanks to your support and encouragement. I want you two to always know that I feel this way, and that I will forever be grateful for everything you have done for me. Yours, Harry.

In mid-October a doctor informed Harry that he was being shipped back to the naval hospital in San Diego for further treatment and convalescence. How long he would be there was unclear, but he told Harry that upon discharge from the hospital he would be entitled to thirty days of home leave.

The hospital ship—one of a large convoy of ships—departed for the West Coast on October 17, 1944—the day MacArthur landed at Leyte Gulf in the Philippines. The news was broadcast by the Armed Forces Radio Service as they steamed out. The wounded men took in the news with some satisfaction, but they knew it was still going to be a long slog with the Japanese. It took the hospital ship two weeks to travel from Banika to San Diego. The weather was warm and sunny. Harry and Ozzie spent hours on deck playing cards and shooting the breeze with other Marines.

Despite the camaraderie, Harry couldn't shake his black mood on board the hospital ship. The more he thought about Swede and Chap, the more depressed he became. He had been told about survivor's guilt, but that did little to assuage his profound sorrow. It also made him think of his parents and his grandmother. Who, really, did he have left anymore?

The day before they arrived in San Diego, in an attempt to find some positive emotion and to grasp a reason for returning, Harry decided that he would write a letter to Ellen. It was the first heartfelt letter he had written to her. He told her that she was the reason he kept going day after day in the heat of battle. He told her that he loved her and longed to be with her. He told her that their reunion would be sweet, and that one day they would be joined forever. It took him a long time to write the letter, even though it was short. He threw away several versions. Finally finished, he reread the letter one last time. As he prepared to fold it up, he looked at the heading of the letter. He took a deep breath and closed his eyes. He had addressed it "My dearest Viktoria."

Momentarily stunned, he sat looking out at the ocean. Harry admitted to himself that as he had written the letter, Viktoria's image had been in his mind. It was Viktoria, and the thought of her, that got him through the darkest, blackest days in the South Pacific. *She* was the lifeline that kept him above the water. It was Viktoria he longed to keep and hold for the rest of his life. He shook his head. Then Ellen's image came into his mind. He knew that when he returned to Houston, he was going to have to tell her that he didn't love her and that he never really had. The guilt weighed heavily on him.

Harry glimpsed American shores for the first time in more than two years on the brilliant sunny day of November 3. He thought of Melbourne when he saw the manicured lawns and white picket fences of San Diego. The U.S. Naval Hospital in Balboa Park was clean and bright. The staff made an effort to create a cheery atmosphere, but one couldn't put a pretty face on the ugly realities of war. Young men—in the best years of their lives—lay in the wards, scarred physically and emotionally. Army and Navy hospitals all up and down the West Coast were full of the harvest reaped in the Pacific. Hospitals on the East Coast sheltered the crop from European battlefields.

Harry had to undergo treatment for his lungs, which involved breathing oxygen from a mask. There was not much more than that. He was off of painkillers by the time they arrived. His left hand was of more concern. The scar tissue tightened the skin of his palm, making it difficult to completely close his hand into a fist. The inability to grasp a fist around a grenade or knife could exclude him from combat. Harry wanted a normal functioning hand, but he no longer cared whether he was kept out of combat. He had decided that when the war ended, he wanted to be as close to China as possible to find Viktoria. There was always a possibility that U.S. forces would invade the coast of China. Once he realized on board the ship that his undying love and devotion were for Viktoria, he never let go of the idea of getting back to Shanghai.

By early November, he felt almost completely normal physically, though his ribs ached considerably if he overexerted himself. Most of all, Harry still needed rest. Mentally he had reached a breaking point on Peleliu. On two occasions in San Diego, Harry visited a psychiatrist to discuss what returning wounded veterans struggled with: adjusting to life in a "normal" setting, the loss of close friends, survivor's guilt, and the inability of family and friends at home to understand what they had experienced. Harry couldn't open up to the doctor, whose manner was more perfunctory than concerned. Oddly enough, Harry had few nightmares during his hospital stay. Men in the ward cried out at night, but Harry didn't seem to—at least no one mentioned it—and he couldn't remember any vivid dreams. He thought it must have been the by-product of sheer exhaustion.

Ozzie left the hospital in mid-November, but he returned to visit Harry on two occasions, including once with his wife, Janet. Harry spoke on the phone with Uncle Walter and Aunt Jo on Thanksgiving Day. They were both relieved to hear from him. At the hospital, camaraderie between the wounded men was strong but not as strong as between the men in combat. Nevertheless, Harry felt comforted being among them. It was like an extended family, one that he was proud to be a part of. He sent another letter to Chappellet's wife in Idaho. He also tried to write a letter to Swede's family in Texas but decided instead he wanted to visit them personally.

On Christmas Day the hospital hosted a performance by singers and actors who came down from Hollywood to try to spread cheer among the men. But no amount of caroling could spread holiday cheer. New arrivals had been coming in weekly from Peleliu, which was secured only at the end of November. "So much for the short but rough prediction they gave us," someone said one day as more wounded were wheeled into the ward. "Operation Stalemate," said another Marine, referring to the official name the Marine Corps had given the battle. "They sure got that part right!" The less-than-festive atmosphere was also a by-prod-uct of the news coming out of Europe about the big German offensive in the Ardennes. It seemed that the war in Europe wouldn't be over soon, which meant that the end of the war in the Pacific would also be delayed. By this time Harry was ready to leave the hospital. The weeks after Christmas passed like molasses.

Sometime after Christmas, Harry encountered Father Byron unex-pectedly in the hospital. He had returned from Peleliu and Pavuvu only recently. The chaplain had been the subject of a painting by Tom Lea that Harry would later see in *Life* magazine. They sat down on the slop-ing lawn of the green grounds and had a long heartfelt conversation. Harry tried to make sense of all that he had been through. Not just the war but his entire life.

"Do you have faith, Captain?"

"I'm not sure anymore, to be perfectly honest, Father. I seek truth more than I seek faith."

"Many people would say that truth—or trust—and faith are the same."

"I just don't know, Father." Harry again brought up *The Pilgrim's Progress*. "You know, I feel like Christian sometimes. Each stage of my life presents me with challenges, and if I'm not up to the task, well, I feel like I'll fall into the Slough of Despond or the River of Death. I see myself drowning all the time. There never seems to be any respite in suffering. Everyone I've known and cared for seems to have abandoned me or to have died."

"Son, we all suffer. Suffering is eternal. It's part of the journey. Life is not easy. Christian understood this. At Journey's End, when the King greets Christian, he quotes from Isaiah: 'That the righteous nation which keepeth the faith, may enter in.' You seem to me, Captain, to be a man of faith, who values truth."

"I seek truth, but to be honest, Father, I find loneliness instead. And maybe that's what I deserve now. I mean, after the things I've done . . ."

"I know it's a struggle to understand all of this trouble that surrounds us every day."

"I just don't know if I can believe, Father."

"In God?"

"No, in myself. I'm tired of being me."

"Captain, you can't blame yourself for what has happened to people you have known and loved. Remember what Mr. Bunyan wrote at the end of his work: 'Do thou the substance of my matter see . . . There, if thou seekest them, such things to find, as will be helpful to an honest mind.' Never quit seeking the truth. From this, good will follow. The path may be torturous, but you will succeed. You have an honest mind, Captain. And I believe you try to do well."

In mid-January, while walking the hospital grounds, Harry thought he saw a familiar face. A young yellow-haired man in a robe sat in a chair on the lawn, smoking a cigarette. His neck was bandaged. Harry stopped in front of him and asked, "5th Marines? 2nd Battalion?"

The young man stood from his chair. "Yes, sir, E Company. Corporal Clarence Rhys." He started to salute, but Harry waved him off.

"Stubby Staley's company?"

"Yes, sir. Cap'n Staley's unit."

"I thought I recognized your face. Mortar man, right?"

"Yes, sir. I knew who you were right away, Cap'n. F Company. Good to see you, sir."

"When were you wounded?"

"November 12, sir. We were trying to clear out a pocket in the ridges. I got shrapnel in my neck and in my back."

Harry couldn't imagine having been on that island in combat for over two months. He hesitated for a moment and then asked, "Know anything about Stubby?"

"Sir, last I saw, he was fine. He's as crusty as ever, of course, but he was okay when I got it. I saw a fellow on Banika from our company, and he made it all the way through to the last day. He never said anything about Captain Staley getting hit. I think he must be on Pavuvu now."

"What about Pinky Dolworth?"

"He was acting company commander. Your unit, F Company. I think he made it through, sir."

"They couldn't be in better hands," Harry said. "Do you know Captain Ferdie Goff from Battalion?"

"No, sir, I don't believe I do."

Harry nodded and thanked the young man. "I hope you get healed up quickly, Corporal."

Hearing that Stubby was alive was the best Christmas and New Year's present Harry could have gotten.

On the evening of January 25, 1945, Harry departed on a Pullman train via Los Angeles for the journey east. He was one of the scores of Marines and sailors who were released from the hospital. Since they were convalescing, they were afforded the luxury of sleeping berths. Harry stood at the window for a while in the corridor, watching the San Bernardino Mountains pass by, black against the cloudy pale night sky. Soon the train passed onto the high desert plateau, the clouds dissipated, and a full moon illuminated the large boulders and spindly Joshua trees. They halted frequently, and in cities like Tuscon, El Paso, and San Antonio, they stopped for longer periods. The clean, dry desert air was bracing to the men who had spent long months in the fetid, stultifying tropics of the Southwest Pacific.

Early on the evening of the third day—January 28, 1945—the train pulled into Houston. With a knot in his stomach, Harry descended from the train in his green dress uniform. He was wearing his "cover," or overseas cap, with the captain's bars pinned on. There on the platform stood Walter, Jo, Jolyn, and Paul, who was nearly two and a half years old. He was wearing a little sailor's outfit. He reminded Harry so much of Henry. Jolyn would be sixteen in several weeks, and Harry hardly recognized the young woman she'd become. Walter approached him first. He firmly grasped Harry's hand. Tears welled up in his uncle's eyes. It was the first time Harry had seen Walter show emotion. Jo grabbed Harry and pulled him toward her. She hugged him for a full minute, rocking back and forth, softly crying. She then pulled back to take in Harry with a long look. She looked deep into his eyes. She seemed to fully grasp at that moment what had happened to her nephew since they had last seen him. She patted him on the cheek. "My dear boy."

Walter said softly to Jo, "He's not a boy anymore."

Harry turned to Jolyn. "Hello, Happy Eyes!" He hugged her and then held her at arm's length and said, "The first thing I'm doing here in Houston is taking you to the Avalon, and we'll have lunch at the counter."

She smiled and said, "Harry, you have to promise you'll wear your uniform."

He answered with one of her favorite expressions: "Like nobody's business."

Harry then bent down and put his hands on his knees. He looked at Paul, who was nervously hiding his face in his mother's skirts. "Hello, sailor. I'm your cousin Harry. We're gonna be good friends." Harry held out his right hand. Paul meekly reached out his hand and placed it on Harry's outstretched fingers. Harry shook his hand, and then took his cover off, placing it on Paul's small head. The boy's eyes widened.

Jo laughed and said, "You'll never get *that* back."

They walked out of the station together, surrounded by hundreds of servicemen and their families—happy in reunion or saddened by departure—all coming or going in the constant motion of war.

Houston was changed. The war had turned it into a boomtown. Shipping, refining, petrochemicals, pulp and paper, and munitions fueled the flourishing city that now numbered more than half a million inhabitants. Harry hadn't spent any appreciable time there since he had left for the Far East in 1937. It was still a sleepy southern town then; it was a metropolis today. The energy was palpable. People were on the move, and you could feel the sense of purpose. Everyone was contributing to the war effort, even something as simple as metal scrap drives or the collection of bacon grease to produce glycerin for high explosives. Everyone knew somebody overseas, and Harry was astonished one day to read in the paper that fifteen million American men and women were in uniform at the beginning of 1945.

The day after he returned home Harry visited Henry's grave with Walter. He left his Marine Corps pin by the tombstone and spoke a few quiet words to his deceased cousin.

As he stood, Walter put his hand on Harry's shoulder and said, "I don't know if we'll ever get over this. But having you back helps to fill the void. Jo has spoken of nothing but you during the last few weeks."

"Nobody can take his place. But I feel better, having a home to come back to."

"She comes here often, but only alone." Walter shook his head. "She's getting better. Having Paul brought out her mothering instincts and helped her deal with her depression. And having you here will cheer her immensely."

"I'll help all I can. But I'm gonna have to ship out again."

"They won't send you back overseas, will they?"

"Not likely, but I'm not entirely sure. The thing is, Uncle Walter, I'd like to get back to Shanghai once this damned thing is over."

"You want to find her? Viktoria?"

"I've never wanted anything more in my life."

For the first few days Harry stayed at the house. He read, played cards with Aunt Jo and Uncle Walter, or sat listening to music or the news on the radio. He wanted to get to know his family again. The pre-war restraint had been replaced by an easy familiarity, and almost every evening after the children were asleep, he, Walter, and Jo sat together on the screened porch and had long talks over a drink. The loss of Henry seemed to have taken the edge off of Walter. Harry could tell Jo was also changed, but not necessarily for the better. She looked older, and the old familiar spark inside of her seemed a bit less bright.

Although he was hesitant to do so, Harry decided one evening to bring up Henry's death in front of Jo, and to tell her how much he too suffered from the loss. "I don't know that there is any person on earth I was closer to."

Walter put his arm around Jo, whose tears welled up and rolled onto her cheeks. "I know, Harry. The Dietrichsons, sadly, know of these things all too well."

"To be so far away, to be so helpless, to be of no use to anybody . . . I just felt so frustrated."

Jo gathered herself and tried to offer some comfort to Harry. "He felt the same about you. You were the first person he spoke of every day when he woke up. He'd point to the map and say, 'I wonder where Harry is now.' Every scrap of metal he saved or scavenged. Every food drive he was in. He was thinking of helping you, Harry. Not the war effort, but *you*."

Harry stared into the distance. "I just can't believe he's gone. And Swede, and Chap."

"Those were your friends who you mentioned were killed?" Walter asked.

"Yes. We'd been together since the beginning. Swede's folks live up in the Panhandle. I'm going to visit them." Harry sighed. "They were my brothers. Just as Henry was my brother."

Jo wiped the tears from her cheeks and sat up. "Harry, we so appreciated the note you sent while you were in the hospital. We want you to know that however awkward you may have felt under our roof it was not your fault. Please, don't blame yourself. We love you and have loved you unconditionally. Nothing has ever changed about that, and it never will."

"She speaks for both of us, Harry," Walter said.

"Well, I haven't been much support for you two. And I've had such hard luck with the people I've been close with, the ones I've been fond of. I don't think you two should particularly want to be associated with me."

Jo put her hand on Harry's knee. "Harry, you needn't feel guilty about anything. Don't think you haven't been loved or that you don't deserve love. You need to forgive yourself. Your parents, your grandmother, Henry, your friends in the war. They all lived richer lives because you were a part of them. Please try to understand that."

"Thanks, Aunt Jo. I'll try to keep that in mind."

"You can't carry this burden of guilt around all your life, Harry. Because one day it will catch up. And we don't want anything to happen to you."

A week after he arrived in Houston, Harry received a telegram with orders from the War Department. He was to report to Quantico, Virginia, by March 1 to be an instructor in an officer's training course. He had expected this assignment, but he was ambivalent about going to Virginia. On the one hand, he would be kept from combat for the time being. He would also see Frenchy, who was stationed there. On the other hand, he would be half a world away from China and from Viktoria, assuming she was even still alive.

One day as Harry sat in his room with Paul and Popeye, listening to music on the radio, Jolyn came in and showed him the photo of Viktoria that he had sent to her. "Is this the gal you were in love with, Harry? Her name is Viktoria, right?"

Harry took the photo and looked at it. He nodded. "I still am . . . in love. But I want you to keep it for me."

"You don't want it?"

"I'll take it back for keeps when this is all over. I'm going to try to get back to her again."

"Where is she?"

"I'm not sure. But I think she's still in China."

"She's pretty."

He handed the photo back to Jolyn. "She's a lot more than that."

He went to his bedside drawer and pulled out an envelope. It was the letter he had penned on board the hospital ship. "You hang onto this letter too, please. If I don't get back after the war, you can open it and you'll know everything about her. If you can, try to find her and get it to her. Will you promise me that?"

"I promise, Harry. But I know you'll come back."

"I just hope she still cares for me."

"What do you mean? Of course, she does."

"I've changed a lot, Jolyn, in these past three years. I've seen things, done things . . ."

"Harry, she's nuts about you. I'm sure. How could anyone *not* be?"

"Well, just in case. You keep those for me."

Harry thought about Ellen and dreaded meeting with her. He knew he owed it to her to give her the truth. One day, more than a week after he arrived, he picked up the phone and called Ellen's parents' house. Ellen wasn't there, but he spoke with her mother, Joyce. She said she'd heard Harry was back and asked if he was feeling well after his stay in the hospital. She told Harry that Ellen would phone him when she returned. The next morning Ellen phoned Harry. They did not speak long, and Harry could sense disappointment in her voice. They agreed to meet that very afternoon at the Avalon drugstore.

Harry arrived first and secured one of the small two-seat booths along the plate-glass windows in the front of the diner. He wore a gray wool jacket that he had borrowed from Walter, along with a black and red tie. Ellen arrived a few minutes later, wearing a bright blue dress and a gold-colored tam o'shanter. Her bright red lipstick set the colors apart well. She wore her auburn hair bobbed, and she swept it back to allow for the tam.

He stood and hugged her. "You look marvelous, Ellen. I can't believe it's been almost three years, right?"

"Yes." They sat down, and she pulled off her tam and smoothed her hair. She looked at him coolly.

"Ellen, I'm sorry I didn't call earlier."

"No, Harry, I didn't expect anything—I mean, it's fine." Just then a waitress appeared with menus. Ellen said tersely, "I'm just having coffee, please."

"Two coffees."

"Harry, I don't know what I was thinking all along. I mean, when I saw you before you shipped out. After the divorce from Bill, you know, I thought I needed someone." She paused as the waitress set down two cups of coffee.

She continued. "I thought I loved you, but maybe I was more in love with the idea of a person, of a man. What I wrote in that last letter . . . I poured everything out to you. It was genuine, but when I noticed the distance in your letters, I wasn't sure."

Harry started to say something, but she held up her hand. "Wait, Harry, let me finish, because if I stop now, I might not be able to begin again." She pulled out a white handkerchief from her purse and dabbed her eyes. She put it back down and started again. "I was crushed when I found out you were in town and hadn't called. We heard that you were back last week. I wanted to call you, but I waited for you to call me first. When you didn't call, I figured that you didn't want to see me and that you didn't really love me. Then as I thought about it, I asked myself: *Do I love Harry or the idea that he represents?*"

She took a sip of her coffee and took a deep breath. Harry waited for her to begin again. She pulled out a packet of Raleigh cigarettes and lit one with a match. She offered one to Harry, and he shook his head. She blew out a stream of smoke and began slowly, pausing at the end of each sentence.

"When you didn't open up to me in your letters, I chalked it up to the war. I just figured that you were so preoccupied with staying alive you couldn't be bothered with a silly romance." She shifted in the booth. "We knew you boys were having a rugged time overseas. I tried not to hope too much. I . . . I tried to put you out of my mind. And I did for a while, so the disappointment faded. Then, when you didn't call last week, I was…disappointed all over again."

Harry started to say something. She held up her hand again. "Don't worry. I don't need an explanation, Harry. We're both adults. We've seen the world for what it is."

"Ellen, I didn't mean to hurt you. You see, I'm terribly fond of you. But all the time we were together, even though I thought I loved you, I was in love with someone else."

"Were you seeing someone before the war?"

Harry nodded and looked down into his coffee cup.

"I always suspected there was a story."

Harry leaned back in the booth and scratched his forehead. "Yes, I fell in love with a woman in Shanghai." He went on to tell her about Viktoria. He described how they met, their romance, and his desire to marry her. Her family was opposed, but initially she was prepared to leave with him. Then it all changed suddenly, and she left him at the altar, so to speak. At first he was angry with her, and that's when he returned and had the affair with Ellen. But his mind kept going back to Viktoria.

"If I could just be reassured that she's okay. If I could just see her one time, then maybe I could put this all behind me. When you and I were together in the beginning, I tried to forget her." He looked down at the table and moved his coffee cup around a bit on the saucer. "But until I do actually see her again, I can't put anything behind me."

"I understand. She sounds like a lovely girl."

"I know it's so inconsequential, given what's happening around the rest of the world right now. But I've just gotta find her, Ellen. I want to know that she's alright. That's all. And you know the funny thing? After what I've been through, what I've seen, I completely understand her decision now. I understand why she chose her family over me."

"Really? How so?"

"When I shipped out overseas, I found a new family. I had brothers, and we all gave ourselves to one another emotionally and without question. Then as I started losing them, I recognized how important family was. I forgave Viktoria. I've lost so many people close to me; I've had put up this defensive shield. But now that I've started to mend my fences here, with my family, I'm determined to find her."

They spoke for a while longer, the conversation growing easier and more familiar.

When it was time to leave, they stood and Harry held Ellen's coat out for her to slide on. Outside the drugstore, Harry walked her to the bus stop. While they waited, they chatted about other people they knew. When the bus arrived, Ellen put her gloved hand on his cheek and said, "Harry, I want to see you back here soon, safe and sound."

"I promise."

"Maybe I'll get to meet Viktoria one day." She turned and climbed on board the bus.

He waved as the bus drove off. He continued watching the bus, even after he could no longer see Ellen's golden tam in the crowd of passengers.

Chapter Thirty

February 1, 1945

Dearest Harry,

I write to you again on a dreary winter day in Shanghai. It seems that ten years have passed since my note to you at Christmas. So much has happened over the past month, I don't know where to begin. Although we survived the cholera epidemic, we continue to struggle to simply live. We've had to rely on the generosity of others for the first time in our lives. It is not something that comes easily to the Savin family, but such is the plight we find ourselves in.

I have been unable to visit Tanya for a variety of reasons. Mainly it's because the household can't do without me for a single day. I have grown more and more into the role of the family matriarch, for better or for worse. Aunty Masha has aged considerably and become so forgetful, so I had to step in. And who else is there but me? Although I should take pride in my new role, I find it onerous and stressful, given all the reasons for it.

Anyway, if you can understand our situation, then you can understand how we have come to this, and how I have been forced into certain things out of necessity. Sometimes I wonder whether I will ever see you again. But perhaps this is for the best. For three and a half years I have dreamt about you returning, but now I wonder whether you may have met someone else, or maybe you have completely forgotten about me.

Perhaps I am being pessimistic, but I recognize the need to understand my situation realistically. But please know that whatever happens, I love you deeply, Harry. The thought of you keeps me going. I pray for a reunion soon. This war can't go on forever. Until then, I dream of you, and cherish the thought of the day we encounter one another again.

All my love,
Viktoria

The decline of the Savins' eminence had been coming for some time, but its actualization seemed sudden. But it was more than just the decline in the mental state of both Grigorii and Maria. The Chinese collaboration government had finally taken the Savin tea warehouse. Apart from Viktoria's aunt and uncle in Japan, the family had no active source of income.

It was around that time that Samuel Gu took up an ever-increasing presence in their lives. It was rumored that he had deep connections with Japanese authorities. To say that he was a collaborator would not be mistaken, but like Grigorii Savin, Gu was first and foremost an opportunist who had an innate understanding of where the politics were going. Viktoria would witness that for herself over the course of the next few months.

Gu was very cultured and spoke more languages than anyone in the Savin household, including English, French, German, Chinese, and Japanese. He wore suits tailored on Saville Row in London, preferred French cologne, and smoked American cigarettes from an ivory holder. He could quote Balzac and Dickens as easily as Lao Tze and Confucius, and he loved classical music. He had been a business associate of Grigorii Savin for more than a decade, but only since the occupation of Shanghai had Gu become a more permanent fixture in their lives. Savin and Gu saw in each other a kindred spirit; they had both been reared in torn societies where chaos bred opportunity. They each knew how to take advantage, and they shared a genuine mutual affection. Gu also worked with Viktoria's Uncle Alexei in Japan, and when he visited Kobe, he was a frequent guest in their home.

Gu dealt in tea, silk, ivory, antique home furnishings, and other luxury items. Of course, he also dealt in guns and—it was rumored—in opium. Like the British before them, the Japanese had taken over the opium trade in coastal China, and it was one of the largest cash cows for the occupiers. Through his Japanese connections, Gu profited immensely from the opium trade. Although he abstained from smoking opium himself, he helped facilitate its distribution among the wealthier and older Chinese families around Shanghai. Grigorii Savin was not involved in the opium trade, but he clung tightly to their relationship through the war because Gu could provide sustenance to him and his family during these lean times.

As he spent more time around the family—at first out of brotherly affection for Grigorii—Gu's attraction to Viktoria was hard not to notice. Throughout the fall and winter of 1944, Gu paid more and more attention to Viktoria, and whenever he was a guest at the household, she was the first and last person he spoke with. Although her Aunt Maria was put off by this behavior, Viktoria could not help but be flattered by this sophisticated, erudite man's attentiveness. Gu also began to bring Viktoria gifts. At first, he brought her flowers, then small things like figurines, candies, or records. Soon he offered her perfume and jewelry. She tried to refuse the valuable gifts, but he wouldn't hear of it. She would put the gifts away, hardly ever looking at them again. Gu was attentive to little Henry too, and he playfully engaged with him when he visited the house. Most of all, Gu knew that the way into the hearts of the Savins was through their stomachs. He brought them such foods as fresh fish or fowl, and even milk on several occasions—a true treat for Westerners in Shanghai, even before the war.

Grigorii Savin was nonplussed by the attention Gu was paying to his niece, but under the circumstances, he chose to remain silent about the matter. After all, given Viktoria's situation, this might not be the worst thing. Grigorii understood he was no longer in control of his own fate. The family had become dependent on Gu, and Grigorii was reluctant to bite the hand feeding them. Viktoria, likewise, kept the needs of the children in mind at all times. Whatever she could do to sustain Henry, she was willing to do. As a consequence, she did nothing to dissuade Gu's attentions.

By early 1945, as she began to lose all hope of ever seeing Harry again, Viktoria yielded to Gu's courting and they became lovers. Their first intimate encounter happened at his house in the French Concession, after a candlelit dinner. Viktoria was lightheaded from the French wine he served, and although she did not discourage him initially, she resisted when he forced himself onto her. Eventually she relented. Afterward, Gu tried to be playful with her, but her shame and anger were too much. She dressed and insisted on going home. After Gu's driver took her back to the house, she silently went upstairs and soaked in a half-filled tub of tepid water. For a moment she wished she could drown herself. But thoughts of Henry asleep down the hallway dispelled all such ideation.

Viktoria was upset at her fallibility, and she cried for hours the next day in her room. When she saw the hungry faces of her cousins and her own child, Viktoria thought of herself as one and the same with the hundreds of fallen White Russian countesses or baronesses in exile who had to resort to selling their bodies to survive. Over the next few months she fell easily into the affair with Gu. Desperation had pushed her to that point, and she made a promise not to torture herself with unhappiness, because, after all, she was doing this for her family and for the children. Gu was not unkind to her and he continued his charm offensive. She thought of Harry, and she knew how disappointed he would be. But now she had to think of her family, just as she had done when she refused to leave with him. She felt so alone.

To help offset her dark mood, Viktoria decided to accompany her aunt the next time she visited Tatiana at the internment camp. It was still dangerous to go out, especially for a young woman, but she was determined to see Tanya.

That next opportunity came on a cold, blustery day in late February. Viktoria left Henry at the house with his cousins and joined Maria on her visit to the Lunghua Civilian Assembly Centre, located near an airfield southwest of the city. They took a bundle of canned food, candles, soap, and boiled water—all of which they knew Tanya would share with her closest friends. Most of the internees—women, children, and some elderly men—were British, but there was a smattering of non-British internees, like Tanya.

Maria and Viktoria boarded a coal-fired bus early that morning and set out for Lunghua. Although the camp was only ten miles from Shanghai, the journey was long and laborious. The bus was crammed with Chinese passengers and even some fowl. The seats were wooden and uncomfortable. Soot came in through broken windows, leaving a fine coat of black coal dust everywhere in the freezing interior. They had to wait almost two hours when they changed buses. The Chinese passengers around them eyed Maria and Viktoria suspiciously, but they kept their distance. Never once did the two women feel threatened, but they remained wary.

They arrived at the camp around noon. The area was desolate and dusty, and no trees were visible for miles. The flat plain stretched out to the south and west, where, in the far distance, they could make out low purple mountains. A cold winter wind blew down from them. The barracks were once part of a school. A Japanese Army airfield lay two kilometers away and had been bombed on several occasions, according to Tanya. The bombings had frightened the internees at first, but then they realized this was an indication that the war was going well for the Allies. Maria was a regular visitor, so she knew the routine well. The routine included a "gift" for the camp commandant. Generally, the Japanese were satisfied with food or spirits, but recently the sums had grown more exorbitant. Today she offered cotton linens to the commandant.

The front gate at the prison led into a smaller pen that was sealed off from the rest of the camp. It was here that internees were allowed to receive visitors. The entire camp awaited the visits of Maria because she was the only non-Asian to come. All the other visitors were either Japanese or Chinese somehow connected to British subjects from before the war.

When the small door in the center of the gate was opened and Tanya saw Viktoria for the first time in two years, she burst into tears and fell to her knees. She was thin, and her complexion was gray. But her large eyes were still luminescent.

Viktoria took Tanya's hand and lifted her off her knees. They hugged one another in a deep embrace. Viktoria uttered soothing words in a whisper. "My dearest Tanya. My kitten. How I missed you! How lonely I am without you." Tanya cried and was unable to say anything at first. Maria joined them and stroked her daughter's hair lovingly. After several minutes, they walked over to sit on the few stools that stood in the corner of the pen. Once Tanya had composed herself, they began talking. They asked each other about general conditions. They also discussed the rumors of war. After about a half hour, Maria took out the goods she had brought with her, explaining what each one was. The last thing she produced was a large piece of ginseng root that they had gotten, naturally, from Gu.

"Make sure you use this with hot water, water that has been boiled. It will cure many ailments," she instructed her daughter tenderly, as only a mother could.

"Thank you, Mama. This will go a long way." Tanya then turned to Viktoria. "How is my darling Henry?" She let out a raspy cough.

"He's fine. All boy. So full of energy, it's hard keeping up with him sometimes." She smiled and took Tanya's hand. Viktoria started to say something else, and then her voice dropped off. She thought of Gu and was ashamed.

"Well, I can't wait to see him. Is he the spitting image of his father?"

Viktoria shrugged. "I suppose." Tears came to her eyes. "You know, it's been so long since Harry left, I'm starting to forget what he looks like."

Maria and Tanya both protested. "No!"

"Look at your son, and you will see his father," Maria said.

"Yes, I know, Aunty Masha. It's the thought that we may never see him again that makes me sad. That Henry may never know his father."

Again, Maria and Tanya both protested.

"Well, even if Harry comes back, I'm not worthy of him."

Tanya looked at Viktoria and said harshly, "Vika! Don't be ridiculous, you are the mother of his child!"

"It's just that . . ." Viktoria couldn't finish the sentence. Maria looked down at the ground.

Tanya looked between the two of them questioningly.

Viktoria said, "I've done things that I'm not proud of, dear sister, and that I know Harry could never forgive me for."

Tanya looked at her mother. Maria shook her head and whispered, "Poor child."

Tanya took Viktoria's hands and said, "Vika, dear, whatever you have done, God will forgive you."

"God may forgive me, but Harry could never forgive me. And one day, when Henry is grown, neither will he."

Tanya, sensing the plight her cousin was in, guessed the nature of her torment. "Have you taken a lover?"

Viktoria nodded through tears. "I'm so ashamed."

"Well, don't be, especially if he's providing for you and the boy. We all put ourselves into demeaning positions. It happens in the camp here all the time. You have a child to feed and a family to support."

"That's no excuse."

Tanya looked through the gate into the camp, where people idled and huddled in groups. "I would give anything to have the dilemma you have right now, Vika. We are all dying a slow death here." She coughed and gripped Viktoria's hands firmly. "Look at me. I'm wasting away. I have no choices, no options. Survive or die. It is out of my hands. But *you*, dear, have choices. You must do what you need to do for Henry, and for yourself. You are still young. You can make it through. And I'm sure this will be over soon. And when it is, you make sure that you and Henry are alive. You will find Harry again. I know it." She shook Viktoria's hands for emphasis at the end of her admonishment.

"You were always so much stronger than me."

"Well, now it's time for you to be stronger than me."

"Bless you, my daughter. I could not have said it better," said Maria. "Henry has become the center of our lives. We all live to see him raised properly in spirit and in body. *His* life is what is important. Yes, we make sacrifices, but they are necessary. Vika has done what she has needed to do to support him and all of us. She has been so brave." Maria smiled and stroked Viktoria's hair.

They all cried for a bit and then tried to cheer one another up. Tanya repeated her prediction. "The war will be over soon. You can tell the Japanese are defeated. You see it in the way they walk, in the way they talk, and in their eyes. It's only a matter of time. Dig deep and find the energy to make it through to the end."

Maria and Viktoria stood to take their leave. They each hugged Tanya in turn. Tanya looked at Viktoria and said in French, "*Courage.*"

Maria and Viktoria passed through the gates, turning to catch a last glimpse of Tanya. She stood with the bag of goods. She didn't wave, and she didn't call. But Viktoria saw a look of defiance in her eyes. She knew that Tanya would be alright.

上海

Chapter Thirty-One

In early February Harry phoned the Swanson household to introduce himself and say he would like to pay a visit to the ranch. Swede's father answered the phone. "It's mighty kind of you to offer to come here, son, but you should spend as much time with your family as you can before you ship off again."

Although he sensed bitterness in the man's voice, Harry insisted.

"Mr. Swanson, I understand your reluctance to see me, but Billy told me just before he died that he wanted me to visit you and the place where he grew up. I made him a promise that I would."

After a pause Mr. Swanson asked Harry if he liked to hunt. Harry answered that he did. "Well, then, come on out, son. The family and I look forward to making your acquaintance." He told Harry where to catch the bus in Stamford for the ranch and that he would alert his foreman to be on the lookout for him at the entrance when he arrived on the tenth.

The bus trip to Abilene from Houston took almost eight hours. At the end of the long day, Harry overnighted in a small roadhouse, near the bus station.

The trip north to Stamford the next day revealed a barren landscape, punctuated only by occasional farmhouses and barns. When he started to see large herds of cattle out of the bus window, Harry knew he was close to the Swanson ranch, one of the largest in all of Texas. Forty minutes from Stamford, the driver stopped the bus and motioned for Harry to come forward. The other passengers looked up at Harry as he ambled down the aisle with his seabag. The driver pointed to a large metal gate on the side of the road. Harry thanked him and got off the bus. Just inside the gate—which was flanked by two stone pillars, each with the emblem of the Swanson branding iron—was a battered Ford pickup truck. A man in a cowboy hat got out of the cab and came toward Harry. He opened the gate and greeted him.

"Captain Dietrichson?"

"Yes, sir, that's me." Harry extended his hand and introduced himself.

The man took his hand with a strong, firm grip. "Bill Palmer. I'm the foreman for this ranch." Palmer's wiry, thin body looked as hard as a washboard. He couldn't have been more than forty-five years old, but he had prematurely wrinkled eyes as all cowboys do. "Hop in. I'll take you up to the main house."

Harry threw his seabag in the bed of the old truck and climbed into the cab. When Palmer climbed in next to him, Harry said, "I hope you didn't have to wait long."

Palmer shook his head. "We know what time the bus swings by. Only comes two times a day. I figured I'd just ride over each time and you'd be there one of them."

The inside of the truck smelled of mesquite and sage. Palmer reached up to the steering column and put the truck in gear, and they drove off down the caliche road. They were silent for the first couple of minutes as the gravel crunched beneath them. Then Palmer started talking, never taking his eyes off the road. "This here section—the main section—is just under a hundred and fifty thousand acres. I've been foreman here since my daddy died, about ten years ago. He was the main foreman before me, so I grew up here on the ranch. My granddaddy come over from Sweden to work for Magnus Swanson about seventy years ago, after the war between the states."

"That's quite a spread."

"Well, we've got other foremen and lots of cowpokes out here. I got two sons helping me out. Another one of 'em is in the Navy, somewhere out in the South Pacific, where Billy and Charley are at." He looked sideways at Harry and then quickly corrected himself. "I mean, where they were fighting."

Harry could tell Palmer felt awkward about the mistake, so he continued the conversation to make him feel more at ease. "Your son on a destroyer?"

"A cruiser. Last letter we got was from Hawaii around Christmas."

"Well, Godspeed to your boy."

After fifteen minutes they came to a slight rise in the landscape. On the other side of the rise was a copse of large oak trees. The ranch house stood among the trees. It was two-story limestone, with a tin roof—modest for such a large ranch. A pack of dogs ambled about in front of the house.

As they climbed out of the truck, a tall, broad-chested man in a gray cowboy hat emerged from the house onto the front steps. His face was weathered just like Palmer's, and the hair sticking out from under his hat was white. He had a pipe in his mouth. Harry immediately noticed the similarity between the man and his deceased son.

At the top of the stone steps Harry extended his hand and said, "Thanks for having me, Mr. Swanson. I'm very glad to meet you."

Swanson took his hand, and Harry noticed his grip was surprisingly soft, though the hands were callused. "You're welcome, Captain."

"Please call me Harry."

Swanson furrowed his brows and said, "I remember Billy calling you Dutch in his letters."

"You may call me Dutch, or Harry. No need to call me Captain."

"Well, son, come on in, get your things settled, and wash up."

Inside, the ornate furnishings belied the spartan exterior of the house. It was also larger than it appeared from outside. Every room was furnished with leather chairs and sofas, gilded mirrors, great landscape paintings, and massive wooden desks and tables. In the great room—the first room in the house—stuffed animal heads lined the wall. Mule deer, boar, antelope, longhorns, and even one bison. Swanson took Harry into the kitchen first, to meet Mrs. Swanson, a fair, buxom woman who looked at least twenty years older than Aunt Jo. She hardly said a word at their introduction other than simply, "Welcome, Mr. Dietrichson."

"We've already had our noonday meal; we eat early here. But my wife is happy to fix something up for you if you're hungry."

"No, thank you, sir."

Swanson took Harry to the guest room, on the second floor. On the way down the hallway, he pointed to Swede's room and said, "There's Billy's room." Harry saw photos hanging above the dresser, and in one corner a rifle leaned against the wall. He remembered Swede telling him how many deer, coyotes, and javelinas he had shot with that thirty-thirty rifle.

The elder Swanson excused himself after showing Harry to the guest room. It was fitted out with a large four-poster bed. In the corner was a washbasin on a stand. When Swanson left him, Harry poured water from a jug into the basin and splashed some on his face. He rubbed his eyes with a towel. He unpacked and waited a bit, sitting on the edge of the bed. He wanted to go into Swede's room but felt he should ask first.

Refreshed, Harry went downstairs and joined Bill Palmer, who had offered to show him around the vast and remarkable property. Stone Indian towers from the days of raiding Comanche were among the various landmarks, and the winter wheat fields used for cattle feed were among the farmed parcels. The sky was slate gray. Another cold front was blowing down off the plains. Since the old Ford had no heat, they spread a blanket across their laps. They didn't get out much except to stop and open gates. Harry enjoyed the peace and solemnity of the void land. Palmer brought them back to the house around five. Harry went to his room and lay down on the bed. When he closed his eyes, he saw Swede's bearded, tired visage from that rainy night on Gloucester.

Harry knew that since Swede's death, all the thoughts and prayers of the Swanson family would be focused on the middle son, Charley, who was stationed at an airbase somewhere in the South Pacific, flying P-38 fighters. Harry knew that the air campaign—though clean—was equally rough. At this point in the war, U.S. planes dominated the skies, but planes went down for reasons other than enemy fire, such as mechanical failures, weather, and pilot errors resulting from fatigue or bad navigation. Flying long distances over an ocean was dangerous. Harry dozed off for a few minutes. He was soon awakened by the supper bell.

Harry walked down the hallway to the staircase and followed it down to the great room, where Swanson was waiting.

"You got an appetite, son?"

"Yes, sir, I do."

"Good. Let's go on into the dining room." Harry followed him across the great room to a swinging door. As he walked in, Swanson removed his hat and said somewhat apologetically, "We don't do too big a spread for supper."

In the dining room the women were already seated, while the men stood by their places. Swede's mother was on the left side of the table near the head. The youngest son, Alfie, was standing to the right of his mother. Billy had told Harry about Alfred—"Alfie"—who was now sixteen and eager to join the fighting. Seated next to him was an attractive young woman who had golden hair and light-blue eyes. On the right side of the table stood two boys, each younger than Alfie, and a man who looked to be in his thirties. The family resemblance among them all was strong.

"Everybody, this is Billy's friend from the Marine Corps, Captain Dutch Dietrichson, but he'd prefer we call him Harry. Harry," he continued, pointing to everyone at the table, "this is our family." Each of the males came forward, shook Harry's hand, and introduced himself. The young man on the right side, Johnny, was the son of Mr. Swanson's older brother, who had had no interest in ranching, and had become a doctor. Harry remembered Swede explaining that his father, though the second son, became the family patriarch and the overseer of the ranch. The doctor's son had returned to the ranch to work and help run it. His wife, Elsie—the pretty blond woman—was the mother of the two boys sitting next to their father. After the introductions, the men all took their seats. Mr. Swanson said grace and then they began passing platters around.

The supper was a huge feast. Fresh veal cutlets, sweetbreads, beef hearts, stuffed quail, grilled peppers, platters of roasted vegetables, hot biscuits, wine, mincemeat pie, and hot coffee. Harry had never tasted sweetbreads nor had he tried beef heart. Each was an acquired taste, but he took some anyway. The veal and the stuffed quail were the best he had ever eaten. The vegetables came from a greenhouse on the ranch. Harry noticed that neither of the elder Swansons took wine, though Johnny and Elsie each had a glass. The other family members drank buttermilk.

The conversation was muted during the first part of the meal. There was no idle talk. Swede had told Harry that his family was a stoic bunch. Mrs. Swanson hardly glanced at Harry. Finally, Elsie broke the ice and asked about Harry's trip up, and then about his family in Houston and what he had done before the war. Harry told them that he was born in Pennsylvania and had been orphaned when he was young. He noticed that they all sat up a little bit upon hearing this. Mrs. Swanson took an interest for the first time and asked Harry about his uncle and aunt, and whether he had any siblings. He specifically avoided mentioning Japan, as he figured it would be a sore topic. But he told them about Shanghai. Johnny, Elsie, and Alfie were enthralled as Harry told them stories of that exotic city. They asked about the food, the lifestyle, and the culture. Harry told them of the churches, schools, clubs, racetrack, and grand homes. They were surprised to hear that it was practically a European city located on the East Asian seaboard.

The elder Swanson took it all in silently. As they tucked into the dessert pie, he finally spoke up. "Well, Harry, it sounds like you've seen your fair share of the world. Billy told us you were an interesting fellow. And I suppose it makes sense—given your time in China—that you'd travel ten thousand miles to fight the Japanese. But I never saw no sense in neither Billy nor Charley going all that way." The rest of the family stayed silent, looking down at their plates. He cleared his throat and then continued. "I figured with the demand for beef around the world now, both Billy and Charley could have served their country by helping run this ranch—given all the food shortages."

Alfie spoke up through a mouthful of pie. "Yeah, but Pa, they didn't want to stay on the ranch while everyone else was doing the fightin'. That's why I wanna go too."

Mrs. Swanson scolded him. "You're too young, Alfie."

Swanson looked at his son thoughtfully for a moment and then turned to Harry. "But I have to ask: Is it worth it? Is it worth having American boys go off and get killed? I know everyone says we're doing this so that there won't be another one, but there'll always be another one."

Harry took a sip of water, put his glass down, and started in on his answer. "Well, sir, I figure that for some people it's worth it, and for others, maybe not so much. But there is one thing we all have to remember: the Japanese attacked us. The Nazis attacked England and France and declared war on us. If those madmen win over there, it's just a matter of time before they attack us here. Hitler has rockets and planes that fly by jet propulsion. Better to fight them there than here." He paused and sipped his water again. "I know all the fellows that I serve with would rather be doing the fighting overseas than here on the home front."

Swanson nodded and said, "You make some good points."

Harry went on. "As for the sacrifice . . . yes, it makes me miserable to think about all the fellows who won't be coming back. But I can assure you that if all those guys were here at this table right now—like Billy or his CO, Babe Babashanian, or my CO, Dave Chappellet, or even Charley—they'd all say, 'Yeah, it *is* worth it.' They're fighting for each other, and I can't think of one time that I heard anyone question the necessity of the war. Everyone to a man knows it *is* worth it."

There was a silence as everyone digested what Harry had said. Then Mrs. Swanson cleared her throat. "Thank you for telling us how the boys feel, Harry."

Elsie nodded her agreement. "Yes, Harry, thank you."

After they finished their dessert, Swanson told Harry, "Johnny and Alfie will take you out deer hunting early tomorrow morning. I think Billy would've liked it if you use his thirty-thirty."

"Thank you, sir."

Harry joined the men in the great room for coffee and whiskey. Johnny proposed a game of cribbage, and they began to play. They spoke into the night about hunting, fishing, and ranching. They all felt at ease discussing the outdoor life of Texas.

Before he went to his room, Harry walked into Swede's. He ran his hands along the desk where Swede had carved his initials and those of past sweethearts. He looked at the photos on the wall. Most of them were taken at the ranch. Swede was on horseback in one, roping a calf in another. The photo above the bed showed Swede when he was at the university in Austin. He was with a group of co-eds at a football game, wearing a raccoon jacket and a straw skimmer. It made Harry smile. Suddenly the realization that he'd never see his friend again made him sad.

The next morning Alfie woke Harry at five o'clock. There was hot coffee with biscuits and sausage waiting for them downstairs. They took coffee, but nobody was hungry, so Johnny wrapped up some sausage biscuits in a handkerchief. They walked outside into the frosty morning. Harry wore a thick hunting cap to protect his ears, but his nose was freezing. Each breath seemed like a dagger of ice in his chest. The men sat in the cab of an old Dodge truck and shivered as they drove.

Located in the forked limbs of a large oak tree, the deer blind was just a plain wooden box covered with a corrugated tin roof. They clambered up the rickety wooden ladder. Inside the blind, they kneeled on the floor and set down their rifles. In the front was a wide opening that looked down at the center of the draw. Many people liked to bait the draws with salt licks or dried corn pellets, but the Swansons relied on the natural shelter of the arroyo to draw game in. They positioned two stools at the window. Harry had Swede's thirty-thirty. Alfie carried a .243 with a scope.

It was still dark when they took their positions, and they sat there quietly waiting—hoping—for the sun to rise quickly. Johnny had brought along two thermoses of coffee, and they took turns pouring coffee into small cups and drinking it to keep out the cold. Harry could hardly feel his toes, though he wore two pairs of woolen socks under his boots. His legs were also freezing, but his torso and hands were fine under the wool-lined jacket and thick gloves. Johnny and Alfie wore felt cowboy hats on their heads, leaving their ears exposed. They were accustomed to the cold after years of living and working on the ranch.

The sun would not rise until well past seven o'clock, but by six the draw was clearly visible in the gray dawn. The first thing they noticed among the brush was a covey of quail. After the quail had passed through, there was a quiet period. A few rabbits appeared and then moved on. Small birds fed in the draw, chirping occasionally. At one point, Johnny raised his hand. He pointed to the left. Harry couldn't see anything. Alfie put his head next to Harry's and pointed forward. Harry could see the movement of ghostly gray forms. There were six white-tailed deer. The largest was a buck, sporting a modest spread of eight points on its antlers.

Harry turned and pointed to Alfie. Johnny raised his hand and deliberately waved his index finger in a chiding motion, and then pointed at Harry's chest. Harry nodded, took off his gloves, and then moved forward onto the edge of his stool and leveled the thirty-thirty through the opening of the blind. He took a deep breath and sighted the deer over the barrel of his rifle. He had difficulty holding it steady in the freezing cold, but he waited a while, hoping that the buck would move closer toward the blind. It did. It was now within fifty yards. As soon as the buck turned to present a profile, Harry exhaled and squeezed the trigger, aiming for the neck. The gun roared and shattered the idyllic early morning peace of the arroyo. Birds flew in all directions, and the deer scattered. Through the smoke, Harry saw the buck stagger and then run into the undergrowth, disappearing into the morning frost.

"Great shot!" Johnny said. "He won't go far."

They climbed down from the blind, found the blood trail, and followed it. The deer had run only fifty yards before collapsing at the base of a mesquite tree. It lay there panting, its tongue curled out of its mouth along with frothy blood. The bullet had gone in just below the base of the neck. As the buck lay there on the ground, gasping for breath, Harry closed his eyes and had a vision of the Japanese man he had shot through the neck on Peleliu, rolling on the jungle floor, grabbing at his throat, trying to breathe.

Alfie leaned down and produced a sharp hunting knife. He calmly slit the deer's throat, and the steaming blood flowed out onto the hard ground. The life drained out of the deer's eyes, and they grew glassy and white. Harry suddenly became sad. He was sad to have killed the buck, and he was sad to have killed men. Men with families. Men with children. He had seen so much killing that he had almost become inured to it on the battlefields. Now that he had seen bloodletting again in a peaceful setting, he was full of remorse.

Alfie and Johnny expertly cleaned and dressed the deer and then loaded the carcass into the bed of the truck. As they drove back, they sat silently, as if concentrating on keeping the cold out. Alfie fidgeted, however, and finally spoke what was on his mind. Without turning his head, he asked, "Harry, how did he die?"

Harry looked straight ahead through the windshield, gathering himself. "He went the way any person would wanna go: his amtrac took a direct hit from a Japanese shell. It happened the first morning we landed on Peleliu. He died instantly." He then looked at Alfie and said, "I know they all say that, I mean . . . when a man gets killed. It's a cliché they're supposed to tell every family. 'He died not knowing.' But in your brother's case, that's the honest to god truth. Our corpsman—that's a medic—he saw it happen."

Alfie nodded, and said, "Thanks, Harry."

"He was a good friend. I miss him."

"Billy was younger than me," Johnny said. "But when we were kids, we were close. We spent hours together out on the ranch: ridin', huntin', and just wanderin'. He had a great sense of humor."

"He spoke about you, Johnny. He told me about the time you two were dressing a deer and a cougar chased you up an oak tree."

Johnny laughed. "Yeah, we left our bullets in the cab of the truck. That big cat must have been hungry to go after us like that."

"And Alfie, he talked about how good of a rancher you are, and how he felt one day you'd take over this entire ranch and run the Swanson Cattle empire."

"He said *that*? Really?"

"He did. More than once," Harry nodded. "I only wish I had known him longer. In those situations—I mean the situations we found ourselves in—you get to know someone real well, real fast. It was a short, intense, and warm friendship. I'll never forget the moments we shared for the rest of my life."

Alfie said in a determined voice, "Boy, I can't wait till I'm eighteen."

"Alfie, enjoy your teenage years."

When Harry left the ranch the next day, the entire family gathered on the front steps of the house to see him off. He promised that he would return when he could. After he had said good-bye to each member of the family, he came to Mrs. Swanson. She hugged Harry tightly. "Billy thought the world of you, Harry, and we know that losing him was also hard on you. You take care of yourself, young man. We'll pray that you and Charley and all the others can come home safely soon so parents like us aren't forced to mourn their children prematurely." When she pulled back, her eyes were brimming with tears.

"Yes, ma'am. I'll be back. I promise."

The last person to speak with Harry was Mr. Swanson. He shook Harry's hand and said, "Son, you can call our home your home anytime."

Harry climbed into the cab of the pickup truck next to Bill Palmer, and they drove off down the caliche road toward the main gate. Harry looked back at the ranch house. The entire family stood on the steps; nobody waved, but they all watched. As the pickup came to a curve in the road, the trees blocked out the view of the house.

Chapter Thirty-Two

Harry's pending departure to Quantico was weighing heavily on the Dietrichson family, as the news of Iwo Jima dominated the headlines across the country. The Marines had lost five thousand men on the first day. Although Harry was headed for Virginia, the war with Japan was expected to go on for at least two more years, culminating in a bloody invasion of the home islands. A need for experienced combat veterans would likely soon press Harry back into the war.

With Walter at work all day and Jolyn at school, Harry spent most of his time with Aunt Jo and Paul. Harry and his toddler cousin soon developed a ritual. With Popeye looking on, Harry would help Paul assemble a wooden train set. By the end of each day, Paul had wrecked it completely. The next morning the two of them would reassemble it. And so it went . . . to Paul's great pleasure.

Harry left on February 27 on an early morning train to Washington, D.C. This time he had no Pullman berth. He sat in an open seating area. He tried to make himself as comfortable as possible, but all the trains were crowded and close to bursting. He got off the train briefly at each of the stops. Harry had never seen the country so prosperous. Apart from the ever-present reminders of men in uniform and war posters, it was hard to tell that the nation was in the midst of a two-front war.

He arrived in Quantico on the evening of March 1. He was dead tired. He needed a shave and a shower, but when he was shown to his quarters, he dumped his seabag on the bare floor and immediately went to look for Frenchy. When they found one another, Frenchy shook Harry's hand and beamed.

"Hullo, Dutch! You're a sight for sore eyes. I sometimes wondered whether I'd see any of you fellows again. Come on, let's go to my quarters. I've got a bottle of whiskey."

Frenchy's room was in the barracks reserved for married officers, though he was alone. He sat down on the bed and motioned for Harry to sit on a chair.

Harry pointed to Frenchy's arm. "How's the arm? Can you use it?'

"Oh, sure." Frenchy poured some whiskey into a glass and handed it to Harry. He lifted up his left arm. "I can hold things, but I can't lift anything heavy, and I can't do anything mechanical with it—you know writing or eating—but it doesn't much matter since I'm a righty. I've gotten used to it anyway. What about you?"

"Took some metal in my chest. Punctured a lung."

"Same thing happened to me. Punctured lung. Had that damn oxygen tube shoved up my nose."

"God, yeah . . . awful. It hurt like hell just to breathe."

"Seems like ages ago." Frenchy shook his head and looked at the floor. He looked up again at Harry. "Rough about Swede, huh?"

"He had a million-dollar leg wound. He was being evacuated back out to the ship and his LVT took a direct hit."

"Goddamn! I had no idea, Dutch."

"I couldn't bring myself to write that to you in the letter. I went to his family's ranch in Texas and met his folks a couple of weeks ago. Good people. I didn't tell them about his leg wound. It would have seemed cruel." Harry took his glass and held it up. "Here's to Swede."

"To our brother, Billy Swanson. May he rest in peace."

After they drank, Harry and Frenchy looked at one another for a few moments, silently pondering the randomness of fate. Harry broke the silence. "Well, at least the third surviving member of the United Nations is alive and well in San Diego."

"What do they have Ozzie doing there?"

"Same as here. Preparing the next group of combat leaders."

"They get younger each year. I guess they're running out of college boys like us."

"You know, Frenchy, you can train a guy till he's a living coiled reaction. Correct in every thought and action. But you can't really *prepare* him. You know what I mean? When you're out there, you just don't . . ." Harry paused and shook his head. "You just can't fathom what it's like.

What you're forced to do on a daily basis."

Frenchy remained silent.

"The experiences you undergo . . . I just don't know if you can teach that to anyone."

"I've been out of it so long, I can hardly remember. Maybe that's for the best."

"You remember that morning when we walked around the spit at Alligator Creek? That smell of corpses?"

"Yeah, sure."

"On Peleliu it was like that every moment. Dead Japs everywhere, all bloated up."

"We heard it was rugged there."

"I was on Peleliu for only three days. We were constantly under fire. I couldn't help my men much. Instead I had to send them off to do terrible jobs and to die." He paused and shook his head. "Every guy's got a breaking point. If I hadn't been wounded in the beginning, Frenchy, I'm not sure I wouldn't have gone off the edge."

Harry ran his fingers through his hair and exhaled. "I'm sorry to be unloading all this on you. I just need to get it off my chest. Nobody can relate unless they've been there and seen it."

"Brother, you can tell me anything you want."

Harry paused for a moment and then went on. "You know, Frenchy, it was all rugged, miserable, and terrifying—in *every* place, in its own way. You remember the feeling that we had about being abandoned on Guadal? The shelling from the Jap ships? The air raids? Being hungry all the time? We kept talking about Wake Island. We were all scared—whether we wanted to admit it or not—about being left behind by the Navy."

"Yeah." Frenchy nodded and sipped his whiskey.

"And on Gloucester, the rain never let up for three months. No hot chow. Everyone caught malaria. We marched and marched and marched and hardly saw any Japs. Then, at random moments, they'd come pouring out of the jungle." Harry shook his head. "And here we are, asked to prepare a bunch of new 'combat leaders.'" He looked into his whiskey glass as if searching for an answer. "The best thing you can teach 'em is to keep their weapons clean and ready to fire. Sometimes that makes all the difference."

"You got that right."

"The more I see, Frenchy, the blacker my heart becomes. Watching friends die, the smell of death—killing people face-to-face. It opens a dark chamber in your soul. I know I'll never be the same again." He downed the contents of his glass.

Frenchy leaned forward with the bottle to refill Harry's glass. "How did Kipling put it? 'God help us, for we knew the worst too young.'"

"'And the measure of our torment is the measure of our youth.'" He looked over at the desk and saw a photograph of a woman holding a baby. "Frenchy, I'm sorry. I've been so self-absorbed that I forgot to congratulate you. How's the baby girl?"

"She's fine, Dutch. She's got a swell mother."

"How old is she now?"

"Thirteen months."

"She's beautiful. What's her name?"

"Pauline."

Harry raised his glass. "Here's to Pauline and her lovely mother."

Frenchy raised his glass and they drank. After a moment, he asked, "What about you, Dutch? No love in your life?"

"Still looking for her. I'll tell you all about it another time," Harry said, not wanting to subject his friend to any more emotion than he already had.

They spoke for a while longer about the officers' course and what Harry could expect. Then they refilled their glasses one last time and toasted absent friends. Harry left for his quarters before midnight. He stripped out of the uniform he had been wearing for two days and took a long shower. When he lay down, he fell off to sleep quickly.

The time in Virginia was monotonous after the intensity of battle. But Harry stayed busy and the training was rigorous; it was good for his body and for his mind.

Starting in mid-March rumors went around that the next target after Iwo Jima would be Formosa or even the Chinese coast. Harry decided it was time to ask about getting back out to the theater. In early April, just after the invasion of Okinawa, he approached an officer in the personnel section. Major Kelly, with his sagging jowls and receding hairline, looked to be well over forty. On his desk was a picture of his wife and three grown children.

The major reviewed Harry's file at length, sighed, and closed the folder. "Captain, don't you think you've seen enough? Bronze Star. Several commendations. Two Purple Hearts. Three battle stars. What else do you want?"

"Sir, I'd like to get back to my regiment, the 5th Marines."

"Captain, all Guadalcanal and Gloucester vets from the First Division have been slotted for home front duty. And you've got the Peleliu landing to boot. These are the orders. You need to help bring the new men along." He looked Harry over dubiously. "Besides, the doctors tell us that men who've seen extensive action are prone to battle fatigue. Surely you discussed that with a doctor in San Diego?"

"Yes, sir. I spoke with a Navy psychiatrist. He told me that a normal man can't be expected to go through more than 240 days of combat. I was wounded early on Peleliu and missed time on Gloucester because of malaria. I'm under the minimum they set. He declared me fit."

"Sure, but will you be 'fit' the next time you get caught in an artillery barrage?" He leaned forward to reach for a pack of cigarettes on his desk. "Listen, Dietrichson, you can submit the paperwork, but I can't promise it'll go through."

"Sir, there is something you won't find in my file. I'm a Japanese linguist. I lived in Tokyo for more than a year before the war. I also spent two years in China. I was a correspondent for United Press."

"But your records indicate nothing about such qualifications."

"I didn't report it, sir, but I can verify all of it."

"I see."

"Sir, I didn't want to spend the war in Washington. I mean, no offense, sir, I—"

"Okay, okay, I understand," Kelly interrupted him. He reopened Harry's file momentarily. "How well—*really*—do you know the language? Because we have plenty of men who speak Japanese now."

"Sir, my intention is not to be an interpreter. I have a friend in battalion intelligence. I was thinking about something like that."

"Is that so?"

Harry continued. "To be frank, sir—I have no great interest in leading a rifle company anymore. But I want to get back out there and help however I can. If it's as a company commander, then so be it. But given my knowledge of Japanese and Japan, I figured I could help. I also would come in handy should we go into China. I can't speak the language, but I know the region and the politics well."

"Sit down, Captain." Major Kelly put away Harry's file and lit a cigarette. He offered one to Harry, who declined. "So you want to get out into the theater, but you don't want to lead a rifle company?"

"Sir, I didn't mean that I wouldn't do it; it's just that I'd prefer another assignment."

Kelly held up his hand. "You don't need to prove anything. Your record says it all. I'm trying to help you." He took a puff of his cigarette and then put it in a beat-up white ceramic ashtray. "Intel positions are easy to get in Washington but not so much out in the field. But that doesn't mean there won't be more popping up as we approach the big one," he said, referring to the invasion of Japan.

"I understand, sir."

"What I suggest you do is get yourself tested for the language. If you do well enough, it will help your cause. It sounds like you don't want to do too well, because you may find yourself translating behind a desk. It might make sense to write up a report about your time in Japan and the Far East: what you did, what you learned about the country and the people. We can send your request through the normal channels, but it'd be best to have the test and your report before we do so. You can do the test here anytime. When you have the spare time, try to write that report. Make it short but punchy." He winked at Harry. "Write it like a correspondent."

"Thank you, Major Kelly."

"We've got plenty of vets to train these guys. I'm more concerned with whether *they*—that is the leadership—are going to be angry that you hid this information. You could have aided the war effort substantially in '42 or '43. Why didn't the skill test they administered catch this when you commissioned?"

"No idea, sir. Maybe I was hungover that day."

Kelly chuckled. "Well, if the aptitude tests didn't show you as language proficient, that's not your fault, is it?" He wrote something down on a slip of paper and handed it to Harry. "Go get tested and come back when you have everything in hand."

Harry stood, saluted, and walked out.

Within three days, Harry had his report written and had taken the

Japanese language exam. As Major Kelly took the form from Harry, he said, "You know, this could take weeks or months if it's done the regular way. But I can put out some feelers on your behalf. The way things are going out there right now, they'll be needing replacements. It's getting uglier the closer we get to Nippon."

The days passed slowly. The news coming in from Okinawa was grisly. Harry noted with interest that Okinawa was only five hundred miles from Shanghai—and Viktoria. It looked like China was being bypassed. He felt stranded. He was restless.

On April 12 the nation received the news that President Roosevelt had died. Harry was sitting in the chow hall with Frenchy and some other officers when he heard the radio announcement. Harry had grown to admire and respect FDR, almost as a father figure. The entire nation mourned. When Germany surrendered four weeks later, the reaction of most of the Marines at Quantico—and this reflected the sentiment of most of the men still fighting in the Pacific—was, "So what?"

Chapter Thirty-Three

Harry grew discouraged about being sent back to the Pacific. It had been six weeks. But finally his request to be reattached to the 5th Marines had come to the attention of Lieutenant Colonel "Cannonball" Gant, Harry's battalion commander on Peleliu, who was now reassigned to Washington. Once Gant gave his imprimatur, Harry was immediately granted release to return to theater. Gant saw to it that Harry was assigned to a position on a regimental intelligence team on Okinawa. But, unfortunately, he would no longer be with the 5th Marines.

Harry would be leaving the 1st Marine Division for the newly formed 6th Marine Division. His regiment would be the 22nd Marines. He took solace, though, knowing he'd be near the 5th Marines and might even be able to see some of his friends on Okinawa. More importantly, he was assigned to regimental headquarters, which meant he would not be leading a rifle company. Instead, he'd be spending his days with the regimental leader's staff officers, doing a lot of writing and briefing. He probably wouldn't even be carrying anything other than a Colt .45 sidearm. Harry—no longer indifferent to his fate—welcomed the thought. He wanted to live so that he could find Viktoria.

He sent a telegram to Uncle Walter, explaining that he was going overseas again. He enclosed a forwarding address in the letter. He said his good-byes around Quantico, making sure to thank Major Kelly. The last person he saw before he left was Frenchy, who had just learned that he would be mustered out of the service in July and would return to his family.

"You be sure to keep your head down, Dutch," Frenchy said with a subdued smile. "I still don't get why you're so anxious to get back out there."

"I'll explain it all to you someday, Frenchy," Harry said as he shook his friend's hand warmly. "You take it easy. Let me know where you land. We'll get together after this is all over. Maybe some place like Chicago. We'll get Ozzie to join us. How does that sound?"

"Sure, Dutch. We'll do the town."

Harry nodded and smiled, looking intently into Frenchy's deep-brown eyes. "You give my best to your lovely wife and your darling daughter."

On May 15 Harry hitched a ride on an Air Transport Command B-17 out of Langley Field, near Norfolk. After several stops along the way, the next morning they landed at an airfield near Sacramento. From there Harry rode on a Douglas C-54 that shuttled him and several high-ranking officers to Hickam Field on Oahu. From Hawaii there were dozens of supply ships sailing for Okinawa every day. Harry boarded a fast destroyer with scores of other replacement officers, and within a week they had joined a massive armada of more than a thousand American warships in the waters off the Ryukyu archipelago.

Okinawa was shrouded in low clouds and mist when they arrived. Harry was glad for the gloomy weather; it meant there would be less chance of a kamikaze attack. The destroyer Harry was on board would replace one of the many destroyers that had been on the receiving end of deadly attacks from the waves of suicide planes coming from bases in Japan and Formosa. They rendezvoused with a Landing Ship, Tank, or LST, in the Kerama group of islands, twenty miles southwest of Okinawa. The Kerama Islands were a staging area where damaged ships could be refitted or repatched before being sent on for more extensive repairs on the West Coast. As they steamed into the anchorage, Harry and the other men stood topside and stared transfixed at the twisted, burnt frames of ships that had been hit by kamikazes.

The LST carried Harry and more than two hundred men and several armored vehicles right onto the beach just south of the town of Hagushi on Okinawa's west coast. Expecting to find a denuded rocky isle like Peleliu, Harry was surprised by the thick green foliage, the pine trees, and the terraced rice fields that blanketed the island. Here and there scars of the war were visible, but it was nothing like the rocky moonscape that Peleliu had been.

Orders in hand, Harry proceeded by jeep to the regimental command post of the 22nd Marines. The commanding officer was Colonel

James Snyder, a tough man who always seemed angry. Harry would be working as the exec under the intelligence chief, Major Marcus Vanhoenecker. Tall, blond, and handsome, the major hailed from New York City. Like Snyder, Vanhoenecker was tough, but unlike the colonel, he was fair-minded and didn't yell all the time. He reminded Harry of the actor Alan Ladd, only much taller. Coincidentally, everyone called Vanhoenecker "Dutch," which caused some initial confusion.

During Harry's first meeting with Vanhoenecker, the major spoke bluntly. "You know, Captain, being an intelligence officer is more than about speaking the language. We've got plenty of people for that. Here at regiment we're interested in tactical intelligence. Where are their forces dispersed? Which forces are we facing? How will their disposition affect our maneuvers?" He paused and lit a cigarette. Harry heard the boom of artillery in the distance. It could have been mistaken for giant thunderclaps in the gloomy rain of Okinawa. "Colonel Gant speaks highly of you, which goes a long way. I'm sure you were one helluva company commander, and the knowledge you gained on the battlefield will come in handy. But here on Okinawa, our results are measured with a different metric. Depending on what we produce, we can spare the lives of an entire regiment of men. Maybe even a division."

"Yes, sir."

"Reports tell us that Japanese resistance is crumbling, so who knows how much longer the battle will continue. But in the meantime, the Japanese are still fanatical, and will fight to the end. And once this one is done, we'll have to prepare for the next one." He gestured to the north toward Japan. "The big one."

"Yes, sir. I'm glad to be here to help out."

"Find your rack and get settled."

Being near the front on Okinawa was a major readjustment for Harry after being out of combat for so long. For the first time in months, he had to endure the sound of artillery. From dawn to dusk the Japanese poured in fire from the south and the east. American land and naval guns answered, but the Japanese were so well dug in across a series of ridges that the guns never seemed to hit anything. At the regimental command post, Harry and the others were sometimes forced to duck for cover against incoming Japanese shells. This wore on his nerves. After particularly bad days of shelling, he sometimes lay awake at night on his cot thinking about Peleliu, and Swede and Chap. He would literally shake.

Okinawa was now at the height of its rainy season. And 1945 was extraordinarily wet. Moving around the island was difficult, even on foot. Japanese corpses were left exposed in the mud. On one occasion Harry slipped while climbing a greasy slope and ended up sliding into the shallow grave of a Japanese soldier. When he stood, he found white maggots all over his dungarees. It was maddening. He felt that he had found hell again, and once more he thought of the Slough of Despond.

Now that his black thoughts had returned, Harry questioned the wisdom of getting back into it. It was utterly depressing on Okinawa. Each evening he listened to the raindrops outside of his tent and tried to fall asleep. When he did manage to sleep, he saw Viktoria. The dreams were more vivid than they had been in the past. She was in trouble, and he couldn't save her. One night it was a burning building on the Bund in Shanghai; another night it was an earthquake. But most of the dreams were about her drowning in the muddy Whangpoo River. He wondered sometimes whether she was even alive.

About a month after he arrived, Harry was in the field with the 1st Battalion of the 22nd Marines, about three miles north of the southern coast of the island. Now that the Japanese were in a full retreat southward, the Marines were securing caves where remnants of the opposition often hid. A rifle company was in the process of sealing a network of caves on a ridge. The rain on Okinawa had given way to a hazy sun, and the humidity was overbearing in the still morning. The blast of explosives occasionally sounded across the ridge. Before each cave was blasted, either a *nisei* Marine interpreter or an Okinawan POW shouted through a bullhorn into the opening to warn any civilians or combatants that if they wished to live, they should come out.

At one cave a skinny POW who was missing chunks of his hair told Harry in Japanese that he knew there were civilians in the cave, and he urged his American captors to be patient. The company commander was a young first lieutenant from Chattanooga named Payne. Payne rubbed his chin and looked at Harry in a querying manner.

"Lieutenant, it's your call." Harry would come to regret that he hadn't been more circumspect. He outranked Payne, so he could decide whether to spend more time trying to convince those inside to peacefully leave the cave. But he'd led a rifle company in the field, and he knew it was up to the company commander, and he didn't wish to step on his authority. He also knew Payne was under pressue to quickly clear this network of caves, as it could save American lives.

Payne ordered in the demolition team. Two men poured jerry cans of aviation fuel into the cave entrance. A third man primed a satchel charge. He then gestured for everyone to move back. Harry and the others moved down the slope of the ridge and kneeled down. The man hurled his charge in and dashed back down the slope.

After a few seconds there was a tremendous roar as the charge exploded, shaking the entire ridge. Rocks and other debris came raining down upon their helmets as they squeezed into crevices of limestone for shelter. Harry thought he heard screams. When the noise from the explosion died down, they all heard it: the screaming and crying voices of females. They all raced to the entrance of the cave.

Harry shouted to Payne, "Send that POW in there to take a look!"

Two *nisei* corporals took the POW to the cave entrance and told him to go in and look. The man was clearly frightened. Harry grabbed one of the bullhorns and shoved it into his chest. He shouted, "*Ike!*"

The POW went forward hesitantly, raised the bullhorn, and repeated what he had said before. The crying and wailing was still audible. Harry grabbed the POW's arm, and the two of them went into the cave. Harry pushed him forward and walked behind, with his hand on the trembling man's shoulder. The interpreters followed. The smoky chamber smelled strongly of burnt flesh and gasoline. The wails and groans continued. Harry called for a flashlight, and a private came into the cave and handed Harry the light. He shined it into the darkness and noticed some movement, a mass of heads with long black hair. There were scattered backpacks and an assortment of other debris, including papers. Harry saw they were wearing navy blue uniforms. It looked like a group of schoolgirls. "Oh, Christ," he said in a low voice. He shouted loudly toward the light at the entrance. "Get a corpsman and some stretchers in here!" Overwhelmed by the smell, Harry sat on the ground and retched. He paused, wiped his mouth, and drank from his canteen.

A corpsman and several men came hurrying down into the cave, following the beams of their own flashlights. Harry saw that a crowd had gathered at the cave entrance, blocking the sunlight coming into the shaft. Payne's voice shouted orders, and more men came into the cave.

Harry numbly walked back to the entrance. Once outside, he dropped the flashlight and stumbled past the assembled men. He sat on the ground, closed his eyes, and tried to think of anything other than what he had just seen. He thought of a beautiful sunrise he saw once while fishing on the gulf in Texas. He remembered the Chinese pagoda in the rain of Reading. He saw Viktoria in the garden at the Savins' house in Shanghai. He envisioned the electric-blue butterflies and tried to smell the flowers. But each vision of beauty was instantly violated by the vision of the torn and mutilated bodies of the young girls. Girls who were probably Jolyn's age. He put his hands to his face.

The shouting and chaos continued. Marines carried out the surviving girls and laid them on the ground around the cave entrance. Harry stumbled farther down the ridge. He couldn't bear to look back. He collapsed at the bottom of the ridge, threw down his helmet, and remained there for several minutes, alone. He noticed men scrambling by him, going up the ridge to the cave entrance. Some of them carried stretchers. He heard Payne shouting at the men to give up their canteens. Then he decided to go back up and see what he could do to help. He stood and wiped his eyes.

At the cave entrance, some of the girls were huddled together in small crouching groups or lying on stretchers. Those who huddled had their arms around one another and were wailing. The girls on the stretchers stared blankly into the sky. Harry kneeled beside one of them. He took her hand and held it. Her small hand lay limply in his own. He spoke to her softly in Japanese. He pulled out his canteen and put it to her lips. She wouldn't take any water. She had no visible wounds other than blood trickling from both ears. He offered his canteen to one of the other girls who crouched nearby. "*O-mizu,*" he said. She hesitated then took the canteen and drank from it deeply. She gave it back to Harry.

Harry turned and shouted, "Anyone have any pogey bait?"

A young Marine came forward. He handed a Butterfinger to Harry. "Here you go, sir." He was a slender lad, probably about eighteen. "I've been savin' it, but I figure they can use it better'n me. 'Sides, Cap'n, I never was a big fan of Butterfingers."

"You're a generous Marine."

The candy bar had been crushed in its faded yellow wrapper and probably had been inside a wet pocket for days, or even weeks. Harry opened it and took out a fragment. He handed it to the first girl and smiled. "*Dozo, chokoreto.*" The girl hesitated. He repeated himself, "*Dozo.*" Then in English he said, "Please." He mimicked a person eating. She took the chocolate and held it in her hand. Harry handed pieces to several other girls. The first girl took the piece and put it in her mouth. The others did the same. They sat there mutely, chewing.

Harry stood and walked over to Payne. A cigarette hung from Payne's lips. He said to Harry quietly, "Captain, they found more than a hundred bodies in there. Plus, there's probably more than that blown to pieces or burned up." He took the cigarette from his mouth and exhaled. "Jesus, I can't believe what I've done."

"It's not your fault, Lieutenant. They've all been brainwashed. They were told never to come out or they'd get raped and killed." Harry sighed. "And anyway, I could have stopped it, but I didn't. You've got no reason to harbor any guilt." He patted Payne on the shoulder. "How many did we get out alive?"

Payne scratched his neck. "It looks like about twenty or so." He put the cigarette back between his lips.

Harry looked around at the carnage and said, "This war here, Payne, it's a war without mercy. The guy you are shooting at looks as foreign as a Martian." He shook his head. "Over in Europe the guy you're fighting may look just like you. But over here . . ." Harry shook his head at Payne's offer of a cigarette. "Over here it's the law of the jungle. We're in the jungle and we behave like our ancestors in the jungle. The guy looks different, so you shoot him. And the Japanese, hell, they'd rather die than get a warm meal if that meal is American."

Payne threw down his cigarette. "I can't even imagine what it's going to be like up there," he said gesturing to the north.

"It's best not to think that far ahead. We've all seen things that nobody back home can begin to understand, Payne. But this . . ." he looked toward the girls and shook his head.

They stood and watched the corpsmen directing men to empty the cave and bring out anybody still alive. The sun was beating down on the side of the ridge, but the girls shivered and huddled together as if keeping out the cold. Farther away, over the sound of locusts, the thump of artillery continued.

"Lieutenant," Harry said. "I've got to move on and find the battalion command post. I'll send whatever personnel I can find to get over here and help you out."

"Thank you, sir." Payne squinted a bit and looked curiously at Harry. "Where'd you learn to speak Japanese?"

"In school." Harry turned and climbed down the ridge, sliding on limestone that had been shaken loose by the constant pounding of artillery.

The last hill on Okinawa—Hill 81—was taken the next day. The morning after that, Harry spoke with Major Vanhoenecker at the regimental command post. It was bright and sunny. A slight breeze carried on it the smell of pine trees. It was a nice contrast to the horrid smells that pervaded the island. A staff officer came into the tent around 1000 and informed them that Army troops had found the bodies of the two Japanese commanding generals. Each corpse was slit open at the belly, and they were both decapitated. The battle was truly over. Vanhoenecker said, "On to the next one."

In early July the 22nd Marines embarked for Guam along with the rest of the 6th Marine Division. Guam was hot and steamy, and it stank of rotting vegetation just like Pavuvu had. The Navy built out a huge facility, complete with barracks and mess halls made from Quonset huts. Each night they were served hot chow and shown movies. But as civilized as they tried to make it, there was no escaping the tedium. Harry felt isolated and even further from Viktoria.

On a Monday night during the first week of August, strange news spread around the encampment: an entire Japanese city had been wiped out with one bomb. The men wondered how that was even possible given the amount of ordnance they had fired off on Okinawa. It was the main topic of conversation for the next seventy-two hours, until a second atomic bomb was dropped, on August 9. One fellow in the officers' mess was overheard saying, "Just one more of them bombs on Tokyo, and it's *finis*, baby!" But most of the men were still skeptical.

Then, out of the blue, on August 15, Japan's surrender was announced. V-J Day. Victory over Japan. Understandably, the men were still wary, particularly those who had been gearing up for an invasion of the Japanese home islands. When the order was given for a temporary standdown from training, they began to believe it was actually true. But, for the most part, there was little celebrating, especially among the

veterans. Many of the rear-echelon men and some of the pilots celebrated the news, but most of the combat veterans—men who had fought
for three long years—simply reflected on the losses and on the friends
they had known.

Harry had survived the war. But at night he saw the faces of people
he had lost. Two impressions would scar his memory to the end of his
days: the vision of Happy Hargrove, dying in his arms on Cape Gloucester, and the image of the Okinawan schoolgirls in the cave.

The demobilization process would be a long one, but those with
battle stars would be given priority. In late August, Major Vanhoenecker
told Harry that the 6th Marine Division would be embarking for China
in September.

Harry could hardly believe his ears. "China? Where?"

"Tsingtao. It's on the coast, a few hundred miles southeast of
Peiping," Vanhoenecker answered, using the new name for Peking. He
took the pipe out of his mouth and said, "But don't worry about it. You
have enough points to get home. You'll probably be on the first boat out
of here."

"What will the Marines be doing in Tsingtao, sir?"

"Our orders are to liberate all interned Western nationals and to
repatriate Japanese troops and citizens back to their home islands. We've
laid such waste to their merchant fleet and navy that they don't have
the ships to ferry their own people back home. There are several million of them in China." Vanhoenecker stood up and walked over to
a map of Japan perched on an easel. He flipped the map over, expos-
ing underneath a map of the eastern Chinese seaboard from Hong
Kong north. Harry walked over and stood next to him. Vanhoenecker
pointed out Tsingtao. "Can you believe it? We're being asked to escort
the Japanese home."

Harry pointed to the map and asked, "What about Shanghai?"

"We were initially supposed to be deployed to the Shanghai/Yang-
tze region, but the decision was made to put our troops farther north
around Tsingtao and Peiping. This is classified, but there's concern in the
leadership about the Chinese Communist troops taking Peiping with
Soviet backing. We will remain there to hold it until Chiang can get his
forces up there."

"But the Russians are our allies."

"Come on, Harry. Don't be so naïve. You know we can't trust the Reds. The Nazis are gone. We have nothing uniting us anymore. You can speak platitudes about the United Nations, but we all know what Uncle Joe Stalin is up to."

Harry nodded. "I suppose it was a matter of time."

Vanhoenecker came back to the main topic. "Anyway, the Nationalists have Shanghai under control, and they don't need us there in large numbers. The Navy will send whatever vessels are necessary to Shanghai to repatriate the Westerners and the Japanese nationals. I'm sure the Brits will be involved as well." He went back to his desk and sat down. He took out a bag of tobacco and refilled his pipe. He struck a match and lit the bowl. A cloud of aromatic smoke filled the tent.

Harry sat down and looked at Vanhoenecker. "Sir, you said we don't need to be there in large numbers. Are there going to be *any* Marines in Shanghai? I ask only because, as you know, I lived there for two years before the war. Perhaps I could be utilized there in some staff or intelligence capacity."

"You mean you don't want to go home?" Vanhoenecker craned his neck in disbelief. "Are you wanted for a crime in Texas?"

"Sir, may I speak frankly?"

His curiosity piqued, Vanhoenecker nodded. "Proceed, Captain."

"The fact is, I know many of the internees there, sir. Some of them are close friends. I'd like to see what I could do to be of help to them—and to the Marine Corps. I also know many of the local Chinese, including former officials. I can navigate the city well, and remember, I can use my Japanese language skills."

"Harry, every man who ever served in the 4th Marine Regiment probably wants to be sent to Shanghai. Anyway, most of the people you knew are probably no longer there—or they're dead." He puffed on his pipe thoughtfully for a moment, then took it out from his mouth and set it down. "What else is on your mind?"

"Sir, there's also the question of the White Russians."

Vanhoenecker arched his eyebrows. "Go on."

"Well," Harry began, "I *do* speak some Russian. I picked it up there. It could come in handy. Many of the White Russians collaborated with the Japanese. You know they were mostly Red haters, so they sided against the Communists. Maybe there is something I can do in that regard."

Vanhoenecker picked up a pencil and tapped it on his desk. He sighed. "Listen, Harry. I didn't expect you to come to Tsingtao with us. You're a fine officer. You've been a credit to the Marine Corps, and you've served your country well. If you want to go home, I can arrange it immediately. If you don't—well, I'll help you however I can. I can't make any promises, but I'll look into it and see what and who will be going into Shanghai."

Harry saluted and said, "Thank you, sir. I'm grateful."

In early September, Vanhoenecker informed Harry that he would be attached to the party accepting the formal Japanese surrender in Shanghai. They would depart in one week.

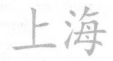

Chapter Thirty-Four

June 20, 1945

My Dearest Harry,

I write this to you today with the knowledge that we may never see one another again. My life has come to such a state that I'm ashamed to be presumptuous enough to think you could still even love me. Whether we do see one another again, I hope that one day you can read these letters to help you understand a little bit about the things that have led me to the current state in which I find myself.

You may be shocked to discover many things about me, but please keep in mind this fact: I love you, have never stopped loving you, and will always love you. The two years we had together were the greatest of my life. I hoped that it could continue forever. I had to make a decision then about my family and our relationship. In the end I chose my family. Now, after all that has happened during the war, I know in my heart that it was the right decision. It is not the decision that I may have chosen knowing what I know now, but my family is better off for my having stayed.

It is impossible to describe on a piece of paper how we have struggled. You need to see the desperation in the faces of my younger cousins, know the hunger that tortures our bodies, understand the compromises that stateless people must make, and feel the fear that grips us each day. The war seems to go on forever, and although we can sense that the end is near, each new day passes as slowly as the onset of a Russian spring. We can no longer imagine our lives without war, as we can barely remember what it was like before the war.

Uncle Grisha went north to Harbin for business, and we have not seen him for nearly a month. We've had no word from him. Aunt Maria is so despondent that she is helpless when it comes to providing for the younger ones. In order to support my family, I have done things that I'm not proud of. Although my infidelity to you was not forced on me at first, once I saw that our family relied on the largesse of the man who became my lover, I was drawn further in. Now I see it as my duty to remain with this man, even though I do not love him. I also have a new responsibility to another, and this responsibility will grow in the coming months . . .

Viktoria had to stop writing because Gu had come into the room. She did not want him to know that she was keeping the diary, not so much out of fear that he would be unhappy with what she had written—frankly, she didn't care anymore what he thought. But Viktoria preferred that her innermost thoughts be shared one day only with Harry. She decided that she would continue writing the entry on another day, when she had more time to sort through her thoughts. Meanwhile, she had people to take care of and mouths to feed.

As she opened the drawer of the desk in the room that she shared with two of her younger female cousins, Gu saw her hastily put the book away. He slowly walked toward Viktoria and put his hand on her shoulder. He then stroked her hair, while she shifted uncomfortably. The rest of the family was either out on the grounds or in one of the other rooms of the guesthouse. Henry was napping in the next room.

"What are you doing, my dear?" Gu asked.

"Spending time alone," she answered. "I don't get to do that often enough."

"Oh, I see. Do you wish me to leave, so that you can be alone?" He took his hand from her head and ran his fingers along the top of the small desk.

"Yes, I do."

"You know I wish only for you to be happy, so I'll leave. But first there's one thing I'd like you to do for me. I'd like you to give me the book you were just writing in. The one in the drawer."

He started to reach down to open it, but Viktoria put her hands on the drawer to keep it shut. "No! You may *not* look at it. It is *my* property, and it is for me alone to look at."

He pulled her hands away and opened the drawer. Initially she resisted, but then she gave up. Gu pulled out the diary and flipped through it. He came across Harry's photo. He looked at it briefly and then started to read one section with interest.

"So, it seems like some lucky man out there has an admirer," he said nonchalantly. "You know, dear, it pains me to know that you reserve a special place in your heart for another. Because you do know, Viktoria, I love you."

He put the diary back down and began stroking her head again with both hands. Viktoria pulled away.

"Don't you have anything to say to me?"

"I have nothing to say to you."

"Well, it seems that you have a lot on your mind. Maybe you'd like to share it with me?"

She leaned back, looked up at him, and said angrily, "What difference does it make to you? You have everything you want. Everything you need. And now you have me. What do I have? A diary? Letters to a man I love, who I will probably never see again. Is this too much for you to handle? Because, you see, I don't even have that," she pointed to the diary. "I have a hungry child, and I have other mouths to feed, and will have yet more. So leave me to my thoughts, if you will, please."

Gu was taken aback. He started to stammer, "Viktoria..."

She said simply, "I don't love you, and I never have."

He sighed, then turned and walked out.

Viktoria slumped down onto the desk. She cried quietly. She was not afraid of what Gu would do. She was devastated by the thought that she would never see Harry again and that he may never know his son. Gu was the least of her problems. Viktoria knew Gu wouldn't abandon her, because she was now five months pregnant with his child and starting to show.

Her relationship with Gu had gone beyond what she had ever imagined. He had drawn her into a web from which she could not possibly escape. She was now totally dependent on him, and so was her entire family. He was not only their benefactor but also their landlord. The memory of their transition passed through Viktoria's mind.

Viktoria was in the kitchen of the Savin house on a warm morning in late May, preparing a breakfast for Henry of crushed wheat softened in powdered milk. Maria walked into the room clutching a paper. Her face was ashen and her eyes vacant. "It's all done for," she mumbled in a low voice, using the simple Russian word *vsyo* to denote all, everything. "Aunty Masha, what did you say?"

"*Vsyo*. They're forcing us out," she answered despondently.

"What? Who? What are you talking about?"

Maria handed Viktoria the paper. Viktoria looked at the document printed in Chinese and in English. It began, "By the order of the municipal government of Shanghai . . ." They were being evicted. They had one day to clear out from the house with whatever possessions they could carry.

Viktoria said to her aunt, "This can't be. We need to speak with the authorities. Perhaps when Uncle Grisha returns, he can speak with the Japanese. Of course, I could speak with . . ." Her voice trailed off, as if she was ashamed to mention Gu's name in front of Henry.

Maria cried aloud, "Where will we go?"

Viktoria found some bread ends and laid them on the table. Henry took them and began gnawing on them. She turned back to Maria and said, "Aunty Masha, we have to act quickly. We have until tomorrow evening to be out of the house. Maybe we can get a reprieve until Uncle Grisha returns." The more Viktoria thought about it, the more panicky she became.

Maria stared ahead blankly. "He *will* come back, won't he? What if he returns and he cannot find where we are?"

"Of course, he will, Aunty Masha." Viktoria took her hand. "But in the meantime, we have to do *something*. We must speak to somebody." Again, she thought of Gu. "If we go, we will leave word where we have gone."

"But where will we go?"

Viktoria stood up and took off her apron. "Please, look after Henry." Maria kept her gaze transfixed on the wall. Viktoria leaned toward her. "Aunty Masha, do you understand? I have to go somewhere. You need to help me out. We still have some *shchi*," she said, referring to soup made from sorrel and cabbage. "You can feed the others if I am not back by supper. Do you understand?"

Maria looked up at Viktoria, focusing on her for the first time during the conversation. "Yes, yes. We'll be fine. Go on, Vika."

They both knew that Viktoria was going to see Gu to find out if he could help in some way. Not daring to venture out of the house alone, Viktoria took along Misha. She changed dresses and put on a scarf to shield herself from the looks of passersby even though the weather was warm. The walk to Gu's house was not far; it was also located in the French Concession, less than a mile from the Savin house.

Gu's bodyguards and house servants all knew Viktoria. She and Misha were led into a drawing room, where they waited for almost ten minutes before a servant came in and asked Viktoria to follow him. He was taking her to Gu's study. She told Misha to wait outside the room. Gu stood behind his desk and beckoned her into the room with a smile. Once the door had been shut, Viktoria immediately came to the point.

"Monsieur," she began. Viktoria still insisted on calling Gu this, though it annoyed him. He preferred the name, Samuel. "We have been given notice that we are to evacuate our house." She walked forward and handed him the paper that Maria had given to her. He took and read it for a moment. He looked up at Viktoria and frowned.

"Please, my dear, have a seat." He reached for his phone and dialed a number. He spoke for a few moments in Chinese. Then he put the receiver back down. "This is not highly unusual, as you can guess, with the way the war is going presently. I'll try to make some calls and speak with some people. It might be difficult to countermand this order. It was done in the name of the police. Were it done for an individual or a family, I'm certain I could do something. But with the police . . ." he shrugged and then lit a cigarette.

"Have you any word from my uncle? Can you tell us *anything*? We heard he had gone to meet with Semyonov in Harbin."

"If I'd heard anything, you'd be the first person to know, Viktoria. But I haven't. He may have been detained by the local authorities. It's hard to say. But it is difficult even for me to get information. The war is going frightfully badly for the Japanese. The bombing raids on Japan have been going on nonstop since the beginning of the year, and every major city has been burned to the ground. The Americans are now on Okinawa."

"Okinawa?" Viktoria knew that it lay only five hundred miles from Shanghai. Was it finally going to end, this nightmare they had been living for four years?

"My dear, I need you to go back to your house. I will make some calls and let you know by tomorrow morning. Please, don't worry right now. Just get back safely to your home. I'll have my driver take you back."

"There is no need, monsieur. My cousin Misha is here with me. We'll walk back." As she turned to walk out of his office, she stopped and looked back at Gu. "You truly know *nothing* about my uncle? Are you holding anything back? Because if you are on account of my aunt, you can tell me."

"No, my dear, I know nothing more than you do. I'm sorry."

Viktoria and Misha returned home. Maria was sitting alone in her husband's study. Henry was with his cousins upstairs. She turned and looked expectantly at Viktoria. "We will know more tomorrow, Aunty Masha. Meanwhile, I think it's best that we pack anyway, and that we make sure we take what we need and what is of most value." Maria nodded blankly. The disappearance of her beloved husband and now the eviction notice were taking the life from her. She looked so old to Viktoria, more like a grandmother than an aunt.

The next morning Viktoria received a note from Gu. He was unable to do anything about the eviction. But, he explained, the entire Savin family was welcome to take up residence in a guesthouse behind his residence. The notice specified that the possessions they could take had to fit into the two suitcases allotted for each person. Anything else had to be left behind in the home. Family paintings, photographs, records, china, flatware, books, and other assorted things that the Savins had treasured for decades would be forfeited. Gu's note concluded with his promise to send a car to pick them up late that afternoon.

Viktoria was now trapped with a man she did not love. And the two remaining adults of the Savin household, Maria and Viktoria, could no longer even console one another. Each expressed her despondency in different ways. Maria had withdrawn into herself. Viktoria—in spite of her repugnance for Gu—had pulled herself closer to him. Unlike her aunt, Viktoria was always able to maintain a positive demeanor in front of the family. She was the glue holding them together in the face of daily challenges for simple existence. She had been forced to stay with them— rather than leaving with Harry—so now she would ensure that she did *everything* possible for them. It was as if she could look at her aunt and uncle and say, "You see? *I* am the one keeping us together." It was a certain point of pride for Viktoria to show that, in fact, she was the leader of the family now. Grigorii was gone, and Maria was useless.

Viktoria was able to support the young family members now, but she knew this was strictly at the whim of Gu.

One day he found Viktoria sitting in his study alone, sobbing. He had taken to chiding her when he found her like that.

"Viktoria, please, when you must act this way, do so in the guest-house, not here. Anyway, why do you cry so? What have you to be unhappy about? I've given you everything you and your family need. Without me, you would be just another starving Russian countess. No—you'd be another starving Russian prostitute."

Viktoria regarded him with a fierce look in her eyes. "What difference is there now? Only that I'm *not* starving? Yes, I know, I *am* a prostitute! What does that say about you? That you can only *buy* my affection, that's what it says."

Gu crossed the room quickly and slapped Viktoria hard across the face. She turned crimson, but she didn't back down. "Go ahead. Have your way with me. This is what you want anyway, right?" She taunted him and started to unbutton her blouse.

He grabbed her hand to stop her. "Quit making a spectacle of yourself. Go back to your family."

As Viktoria stood up to leave the room, Gu suddenly softened his tone and said, "Viktoria, I'm sorry I did that. I've also been under a lot of strain. Things are starting to change in Shanghai. The light has come into the room and everyone is being revealed for what they are. It is dangerous. I have more enemies than I have friends."

"What does that have to do with me?"

"I've been protecting you because I care about you and your family. Don't make me rethink my decision. Do you want to end up like your cousin? Behind the Japanese barbed wire where the children will die of cholera or typhus?"

Viktoria marched out the front door of Gu's residence, but instead of returning to the guesthouse, she brazenly walked out of the front gate of the compound into the deserted streets of the French Concession. She walked and walked until she came to the river. She stopped at the embankment and watched the brown water flow by. She was so lost in her misery that she gave no thought to her personal safety. She looked out over the river, searching for some sign that the war would end. But, as she strained her eyes to the north, she saw only Chinese junks and the

Japanese patrol craft, and her heart fell even deeper into despair.

Viktoria knew that Gu's patience could wear thin at times and that he would blow with the wind. Now that they were all in a hurricane, there was no telling which way the winds of change would ultimately take them.

Viktoria once heard her uncle say that the most dangerous times during a war are at the end. That is when the discipline that has been strictly maintained starts to crumble. In eastern China in 1945 there were a number of competing forces tearing at one another, leaving normal people to bob like flotsam in an unruly river. For now, Gu's attraction—and genuine affection—for Viktoria kept the Savin family protected. Viktoria knew that could change overnight and that if Gu ever needed to choose between his Chinese family and the family of his Russian mistress, she and her cousins would find themselves cast out onto the street.

Physically Viktoria had never felt worse. Each day was a burden to rise. She despaired of spending what should have been the best years of her life as a subject in a foreign land during wartime. She thought of Harry constantly. But she found it difficult to summon the physical and emotional energy to write for him in her diary, to try to give him an understanding of all that she had gone through. And now she was certain that Harry would never forgive her and that he could never love her again. She actually took solace when she imagined that Harry had found someone else, and she made herself believe it, so that her own guilt might be assuaged. She had to suppress the blackest thought that sometimes occurred to her: maybe Harry had been killed and was no longer even walking the earth. The minute such a thought came to her, she quickly pushed it out of mind and crossed herself.

Chapter Thirty-Five

The cruiser USS *Rocky Mount*'s turbine engines slowed as the ship swung around, anchoring at Number One buoy opposite the Bund on the Whangpoo River. For most people in Shanghai that day, September 19, 1945, the significance of that particular action went unmarked against the larger meaning of the celebrations under way. But for those who knew Shanghai—and China—there was a special symbolism associated with Number One buoy. For a century that buoy had been reserved for the flagship of the British Asiatic Fleet. Now the flagship of the U.S. 7th Fleet had taken its place. Some of the older veterans of the 4th Marines who were there that day understood the significance. Harry did too. But now was the time to put the past behind him in order to get on with the future. Harry was in Shanghai for Viktoria. The four years of war he had endured, as well as the surrender, were mere sideshows. It was all about her.

An elbow nudged him softly in the arm. A young man's voice spoke. "Hey, Dutch, getta load of that group. You think it was like this in Tokyo Bay when the *Missouri* took the surrender?"

"I doubt it," Harry answered.

They were both looking off the starboard bow, where a flotilla of dozens of sampans and junks had pulled out to greet the incoming American ships. Overcrowded to near tipping, the boats acted as individual stages for any number of impromptu celebrations. The people on board madly waved their arms, hats, rags, ersatz American flags—whatever they could get their hands on. Tugboats and other smaller craft tooted their horns and whistles, their crews joining in the celebration.

Fireworks punctuated the chaotic scene in a cacophonous barrage. Occasionally a noiseless splash in the distance would mark a celebration temporarily gone awry, somebody falling over the side of an overcrowded boat. Harry watched as a tall, skinny man with red trousers fell over the side of a sampan. He struggled in the water as the sampan moved away from him. A tug happened to be passing by, and it appeared to steam right over the man. Far in the distance it was hard to see what became of him. No one on the sampan even seemed to notice or care. But this was China. For over a decade the people had endured wartime hardships. What was one more casualty at war's end?

Along the waterfront, crowds had also massed on the Bund to greet the incoming ships, many hoping for some sort of salvation from their interminable suffering. The American servicemen perched along the incoming ships' rails took in all the madness, their heads shaking in disbelief. More than a few of the soldiers and sailors on board reflected on the difference between this reception and the one they likely would have gotten in Japan had the war not suddenly ended.

Harry, who recently had been promoted to major, was among the few men selected to board the first launch from the *Rocky Mount* bound for the quay along the Bund, where they would accept the formal surrender of Japanese troops. A small number of American troops were already in Shanghai. Elements of Army personnel had been airlifted in, and smaller detachments of Marines, sailors, and soldiers had landed earlier in the month. The official surrender had been signed at an airfield on Shanghai's outskirts a week earlier, but now, with a large American presence in force, it was time for a ceremonial handover of power. The Marines would take the surrender as a symbolic gesture, given their colorful history of service in this city. General Alvin "Al" Stevenson led the delegation. He had served in the 4th Marines—a "China Marine"—and had been stationed in Shanghai in the 1920s.

The shore party was joined by a group of news reporters and Navy photographers at the embankment. They waded into the celebratory mass of people on the Bund. Shanghai—though a liberated city—was on death's doorstep. The crushing poverty that Harry had known before the war had worsened. Shanghai had always been overrun with the destitute, but now beggars, young and old alike, seemed to outnumber ordinary people. Some of the needier were mutilated and crippled; others were simply starving. The city had suffered more than seven years of Japanese encirclement and four years of occupation. Before the war, begging mothers would push forward babies that cried and screamed. Now the babies were despondent and the mothers' eyes hollow. The city was celebrating its liberation from the hated Japanese, yet most people dreaded the upcoming months of uncertainty and the famine of winter that was sure to come.

Chinese Nationalist troops kept the crowds away from the party of Americans, but the desperation surrounding them was obvious. For weeks Army Air Corps planes had been airdropping parcels of foodstuffs and assorted items. Although they were intended for the Westerners crowded in the POW camps across the region, many of them ended up in the hands of Chinese black marketers. The parcels were nothing more than drops of water in an ocean. Millions of Chinese and Japanese civilians and soldiers were starving in and around Shanghai. The same situation existed along the entire Chinese seaboard, from Canton to Tientsin. But for this group of Americans who had come to take the surrender, the issue of paramount importance was the fate of the thousands of American, Australian, British, Dutch, and other Western POWs—civilian and military. And the displaced White Russians, of course. They were not a priority for the Americans, but for Harry they represented more than a passing interest.

On this day, however, it was all about the surrender. The Japanese delegation was waiting in the ballroom of the Cathay Hotel. Though dressed in their finest uniforms, the officers looked shabby. A cadre of Nationalist Chinese officials was present, ostensibly to take over the reins of government from the Japanese. They had been brought into Shanghai to fill the vacuum before the Chinese Communists could do so, as Major Vanhoenecker had alluded to on Guam. Even though they had been on the winning side in the war against Japan, China was in the middle of its own civil war.

The head of the Japanese delegation was a colonel named Uga. Half a dozen other officers accompanied him. The ranking Japanese general in Shanghai had committed *seppuku*, disemboweling himself upon hearing Emperor Hirohito's call for surrender. The Japanese admiral who had been next in line for the regional command had been assassinated the week before the Americans' arrival. The Japanese claimed it was the work of Communists. More likely, it had been carried out by criminal elements, perhaps a black-market deal gone wrong.

Uga was tall for a Japanese man, his height accentuated by the ramrod posture of all career soldiers. He had thick black hair, which set him apart from the many other Japanese officers who preferred a shaved head. He came forward to present his sword to General Stevenson. The ceremony was brief. The photographers and reporters who were on hand to record the event snapped photos and shot film. General Stevenson read a statement. He stressed the urgency of the complex task at hand: securing the Shanghai area, which was being overrun by "bandits and Communists"; locating and rescuing the thousands of Westerners—primarily American and British—who were languishing in camps; repatriating more than half a million Japanese from the area; and lastly and most importantly, feeding all those groups of people. Uga—who didn't require a translator—affixed his seal to a document that had been prepared by the American staff. The other Japanese officers came forward one by one and laid down their swords and pistols on a table.

Stevenson's chief of staff, Colonel Keith Davenport, called Harry forward after the ceremony and introduced him to Uga. "Major Dietrichson is going to assist you with the disposition of all Allied POWs and the remaining Imperial Army troops in the greater Shanghai area. You are to afford him whatever he may need in the way of cooperation. Is that understood, Colonel?"

"Yes, Colonel." Uga bowed deeply.

Uga then called over a man and introduced him as Major Katada. He was a full head shorter than Uga. When Katada spoke to Uga, Harry noticed his mouth was filled with gold teeth. Uga explained that Katada was to be Harry's primary liaison officer should the need arise for anything such as transport or security. Harry introduced himself in Japanese, since Katada spoke no English.

As the two parties assembled to leave, General Stevenson and Colonel Davenport took Harry aside. Stevenson spoke first. "Major, I know you've been fully briefed on the situation, but just a few last-minute words of advice. This repatriation is going to take several months. It's good to have someone here who knows the city. That's why we selected you. As much as I hate to say this—as an old China hand and as a Marine—the Japanese may prove to be the best friends we have here in China before all is said and done. Use them to the fullest extent possible. They're good soldiers, and they know the lay of the land. More Americans are on their way to help you out in the next few weeks, but for now, you're on your own. It's a big responsibility, but I know you'll do a fine job. My friend Cannonball Gant speaks highly of you."

"Yes, sir. Thank you, General." Harry thought of Gant, limping around Peleliu, shouting orders and encouragement. It seemed a thousand years ago.

Colonel Davenport added, "We've managed to commandeer two Japanese trucks and a small car. You'll have three Marines to drive you around. Hopefully, in the next couple of days a motor pool will be set up, and you'll get a staff. But the first order of business is to escort Colonel Uga and his group to their headquarters." He paused and chuckled. "I guess we're sending you into the hornet's nest, Dutch. Jap headquarters for Eastern China. There you'll meet a Colonel Gu of the Nationalist Army. He will be your contact on the Chinese side. He's been there for several days and is expecting you. Good luck."

General Stevenson extended his hand. "Best of luck to you, Dutch." With that, he and Davenport left.

A squad of KMT soldiers stood at the ready to escort Harry and the Japanese. This oddball assemblage of former enemies made their way together out onto the Bund to the waiting vehicles. The Japanese were the object of great venom from the crowds that had gathered. As they walked toward the vehicles, the group was struck by no fewer than a dozen projectiles, among them rocks, pieces of wood, glass, and at least two teacups. The Japanese exercised self-control. The Nationalist escorts seemed to enjoy the spectacle.

Harry was surprised to see in the driver's seat of the requisitioned car—an old Citroën—a Marine driver he knew from Okinawa. He was a squat youth with cropped brown hair. Corporal Alston stood out because he always carried a small hand accordion.

"Got your squeezebox, Corporal?"

"Yes, sir."

"Outstanding. I can't wait to hear it later."

After making a quick detour to visit the shop where the Savin teahouse had stood, they drove across Soochow Creek into Hongkew, known before the war as Little Tokyo. As they approached Jiangwan Road, squads of KMT troops became more conspicuous. They came to a checkpoint. A KMT officer strode forward, and Harry produced his orders. The Citroën was quickly waved through. Alston pulled up at a massive concrete and steel building within high walls. The convoy of trucks had only just arrived a few minutes before. The compound, from which the Imperial Japanese Army brain trust had ruled most of Shanghai for the past eight years, was in surprisingly good order. It showed pockmarks where bombing raids had left scars, but for the most part, it was tidy and well kept. The main building appeared to be deserted except for a few Japanese soldiers.

Colonel Gu strode out into the compound to greet the contingent. He smartly saluted and said in perfect English, "Good afternoon, Major. I'm Colonel Gu. I wish to extend to you my greetings."

"Thank you, Colonel."

"I understand you lived in Shanghai before the war."

"That's right. I was a correspondent for United Press."

"I see. Well, as you get reacquainted with our city, I welcome any questions or any requests you may have. We have a difficult task ahead of us." As they walked toward the main building, Gu asked, "How does it feel to be back, Major?"

"It's been four years since I was in Shanghai, Colonel. Everything looks familiar—and different."

"Yes, Major Dietrichson. Much water has passed under the bridge since you were here."

Chapter Thirty-Six

The Savin family received news of the Japanese surrender in mid-August, but their daily pre-occupations and simply surviving were all that really mattered. Uncle Grigorii was still missing, and as Russians, they were still a stateless people without a home. Since the Soviet Union was a victorious ally in the war against Japan, they could probably never return to Russia. For Viktoria the August heat was making it hard on her, and she took to bed more often as she neared her date of confinement. Henry spent most of the time with his cousins, when they weren't out trying to scrounge food for the family. Gu's munificence went only so far at this point, even with Viktoria carrying his child.

Viktoria and Maria both knew the end of the war meant that Tanya would be freed any day. It had been months since they had had any word from her. One day Maria decided she would go out to the camp to try to find out what had happened to her daughter. It took her the better part of a day to get there. She was accompanied by two of her sons. Much to her surprise and disappointment, she found out that the internees had been moved to another camp. Nobody knew where. On the way back, they saw a huge American Dakota transport plane, flying low over the area where they were walking. The boys waved their arms, and the plane dropped a parachute that they realized would fall near them. It held a long metal canister. As it landed in a field the shiny canister popped open, spilling out the contents. The boys ran to it, and when Maria reached them, she saw they had already gathered piles of canned goods, including condensed milk, Spam, tuna, and chocolate. They were both eating Hershey bars, grinning broadly. Maria came forward, her brows arched, dumped the meager contents from her bag, and filled it with cans. They took all they could carry. They avoided crowds for fear of being robbed and didn't arrive back in the French Concession until past midnight.

Throughout the rest of August and early September, the boys canvassed the region, looking for more airdrops. On most days they found nothing or were beaten to it by Chinese locals. But on some days, they returned with bags full of canned goods. They hadn't eaten this well since 1941. But each time they saw an American plane, they asked themselves, *Why won't they land?* By early September, as Viktoria became heavier with child, she was in bed most every day. Henry, meanwhile, was having the time of his life. There were no longer any restrictions, and he and the other boys could do as they wanted. He tried chocolate for the first time. Viktoria was happy to see him having fun and growing up surrounded with such affection. But she grew depressed about her own condition. She had no appetite and only ate for her unborn baby. Gu was absent for long periods now. Once she saw him leave the house in a Nationalist uniform. She was curious, but she never asked.

One day in mid-September the two youngest sons, Sergey and Pyotor, returned after a long day searching, with a sack full of soap and powdered milk. They excitedly told the family that they had spoken with American soldiers at the airfield northwest of town. The soldiers gave them two cartons of Chesterfield cigarettes and candy bars. They explained to the boys that they had come to take the surrender, but that they wouldn't be staying. They said more Americans would be coming soon on ships.

Gu came to see Viktoria the next day and confirmed the story. He told her that a fleet was expected to arrive soon. Gu noticed that Viktoria wasn't burdened by her customary despondency, so he asked sarcastically, "Are you expecting your man to come and rescue you? You, with a bastard son and another bastard child on the way?"

"Henry is no bastard. He knows his father, and I know his father."

"And I'm sure this man is so generous. Didn't he leave you behind?" He said, ridiculing her. "And what if he *does* come back? You think he's going to take you and your half-breed child back to America? Stop with your fantasies."

Viktoria lay back on her pillow. "Go away, please."

"Listen," his voice softened, "I'm sorry, Viktoria. I didn't mean to sound so harsh. It's just that I want you to be with me. I want to raise the child with you. Can you understand that?"

"Please leave me."

Gu left and she lay there. *He's right*, she thought to herself. *Harry isn't coming back*, she despaired.

Three days later Tanya returned to the family, along with Edward. They had gone first to the Savin house, only to find it abandoned. She and Edward were able to figure out where the family had gone by asking around. After the initial joy of the reunion passed, Tanya recounted their story to Maria and Viktoria. When the Japanese surrendered, the interned women moved to a new camp for security purposes. Japanese troops still guarded the camp, but they were free to come and go as they pleased. They left the camp only to gather foodstuffs from the American airdrops. One day the Japanese soldiers simply opened the gates and walked away. The women decided that they should all stick together, so they stayed in the camp. Two days later a group of British men—who had also been liberated—came and found them. Edward was among the first to come into the camp. He located Tanya. They had both made it. They were hungry, sick, and exhausted, but they had survived. Once the first Allied troops arrived, Edward found them a billet in a smaller camp that was guarded by Ghurka troops. Soon they were moved to the Palace Hotel. Ensconced there, Edward and Tatiana set out to find the Savin family.

They arrived bearing more food and medicine. Tanya was shocked to see the state Viktoria was in, but Viktoria rallied, buoyed by the sight of her cousin.

Alone with Tanya, Viktoria recounted her plight.

Tanya hugged her, trying to soothe her. "Dearest, you must understand. It's okay. You did what you had to. And now it's all over. We survived."

"But it's not all over. What will become of me?"

"We will take care of you."

"No." She looked up at Tanya and said with a pained expression, "I want you to take care of Henry and take him back with you to England."

"Vika! Don't be silly! Edward and I will take care of both of you. We will all go to England."

"No. I don't want any help. I'm not going anywhere. Once I have this baby, I'll be stuck here. With *him*."

"Vika, that is out of the question. You'll come with us."

"Don't you understand, Tanya?" Viktoria shook her head. "I could never go to England with his child. I have lived with enough shame for too long now. You take Henry. And I'll stay here to fend for myself and the baby."

Just then, a loud shout came from another room. Misha burst in. "The American Navy is here! We just heard from a man who was on the Bund, and he said there are the three American warships—big ones—on the roadstead off Hongkew."

"What?!" Tanya and Viktoria looked at one another, wide eyed.

"Are you deaf? The Americans! The Navy! Everyone is going to the Bund. Pyotr, Sergey, and I are going."

Maria came in behind Misha. "Yes, it's true. They say that they are finally here." She looked at her son. "But please, I don't think you should go."

Misha looked at his mother and said determinedly, "Don't worry, we'll be safe. But we *are* going." He turned and left the room.

The three women remained silent for a minute, looking at one another and absorbing the information. It seemed like a dream. They had all wondered for months when it would be over. And now, there were American ships on the Whangpoo.

Tanya stood and asked her mother. "Is Edward out there?"

"He is in the back, outside."

"I must go talk to him." She turned back to the bed. "Think about what I said, Vika."

Viktoria looked at the foot of her bed and said in a monotone voice, "This changes nothing for me."

That evening the boys returned with more canned goods. They recounted to Maria and Viktoria how they had seen a group of American soldiers and sailors ride launches up to the quay, but they couldn't follow where they went from there. The crowds were too big. They confirmed there were three warships. They had also seen British Indian troops to the west of town. The Allies were coming in large numbers now.

Over the next three days, Tanya came back to check on Viktoria in the morning and the evening. They had to make a decision whether she would deliver the baby at the house or whether they should seek out medical care. Maria and Tanya agreed that given Viktoria's frail state, it would be too dangerous to attempt a home delivery. Edward asked around about British medical personnel but was told that they were all dealing with the hundreds of internees who needed urgent medical attention. Viktoria told them that she would speak with Gu and that he would arrange for everything. She could tell the baby would come any day.

On the fifth day after Tanya returned, she recounted to Viktoria and Maria a curious event that morning, when she and Edward had gone again to the Savin house. "We didn't see much the first time we went, because we were so anxious to find you. But this time we walked all around the house. It was so sad. It's in shambles and several poor Chinese families are living there. I tried to look for old photos, pieces of art, anything. But the place had been stripped bare." She paused a moment, then said, "Something funny happened, though: we spoke with a young man, who was living there with his family. He understood some English. He said that right before we came, two white soldiers had been at the house, going around looking at everything. We asked him whether they were British or American. He said that he hadn't been there, and when he asked his father the old man said he didn't know. But they gave him a pack of American cigarettes. When we asked what the soldiers looked like, he just said they were tall and white." She looked at her mother and Viktoria for a minute with a perplexed expression.

"Why were they in our house?" Maria wondered aloud.

Just then Viktoria cried out in pain. "Oh!"

They rushed to the bed. "Is it time?" Tanya asked.

"I don't know," Viktoria grimaced. "Please . . . go find Monsieur Gu!"

Chapter Thirty-Seven

Harry was billeted in a mansion in the French Concession with four other officers, two of them from the Navy, the other two from the Army. Harry was the ranking officer. They had a staff of two dozen enlisted men. Accomplishing their goal of repatriating Allied POWs and Japanese civilians, while trying to sort through the postwar chaos, was a big task for such a small team. The Chinese Nationalists and the Chinese Communists were consumed with deposing each other, and each was bent on using American power to do so. Then there were the Chinese warlords, who were intent on reestablishing their fiefdoms amid the chaos. Old scores were being settled. Additionally, marauding bandits were a serious and lethal issue that Harry and the others had to confront on a daily basis.

In the middle of all those competing actors and interests was the Japanese military. They were heavily armed, disciplined, and most importantly, excessively submissive to American authority. In addition—as General Stevenson had pointed out—the Japanese were perhaps the only trustworthy partners the Americans could rely upon in China. They would do whatever the U.S. military authorities asked them to do, including protecting Western nationals and property. Ironically, the people the Americans were sent over to protect—the Japanese—were the ones doing the actual protecting. In the beginning, Harry and the others had to readjust their thinking because only a few short weeks before the surrender, they had been in the midst of a titanic and barbaric struggle with the Japanese. The war was supposed to be over, but the Marines, sailors, and soldiers in China found themselves in a seething cauldron that presented its own dangers.

Daily flyovers of warplanes and the presence of U.S. Navy warships on the roadstead reassured the men only so much. On the ground, a life could be snuffed out in seconds. Nationality or the color of a uniform didn't matter. Several hundred U.S. troops in Shanghai could not guarantee safety for anybody. Japanese troops, on the other hand, were present in the tens of thousands. Accordingly, the Americans in Shanghai found it necessary to rely on their former enemies. The black-and-white truths of the four previous years were now distorted by gray ambiguities. For Harry, who had lived in Shanghai before the war, it was easier to grasp the political complexities and nuances than for the others. But that was of no great reassurance to him; knowing it made him no safer on the streets than anyone else.

The American officers in Harry's billet had either Chinese or Japanese language skills. Each man was assigned separate sleeping quarters in the spacious house, and they shared an office in the converted living room. The five of them were given the onerous task of sorting through the files and records that the Japanese had put together for the internees. The enlisted staff completed whatever administrative tasks they needed, and Japanese officers helped them collate and interpret the files when questions arose. Every day the Japanese would come down from Hongkew with a new batch of records. Harry kept his eye out for any written word of the Savins, but he found nothing.

Three days after they had visited the Savin teashop, Harry had Alston drive him in a jeep to the Savin compound, about two miles from their own billet in Frenchtown. Harry had been seeing Viktoria in vivid dreams since he had arrived. He could sense she was near.

Harry's stomach churned as Alston turned onto the gravel driveway. The jeep came to a crunching halt in the gravel driveway in front of the house. Harry saw Chinese posters tacked on the columns there, but he couldn't make out what they said. He understood, however, that the Shanghai municipal authorities had put them up. He and Alston got out of the jeep and walked up the steps and into the house. Alston held the Thompson at his side, just in case.

Harry pushed open the door and called out in a loud voice. Nothing stirred. The house was so unkempt he hardly recognized it. In the front hallway, someone had recently built a fire on top of the checkered marble floor, which was pockmarked. The ceiling above was blackened with soot. Harry saw that some of Grigorii Savin's books had been used as fuel. Every item in every room had been ransacked: fixtures were looted, furniture taken or smashed. Because the windowpanes were missing from many of the windows, there were bird droppings in most of the downstairs rooms. Harry glanced out and saw that the garden was weed-choked, and all the fruit trees had been chopped down. *No place for the butterflies anymore,* he mused to himself.

They heard a loud bump upstairs. Harry called out again. "Hello?!" He pulled out his .45 and looked up from the bottom of the stairs. He noticed that the Persian rug runner on the stairway had been ripped out. Just then a figure appeared at the top of the staircase. It was an elderly Chinese man. Harry looked at him and said, "My wanchee savvy, s'pose Russia man have got, no got?" The man shook his head. Harry repeated himself, and then he asked a third time in English, "No Russian family living here?" Again, the man shook his head then turned, walked down the hallway, and disappeared.

Harry looked at Alston and said, "Come on." As they ascended the stairs Harry called out again, "Hello?!" At the top of the stairs, he looked down the hallway. The room Viktoria had shared with Tatiana was on the left side, and to his right he saw the old man standing outside the Savins' master bedroom. The man looked at them then went into the room, leaving the door slightly ajar. Harry and Alston walked slowly down the hallway and gently pushed the door open. Inside was a group of seven Chinese of all ages, huddled with their possessions in the corner of what was now a bare room. Except for the old man, there was no male over the age of ten. All the women and children were modestly but not shabbily dressed.

Harry addressed the group, pointing to the other rooms and making a circular motion with his finger. "Hab got this side?" The old man shook his head and said something in Chinese. He went on for about ten seconds. From the old man's gestures Harry surmised that other people had been here—perhaps other Chinese—but they had gone away. Harry pointed to Alston and to his own uniform. "*Shebang?*" The old man nodded. "*Urban?*" The man shook his head. Harry turned to Alston. "He said soldiers were here, but they weren't Japanese. You got any coffin nails?" Alston pulled out a pack of Chesterfields and handed it to Harry. Harry tossed it at the old man's feet.

Harry turned and walked out of the room. Alston followed behind him. Harry looked into every room along the hallway. They were all the same: barren or with smashed furniture and broken glass. All the drapes and carpets had been removed. He looked everywhere for a clue, but there was no sign that the Savins had ever lived in this house. When he came back to Viktoria's room, he exhaled loudly before pushing the door open. Harry walked into the room and suddenly thought he could detect a faint scent of Viktoria. In the corner closest to the door, he saw a small object. He knelt down and picked it up. It was an old icon. He recognized it. The family had brought from Russia, and it had once hung above the door of this room. It showed the Virgin Mary with the Christ child in her arms. Their faces were careworn but beautiful. Harry clasped it in his hand and stood. He walked to the window, which looked out onto the garden. He closed his eyes and took in a big breath, hoping to catch a hint of Viktoria again. Nothing. Releasing another sigh, he walked to the doorway, where Alston was waiting. Harry paused and took one last look around the room before heading toward the staircase.

Downstairs, Harry made his way to the hunting room. From there he opened the double doors that led into Grigorii Savin's study. The huge desk had been shattered; only a few books remained, scattered on the shelves or strewn on the floor. He stood a moment, taking it all in. Alston waited vigilantly in the doorway, keeping an eye outside the room. As Harry started to walk out, something caught his eye. It was spherical in shape, and he recognized it as Savin's globe. It had been lifted off its mounting and left on the floor. The globe was positioned so that the country most immediately visible was Russia. It was not labeled L'Union Soviétique, however, but the pre-1917 term L'Empire Russe. Harry shook his head and said aloud, "All great empires must come to an end."

They walked outside together. Harry climbed into the jeep and Alston got in behind the wheel. As they drove away, Harry didn't look back at the house, but he sensed the Chinese family was looking out the window at them. On the road they passed an oncoming car, but he couldn't see who the passengers were. Harry didn't turn back to look at them either, but had he done so, he would have seen the car turn onto the gravel driveway they had just left.

At the end of the first week, Harry went to Hongkew to meet with Colonel Gu and Major Katada. While he was there, he asked Katada about the White Russians.

Katada shrugged and said, "They weren't our enemies, so we didn't intern any of them. Some of them were married to British and French men, though, so they went with their husbands to the camps. The others stayed in their homes. Some of them continued on with their businesses, mostly in the *mizu shobai*." Harry noted he had used the term for the nightclub establishments.

Harry asked him about the tea merchants, the Savins. "Did you know them?"

"The businessman Grigorii Savin? Yes, we knew him. He disappeared a while back. We haven't heard about him since."

"And his family?"

"I'm not sure. He had so many children and other relatives; we couldn't keep track of them. Grigorii Savin was a very important man. He was a friend of Japan. He hated the Communists. Some people say he went back to Russia, but I don't think he would ever do that. It would be too dangerous for him there."

Harry spent the rest of the afternoon at the Japanese headquarters in Hongkew and was treated to an early supper. They served grilled fish with pickled vegetables and brown rice. Harry was offered sake, but he declined. He didn't want to stay in Hongkew past dark.

As Harry prepared to leave, Gu approached him and engaged in a short conversation about Grigorii Savin.

"You *do* know about him, then?" Harry asked.

Gu spoke in a guarded tone. "He was a collaborator with the Japanese. He probably fled to Harbin to escape the KMT. He had a connection with Ataman Semyonov, the Cossack. No telling what happened to him there. If the Soviets captured him, he is probably dead. No one knows what happened to his family."

Harry nodded and said, "I see." He had a sick feeling in his stomach.

Gu continued, speaking furtively. "I don't think it is worth following up on this. You can consider him dead."

Gu seemed determined to put the Savin story to rest, that much was clear. But Harry sensed that he was holding back something, and he couldn't imagine why.

Alston drove Harry back to the Bund from Hongkew, but there had been an accident at the Garden Bridge, and all traffic was stopped. Harry directed Alston to let him out there and to take the jeep back to the

French Concession the long way, across the Louza Bridge. "I'll meet you at the house later. I feel like walking and clearing my head a bit."

As Harry approached the Garden Bridge, he could see that the accident had been a serious one. A coal-powered lorry had overturned, and several rickshaws were crushed underneath it. KMT soldiers were keeping pedestrians from the bridge. One of the guards looked at him, but when Harry pointed toward the Bund, the soldier waved him through. As Harry walked by the wreckage, he saw the carnage firsthand. Three pools of blood indicated at least three fatalities. Bloody skid tracks led from two of the pools to the corpses splayed out on the far side of the wreckage. There was no sign of the third body. Harry's thoughts immediately drifted back to the airfield on Peleliu, where wounded and dead Marines were dragged to cover by their buddies during shellfire, leaving telltale bloody trails like these.

Having crossed the bridge, Harry was allowed through the barbed-wire barrier marking the beginning of the Bund. He shook his head in wonder that the barrier was still here. It had survived the war unscathed, perhaps the only thing in Shanghai to do so. Harry pushed his way through the crowd that had gathered to gawk at the bloody spectacle. Walking south down the Bund, he was immersed in thoughts of Viktoria and the Savins. He had no leads, and it began to dawn on him that he may never find her. He muttered, "Why the *hell* did I get myself sent here?"

上海

Chapter Thirty-Eight

Harry could barely go through the motions of doing his work the next day. An interminable number of files came across his desk. He was curt with his fellow officers, so they left him alone. When the others went out for an early lunch, Harry stayed back and decided to write a letter. Uncle Walter and Aunt Jo had sent Harry several letters since the end of the war, in each one saying they couldn't wait to see him again. Harry had told them nothing about his current assignment, so they probably figured he was somewhere in the Pacific or Hawaii. He wrote and explained that he was in Shanghai, that he had come to find Viktoria. He wrote about all the memories that had come back, and that the city was in its typical semipermanent state of crisis. He described the internment camps, knowing that everyone back in the States had seen newsreels of the Nazi concentration camps and the camps in the Philippines that held American POWs. It was a topic of great interest.

When the other officers returned from lunch, Harry realized he needed to get out of the mansion. He decided to go to the Cathay for a quiet lunch alone. He would go by foot to clear his head. It was warm and sticky after heavy rains the night before. As he walked north, he noticed that a large British liner had appeared on the roadstead. It sat clean and brilliant, presenting a contrast to the drabness of Shanghai and the cold gray lines of the American warships. It must have seemed like a mirage to the people in the junks sailing around it.

Further up the Bund he saw a little boy, obviously a Westerner, walking along holding his mother's hand. The woman wore a maroon dress and a black hat. They were headed—it seemed—toward the nearby Palace Hotel one block away. The mother had her back to Harry, but something caught the little boy's attention and he kept turning around and looking behind him. Something struck Harry about this boy. He wore a cap, but at one point the boy took the cap off. At that moment Harry saw that he was almost an exact replica of his deceased cousin, Henry. He tried to hurry and get a better look at them, but traffic blocked his view. By the time he could cross the street the mother and son had gone into the hotel.

Harry stood on the corner for a moment, wondering whether he was seeing ghosts. He decided to go into the hotel to try to catch a glimpse of them in the lobby. As he arrived at the Palace Hotel, a tall distinguished-looking Western gentleman passed in front of him and started to climb into the backseat of a parked Packard. The man stopped, stood straight up, and looked at Harry.

"My God, Harry?"

Harry stopped and turned to look at the man, who stood at the open door of the car. The man was thinner, and he looked older, but there was no mistaking the Douglas Fairbanks Jr. look-alike. It was Edward Muncy. The blood drained from Harry's face. "Edward?"

"Yes, old friend, it's me!" He stepped away from the car. "My God, Harry, I almost didn't recognize you in the uniform. I can't believe it's you! I'm so glad to see you! You made it! Why . . . how . . . what are you doing here?"

They shook hands. Harry said, "Never mind. I'll tell you all about it later. Where is Tanya? Do you know what's become of Viktoria?"

"Yes, old man, lots of questions. And I have lots to tell you. But what are *you* doing here? What brought you back?"

"I think you know, Edward."

Edward put his hand on Harry's shoulder and said in a voice that suddenly grew soft, "Of course. Come on, let me buy you a cup of coffee. I was running to the British consulate, but that can wait."

Harry followed Edward into a café on the ground floor of the hotel. Food for select Westerners in Shanghai was now available in abundance, and the café was crowded with people taking their lunch or having tea. Edward bid Harry to sit at a table near the front window. Harry sat down and removed the cover from his head. The other patrons of the café—many of whom had been interned throughout the war—momentarily turned to look at him. American servicemen in uniform always drew attention; the internees had not forgotten their role in freeing them from the Japanese.

Edward sat and rubbed his chin with his left hand, and said, once again, "My God, I can't believe you're here." He offered Harry a cigarette. Harry shook his head. Edward called for two coffees.

Harry couldn't wait for him to get through the formalities. "Edward . . ."

Edward held up his hand. "Please, Harry, allow me. I know you're wondering about the Savins, and I know you have so many questions. But I will say this up front: Viktoria is okay. The good news is she is alive and well." He paused for a second and then went on. "I don't know the proper way to tell you, but she is in a hospital at the moment . . . She delivered a baby . . . only yesterday."

Harry closed his eyes for a moment. He had told himself repeatedly that he had only wanted to know that Viktoria was alive and well. And now he had this confirmation. But the realization that she had had another man's child was a tremendous blow. He sat back in his chair and looked out the window, trying to absorb the news. Years of wondering about her, thinking he would probably never know what became of her, and now to know he could never have her again.

Harry looked at Edward and said, "I'm so relieved to hear that she's okay, Edward. I never stopped thinking about her. Even though this news is a shock, it makes me feel so much better to know she survived." Edward looked at him sympathetically, nodding his head. Harry then asked, "What happened to her during all these years?"

"How long do you have?"

"As long as it takes."

A waiter came and put two cups of coffee on the table along with two glasses of water. "Harry, I really don't know where to start." He exhaled. "But your appearing here today is miraculous. We've been wondering about you too, not knowing what became of you. Tanya is fine. She just went upstairs. We'll go see her shortly, but first let me try to fill you in on the Savins." He took a sip of his coffee. Harry ignored his own.

"Tanya and I were married, and we left for Hong Kong around the time you left for America. We actually eloped. We wanted to get away from all the prying eyes here in Shanghai; you remember our conversations about my family. Her parents, as you know, were also very much against our marriage. Anyway, I needed to arrange things for myself and for us back in England, so we decided to stay temporarily." He paused and took another sip of his coffee. "Before we booked passage back to England, I was offered a position at a bank and I accepted." He shook his head. "The worst decision I ever made. Then December the eighth happened. You know the story. Hong Kong was attacked. The Japanese marched in. We were placed under house arrest for almost a year. Then they decided to send the top British administrative officials from Hong Kong and the rest of China to one consolidated camp outside of Shanghai. A *VIP* camp," he added sarcastically. "So, in November of '42, Tatiana and I were returned to Shanghai. We were incarcerated separately. We spent the war in different camps. We never had word from one another. They only just released us late last month. I immediately found Tanya. Then we set out to find her family."

"What about Viktoria?"

Edward put up his hand. "I'll get to all that, Harry. I know you're eager to hear about Vika, but I'd like you to hear the full story in context." He crushed out his cigarette. "The Savins were left alone for the most part during the war. The White Russians, stateless as they were— but more importantly, anticommunist—could live in their homes and come and go as they pleased. And Grigorii Savin . . . you *know* how he played every side. He conducted his business as before. Viktoria and . . ." He paused a moment. "Viktoria continued living with her uncle. Mind you, this was all related to me by Tanya; I had no knowledge about any of this during the war. Tanya stayed with her family for a bit before she was sent to a camp for British women and children. Maria would occasionally go out to the camp to deliver parcels." He stopped, lit another cigarette, and then went on. "Anyhow, things got dodgy for the Savins in late 1944. Maria began complaining about the Japanese to Tanya. They were putting the screws to Grigorii, and his business dealings were under severe pressure. Things around Shanghai were never really settled—the low-level war never stopped here—but by the end of 1944 it was going badly for the Japanese."

Edward took a sip of his coffee and went on. "Savin was getting pressure not just from the Japanese but also the collaborationist government the Japanese had installed. The Chinese traitors were given almost complete power over the city in 1943. They fancied themselves the lords of Shanghai. They were brutal. Execution squads went around the city, rounding up Chiang supporters and suspected Communists. But Savin had gotten into bed with them, so now they decided they would take what they could from him, and he could no longer count on the Japanese to protect him."

Edward sat and stared out the window for a moment, trying to find the right words to continue. "Viktoria missed you. She visited the camp once with Maria. But the visits to the camp were coming under increasing scrutiny and they stopped altogether early this year. By this time, Savin was under pressure by a local boss, a man by the name of Gu. They had been associates before the war."

Harry started at the mention of Gu. His mind flashed to his counterpart, the Nationalist officer. "A tall man? Speaks American English perfectly?"

Edward nodded. "That's the one." He dropped a long ash from his cigarette into an ashtray. "Did you know him?"

The shock of hearing Gu's name in connection with the Savins left Harry momentarily speechless. He recovered, and nonchalantly answered, "Uh, yes, somewhat."

"Gu took over all of Savin's affairs. Took his properties, including the tea shop." Edward paused. "Viktoria became Gu's mistress." Edward stopped for a moment and looked at Harry.

Harry sat impassively. "Go on, Edward."

"Evidently, Savin was beside himself. Maria as well. But what could they do? Sometime in May, Savin went off to Harbin to see some Russians there. Nobody heard from him afterward. And you know the Soviets are in Harbin now, hanging or shooting all the White Russians. Maria and Viktoria stayed in Shanghai. By this time, they were both living with the children at a house provided by Gu. He was the only person able to protect them and the family." The two men fell silent for a moment before Edward continued recounting the events.

"After many months, Viktoria became pregnant . . . with Gu's child." He stopped and waited for Harry to say something.

Harry buried his head in his hands.

"Listen, Harry, I know this is damned difficult for you to hear. And there is more, so it's important that you hear me out. You have to understand what it was like for people living under occupation. You do whatever you have to . . . to survive. Especially if you have others to support, like Viktoria did. Most of the Russians have been demeaning themselves to survive in China for the past three decades. Viktoria had to think about her family. God knows, we all did things we regretted. Please don't rush to judgment. She loves you, and only you. Tanya will tell you all that herself."

Harry looked up and let out a long sigh. "No, Edward, I'm not judging her. I understand. It's just . . ." He paused, looking for words. "I saw her all these years, in my mind—my dreams." He sat back and exhaled. He looked out the window toward the river. Its brown presence was always there, flowing past. "I don't begrudge her doing what she did." He shrugged his shoulders resignedly. "I'm sure she'd given up hope she would ever see me again. It's only by God's grace that I'm even here." He took a sip of his lukewarm coffee. "To be honest, sometimes I feel guilty about being here at all, about being alive."

Edward nodded. "I'm sure it's been difficult for you—like it has been for all of us. In the future will anyone really understand the horrors we all faced these past few years?"

"It wasn't as bad for me as it was for others. I kept my head above the water. I survived. That's what Viktoria was doing."

"Viktoria went to the hospital to give birth yesterday."

"Where?"

"There's a hospital for women in the French Concession that is run by nuns. We were told that we can go and see Viktoria later this afternoon." He paused and looked expectantly at Harry. "Would you be up to it?"

"I'm not sure I need to see her. I'd like to, but maybe it's best if we leave it at that."

"No, Harry, I think you *should* see her. She still loves you. I know it's difficult, but I think it would do both of you a world of good to see one another."

Harry looked at Edward thoughtfully for a moment, and then nodded. "You're right, Edward. I'll go see her. I owe her at least that much. Can you take me there?"

"Yes, but that isn't the entire story."

"What else is there to say?"

"You need to come upstairs with me to see Tanya."

Harry exhaled and looked out the window again before turning to face Edward and nodding. "Alright. I'd love to see her. But do you mind if I sit here for a few minutes by myself? I need some time to think about all this."

"Of course. Take as long as you like. I'll be having a smoke in the lobby." Edward stood, fished in his pockets, and left some script on the table to pay for the coffee. Then he walked out.

Harry sat there, alone in his thoughts. His instincts had been right about coming back. But just like in his dreams, he was too late to save Viktoria. He was both drained of and flooded by emotion. He closed his eyes and thought about the epiphany he had had on the hospital ship when he was writing a letter to Ellen. Viktoria had been with him the entire time the war had separated them. He had never quit thinking about her, even when he was with Ellen. Vika was the guardian angel who had kept him out of harm's way. He pondered the inanity of it all—the past four years of his life. Historical forces. The sheer will of a handful of men. A world thrown into war. And now it had all ended with a single bomb. Tens of millions of people dead. Through it all he had finally returned to Shanghai and found Viktoria, but she could no longer be his.

He remembered that Edward was waiting for him in the lobby. He walked out of the café and found him, and the two of them went to the elevator bank. Edward said to the elevator boy, "Eighth floor."

Harry and Edward exited the elevator and walked silently down the carpeted hallway to the door marked with the number 88. Edward knocked once and then produced a key. He explained that they had been lucky to get a suite. As he opened the door, Harry heard Tanya's voice. "Edward, is that you?" Edward motioned for Harry to go in first.

As Harry walked in the door, Tanya stepped back in surprise initially. "Harry?!" She came toward him. They embraced. She pulled herself back to take him in. Tears filled her eyes. She looked over Harry's right shoulder at Edward, who was standing behind him. "How in the world?" Then she whispered to herself in Russian, "*Bozhe moi. Ya v'shoke. Ya ne mogu verit, shto ty zdez.*" Almost too stunned to speak, she stammered, "I . . . I can't believe it's you!"

Edward came and took her hand. "I'm as surprised as you are, Love. I was just about to get into the car when I looked up and saw his face." Edward turned to Harry and explained. "You see, we have passage on that liner in two days time," he indicated the ship out on the roadstead. "If I hadn't run into you, we'd have never found you."

Tanya looked at Edward through the tears pooling in her eyes. "Does he . . . did you . . ."

"He knows about Viktoria."

Tanya put her hand on Harry's cheek. "She never stopped thinking about you."

Harry shook his head. "I don't know what to say. I came to Shanghai specifically to find her. I just wanted to know if she was alright. But now . . . I just . . . I don't know what to say."

"Harry, Vika never stopped loving you. She thought of you and spoke of you all the time. You were present in more than one way all these years, you see." She saw how her words puzzled him.

Edward spoke up. "There's something else you need to know, Harry. We've been trying to find you, to somehow communicate with you since the war ended. We didn't know your address. We only knew you lived in Texas. And of course, the war . . ." His voice trailed off. He looked at Tanya. He gestured toward the door of a bedroom off the main room. "Is he asleep?"

"I don't know. I just put him down." She bit her lower lip, then said, "But I'll wake him."

Edward walked toward Harry and motioned for him to sit down. He gestured toward a chair, its light-blue velvet upholstery marred by a few cigarette burns. Harry took a seat, wondering what was going on.

Edward began, "You see, when you left Shanghai that summer in '41 . . ."

Tanya returned and said, "He's awake, shall I bring him out?" Edward nodded.

Harry stood up again. "What's this all about?"

Tanya emerged from the bedroom with a little boy. He looked about three years old. His hair was tousled, and he squinted his eyes half in sleep. Harry recognized the blond hair. His mouth dropped open. It was the boy he had seen on the street, walking with Tanya, before he encountered Edward. He was almost an exact copy of Henry.

Confused, Harry looked back at Edward, who nodded. "He's your son, Harry."

"What? Viktoria was—"

"When you left," Tanya interrupted, "she didn't know she was pregnant. She decided not to tell you. There was really nothing you could have done about it anyway. She thought about trying to stop the pregnancy. My parents were angry at first, but they promised to support her, so she decided to have the baby. He was born on March 21, 1942. His name is Henry. Henry Garrievich Dietrichson."

Harry stood there stunned. Edward walked up, put a hand on his shoulder, and said, "Harry, why don't you go over and introduce yourself?"

Harry looked at Edward for a moment and then walked over to the boy, who was holding on to Tanya's left leg. Harry crouched down. The boy looked shyly at him. Harry reached his hand out and said, "Hello, Henry. My name is Harry." The boy meekly took his hand. He quickly released his grip and clutched Tanya's leg again.

Tanya leaned down and quietly spoke to little Henry. "This man is a good friend. He knows your mother very well. He's an American."

The boy looked at Harry. Then he looked up at his aunt. "Tyotka Tanya?"

"Yes, dear?"

"*Khochu peet.*"

"*Konechno, Lyuba.*" Tanya took him back into the bedroom to pour him a glass of water.

Edward touched Harry on the arm. "Viktoria speaks to him in English and Russian."

Harry said numbly, "I just can't believe it. I . . . I don't know what to say."

"This is why we've been wondering how to get in touch with you, Harry—to somehow find out what happened to you. Believe me, throughout the war Viktoria ardently sought some way to contact you, but it was forbidden. Then when the Savins were evicted from their home, she lost your address."

Tanya and little Henry came back into the room and sat together on a sofa. She began singing to him in Russian. It was a child's song, "*Soro-ka-vorona.*" She played with the boys' fingers while they sang.

Harry and Edward sat down in the chairs facing the sofa. "I . . ." Harry stopped, then exhaled. He looked at the woman and child on the sofa. "For four years I've been doing what I could to survive and make it back to find Viktoria." He shook his head. "If you knew what I went through—these last few months, especially—to arrange my being here."

Tanya smiled and said, "And now here you are."

Edward said, "They've also been waiting for you to come back. Viktoria had no word from you. With the Americans fighting all over Europe, Africa, Burma, and the Pacific, we weren't sure where you might be or if you were even alive. She understood that she might never see you again. But she held out hope." He pointed to Henry. "He knows about you. His mother has explained to him. But . . . a child . . . well, he just can't understand very well. It must be confusing for him."

"And this whole business with Gu. How did that come about?"

Edward looked at Tanya for a second and then said, "It was bad here. Not just in the camps, but in the city as well. The Japanese let the worst elements run the place. They did nothing to stop the killings, the loot-ing, the starvation. Viktoria did what she could for the family. And keep in mind, she had someone extra special to take care of and look after." He nodded toward Henry. "You know this yourself. When there's a war on, you find yourself in compromising situations. We do what we have to do to survive."

"I know . . . you're right." Harry sighed and looked out the window toward the river. "You know, all these years I've had dreams in which Viktoria was in trouble. Most of the time she was drowning. I would try to save her, but I couldn't." He paused momentarily, and then went on. "I'd wake up and be gasping for breath. She was calling out to me."

Tanya stroked Henry's head. "*They* needed you, Harry."

"He looks just like my little cousin Henry. He died of leukemia at the beginning of last year. And now, it's as if he's come back." A lump grew in his throat. He wished so much at that moment that Walter and Jo were here with him to see the boy, this little Henry, *his* son.

Tanya said, "He looks just like you, Harry."

Edward said, "Harry, I know this is all so sudden, and you probably want to have some time to yourself. But we're going back to England. And, well, we were planning on taking Henry with us. That's why I was going to the consulate. Viktoria wants us to take him with us as our child. Given the circumstances, it's challenging to get an entire family out. And Vika would never leave without them. But we plan to send for her, Maria, and the children afterward."

Harry couldn't take his eyes off the boy, but he nodded, indicating that he understood.

"Harry, I know this must be so overwhelming." He stood up and began pacing. "But it seems only right that you take your son back to America with you. Viktoria would want that. Maybe you three can be together. Perhaps there is some way . . ." His voice trailed off for a moment. "Listen, I know this is devilishly difficult for you, but if you still have feelings for Viktoria, you *can* be happy. I know the business about the second baby must be tough for you. But think about it."

"There is no right decision; there is only the decision you must make. And this is something to which only *you* know the answer, Harry," Tanya said, unconsciously summoning the spirit of Batushka Dmitry.

Edward added, "Right now, Harry, the most urgent need we have is to get out of China and get home."

"When can we see Viktoria?"

"Tanya and I were planning to go this evening."

"I want to go."

Harry stood and went to Tanya and the boy.

Tanya said, "I have something for you that you should read before you see her." She walked toward the desk in the sitting room. She opened a drawer and pulled out a small book. It was old and worn, and it had an attractive gold leaf cover in a Japanese style. She walked over to Harry and handed it to him. "This is Viktoria's diary. There are some entries that are meaningless, mostly about daily affairs. But you will also find the letters she wrote to you over the years. It will help explain everything to you."

Harry took the book and paged through it for a few seconds. He recognized Viktoria's handwriting.

Edward said, "If you'd like to go down to the café and read it alone, please, feel free. We can go to the hospital after you return."

After saying good-bye to the boy, Harry walked out and descended the elevator in a daze. He sat for a while on a bench in the lobby, trying to gather his thoughts. He looked at the diary in his hands and thought about going into the café and reading through it. He decided instead to return to his billet. He walked down the Bund beside the ever-present river.

After he arrived at his billet, he sat down, pushed aside the files on his desk, and set the diary down in front of him. He stared at it, going over the designs, noticing for the first time the electric colors of the butterflies that graced the gold leaf cover. He smiled to himself, thinking about the time Viktoria told him that butterflies represent the souls of loved ones who have passed away. He opened the diary and began leafing through it. Viktoria had started it in late 1941, a few months after Harry returned to the States. He read all the heartfelt letters she had written for him. He understood now how bad it must have been, and how the horrors of life in wartime Shanghai must have drained Viktoria of any hope. He read of Grigorii Savin's troubles with his business, leading ultimately to his disappearance. He read about Gu, and his cheeks flushed.

Viktoria had started her final letter in June, but she finished it on July 15, 1945.

Something I have not told you that you now probably already know is that we have a child—a son. I named this beautiful boy Henry, in memory of your cousin whom you love so dearly. As he has grown, I recognize your face in his face. I didn't know that I was pregnant until after you left. I thought to tell you in a letter, but I decided that our separation was fated. You had returned to your family, and I couldn't tell you the news because I know you too well. Had you known, you would have tried to come back, and where would that have left you? You would have ended up in the hands of the Japanese in one of the camps. I couldn't make you return, and as much as I wanted to, I knew it was for the best. But I've been able to raise a beautiful boy, so full of life, energy, and happiness. Everything I have done—every scrap of food I saved, every demeaning act I undertook—was for him. God willing, when this war is over, you will be able to finally see him and see what a remarkable person he is and what a fine man he will become.

As for my indiscretions with the other man, God will judge me, and I have no expectation that you could ever love me again. I make no excuses. I had to do what I did. And now I am going to have another child. I shudder at the thought of bringing another baby into this horrible world. I don't know what the end of the war will bring. But I will do what I need to do to support my two children. Perhaps we can be optimistic about the future. Should I not be able to go on, and should something happen to me, Maria will take the children. She will reunite with Tanya when the war ends. If they do manage one day to find you, you must be the one to raise our son. You must care for him and see that his upbringing is wholesome and Christian.

For now, we know that the end is a matter of weeks or even days. We just all need to hold on. Every day I fervently pray for you and I pray for Tanya, my two dearest and most beloved friends.

I know how disappointed you must be in me, but always know that I love you and have always loved only you. My heart aches to think that you may never forgive me and that you may never see me again. But I also take solace in knowing how proud you will be when you are reunited with your son one day. He will also be overjoyed to know you. I speak of you to him every day, so he will be sure to recognize and respect and admire his own father. My heart thrills when I think of the two of you together.

I close this entry feeling better that I have cleared the air. You need to know the truth, and for this, everyone will be better off. You will always remain the largest part of my heart and my soul.

All of my love, V

Harry slowly closed the book and pondered for several minutes. He had never been so moved in his life. He understood the difficulties; all the pain and anxiety; the life and death choices she had been forced to make on a daily basis, just as he had over the past four years. He knew deep down that once he saw her, he would never be able to walk out of her life again. Viktoria had explicitly written that she wanted him to care for their son. But he had to consider the situation he was in and the likelihood of his being able to take the child. And what about Viktoria? He still loved her. Then he understood at that exact moment that he would be taking them *both* back home with him. And yes, he would also take her new baby, assuming he could. He would love Viktoria with all his soul and be the best husband she could hope for.

Harry shook off his pensive mood. He wiped his eyes, looked up, and saw that it was close to five o'clock. By this time the others were getting up from their desks, putting on their tunics, and preparing to have a night on the town. Harry stood and put on his own tunic.

"You coming with us to the Cathay for dinner and drinks, Dutch?" one of the men asked as he put on his cover.

"Yes, but I won't be joining you for dinner. I'm just hitching a ride. There's something I need to attend to."

All five of them crammed into one jeep for the drive over to the Cathay. Harry sat quietly but the others bantered among themselves the whole way. They hollered at pedestrians or whistled at women on the side of the road. They parked the jeep near the crowded Cathay. People were congregated in the front and in the lobby. Most of them were British families taking in their last meals in Shanghai before departing on the liner. They were toasting both their imminent homecoming and the end of their long stay in the Orient. A celebration of past times in China, both good and bad.

Harry left the group and walked toward the Palace Hotel. He entered the lobby and approached the front desk. He asked the clerk to ring Edward's room. The man handed Harry the receiver. Tanya picked up the phone.

"Tanya, it's me, Harry."

"I'm so glad you phoned. We're getting ready to go see Viktoria. Where are you?"

"I'm in the lobby."

"Wonderful. We weren't sure if you would make it. Please come up. Edward is having a bath."

Harry took the elevator to the eighth floor. He knocked on the door. Tanya let him in and greeted him with a kiss on the cheek. He removed his cover. Henry was seated on the floor near the window, playing with a small toy train. He looked up at Harry briefly then resumed playing. Tanya was in a plain blue dress, but she looked beautiful. Her deep brown eyes sparkled like they always had.

"Edward will be out in a minute. Can I offer you something in the meantime?"

"No, thank you."

"Not even a cigarette?"

"No, I don't smoke anymore."

"I see. Were you able to read Vika's diary?"

"I read every page. It was beautiful. It broke my heart."

Just then Edward emerged from the bedroom, his hair still wet. He smiled at Harry. He wore shirtsleeves and gray trousers. He was tying a necktie. He walked by Henry and rubbed the boy's hair. Henry looked up at him. Edward said, "Hullo there, chum." Then Edward came and sat down next to Tanya. "Hello, Harry."

"I've made a decision," Harry said calmly.

Both Edward and Tanya sat up expectantly.

"I'm going to take them back with me. I'll take Gu's child too, if that's what Viktoria wants."

Tanya let out a small yelp and smiled broadly. She stood up, came to Harry, and they embraced. Through tears she said, "I'm so happy."

Edward stood and put his hand on Harry's shoulder. "Are you ready to go see her?"

"Yes, I am."

"I think the two of you go on alone. I'll stay here with Henry." She looked at Harry and smiled warmly. "I know Viktoria will be happy again for the first time in a long time."

Harry put his cover back on and walked to the door, where Edward waited. Before Harry walked out, he paused, turned, and said, "Henry, I'll see you later."

The boy looked up at Harry, smiled, and waved good-bye.

上海

Chapter Thirty-Nine

Harry and Edward took a car from the hotel. They drove for fifteen minutes south into the French Concession and located the hospital. Harry's heart pounded in anticipation of seeing Viktoria for the first time in four years.

The hospital was located on Route Lafayette. It was crowded and in poor repair. The staff were overwhelmed as they struggled with the influx of the sick and the poor. The nuns were loath to turn away anyone. Harry wondered why Gu couldn't have found a more suitable place for Viktoria. But in postwar Shanghai the chaos and disorder no longer knew class distinction. Harry followed Edward inside. They inquired at the admittance desk about the maternity section. A small, thin Belgian nun directed them to the third floor. They ascended the stairwell, which reeked of ether and urine.

On the third floor Harry noticed the large number of Eurasian women in the maternity ward. People made way when they saw Harry in uniform. Finally, he and Edward located a desk where another nun was seated. Edward asked her about Viktoria. She looked at her list and then stood up abruptly, looking first at Edward and then Harry. She told them to wait at the desk. She disappeared into a room farther down the hall. The two of them stood there alone, conspicuously, with hats in hand. Finally, the sister emerged followed by another nun. This older nun had a round face that framed kind gray eyes. As she came forward, Harry and Edward looked at her expectantly.

"I am Sister Anna." From her accent, Harry guessed she was probably Ukrainian or Polish. After Harry and Edward had introduced themselves, she continued. "We sent somebody early this morning to the gentleman's house." She looked at them, and Harry noticed the concern in her eyes.

"The Chinese gentleman?" Edward asked.

"Yes, that's right. Monsieur Gu." She paused and then asked, "Are you related to Madame Savina?"

"I am married to her sister."

The sister shifted uncomfortably. "Yes, I see. Well, the baby died this morning. Madame Savina is resting, but she is very weak. It was a difficult delivery; she lost a lot of blood."

Harry grew light-headed, but he continued listening quietly.

The sister seemed to notice Harry's distress, and she began directing her words toward him. "There are so many diseases ravaging this city. In her weak state, we are concerned she is vulnerable. She has been running a very high fever, and we are worried this could develop into pneumonia."

"Can we see her now, Sister?"

Sister Anna answered hesitantly. "Well . . . yes, of course. I think it won't harm anything if you see her."

She directed the two men to follow her. They passed a number of small anterooms, curtained off from the corridor. There was no such thing as privacy in the overcrowded hospital. As they walked, she told them more of Viktoria's condition. "She has been delirious at times. She cries out about the baby. Also about her son."

Sister Anna came to one curtain and opened it. There, before them, lay Viktoria in her bed. Her eyes were closed. As Harry walked toward her, he saw that her cheeks were shrunken and she looked waxen.

He put his hand on her arm. "Viktoria, dear, it's me, Harry."

Her eyes fluttered opened. They widened as she took in Harry's figure. She looked him up and down. She closed her eyes again. Then she slowly reopened them.

A smile slowly spread across her lips. "It's you, dear," she said weakly.

"Yes, it's me. I came back for you, Love." He bent down and kissed her cheek. He kept his face next to hers.

"I can hardly believe it." She looked Harry in the eyes. "I'm not dreaming, am I?"

Harry grasped her hand firmly. "No, Love. I'm standing before you in the flesh. There are so many things to tell you. But don't worry, I'm not going anywhere. I came back to take you and Henry home."

She closed her eyes again, and tears formed at the corners. "You shouldn't see me like this. I've done so many things I'm ashamed about."

"Vika, My Love, so have I. I've done much worse than you ever could have. What matters is that we're here. We survived." He stroked her head, "And I've seen Henry. I'm so proud of you, so proud how you raised him."

She opened her eyes again. "You saw him? I'm so happy. I never stopped thinking about you. Forgive me for not sending you a letter and telling you." She coughed thinly.

"No, Vika Love, don't mention it." He took her hand and kissed it.

"And now, I've made this mess of my life, and I lost my baby." She began crying.

"Viktoria. It's okay. I'm here. I read your letters."

"You did?"

"Yes. They were beautiful. But even before I read them, I understood you. I understood why you couldn't come with me. I understood why you couldn't tell me about Henry."

"I love you so much, Harry."

"I love you too. We're going back to America. Me, you, and Henry. And this time you're not backing out."

She smiled weakly and then began a long, raspy cough. It took her several moments to regain her breath. Harry looked at Sister Anna.

"Viktoria, Love. Rest now. I'm going to get you good doctors to make sure you recover quickly. The sooner you're better, the sooner we can leave and put these awful four years behind us. We'll start over again and make a wonderful home for ourselves. We'll have long picnics under peaceful blue skies. We'll go to the shore and swim together. We'll dance at the swankiest nightclubs. That's all I've thought about for the past four years."

"You have no idea how happy that makes me, Harry. Please, tell me what else we'll do."

"We'll listen to records together on rainy afternoons. We'll cozy up to a fire when there's two feet of snow on the ground."

"Snow?"

He smiled through his own tears. "You bet. We'll go to New York and to the theater. I'll take you to jazz clubs in Harlem. I'll teach you to ride a horse. I'll teach Henry to throw a baseball and bait a hook. We'll have more kids. We'll grow old together. And one day we'll have grandkids."

"But can you ever forgive me?"

"Can you ever forgive me for leaving you?"

"You didn't. You were always here with me. In Henry."

"I'm never leaving you again, Love."

She coughed again. She paused to regain her strength. "Harry, I can't believe you came all the way back. I'm happy for the first time in so long. I'm so happy . . ." She smiled and closed her eyes again. "I'm tired."

"Sleep, Viktoria. I'll be here. Right next to you."

Sister Anna agreed to let Harry stay the night. Edward went back to the Palace Hotel and promised to try to find a doctor. During the night, Viktoria occasionally awoke and called Harry's name. He took her hand, to reassure her that he hadn't left her side. She breathed with difficulty through the night, and her fever wouldn't abate.

By the next morning, her condition had worsened. Not waiting on news from Edward, Harry told Sister Anna he himself would try to get whatever medication she needed. He waited until Viktoria was asleep again and then raced back to his billet. He had Alston drive him to the Cathay, where he was sure he could find an Army doctor.

Harry was able to find a flight surgeon who served in the Army Air Corps. Major Humphrey was skeptical, and had he outranked Harry, he may not have come. But Harry was able to convince him by simply stating, "She's my wife."

Alston drove them back to the hospital. Harry was surprised but pleased to see Edward smoking a cigarette in front of the hospital. "I came to find you, Harry, but the news isn't good. We couldn't find any-one to help. I'm so sorry."

"It's okay, Edward. This is Major Humphrey. He's a doctor."

The three men went into the hospital and ascended to the maternity ward. Humphrey took the repugnant condition of the hospital in his stride. Doctors all over the world had grown inured to horrific condi-tions over the past four years.

They came to the anteroom where Viktoria's bed was partitioned off. A young nurse tended to her with wet compresses on her forehead. She looked at the three men with surprise. She left to find Sister Anna. Doc-tor Humphrey took Viktoria's wrist and felt her pulse. He then felt her forehead. He instinctively looked for a chart but found nothing. "She's extremely weak. We've got to get this fever down." He shook his head. "If we only had ice."

"Doc, don't you have aspirin or something for the fever?"

"Yes, but we need to get the fever down immediately. She may be too weak to swallow any pills."

Humphrey put his hand on Viktoria's cheek. "Young lady, can you hear me?"

Viktoria opened her eyes and tried to focus. "*Vy kto?*" she asked in Russian.

"Vika, dearest, it's me. I've brought a doctor."

"Harry? Where did you go, Love?"

"This is Dr. Humphrey. He's going to help you get better."

Humphrey took a stethoscope. Harry helped him prop an emaciated Viktoria up in the bed. Humphrey briefly listened to her lungs. They laid her gently back down.

Edward asked, "What exactly is her condition?"

Humphrey sighed. "Pneumonia. Anemia. Severe dehydration. Dangerous fever. Maybe meningitis. She needs penicillin and vitamins."

"Do you have any?"

"Not on me. Penicillin is very strictly controlled."

Harry's shoulders sagged. Humphrey reassured him. "Don't worry, I can get some. But I'm telling you right now, she's in extreme danger. I should leave immediately."

"Edward, can you go with him?"

"Yes, of course. Anything you need, Harry."

Humphrey put his hand out to Harry. "First, try and get this aspirin down her. See that she drinks some water. I'll try to bring back some ice as well." With that Edward and Humphrey left and closed the curtain.

By this time, Sister Anna had returned. "She weakened over the night. We are trying to keep her cool, but . . . not even one fan in this whole hospital." She resignedly threw her hands up to signify the almost impossible task she was facing at the understaffed, crumbling facility.

Harry sat next to Viktoria. He took her hand.

She opened her eyes. "Harry. It's you." She closed her eyes again.

"Yes, dear, I'm not going anywhere."

"Tell me what else we'll do. You know, in America?"

"I'll teach you how to drive a car. We'll go camping out in the Texas Hill Country and see the wildflowers in the spring. I'll take you to Los

Angeles. We'll go to Hollywood. I'll take you to see the Golden Gate Bridge in San Francisco."

"San Francisco?"

"Yes. I'll cook you eggs and bacon and serve you breakfast in bed every day, not just on your birthday. You'll hang your wet stockings on the wash-basin when I'm trying to shave. I'll track mud into the house with my hunting boots. And we'll argue about stupid little things like that."

"I'll never complain, Harry." She closed her eyes. When she opened them again, she said, "Harry, you don't know how happy you've made me."

"You make me happy too. Say, you remember that day when we got caught in the rainstorm in the English Gardens on the Bund? And we stole that poor coolie's rickshaw? And I pulled you all the way home?"

She nodded and tried to smile.

"Or the day when we asked Willy to cook us a duck in my apartment?" Harry chuckled. "I still think it must have been a crow or something."

Viktoria smiled. "Walkee-walkee duck." She coughed and motioned to Harry. He came closer. "Henry—" she said weakly, "how is Henry?"

"He's with Tanya. He's fine."

"I've tried to raise him as best as I could."

"You've done a marvelous job, Love. He's a fine boy."

She shook her head. "All the bad things . . . I'm so ashamed."

"No, Vika! You've been wonderful. Enough of that."

"If something . . ." She closed her eyes and coughed. "You must take him."

"Viktoria, we'll go together."

She shook her head. "I don't know—"

"I'm *not* leaving without you."

She nodded. "If something . . ." she murmured again.

Sister Anna came forward. "She needs rest."

Harry nodded and sat down.

He stayed by Viktoria's side for several hours, looking up every five minutes in expectation of Humphrey's arrival.

In the afternoon Viktoria cried out in delirium. She spoke in Russian, asking for Henry and Harry.

He took her hand. "I'm right here, dearest." She looked at him briefly before closing her eyes. She didn't appear to recognize him. She nodded off again.

Her fever raged and the nurses kept bringing in new compresses. She coughed and slept fitfully. Her skin looked even more waxen. Harry walked out into the corridor and paced. He looked down toward the stairwell, impatiently awaiting Humphrey.

Finally, just after five o'clock, Humphrey and Edward appeared. Harry rushed to them. "I'm sorry it took so long, Dietrichson. We tried to get here sooner but I had to pull favors to get the medication. And ice is almost impossible to find. We combed all of Shanghai. How is she?"

"Very weak. Come quickly!"

They went to Viktoria's bedside while Edward busied himself chipping the ice into a basin. Sister Anna stood over Viktoria with a look of great concern. "We cannot get the fever down. She's having difficulty breathing. We could get her to take only one aspirin."

"Please, Doc, do you have the penicillin?"

"I do. But you must understand, the fever is what we need to treat right now."

Viktoria's breathing was irregular. Humphrey leaned over her and applied a compress of crushed ice to her forehead. He looked at Sister Anna. "How long has she run such a high fever?"

"More than seventy-two hours."

Humphrey looked at her with concern. "That long? Let's get some compresses underneath her, as well."

Viktoria coughed and gurgled as they turned her.

Harry took Humphrey aside. "What do you think?"

Humphrey shook his head. "She's weak. I just don't know if a course of penicillin will help her. We'll try, of course, but the main thing is the fever. She may have sustained brain damage. Plus, she's basically drowning in her own lung fluid. I hate to sound so dire, but I figured I should come straight with you."

Harry nodded. He went back to Viktoria and sat with her. She opened her eyes again after a while. Harry took her hand. She looked at him. "It's me, Love. I'm still here. I won't leave."

She nodded and closed her eyes. Another thirty minutes passed, and her breathing slowed. Her pulse grew weaker. Humphrey took her vitals. He looked at Harry and shook his head. Harry looked over at Edward, who stood with tears in his eyes.

Harry leaned over Viktoria. His voice choked with emotion, he said,

"I'll take you to my favorite drug store counter. We'll have chocolate malts, lime rickeys, and ham and cheese sandwiches. I'll take you to Shibe Park in Philadelphia. We'll see the A's. We'll eat hot dogs and drink root beer." He began crying. "You'll spill mustard on your blouse . . ."

Viktoria's breathing became intermittent. Harry stroked her hair and cheeks. He repeated his love for her and assured her Henry would be fine. Soon after, she took her last breath. Harry leaned down and kissed her lips. "We'll see each other again, My Love, in the Celestial City."

Suddenly all the dreams about Viktoria drowning in the river that had haunted him for years came rushing back. They were no longer dreams. He had foreseen it all.

Some minutes after she passed, Harry sat on a bench in the corridor and buried his head in his hands. Sister Anna sat beside him, with her arm around his shoulders. Edward kneeled next to Harry, with his hand on Harry's knee. They stayed there for a quarter of an hour. Not a word passed between them. After a while, Harry heard Humphrey's voice.

"Is there anything more I can do for you, Major?"

Harry looked up and shook his head.

"I'm sorry. She was too far gone. There was really nothing I could do."

Harry nodded and then put his head back into his hands. Humphrey left after a few minutes.

Finally, Harry pulled his head up. "Edward, we have to go tell Tanya." He turned to Sister Anna, "Thank you for being so kind to us, Sister. Can I come later and ask about her burial?"

"Of course. I'm so sorry. I wish I could have done more to help." She began to choke up.

Harry took both her hands. "You did all you could."

Harry and Edward exited the hospital and wordlessly walked onto the streets of the French Concession. They walked side by side, shoulders hunched under the grief they shared. Harry remembered that they were not too far from his billet, so they walked to his mansion. From there they had Alston take them by jeep to the Palace Hotel.

When they arrived in the suite, Henry was already asleep. They told Tanya the news. She collapsed in grief, but Edward was able to give her some brandy and get her into bed by the time Harry left.

Harry spent the entire night alone in his room in the mansion, thinking it all over. He sat and tried to envision Viktoria's life over the past four years. Her life had been no easier than his own. Who had not suffered—truly—during the war? She had shown immense courage and had never stopped thinking of him or loving him. They had been together all these years. Each time he looked at the stars in the night sky to find her, she had been doing the same thing. Harry was glad to know that, but he also knew that it wouldn't bring her back. They would never see one another again, until they were joined in the Celestial City.

As he thought about her, he grew sadder. At the same time, he gained a deep appreciation for what she had done. She had sacrificed herself for her family, for the people she held dearest. Harry then thought about his friends in the war. They had all done the same thing. With clarity, he came to the realization that he understood her and loved her more than he ever had before.

Harry knew that Viktoria wanted him to take Henry. Harry knew that with Henry he could build a life with his family in Texas. Harry had been ashamed to admit that he had turned his back on Walter and Jo at times for fear of getting too close to them. He could redeem himself in their eyes. But he had to consider the situation he was in and the likelihood of his being able to take the boy now. He had a commitment and couldn't just bring a young boy into his billet and go on as before. He sat and thought through the scenarios until the sun rose.

Early the next morning Harry had Alston take him to the Palace Hotel. In the lobby, families were gathering with bags and trunks, getting ready for the steamer to take them back to the homes they had not seen in more than five years—in some cases much longer. He sensed their elation, and the excitement and innocence of the young children who had endured the Japanese camps.

Harry took the elevator to the eighth floor. Edward opened the door. Tanya stood near the window. There were dark circles under her eyes. Henry was on the floor playing with his toy train.

Edward invited Harry to sit but he chose to remain standing. He watched Henry play. After some time, Tanya came to him.

"I'm so sorry, Tanya."

"I'll never get over losing her."

"I know."

Tanya wiped her eyes. "Her losses, her compromises, and all the bad things that happened to her finally caught up with her. The guilt and shame must have been unbearable. The nobility of self-sacrifice holds its beauty only for so long."

Harry looked Tanya directly in the eyes. "Over the past few days I have come to understand myself so much better, through Viktoria's example. I've never loved her more."

Tanya turned and looked at the boy, who continued playing. "We tried to tell him, but he doesn't understand. But with time he'll come to understand."

Harry nodded. "I have something to tell you. I understand what I need to do: I'm going to take him with me." Tanya nodded and gave a wan smile. Harry went on. "But I can't right now. There is no way—given my assignment—that I can keep him with me. I'll probably be in Shanghai for several more months. She wanted me to take him. And I want to. But I just can't right now." Harry looked at Edward. "So I ask this of you two: Please take him back with you to England. Care for him, love him, treat him as your own son. Let him know that I'll come back for him, as I came back for her. I don't know how long it will be before I'm able to come and get him. But I will." The boy had stopped playing and was looking at them. He sensed that he was being spoken about.

Through tears Tanya said, "Of course, we will. She would want that."

Edward said, "You can count on us. We'll be waiting for you in England, Harry."

"Thank you." Harry turned back to Tanya and took her hands in his. "I'll carry this grief the rest of my life, but through Henry I'll also carry her love."

Tanya said, "It's truly God's miracle. For you to come all the way back here and find him. I couldn't be happier for Henry, and I know Viktoria is now looking down on us, and she is happy."

Harry walked over to Henry. The boy was playing with the engine again. Harry crouched down and stroked his hair. The boy looked up at Harry.

Harry smiled and said, "Henry, we're going to see each other again soon. You hear? I'm going to show you Texas and introduce you to your family in America. But for now, you're going to go to England with your aunt Tanya and your uncle Edward. But we'll see one another again soon. Okay?"

The boy had looked at Harry blankly at first, but when Harry finished speaking, he smiled. Harry continued to stroke his hair. The boy's attention then went back to his toy, and he began making engine noises again.

Harry stood, turned back to Tanya, and said, "Remind him every day of his father and his mother."

Edward spoke, "Rest assured, we will."

Tanya nodded, "Yes, he'll be ready when the time comes."

Harry produced the photo Viktoria had kept in her diary. The one of Harry in his white suit and skimmer at the racetrack. "Keep this as a reminder for him."

Edward took the photo. "Of course. Will you see us off at the quay this evening?"

"You can bet on it. I'll be there."

Tanya took Harry in her arms, and they embraced once more. She pulled back and looked him in the eyes. "We will miss you. But we'll be waiting for you."

Edward went over to the table and wrote down something on a slip of paper. He came to Harry and handed him the paper. "This is where we can be found. It is my parents' address, and though we may not be living there by the time you come to England, they will forward any mail or telegrams to me."

Harry nodded, took the address, and then fished in his pocket for a large coin. It was a Mexican silver dollar dated 1931, the same year his cousin Henry was born. He then pulled out the yellow handkerchief he had kept since the day Happy Hargrove died on Cape Gloucester. It still showed faint bloodstains. He went over to Henry and handed him the silver dollar. "Henry, I need you to keep this for me. Can you promise? It's special. Keep keep this wrapped up in this handkerchief. When I see you next time, you can give it back to me. Okay?"

The boy took the coin and turned it over, looking at it admiringly. He first looked over at Tanya and then at Harry. He smiled and said, "Okay."

Harry rubbed the boy's head one last time, stood, and walked back to Tanya. He handed her the icon he had found in Viktoria's room. She gasped. "How did you get this?"

"It came back to you. It's Viktoria's final gift."

He turned and walked to the door. Before he opened it, he paused and said, "She *is* looking down on us and smiling."

Tanya answered, nodding. "Yes, she is."

After he had seen the three of them off to their boat that evening, Harry wandered slowly back to his billet, taking in the sights and sounds of the city. He stopped whenever he came upon a place where he had been with Viktoria, and reminisced. The smells, the chaos, the river, the high moments, as well as the low moments, would stay with him forever. He would see the city in his dreams, he would see the Savins' garden, where the electric-blue butterflies danced, and, of course, he would see Viktoria.

Along the quay a young boy came up to Harry. He was wet and had probably just emerged from a swim in the muddy river in the warm evening. He extended his open palm toward Harry, "No mama, no papa, no whiskey soda."

Harry held his hands out to either side, "Me neither, kid." Then he remembered and reached for his breast pocket. He pulled out a stick of Juicy Fruit and handed it to the boy. The boy took the gum, unwrapped it from the foil, and quickly shoved it in his mouth. Harry chuckled and patted him on the top of his head. As the boy ran off, Harry put his hand up to his brow as if to salute the boy good-bye. He stopped and looked at his wet hand. There it was again—the smell.